Jane House began her career as a psychiatric nurse and worked in that field in hospitals and in the community for 17 years before moving into the forensic drug and alcohol field which is ongoing today. She is dedicated to her family, husband, two sons and extended relatives. She is passionate about animals and the environment.

I would like to dedicate this book to four very significant ladies in my life. My grandmother, Marjorie Kennedy and mother, Mary Sears (both deceased); my aunt Shirley Richards and my mother-in-law Pat House. Each has played a very important part in my life.

Jane House

THE TRAUMA VACUUM

AUSTIN MACAULEY
PUBLISHERS LTD.

A CIP catalogue record for this title is available from the British Library.

ISBN 9781786291325 (Paperback)
ISBN 9781786291332 (Hardback)
ISBN 9781786291349 (E-Book)
www.austinmacauley.com

First Published (2016)
Austin Macauley Publishers Ltd.
25 Canada Square
Canary Wharf
London
E14 5LQ

Part 1

Chapter 1

Samuel Nelson was just getting ready for work. At twenty-three he had lived a very privileged life and materially had wanted for nothing, but there had always been a huge 'something missing' that he couldn't articulate. What did he lack? What had he missed? He never knew. He simply thought of it as a 'gap', which he pointedly, and wholly, placed at the feet of his father and grandmother. His grandfather had been the only person in his family who had shown him any demonstrative love, the only one to give him a slap on the back and say, "Well done." He remembered, with a smile, how his grandfather would only let him have presents after he had given him a huge hug. "Never too old for a cuddle, young Sammy," he'd chortle and wrap his arms about his torso, patting his back and, when he was still little enough, lift him off his feet and into the air: but his grandfather was dead now. As for his grandmother, she was like ice, non-responsive and devoid of life. She had been that way all his life and he never knew why, she just seemed to… exist; she too was dead now. His father he viewed like a valued vase that sat on the mantelpiece. It was something to be admired but never touched and never interacted with in any personal way. And yet, deep down, he knew his father loved him and only wanted the best for him. Sam, as he was better known to all except his father, was always on tenterhooks around him. He was obedient to his father's wishes and took whatever his father offered, but he always wanted more. He mused to himself as he finished cleaning his teeth that it wasn't his father's fault, he was who he was; a man who had no time for people and few people had time for him.

Sam was currently working at a local Adelaide pub, 'The Cumberland', as a barman and he did not aspire to do more. *"What's the point,"* he often asked himself. He knew full well that the only reason he was allowed to work at the pub was because there was some business arrangement between his father and the publican, Geoff. Geoff was Thomas's eyes and ears and whilst that worked, then Sam could continue his part-time job. Sam never questioned the arrangement, it suited him well enough. He'd been working there since he was 18 on a part-time basis, and to all intents and purposes being part-time afforded him time to engage in the only thing he really cared for and that was staying fit. He tried to run 10 km a day or cycle 25 km or more, weather permitting, and in between all that he'd go to the gym. He did not believe in supplements to enhance his fitness, just hard work, and somehow his fitness regime had made up for the emptiness he felt somewhere in his core. Whilst he was looking about his room for his shoes he remembered confiding in his friend, "Billy, I don't know what it is but when I am working out it is the only time I feel 'whole'. Do you know what I mean?"

"Not really mate," Billy chimed. "What's not whole about you? You have a great life, plenty of access to money, a car, good looks, a father who indulges your every whim and,"… he stopped, looked around furtively, as if checking no one was listening and added … "I don't know, did I say, you have access to plenty of money? You don't even have to work yet you choose to. What's not 'whole' here?" and he smiled broadly, giving him a not so gentle punch in the bicep.

"You don't get it. I feel… hell, I don't know. It's hard to describe. I suppose I miss my grandfather. At least when he was alive I had someone to talk to but he's been gone for the past five years and living in that house with dad is like solitary confinement. Well, that's what I assume solitary confinement is… cold and bare."

Billy had laughed then, given him another punch to the bicep and said, "Don't overthink it mate. Come on, let's go shoot a few hoops."

What Billy didn't understand though, was most of the things Sam was allowed to do were hard fought for. Even being allowed to ride his bike anywhere near the roads had been a challenge. He had bemoaned to his father that he would be careful, "No I won't ride on the road, just to the side, yes I know motorists are stupid, please Dad, it's the only thing I really love. What is it with you and bikes, everyone rides these days." But without his grandfather to back him up it had been months of arguing and debating before Thomas, finally, and reluctantly gave in. "Dad, you CANNOT protect me from everything," he had yelled. And Thomas had looked at his then seventeen year old son and thought, *"I damn well will try Samuel. I've done well so far."* But to Sam he had said, "Okay son. I trust you." What Sam didn't know was that Thomas had a person follow him for a month before Thomas felt comfortable enough with his son riding kilometre after kilometre to call the follower off.

It had been four years ago when he'd had that conversation with his mate Billy, and he still felt the same. Shaking his head he spied his shoes, slipped them on, grabbed his car keys from the front door table and yelled out, "I'm off," to his father, knowing he wouldn't get an answer. He headed to the garage, jumped in his car and headed to The Cumberland for his afternoon shift.

Chapter 2

In the study Thomas Nelson heard the front door slam shut and the car racing down the driveway. He never gave a lot of thought about his son and where he was heading in life but he thought that now Samuel – he never called him Sam – was twenty-three he probably needed more responsibility. Having thought that he quickly returned to what he was doing, that being; reading the Financial Times. Before the shout, the door slam and the car noises he had been musing as to whether he should buy some shares or invest in more real estate. Thomas thought about how his life in shares took on an obsession to a degree. He remembered when he first met a man named Tim O'Rourke, he was a trickster, a shonky moneylender, the under the counter, excessive interest, hard line tactics man who was only out to line his own pocket and be damned who ever got in the way. Not many people got away without being burnt when dealing with Tim. He was basically groomed by his father Max O'Rourke, who was well known in the who's who of all Australia's capital cities except Canberra, "Tim, boyo. You don't mess in the Poli's backyard! You remember that," but Tim was one degree more ruthless than Max and he messed wherever there was a penny to be made.

It was back when Thomas was still living in Ballarat and he'd gotten into stocks and shares and was just learning the trade. He remembered because it was around the time of his up and coming 21st birthday. Thomas was determined to show his father Oscar that he could be financially responsible and pay for his own trip to Europe which, at that time, had been a dream of his. He was mesmerised by the market and his study of it had him dabbling in all sorts of areas; gold, domestic insurance, horses, overseas investments. One day in his researching he had come across a paper mill company that was currently struggling financially and Thomas was determined to buy shares in it. His research told him it was their poor management and not due to lack of demand that had landed this family business in trouble. He knew there was more to it than that but, bottom line, he figured he could turn it around quickly with the right man at the helm and that would be him to begin with. He didn't have enough money to really make a difference and he feared if he waited he would lose the opportunity. He decided that if he borrowed money now he could pay it back in no time at all, as long as the predictive data on the shares and the company's growth eventuated. Thomas did not think of the alternative that he could be buying into a failed venture. He felt in his core that this was the right decision.

He went to see O'Rourke Brokers and Finance, with no knowledge of the firm. The shop front was on Lydiard Street and advertised as a legitimate moneylender who was keeping 'the big banks' honest, lending small and large amounts with few questions asked. O'Rourke brokers were on the side of the battlers… the true Aussie spirit.

Thomas walked in and read a sign sitting on the front counter. Please fill out the form on the right and place it in the basket on the left. Once completed, someone will be with you soon.

He took the form and sat down at a small table and chairs, completing it in five minutes. It asked the usual details, name, address, assets and amount wanting to borrow. Thomas listed his car and an investment home he had and requested a loan of $3000.00. He placed the form in the basket as required, watched it slide from the front of the counter through an opening in the back wall which he hadn't noticed before and he watched it disappear. Thomas was instantly on alert. He had been watched, he began to doubt himself, and he became agitated. In a matter of seconds he had gone from a confident young man with a plan to feeling fretful and having a sense of doom. Doom so complete that he was finding it hard to breathe. His thoughts raced, *'What have I done? They know me now, they know my assets…, take it slow, breathe.'* he stressed to himself. *'Yes, breathe, yes, okay.'* But he did not sit down; he was at the counter with both hands on the edge, head hanging down and feet apart. Just as he was about to start ordering someone to come out immediately a man came out the side door on the left. Another feature he had missed! And he walked up to where Thomas was and from behind the counter Thomas thought idiotically, *'He's smiling at me!'* but before he could speak the man was saying,

"Hello, Mr Nelson, how are you? Sorry to have kept you waiting," and extended his hand. Thomas didn't take it. Thomas did however straighten up and began demanding this man explain himself. With a slight look of puzzlement on his face Tim O'Rourke said, "You came to ME," in a raised voice. "Perhaps," and he paused, "you should explain what you want the money for so I can determine if I will lend it to you," and he fixed a stare on Thomas that made him flinch.

Tim O'Rourke was no fool and did not indulge anyone; least of all a young upstart like this bloke. Tim wasn't much older that Thomas, maybe 28 to Thomas's nearly 21 but Tim O'Rourke did not suffer fools and he had decided Thomas Nelson was one. Thomas was taken aback with the directness of the request and his apparent dismissal and so he quickly explained the business he wanted to buy shares in and how the money would help tip the edge in his favour to owning the paper mill. "I will resurrect it and be able to pay you back quickly."

"Well, I think I can help you then." Glancing down at the application form in front of him, "Mr Nelson, Thomas, before I can say to what extent I can assist you I will need to research the business myself. It's a safety precaution in case I think it looks like a bad choice. You would totally understand that; being a business man yourself." There was a pause and he proceeded, "Still, I am sure you are on to something. Come back tomorrow, around 3 pm and we will talk business."

Thomas left the shop but had a deep sense of unease.

The next day he was walking into his local stock broker's office on Sturt Street with $3000 in his hand. *'Well that had gone smoothly for sure,'* he thought. He had been in and out of O'Rourke's office in three minutes. Now Thomas could put all his plans into action, $3000 of shares equalled a large chunk of the Paper Mill.

"Hello sir," a friendly old man of about 70 with a white shirt, black vest and thick glasses said, whilst adjusting his bow tie. "Oh! Mr Nelson, it's you? How can I help you today?" Isaac Pender had been working as a stock broker for years and prided himself on remembering his clients.

"I want to buy 10,000 shares in the paper mill business of Rollins and Sons."

"Well, well, this is a popular little business today," Isaac said with a rise of his left eyebrow.

"What do you mean?" Thomas retorted in a rather aggressive tone.

"I mean that I sold a large packet of shares this morning which means that, at present, there are fewer than 7,000 shares left and the share price rose immediately, proportionally to that large buy up. Just about doubled, in fact," and his voice tapered off as he reached for his calculator and began tapping numbers. "Hmm, yes now," but Isaac Pender stopped midstream. He was staring at an enraged Thomas Nelson who was rubbing his eyes very hard and, saying to himself, more than to Mr Pender, in an almost inaudible tone, "Yes I know the bastard. Do you think that's a good idea? Okay, alright. Yes."

"Umm, Mr Nelson do you want to buy the rest?" Isaac was feeling a little concerned.

Thomas returned to the counter, red-faced but apparently calmer and said, "But how can that be? Who bought those shares? I had calculated 10,000 shares and I have the money. Look, $3000," and he waved the money in front of a very confused and quickly becoming frightened Isaac Pender. Thomas was still speaking,

17

"Now you are saying someone has taken up the bulk of the shares pushing up the price and reducing the amount to buy!" He was shouting now. "How, why, who? This is NOT the plan!"

"Calm down, son. I can't tell you who. That's not ethical. All I know is this woman came in first thing this morning, said her husband had been given a very good tip and he wanted her to come in and buy some shares. Now, do you want the rest of the shares or have you changed your mind?" Thomas was livid. He knew it had to be Tim O' 'bloody' Rourke and he was thinking murderous things.

"Hey son, come on. I haven't got all day. If you want the shares let's do business; the shares at the current market value, and my fee of $275.00. What are you going to do?" Isaac wanted him out of his shop.

Thomas knew it was a good business, he'd done the research and he quickly calculated that even with the reduced shares he could still make good money. He felt flat and very angry but he was determined to go home with some pride. He was also determined to pay Tim O'Rourke back, as soon as possible, and never have anything to do with him, ever again.

He left the stock broker's office with 5,900 shares. As it turned out, that was enough and he had profited well regardless. It was from that transaction and the manner he found himself that his love and interest in stocks, shares and bonds was cemented. He had been able to pay the loan back to O'Rourke in full with minimum interest. He had determined that the quicker he was rid of Tim O'Rourke the better.

From that point on he had found his interest in the stock and shares market. He was mostly a technical trader because he loved following charts and looking for patterns, it suited his personality, but he knew he could not pigeonhole himself and also moved in fundamental trades as well.

Like he had done with the paper mill business he surveyed the wider business environment looking for opportunities. On one occasion he had seen world prices of oil and petrol go up due to civil unrest in the Middle East and other foreign lands and how that hike had affected people's ability to travel as much and as a consequence of that, tourism was being affected. He decided he needed to sell shares in his tourism portfolio and he bought into cochlear ear implants, a new but innovative invention that hoped one day to help deaf people hear. It was a risk but Thomas had researched and felt that over time this would pay off and it had. On the occasions he lost money he would spend days mooching around the house and his parents and brother knew to keep well away, but he didn't lose often. Thomas's intuition for money, buying and selling was amazing and rarely did he steer in the wrong direction.

Returning from his memories Thomas smiled. He was a handsome man of fifty-seven who had been born into money and he had taken the job of looking after his parents' property and growing more wealth very seriously indeed. He stood up and went over to the home bar and poured himself a brandy. Returning to his chair, he didn't pick up the paper again but sat thinking about his parents, their history, the history that his mother had never failed to remind him of throughout his life.

Chapter 3

His father, Oscar had a big break when he was eighteen, having won a Tattersall ticket worth a thousand pounds. His parents had encouraged him to buy a home with the winnings. Thomas's mother, Sharon, came from a wealthy farming family and at age seventeen she met and married Oscar. Thomas recalled this part of the family history as his mother's favourite and the only time she really showed her true self. She'd say, "Your dad literally 'swept me off my feet." Sharon had been walking home from the local shops with a girlfriend when, from nowhere, a group of young men came running around the corner, the group separated around the girls just in time but Oscar was not as quick and with a flurry of arms and legs he side-glanced Sharon, knocking her off balance before grabbing her by the arm and saving her before she fell. "What the hell do you think you are doing?" she yelled.

And in a spray of words he had said, "I'm sorry I didn't see you. Are you OK? It wasn't my fault really."

"Oh, forget it," she'd retorted angrily and with that she marched off with her friend in tow.

"Bloody hell," she said, turning to Lucy, "that was a close one. Do you know who that idiot was?" Lucy replied that she thought it was Oscar Nelson, whose family had just moved into the district from New South Wales. "Mum was telling me," continued Lucy in a conspiratorial tone, "that his mother was 'convalescing' after the death of Oscar's sister who was killed in a tractor accident. Apparently the mother couldn't live on their farm anymore. Too many memories, you know, so they moved here to try and get over it."

"How does your mum know that?" Sharon asked, with eyes wide and loving the gossip.

"Mum popped over to welcome them and the father told her as much." Mum said, "He told me; 'my wife will not be socializing within the community any time soon but thank you for coming over.' And Mum said he went on to explain about the accident and, that was that. He dismissed her."

"That was about four months ago and no one's seen the mother to this day! Odd isn't it?"

Sharon had said that she thought it was but didn't think much more about it.

However from that day onwards she would stop and talk to Oscar when she was walking either to or from school. Within four months, to the day, of their meeting, Oscar Nelson proposed to Sharon and six months later they married. For a wedding present Sharon's parents bought them their first home – a sturdy four bedroom weatherboard with polished floor boards and all the mod cons of the time. Oscar decided to rent his home out to one of his mate's parents. Sharon and Oscar settled into married life with Oscar proving to be very handy with his hands and being business smart. He opened his own business at age twenty in home maintenance and found there were plenty of people needing odd jobs carried out around their homes. During those years he worked hard but like so many, he struggled to keep his business going when WW2 broke out in 1939.

People could not afford home maintenance. Sharon travelled every day to the family farm and assisted her family, for which they paid her in meat and other farm goods, but money was very tight. Sharon had been in the kitchen of her parents' home one day, helping with cooking, when her mother mentioned that their neighbours, the English, were being threatened with eviction for unpaid mortgage repayments. "It's terrible what the war is doing to families. I heard this will only be the beginning of trouble for lots of people. Oh, I feel so sorry for them," and Sharon had nodded her agreement.

That evening she had related the story to Oscar over dinner and Oscar had replied, "The English? I know the husband, William, 'Bluey' we call him. He pitched in and helped when that kid went missing last year, remember? The child was only three years old. Bluey walked with me whilst we searched the Slatey Creek area. He seemed a really descent bloke. When that child was found murdered he actually cried." He bent to pick up his mug of coffee and taking a sip said, "I am sorry to hear the family's in strife."

The following day Oscar was thinking about the English's plight and was trying to think of how he could help. The local paper was reporting on many families struggling to make ends meet and he knew he couldn't help everyone but maybe there was something he could do.

It was about three weeks later that Oscar went to the local National Bank on Armstrong Street in Ballarat and put a proposal to the bank manager.

Oscar's idea was to buy out the English's mortgage and organise a rental agreement that suited all parties. In this the English would sign over their home but rent it back from Oscar for a minimal cost and the bank would benefit because they had a functional mortgage again. The tricky part was first to convince the bank, and then to convince the English, that this was good for them. Oscar was also aware it was good for him too. The bank was indeed difficult to negotiate with. It was unknown times and they were reluctant to lend any money, but, with the title of his home which he was renting and since marrying Sharon, and with Sharon and his home put up as collateral, the bank finally relented.

The following day Oscar went to the English farm around 10 am and knocked on the door. The home was a large ranch-styled weatherboard with wide verandas all around. There were two steps up to the front door which was painted in soft sky blue paint. As he waited for the door to be opened he looked at the window sills and the veranda decking and thought, *"Hmm; could do with a bit of maintenance."* Just then the door opened and a large lady carrying a small child on her hip answered the door. She looked very tired, as if she hadn't been sleeping well. Oscar wondered if she had been crying, such were her red eyes. Taking off his hat he said, "Mrs English, I am Oscar Nelson, my in-laws live next door." She interrupted and said,

"Yes, I know who you are, Mr Nelson. How can I help you?"

"Please call me Oscar," and quickly added, "Is your husband William home?"

"Yes, out the back chopping wood. Please come through," and she stepped to the side of the doorway and Oscar entered. He was immediately impressed by the large ceilings and the ornate decorative cornices and pressed metal on the walls and ceiling. The home had a long corridor splitting the house in half and he noticed as he walked behind Mrs English that the bedrooms seemed to be on the right and the lounge and study on the left before opening up at the bottom to a large, warm and homely kitchen. She continued to march him through the kitchen to the backdoor where she opened the flyscreen and called, "William, we have a visitor," and turning to Oscar said, "please take a seat," pointing to a large, cluttered dining room table that could easily seat ten people.

Oscar sat down where he was directed and waited whilst Mrs English placed the child on a rug and started to put the kettle on. "Tea? I'd offer you coffee but I don't have any," and with a chuckle in her voice, "hard to get anything in these times."

"Yes. Indeed it is." Oscar agreed.

The back door swung outwards and William English came into the kitchen. He looked at his wife and then quickly to Oscar and it was obvious he was taking a little time to place the man at his table. Then, as if a light bulb had gone off, he was over to the table, hand extended to shake Oscar's. "Oscar, Oscar Nelson, How are you mate? Hell, I haven't seen you since that little boy got lost. Oh! That was a terrible day, terrible," he uttered shaking his head. "Now, what can I do for you?"

"Well, this is kind of delicate," looking from Mr English to his wife, and William understood his hesitation.

"Yes, spit it out. Whatever you have to say you can say in front of Bekky here," and he moved to pick up the child and stand next to his wife, who was at the kitchen sink.

"Ok, I will simply say what's on my mind. The other day my in-laws, Sharon's parents, next door, mentioned that you were on the brink of being evicted from here," and he swept his hand and arm out in an arc. Oscar was feeling very self-conscious and wished they would sit down, but both stood and looked at him as if to say, "*So!*" So he stumbled on, clearing his throat. "Yes, well I was hoping that we could talk so as to, well I was thinking," eyes dropping to his hands that were in his lap, "I was thinking I might be able to help."

"Really!" It was William who spoke. "And why and how would you do that?"

Oscar sat up and straightened his back, looking straight at 'Bluey'. "Look, that's a fair question. The why is easy, you and I went through a time back there a few years ago and I knew straight away you were a good bloke and I just thought if I could help I would. I know Sharon's parents think a lot of you both." He was getting thirsty and asked for a glass of water which Bekky got pronto. After downing the water he continued, "As to the how I can help, I have an idea but, obviously, it is up to you if you want to consider it."

"We are listening," William said with a slight sceptical tinge to his voice.

Oscar cleared his throat again. "I thought I could buy your home, take over your mortgage and you could live here renting." He blurted it out and waited.

The look on the English's faces was priceless, Oscar thought, as he looked at them staring at each other and then him. Bluey sat down on the chair next to the sink and Bekky followed suit. "So you're proposing... that we sell the house to you and then we rent it? Rent it!" his voice was getting louder. "Why would we do that, Oscar? Why?"

"Well, I've been reading the papers and listening to the wireless and know that many people are being displaced by the banks because we are in hard times and they are ending up in boarding houses and squats or piling in with family and I thought..." Oscar was stumbling with his words. He had anticipated, no expected, some hesitation when he first mooted the idea but ultimately he had been thinking quietly to himself that they would see the benefits and even, possibly give him words of praise and thanks. The negativity and incredulous looks were taking him aback and he was feeling distinctly unsettled. He stammered, "Look, I'm sorry. I didn't mean to offend you or pry into your business, it's just that I thought I'd be able to help."

Bluey had stood again and was placing a hand on his wife's shoulder. "Look mate, I see what you're doing and that's fine but if we need help we will ask for it. Okay? We have some ideas to keep the bloody bank at bay and it doesn't involve selling."

"Well, that's great Bluey, really I am pleased. I hope you don't hold this against me. I was just trying to help."

"Thank you, Oscar, we understand." It was Bekky speaking, "Please say hello to Sharon's parents for us. How are they faring?"

Oscar was thinking to himself, *'Well that went down like a lead balloon. What was I thinking? And get me out of here.'* But when he realised that Bekky was speaking to him his eyes shot up and he said, "They are struggling like so many but they are just keeping their heads above water at this point in time."

"It's a nasty business this war. How it destroys lives. Very nasty," and then, as an afterthought, "can I get you that tea?" but Oscar declined and left.

About four weeks later Oscar was at home whilst Sharon was at her parents. Hearing a car pull up he rose and, answering the door, saw a very distraught William English on the doorstep. "William, what's wrong?" was his initial question, whilst at the same time he ushered William into the house.

"I'm sorry to just turn up here but…," and his voice trailed off.

"Here, here, please sit down," offering him the chair next to the fireplace. "Can I get you a drink? Tea, whiskey, anything?" and after a moment's hesitation William said, "Yes, I'd love a whiskey, if you wouldn't mind."

Oscar went over to the bar. "It's cheap but hits the spot." He got two glasses out and poured them both a decent slug of single malt whiskey and handed one to William and then sat opposite him in the other chair.

They both sat in silence and sipped the whiskey until William ventured, "Oscar, I feel really foolish but I don't know who else to turn to. Remember your offer of buying the house?" and he looked up, staring at Oscar. His eyes were a deep blue but were rimmed red from crying and his chin was covered in stubble, suggesting he hadn't shaved for a few days, which Oscar noted was probably unusual for him.

"William, what's wrong, mate, has something happened? Is Bekky alright?"

"No, that's the thing, she's sick, doctors aren't sure what it is but they have sent her to Melbourne for tests and, and I'm worried, really worried. We had plans to help us get through, like I told ya that day you came, but now I can't do it. Not without her and I'll have to be in Melbourne to be with her." He gave a deep sob and a sigh. "You see we were going to double the veg patch, you know," and he chuckled, "if it's one thing we can do well it's the veg patch," and Oscar did know, everyone in the area bought, when they could, vegetables from the English, they had that knack to get things planted just at the right time and they were so sweet. Pumpkins were the best. Oscar looked up from his musing and William continued, "Well I have been talking to a company in Bendigo and they were keen to distribute our veggies in that region 'cos they had failings in the weather. You know, rain, frosts etc. It wasn't going to be a lot of money but it was going to get us through, we were really looking forward to it. But," and again he faltered, "now," and he dropped his head in his hands, "now we can't, I can't commit to it. We just don't know when Bekky will be back and how long it will take for her to recover."

"I'm so sorry to hear this, it's so sudden!"

"Yeah, she's been fine but last week she began to feel breathless and very tired. She's stubborn and wouldn't go to the doctors but yesterday I could see she was getting worse and made her go. And straight away she was off to Melbourne… I'm bloody worried, Oscar."

Oscar refilled the whiskey glasses and handed William his. "Thanks. Anyway I want to talk to you more fully about your idea of buying the house and us renting."

The two men sat by the fireplace and Oscar outlined his idea that he would buy the home, effectively taking over the mortgage because selling real estate in this climate was not good and then the English could remain in their home and pay a modest rent. "How modest?" he asked a little too abruptly and Oscar said he wasn't sure but how would a quarter of the mortgage he usually paid per month sound.

Oscar could tell William wasn't happy but he also knew what he was offering was a fair deal. Eventually William looked Oscar squarely in the eyes and said, "You know I hate being in this position but this is about Bekky, not me, and she will need as much stability as possible. I don't want her to know that I have come to you Oscar, do you understand? This is between you and me."

"I understand," and they shook hands.

Two weeks later Oscar owned his second investment property.

Oscar went about buying up other people's mortgages as they struggled to make ends meet, and like he had with the English he gave them options to rent their homes at minimal cost.

Within years Oscar's real estate business was booming and his reputation as a fair and decent bloke was known far and wide.

Chapter 4

At twenty-two Sharon was pregnant with their first child and, although the labour was long, 30 hours, she gave birth to an 8lb 2oz boy and they named him William. Sharon soon fell pregnant again and her second son, Thomas, was born eighteen months later. Sharon was quiet strict with the children but loved them equally in her own way. William looked more like his father and Thomas tended to have features more from Sharon's side of the family. Even though there were only eighteen months between the boys they did not get on all that well and it seemed to Oscar that Sharon was at fault because she tended to play them off against each other. Some days William was the 'good boy' and Thomas the naughty one and then the next day the tables were turned. The children were forever trying to get in her favour which meant they pitted themselves against one another. Of course William often won out being that little bit older. One thing she would never tolerate from either boy however was if they cried. She had told Oscar one day, "It's the best way, Oscar, they need to be tough these days. I grew up on a farm. I know the extremes of life and I insist that my children will be survivors. I've seen other children in the area being brought up in cotton wool; and mark my words they are not doing them any favours." Although Oscar didn't necessarily agree with this tenet he simply allowed her to have her way, she was their mother and besides he had too much to do with his business to bother with the raising of children.

Oscar was however very attentive to the boys when he was home. He would take them out to the shed where, although he wasn't a man of carpentry skills, he liked to dabble and with the boys in tow they built a little billy cart. William was around five and Thomas only three. William loved it, the little wheels on the front of a T bar running the length of the cart with a packing box for the seat. String attached to the front axle between the front wheels and it flew. There weren't many sealed roads around but there were enough with a good incline that would see them pushing the cart up the hill, William getting in first and Thomas squizzing in behind and Oscar, with cigarette in mouth, saying, "Now take it easy Willy, have your feet ready to hit the road if it gets too fast," and then he'd give them a shove and away they'd go with him running behind. Many a time they came to grief but they laughed a lot too. Sharon would clean their gravel rashes and hear no sooking from either boy. When alone with Oscar she'd have a laugh about how brave they were, recalling the day before yesterday when Oscar had taken them out billy cart riding. "Oh, Oscar, you should have seen Thomas when I was cleaning his knees and elbow, he was going to cry, he wanted to, but he just looked at me and said, 'It hurts a lot, mummy, but I didn't cry'... Honestly Oscar, I just hugged him and told him what a brave boy he was, and over my shoulder I told Willy what a little man he was too," and she had smiled one of her rare but radiant smiles that seemed to shimmer across her face showing deep dimples and smiley eyes. It was one of the things Oscar had first noticed about her.

"Yep, great kids, love. And you're great too," and they held each other close enjoying a brief, and to Oscar's mind, all too few, moment together.

Chapter 5

In June of 1963 Oscar had come home from work at lunchtime in a foul mood. He stormed up the steps of their verandah and pushed the front door open with such force that it rocked the small table in the hallway sending the daily mail flying to the floor. Oscar ignored this and went straight to the kitchen, where he found Sharon with William, now aged six, and Thomas aged four at the kitchen table, chatting and laughing at something William had said. Sharon took one look at Oscar and jumped up and with an alarmed voiced said, "Oscar, what's wrong?" At the same time she turned to the boys and said, "Boys, will you go out and play in the back? I need to talk to Daddy." They didn't move straight away and Oscar then raised his voice, "Go, now, boys, go!" pointing frantically at the kitchen's back door. Having rarely heard their father raise his voice William looked terrified and Thomas looked between mother and father not knowing what to do. "Go boys, do as Daddy says, it is OK," and Sharon smiled at her sons. William grabbed Thomas's hand and the boys ran out the back door.

Outside they quickly realised that it was very cold but they were too scared to go back into the house for their jackets. William, still holding Thomas's hand, began walking towards the cubby which he and Oscar were building with a little help from Thomas. It was their latest building project and Oscar had made William the foreman and he was taking that role quite seriously. "Come on, Thomas, grab your tools, let's get the ladder and go in the cubby. Mummy will come get us soon." The boys started walking down the backyard towards the big gum when all of a sudden Thomas pulled away and shouted, "I want Mummy, now!" But William tugged at him, "No Thomas, something's wrong." But with a sudden burst of strength Thomas pulled hard, breaking free of William's grasp. He quickly turned on his chubby legs and ran around the side of the house. William followed slowly, calling and teasing, "Thomas, Thomas you are such a cry baby. Come back here. Come on. Mummy doesn't want you in there."

At hearing William's voice Thomas ran faster but instead of up the steps to the front door he ran to the gate, out onto the street and out of sight. At the same time as this occurred William came around the side of the house and saw him disappear. William knew that this was bad because his mother never allowed them out on the street on their own. He stood very still at the gate, undecided as to what he should do. After a while, having thought about how angry his Daddy was and how mad his Mummy would be because Thomas had gone into the street, he decided he better get Thomas back now before there was more trouble. Stepping gingerly through the gate and onto the dirt footpath he headed right, passing three of the neighbours' homes before coming up to a corner. As he drew nearer to the corner he saw Thomas on the other side of the road crying and looking around as if he was totally lost. William was standing beside a large elm tree on the nature strip. He called, "Hang on Tom, I'm coming." But William was scared. He was not allowed out on the street alone, and he was definitely not allowed to cross the road without an adult. He was still trying to work out what he should do whilst at the same time stepping out towards his brother. The instant he stepped on to the road it was too late to turn back. He had not looked for traffic; he did not see the bus until it was too late. It happened very quickly, William saw the bus and the driver had no time to stop; running over William and killing him instantly.

Chapter 6

Sharon still hadn't gotten to the bottom of what Oscar was so furious about when she heard an ear-piercing scream, then silence. In a flash she had pushed past Oscar and was running out the front door looking left and right and calling the boys' names. She ran around to the back of the house and down to the cubby house but the boys weren't there. She fled around the side of the house to the front yard again and this time she noticed the gate open. *'Oh no,'* she mouthed and ran. Once outside the gate she followed the road to the right and upon rounding the corner stopped abruptly. The scene before her was chaotic. She could see the bus stopped in the middle of the road and people milling about, shouting, "Get an ambulance," "Get help", "Oh that poor child." Nothing registered for Sharon. In her mind she was watching a show on the black and white TV. A show where people were looking around waiting for the funny man to come out and make them all feel better. Yet every instinct within her body, and that of being a mother, told her, her children were in danger or worse. With that clear thought she got moving again. Sharon ran up to the people saying, "What's happened?" the faces were blank, "let me through," and she began to push and shove people in an effort to find her children.

But a hand grabbed her arm and she was pulled backwards and gripped, vice like, by someone. Sharon couldn't see who it was and she continued yelling, "Let me go, what's happened? Please…" Then a voice, very close to her ear said, "Sharon, it's me Mrs Jacobs, from next door. It's your boy, William. It's terrible. Don't look. Let me take you home." She heard the words like someone talking through a hollow pipe, echoing and eerie. She just stood there in Mrs Jacobs' large arms taking nothing in. Her legs were beginning to buckle. Sharon had no idea of time but all of a sudden, when Mrs Jacobs began to move backwards, she came to life. "No, what are you talking about," she screamed, spinning on her neighbour and spitting out the words, "Where's William?" Her eyes were slits and her brow was knitted and Mrs Jacobs held up her hands defensively believing she was going to be hit but Sharon turned from her and called in a soft, almost dream-like way, "William! William!" before collapsing, in a faint, on the spot. The next thing she clearly remembered was sitting at her kitchen table with a strong cup of tea and Mrs Jacobs at the refrigerator. She slowly looked up and said, "Mrs Jacobs, where's William. What's happening?"

The older woman closed the refrigerator door and came to Sharon's side. "I am so sorry," placing her hand on Sharon's shoulder, "your son, William has died, the bus driver couldn't stop, the driver said he just stepped out in front of him. I am so sorry, my dear. It is awful."

"No," she cooed and dropped her face into her hands, "that can't be right." She repeated this over and over again. But in her heart she knew it was. "Where's my husband, oh God!" and she jumped to her feet. "Where is Thomas?" In all the confusion and chaos no one saw a little frightened four year old boy on the side of the road. No one that is; except Peter Cambridge.

Chapter 7

Thomas came out of his reflections, moved stiff-legged to the bar and refilled his brandy glass. He shook his head whilst raising his glass, "Here's to you, mother. To the Nelson history. But there was some history you never talked about, wasn't there? Oh yes, some things were to stay hidden, unspoken, forgotten; the secret, yes, you were good at that. Here's to you," and he downed the brandy and once more filled it, slumping back into his arm chair. Thomas never knew that Oscar held that secret too. Thomas's mind quickly drifted back to the day of William's death, his brother, he could never forget his brother. Thomas remembered watching in horror as his big brother William was hit by the bus. He saw the red blood on the road and he told William quietly, "Don't cry, Willy. It's alright. Mummy is coming." He recalled he was about to go to his brother when Peter Cambridge came up beside him and said, "Oh, you poor little thing. You better come with me. I will take you to your mummy," and Thomas had taken his hand and walked off with him without looking back at the road because Mummy was going to make William better.

Thomas remembered the house with the painted fence and the bushy garden path. The man was still holding his hand and talking to him but Thomas couldn't work out what he was saying. "Now you go inside and your mummy will be there," and Thomas had looked up at him and the man shook his head in the direction of the front door and shooed him with his hands. "Yes, just up there. Off you go," and released Thomas's hand and Thomas ran up the steps and into the house with the man following behind. With a quick look left and right Peter Cambridge walked through the front door, locking it behind him.

Thomas knew he had been with the man for exactly 48 hours before he had been released. His mother had told him that. Sharon had told Thomas years later that when she had realised Thomas was missing she went hysterical and the local GP was called and he sedated her, telling Oscar not to disturb her. "Oscar, it's better that she rests." In the meantime Oscar had called the police about his other son and a search was underway.

There was no sign of Thomas that day or the following day and Oscar had had very little sleep. A working party had gathered at his home and was asking questions: "Where do you think he might have gone?" "Has he taken off before?" Bluey was there and he ordered, "Jake Bussell, Bill Smith, you two go door to door and double-check none of the neighbours have the lad." He turned and spoke to the rest of the men. "Look, he cannot have gone far in this time, spread out and check the old quarry up there on Rose's Avenue, also under bushes." To Oscar he said in a calm and caring voice, "We will find him mate. Don't lose hope," but

Oscar was numb to the bone and absolutely no assistance to anyone. He refused to talk, he could only berate himself for being the absolute and total cause of all this and in his head he screamed for his sons.

The working party worked tirelessly with no luck and everyone, including the police, were at a total loss as to what had happened to the child. Around 12.30 pm, 48 hours after William had been killed and Thomas had gone missing, a neighbour spotted young Thomas in a confused, dishevelled state not far from where his brother had died. "Oh my goodness,' she called, as she rushed to the boy and ever so gently coaxed him to go with her. "It's not far dear, please come with me. I will take you to mummy," and Thomas Nelson screamed but walked holding her hand.

Oscar came to the door before the bell could be rung. He took one look at the screaming child and dragged him from the hand of Esme Catter and said, in a not so friendly voice, "Where did you find him?" To whit she replied, "I'm so sorry, Mr Nelson, William was such a lovely boy, I used to stop at the garden gate on my way home from the shops when the boys were playing outside and he was such a little chatter box. It's tragic, just tragic."

"Yes, yes, Esme," his voice more controlled now, "But where did you find Thomas?" and then protectively he picked his son up and Thomas stopped yelling.

Esme was saying, "Oh sorry, he was just standing on the footpath where the tragedy happened. I just looked out and there he was."

With that Oscar mumbled his thanks and walked inside and shut the door. Mrs Catter called out, "If there is anything I can do, please let me know." But she knew Oscar Nelson was nowhere in earshot.

Inside he placed his son back on the floor and Thomas stood mutely scanning the room, which he knew like the back of his hand, and yet at this moment, he did not recognise it. He trembled and moved slowly but deliberately towards the couch.

Oscar stopped him and bent down. "Thomas, where have you been?" but the child didn't speak. He hugged his son and repeated in a quiet but firm voice, "Where have you been, son?" but Thomas gave no indication that he had heard him. He just continued to scan the room.

"Ok. Thomas, you better go and see your mum, she's been frantic," and he let the child go.

"Where's William? William! William!" the little boy cried before running up the corridor looking in all the rooms. When he got to his parents' room he stopped and, looking through the open door, saw his mother on the bed not moving. He walked tentatively towards her but before he got to the bedside Sharon was saying, "William's gone, Thomas. Stop calling him. He's gone."

Chapter 8

Thomas took a quaff of his brandy and thought *'I'd better stop drinking. What time is it?'*, and he looked at his wrist. 5.16 pm, *'Dinner soon'* but he didn't do anything, remained seated, empty glass in hand and returned to his reminiscences – even though I had seen the bus hit William, even though I had seen the blood and heard the screams of people I was still not sure what that actually meant for William and no one bothered to tell me. He recalled that whilst his mother was saying "William's gone, Thomas. Stop calling him. He's gone," his father had entered the bedroom and coming up behind him he was saying, "Sharon, you better get up and tend to Thomas, he's a mess," and she had responded, as if in a daze, "Yes. In a minute."

His father had gone to his mother then and holding her by the shoulders he had said, "Sharon, it's been two days, love. I have to go to work. I've had no sleep but I can't sit around just thinking. I have to keep busy. Oh dear God, why us?" he bemoaned, adding, "Sharon, lying about is not going to bring William back. We have to get it together, for Thomas's sake. Come on," and with that he left.

Thomas remembered vividly standing in that room feeling terrified, hurt and frightened but she never came to him, never comforted or consoled him. He knew now William had always been her 'little man' with his funny little jokes and great big hugs and kisses. That Sharon had gravitated closer to William than him and he remembered crying at that point. Quietly at first, and then more loudly. Between gasps and sobs he called his mother but when she finally acknowledged him it was to tell him to, "Shut up and don't be a sook. Just stop that crying."

Thomas stopped immediately. He remembered she didn't like crying and he had not cried from that day forth.

She had reluctantly gotten up then and was about to take Thomas to the bathroom when there was a knock on the door. Mrs Jacobs was on the doorstep. "Yes?" Sharon asked and Thomas heard her saying something about wanting to help and having time to cook or clean. His mother had stood aside and asked Mrs Jacobs, "Can you see to Thomas, he's upset?"

"Oh, you've found him. Oh yes, wonderful Mrs Nelson."

"Yes, he is found." Then as she passed Mrs Jacobs in the hallway she said as an aside, "Mrs Jacobs, could you let the authorities know Thomas is back? I don't have the energy."

"Yes dear. Of course."

As it turned out Oscar had informed all the relevant parties, thanking them for their time and concerns. "Yes he was overjoyed his son was back... No he did not know where he had been… No he did not want any help… thank you."

Thomas had pieced together the next memories from bits and pieces he had heard, remembering how Mrs Jacobs had followed Sharon down the corridor and into her room where she saw Thomas sitting hunched up under the window. His eyes were red with crying and his clothes were scruffy and dishevelled. Mrs Jacobs went over to the child and taking him gently by the hand asked, "The bathroom dear, which way?" and his mother had pointed to the right and Mrs Jacobs led him out of his mother's room and to the bathroom.

"There, there, Thomas, let me help you into a nice warm bath and we will get you your pyjamas and then something to eat. How does that sound?" and Thomas looked at her with such pain and suffering that her heart just about melted. "Come love. I'll look after you," and with those words he clasped her hand tightly and hugged her leg. They stood in this position for some time before Mrs Jacobs felt comfortable enough to get Thomas off her leg. "Come along, I will draw the bath and you get undressed, that's a good boy."

As Thomas was taking off his clothes she noticed bruising and scratches on his legs, arms, back, in fact all over the child. "My goodness, how did that happen?" but he did not reply.

"Thomas, I am going to get your mother, darling. You jump in the bath and I will be back straight away." Thomas did as he was told.

Mrs Jacobs found Sharon lying on top of her bed staring out of the window. "Mrs Nelson, you have to come with me, it's your son, Thomas. He is covered with bruises and scratches. Do you know where he's been these past two days? Did you find out what happened to him after William's accident?" and Sharon replied she did not know where he had been and had not asked but she would come to the bathroom and help.

When Sharon saw the extent of the injuries on Thomas her instinct to protect kicked in from nowhere and she instantly turned to Mrs Jacobs and asked her to call the doctor. She then knelt beside the bath and very quietly stroked his hair from his eyes and said, "Thomas where have you been for the past two days since William got hurt? Where have you been? Who was with you?" but Thomas just shook his head and said nothing.

Mrs Jacobs came back into the bathroom a few minutes later saying that the doctor would be there within the hour. The two ladies worked together to get Thomas bathed and into his pyjamas and Mrs Jacobs made a pot of warm, sugary, milky tea saying, "Here is what you both need," and Sharon was very grateful to have her there.

When Dr Flannigan arrived Thomas was in the lounge room and he still had not said anything to anyone. "Well, young boy, you gave your Mum and Dad a fright alright. Can you let me look at your injuries?" and Thomas nodded and pulled up his pyjama top. "Hmm, yes I see, I see. Can I see your legs and back as well?" Gently he looked at the boy's small body and cringed at seeing fresh blood streaks on the cheeks of his bottom emanating from his anal area. "Hmm OK, young man, you have been very brave," and gave him a little rub on his shoulder. "Thanks Thomas, that's all." Dr Flannigan then went over to his black bag and took out a small toffee and handed it to Thomas, who took it gratefully. "I'll be back in a minute. I just want a few words with your mummy. Okay?" He pointed to Sharon to follow and whispered as she came close, "I want to speak to you in private." Sharon nodded and led him to the kitchen where Mrs Jacobs was washing up. Upon seeing the doctor she exclaimed, "Oh doctor, how's Mrs Flannigan? I heard she had to go to Melbourne for some tests."

"Yes Claire, that's right we cannot have any secrets here can we?" smiling widely, "no, she is fine, just a bit of arthritis is all. But thanks for asking. Now if you wouldn't mind going and sitting with Thomas for a minute I'd like to talk to Mrs Nelson."

"Of course," and she dried her hands and decamped quickly.

As soon as she had left the doctor turned to Sharon and said, "It looks to me like someone has been manhandling Thomas. The bruising on his arms and legs are consistent with someone holding him like this," and he demonstrated on Sharon's arms by enfolding his hands around her biceps and squeezing, and then indicating, but not touching, a squeezing action around her upper thighs. "His back is covered in scratches and bruises and he has laceration around his anal area. We need to call the police. I've seen this before. Sharon, I believe your son has been molested." Unseen by Sharon and the doctor was Oscar, who had been standing just off the back porch listening to this conversation, but upon hearing the words, "Call the police," he blurted, as he burst in through the back door, in a sad but adamant tone, "That is not going to happen, doctor."

Doctor Flannigan jumped when Oscar entered the room but settled soon after and exclaimed, "Why in

God's name not, Oscar? The child has been violated. He will need help and this monster needs to be caught."

"I said no and that is the end of that. We can handle this ourselves. Do you think we haven't suffered enough with William's death two days ago and now this! I will not have Thomas exposed to any prying eyes and dragging our family through more grief. Thomas is young; he will get over it. Just do what you have to do, doctor, from a medical point of view and that will be the last we will speak of it."

"Oscar." It was the doctor again, "I believe you are making a big mistake." Turning to Sharon he said pleadingly, "Sharon, talk to him, make him see sense." But Sharon was already silently agreeing with her husband. The shame and scandal of it all. How they couldn't look after their own children, protect them. She knew she was a failure, she didn't need all of Ballarat knowing too.

The doctor could see he was wasting his time and so he excused himself from both of them and returned to the lounge, where he applied Mercurochrome to the scratches and asked Thomas if he had any pain, but the child looked vacantly at him saying, "No doctor. No pain. It's alright, William will look after me." Dr Flannigan gave the boy's hair a ruffle and said, "That's nice Thomas, very nice. Yes. Would you like another toffee?" and he said he would.

Chapter 9

William's funeral came and went without Thomas being in attendance. As the weeks drew on and the household got back to some semblance of routine Sharon noted that Thomas remained aloof and virtually non-communicative. Although deep down she knew the child was traumatized she would quickly push the thought to the back of her mind and justified her inability to connect with the child by saying to herself – Oscar is alright, he's young, he just needs time.

But Thomas was struggling. His four-year old brain was swimming with images of the man who said he was going to help him but who had hurt him. He didn't know why but he did understand that his parents were unhappy with him. They didn't talk much or do any of the things they used to do. His parents' total rejection of him made him want to disappear and in his mind he had. He was gone and the only person he spoke to was William. Yes, William was there and William understood. William loved Thomas and Thomas loved William. As long as William was there Thomas felt he was alright. He didn't need anyone else.

It was about four weeks after the funeral when Sharon had woken and felt a little energized. The heavy burden of grief and having to do day to day tasks had been exhausting and so she revelled in the feeling that a veil had lifted and that perhaps life could go on. She didn't know why but she just felt stronger. That morning she watched Thomas in the lounge playing with his trucks and decided to take him to see where his brother was buried. She felt that this would help him understand that his brother was not coming home. It had bothered Oscar and Sharon that since his return home to them he had spoken little but when he did speak it was as if William was still there or that he would be home soon. Seeing his grave might help him understand his brother was gone forever. With that thought she suppressed the overwhelming surge of emotion that threatened to overtake her any time she thought of William. Determinedly she entered the lounge room and said, "Thomas, can you come here dear?" He got up immediately and went to his mother and she bent down smiling and gave him a hug – something she hadn't done since William left. "Thomas, how would you like to go and see William?" Thomas's eyes shot up to hers and he tilted his head to one side as if sizing her up. "Yes Thomas. Just you and I. It's time, darling. You'd like that wouldn't you?' and Thomas threw his arms about his mother's neck. "Yes please, mummy."

"Then go get your jacket and we'll be off," she chimed.

As his mother helped him with his jacket Thomas was confused, scared and excited. He was going to see William. Where had he been? Why had Mummy and Daddy been so upset, yet they knew where he was. In the end he didn't care, he was going to see William and that was all that matter. Then everything would be back to normal.

They drove up Sturt Street and Thomas knew this road well. He and William had often travelled along it in their mother's car when out shopping. Turning right into Doveton Street they travelled another five minutes before Sharon stopped the car and got out. As they had been slowing down and stopping Thomas had felt a slight change in his mother's demeanour, a sadness that hadn't been there when they left home, but here it was again. Sharon opened the car door and Thomas hopped out and held his hand up to hers, but she didn't take it. "Where's William?" he asked his mother and she replied, "Shh, Thomas. Follow me," and with that they entered the cemetery and headed left.

He was looking all about him and was feeling very worried and confused, wanting desperately to call out, "Come out, come out wherever you are." A great game he and William played all the time but he knew instinctively that his mother would be mad at him. Instead he wandered slowly behind her and scanned the area for any signs of William in amongst all the concrete trees with funny writing on them. He jumped when his mother said, "Ah ha, here we are, Thomas dear. This is where William is. I am sorry you couldn't come to the funeral but now you know where your brother is that should help, I think. Next time we come we can bring some flowers, he'd like that wouldn't he?"

Thomas looked at her and saw she was crying, tears on her cheek. How can that be, he thought. *'To sook.'* He then looked at where his mother was looking. Freshly dug ground covered with wilted flowers and a lump of stone – like everywhere in this place. He looked about him and said innocently, "Mummy, where is William?"

"There, Thomas." With a touch of annoyance in her voice as she wiped her eyes, "There," and she pointed to the ground at their feet. "See. There. That's where we buried your brother, there."

And Thomas was horrified. He knew the word buried. Hadn't he and Daddy and William and Mummy buried little Dynna? He remembered that day very well. Dynna was a little hairy terrier who Thomas had known all his life and one day he got sick and Daddy said he was dead. Sharon and he were talking in the kitchen but William and Thomas could hear them. "We will have to bury him. But I don't want the boys to watch," and Sharon had said, "Don't be silly, love, that is what life is about. Life and death. Like on the farm and the boys need to understand that."

"Alright then, if you think so," and Oscar called the boys and explained that Dynna was dead and that they had to bury the body. Thomas began to cry as his father wrapped Dynna in the blanket and they went out the back door. After digging a hole under the Peppercorn tree in the back yard Dynna's small body was placed in the hole and both boys were horrified watching their father throw dirt over his body and then stomp the ground with his foot.

On remembering what had happened to Dynna Thomas screamed, "No Mummy, no," and then "William!" as he threw himself onto the gravesite, scratching frantically with his little hands to save William, all the while continuing to cry out his brother's name.

It had happened so quickly that it took Sharon a moment to kick off her stunned disbelief of Thomas's reaction. When she did respond it was to grab him by the left arm and drag him off the grave and push him forcefully along the footpath away from the grave, all the while saying in a harsh but hushed voice, through gritted teeth, "Stop it. Stop it. What do you think you are doing? People will be looking at us. Thomas, calm down now. I don't want to smack you but I will. You are being silly, Thomas. STOP," but Thomas was inconsolable. His brother had dirt on him and he wasn't coming back – Dynna never came back – in his mind he screamed *"What's going on? William. Help."*

It was a terrible day in every way possible and Thomas knew, even though he was only four, that big people were scary and mean and hurt. He gave up struggling. They drove home in silence but William had come to help him and Thomas knew he would be ok.

Chapter 10

Thomas was never the same outgoing little boy he had been, but things had moved on. Oscar worked hard in the real estate business and Sharon busied herself between her parents' farm and her home-making endeavours. In private, Oscar and Sharon spoke of Thomas in terms like, "He's a strange boy. Very shy. Far too serious, a loner, he doesn't need a lot of company," and at the same time they each worried for their son. At school he kept to himself and there were times that he lashed out with violence towards other children in the class. In particular his grade 1 teacher raised concerns and invited Oscar and Sharon to the school to, "Discuss your son's behaviour."

"Yes, No worries," Sharon had said, "what time and where?" She listened and said, "Fine, Ms Butler, Oscar and I will be there." Oscar and Sharon attended the Black Hill primary school the following day. It was a small school of about 80 children with a huge playground divided with an invisible line that marked the area where the preps and grade 1's and 2's could play and the rest of the school in the other section. Thomas's classroom was in the original brick building with the large windows and high ceilings. Over the years extensions were added to match the recent designs of that particular era. As they entered through the front gate Oscar noticed all the children lined up waiting for either their parents or the bus. Oscar had not been to the school for a long time and definitely not since the death of William. He was deep in self contemplation, as he often was, about what he could have done to save his son, knowing full well there was nothing, when Thomas came around the side of the building and stopped dead in his tracks. With a casual wave Oscar called him over and after a moment's hesitation and a look from left to right the child went to his father. "Hey young man, how's school been?"

"Good," and he diverted his eyes back and forth between his parents. "It's ok. Ms Butler just wants a word. Go play on the swings and we will be out in a tick." As Oscar turned to the school entrance he saw Ms Butler in the doorway.

They followed her into the classroom which was decorated with all the children's drawings, paintings and examples of writing. "Thanks for coming," shaking both Sharon and Oscar's hand. "Please sit down,' indicating the half-sized table with the half-sized chairs. Awkwardly they all sat.

"I'll get to the point. I know we are all busy and Thomas will be fretting. Thomas will be turning eight at the end of the year and I have some concerns about his social interaction skills. Now I know it is none of my business but I feel I need to express my concerns regardless. Have you noticed any strange behaviours? Things that you think are 'odd'?" Sharon and Oscar looked at each other and then Sharon said, "What do you mean 'odd'?"

"Look, he simply doesn't socialize with any of the children; this makes him the brunt of their attention, which I may add is not always good. On these occasions Thomas can be quite explosive, yelling and thrashing his arms wildly. Thankfully he will quieten quickly once an adult intervenes, but upon questioning him as to what was wrong he will not speak nor give eye contact, just stares blankly out the window or at some other object. I and the other teachers feel there is something wrong." She stopped for a breath and then proceeded. "Look, we know he suffered the tragic loss of his brother three or four years ago, perhaps that has something to do with his oddness. I am sorry but I only speak because I care and firmly believe that we need to do something sooner than later. If you know what I mean!"

It was Oscar who responded, "Thank you, Ms Butler, for your concern but what I am hearing from you is that our son is being teased and bullied and you blame him for reacting. This is preposterous, obviously you know these children," and he swept his arm in an arc, "I don't see their parents here. What is it you want us to do?"

"Oh Mr Nelson, you misunderstand. If the children are caught upsetting Thomas of course we discipline them, but it is more than that. Thomas doesn't talk unless spoken to and even then it is minimal. He is often seen staring into space and occasionally I have observed him talking to himself."

Oscar laughed at this and turning to Sharon, "Well Sharon, it makes sense to me. Having been bullied and not liked he would obviously prefer his own company or that of an imaginary friend. I never told you but when my sister died I had an imaginary friend too." Turning to the teacher he said, "And it did me no harm. My wife and I appreciate your concern and bringing this to our attention. I suggest you get these children to leave my son alone or we will have no other choice but to move him from this school." With that he stood and stretched with Sharon following. He proffered his hand and Ms Butler, clearly understanding that she had been dismissed, took it and walked them to the door. "G'day, madam." Once in the playground they found Thomas and left. Sharon and Oscar never discussed it afterwards because Oscar had clearly stated the 'matter was closed.'

On another occasion, when Thomas was turning eight years old, Sharon decided that she would invite the entire class of grade 2 to their home for a party, dismissing Thomas's protests that he categorically didn't want a party. "I don't like the kids in the class." But she had gone ahead regardless and only one child responded with an affirmative to come over. That person was Miles. Miles came from a family of six brothers and two sisters and he loved coming to the Nelsons' home to get away from the racket that was understandably the Smith family's life. Thomas liked being around Miles too, he couldn't say why but when Miles was around he knew he didn't have to – do anything or say anything. Miles was Miles and he would chatter and chatter and Thomas had no time to think, it was a break time away from his own thoughts.

When it was obvious that no one else was going to come to the party Sharon decided to take Miles and Thomas to the Zoo for the day. The train ride to Melbourne was very exciting, followed by a tram ride and then the Zoo with all the beautiful animals. Thomas was rapt. Sharon told Oscar later that evening about how the boys had run from one enclosure to the other and made up stories about the lions and the monkeys escaping and the zoo keepers having to run around and catch them all. They had laughed and chattered, eaten ice-cream and hot dogs and, "Thomas was relaxed Oscar, really relaxed, his face was soft and less concentrated and he even gave me a hug!"

"Well that's great, Sharon, perhaps he is going to come out of his shell. Let's hope, hey. I have always thought time would tell."

The morning after his birthday, and the zoo expedition, Thomas woke hearing his parents' raised voices. He hadn't heard them argue and yell for a long time. In fact he hadn't heard them speak to each other much at all. It seemed to Thomas that his father worked all day, came home at night, ate dinner and retired to the lounge to watch TV before going to bed having consumed brandy. He hated the evening ritual of kissing his father goodnight and smelling that smell. Sharon on the other hand mostly sat in the kitchen and drank something else which no one labelled or named but to Thomas's mind it was just as bad as Daddy's. She would sew, read or simply sit. So when he awoke to them in loud conversation it was a shock.

Thomas moved down the corridor to listen. Although frightened of being caught by his mother he was inquisitive, and besides, he needed the bathroom which was beyond their room. He stopped just short of the door and heard his father say, "No Sharon, I don't believe it. Really," and she responded, "Yes, I saw Dr Flannigan a week ago and he has confirmed it, we are going to have a baby, Oscar. Do you believe it? Oh! My love, I have prayed for this. I didn't know what you would think but I couldn't keep it to myself any longer." Thomas waited for his father's response. There was a pause and then he heard his father say, "Sharon" then there was silence before he spoke again,

"He will not replace William. You know that don't you?" and she said in a lowered voice,

"No but…" however before she could finish her sentence Thomas marched into the bedroom and said, without a doubt in his mind, "Of course you can't replace William because William has never left. William is here, don't you know that?" and he categorically stamped his foot. Oscar and Sharon looked at each other, unsure of what to say for a split second, and then she laughed and Oscar laughed too. "Yes, you are right. Of course we know William is here," and she touched her heart and then Oscar's. Then with a winning smile she turned fully to her son and said, "And now you can get out of here you eavesdropping mite. I was going to tell you later." Oscar joined the mock anger adding, "Yes, young Thomas get back to your room, you naughty boy, and get ready for school," Thomas left but not before he heard them both say, "This is so exciting."

At age nine Thomas had a brother again. It was 1968 and they named him Roger. Roger was the spitting image of William as a child and the instant devotion of his parents was palpable. Mrs Jacobs had come over to wish them well and it was the first thing she had said, "Oh! My lord, isn't he the dead spit of young William?" Other comments cemented the fact that Roger tended more towards his father's side of the family which had the finer features like William had. "He looks like you dear." Mrs Jacobs had said to Oscar with a beaming smile. Everyone was happy except Thomas who didn't care about the baby. He could see Roger was dominating his parents' attention so he, Thomas, withdrew completely.

From nine until age seventeen Thomas's life was fairly static and predictable. He studied hard and excelled in academia. If he wasn't studying he was reading novels or in his room listening to music, mainly Bob Dylan, Joan Baez and other American stars of the time. He rarely had friends over although Miles remained a close mate but Miles was into sports and that left Thomas cold. When Thomas was seventeen Miles had called by and invited him to come with him to the local basketball game being played at the basketball stadium. "Come on, Thomas, you can't sit at home forever. Come on out, it will be good for you." Thomas was going to argue the point but realised it was probably pointless. Putting his book down, he grabbed his duffle coat, shouted out to his mother where he was going and left.

The stadium had been quite packed, with Ballarat Tigers playing against the Wild Cats. "This is always a great game, Peter Cain number 24, on the Tigers' side hates Jessie Walker number 3 on the Cats'. Last time they played they got into a big punch up. It was great," Miles was saying as they shuffled through the crowd and found two back seats up high. "Look, there he is," Miles pointed, as number 24 did a layup and missed. The game started and finished with Thomas hardly registering any of it except for the running commentary of Miles by his side. When the final siren sounded the Wild Cats had won by three points and there had been no incidents between any of the team players. "Well, that was disappointing," Miles was saying as they came outside.

"I was sure Pete would have had a go, especially when he was tripped!" and without waiting for a comment from Thomas he continued, "anyway what did you think of the game?" Silence. "Thomas …Hellooo Thomas. Is anyone home?" But Thomas was not responding, he had stopped walking and was staring across the road. Miles looked in the general direction but couldn't see anything specific. "Hey Thomas, you OK?" and Thomas turned to him and said, "Yes, yes it was good. Miles, I have to go now. Thanks," and walked across the road in the direction he had been staring. Miles called to his back, "Hey Thomas, where are you going?" but Thomas was oblivious to all around him.

Chapter 11

Peter Cambridge had been 42 years old when he moved to the Ballarat district, having relocated from Wangaratta after he was released from prison, although no one in the district knew this, in fact no one really knew him at all. He was a tall man and had always prided himself on the fact that he kept himself fit. Being born in Wangaratta to an Italian father and Australian mother Peter Cambridge was the fifth child of seven, having an older sister and five brothers. The family was close knit and they lived on a small acreage where his father, Giuseppe Tascotto, had two industries. He planted tobacco and he also grew wine grapes. Both proved very profitable. During the years of Peter's childhood his father's extended family all immigrated to Australia, initially working for his father on his farm but then buying property of their own. Giuseppe's property backed onto the Ovens river and he irrigated both crops from it. When Peter was only five years old tragedy hit the family with his two older brothers, then aged nine and ten, being bitten by tiger snakes. The area was riddled with the snakes and in breeding season it was nothing to see the snakes roiling behind the tobacco sheds, mating. Although it was a fascinating thing to observe, the snakes entwined in circles and constantly moving, heedless of anything else about them, Peter and his siblings were cautious. One day his mother happened to notice him walking towards the snakes, trancelike. The scolding and berating he received meant that thereafter, his only reaction to a snake was to run in the opposite direction. It was a Saturday afternoon and the two older brothers had been helping their father in the seedling section of the tobacco patch. The task was simple; the boys would dig up the seedlings from the ground and pack them neatly into prepared boxes ready to sell to other farmers for their crops. Both James and Buddy had done this countless times. The pocket money was well worth it.

On this particular day they had stopped working and headed off to the river for a swim. Buddy, the older of the two, ran ahead and was throwing a tennis ball over his head calling out, "Catch it." Inevitably the ball was caught by James, who then threw it forward over Buddy's head for him to catch. It was a great game and one they played often.

"Catch it," Buddy yelled, as the ball flew high and crooked off the path and into last year's paddock of tobacco plants. James ran after the ball, seeing exactly where it landed and swooped on it with his right hand. "Got it," he yelled, followed by a sickening scream, "Snakes. Buddy. I've been bit," and he stood and ran back towards the house. Buddy took only a few moments to understand and ran after his brother. For some reason, something Giuseppe would lament later, "He ran to where the snakes were, he followed exactly where James had been, why didn't he run back along the track and catch up to James further along? Why? Oh, I know this is true but why?" Buddy and James were found together on the track half way between the Ovens river and the homestead later that afternoon, dead.

The family grief was enormous and the children were sent to live with uncles and aunts until Giuseppe and his wife were ready to take them back. Peter and John went to live with Giuseppe's older brother Franko and Victoria; Joe, Christina and Louis went to stay with Giuseppe's older sister and brother-in-law, Salina and George. The family remained in close contact but Giuseppe and Helen took five months to return to some semblance of functionality.

During the five months with his father's brother five-year old Peter and eleven-year old John were subjected to the most heinous acts of abuse both sexually, mentally and physically. Their uncle controlled them with fear and mental torture. The day the boys returned home, Franko told Giuseppe and Helen he was glad to hand the boys back. "They were a little hard to handle at times, brother, but I made compensations for their bad behaviour knowing they were grieving. Yes." He smiled and they thanked him for all his help in this terrible time. Five years later the family met with another tragedy, the suicide of their eldest son, John, age sixteen. No-one could understand why.

Peter Cambridge hated it when his memories floated back to those days. He changed his name as soon as he could at age eighteen from Tascotto to Cambridge and he never saw his family again.

As he walked amongst the crowd coming out of the Basketball stadium he was musing about his past and following on from his childhood memories he recalled the day he left his home, the one he still lived in today, and went for a walk. Upon turning a corner he saw a bus in the middle of the road and people everywhere shouting and a child on the ground obviously dead. *"How sad,"* he had thought. Then he noticed the little boy on the side of the road staring at the commotion. Cambridge watched him and he was saying to himself, "Let him go, you don't ever want to go back to prison, it's not worth it." But the urge was strong and he convinced himself, *"The child is in need, he is scared, abandoned, why didn't these people see that? I can help,"* and before he even knew what he was doing he had sidled up to the child and told him he would take him to see his mother. *"Well, that was a long time ago,"* he said to himself.

Cambridge was now fifty-five and he had managed to stay out of prison for the past thirteen years. Yes, he'd been hassled by the cops repeatedly whenever a sexual crime was committed but they had nothing on him. *"I'm a model citizen,"* he would say to himself. He had established a small circle of friends to socialize with. He didn't work but volunteered at the local Anglican Church, assisting in any activities that might need his attention; fetes, driving a bus for older people of the congregation when they went on outings, that sort of thing. And, importantly, he made sure that he did not work around any children, not after what happened two years ago. That memory would forever hound him and had left him always looking over his shoulder. He had nightmares about that day and knew he would for the rest of his life.

It had been a Saturday and he had been shopping at Safeway in Sebastopol. He didn't normally shop there because it was across town from his home but there had been a magazine delivered with a number of specials and, in particular, a buy one, get one free for a scented moisturizer he enjoyed using. He would smear it over himself when he showered and it often aroused him with thoughts of being with young boys. He knew society abhorred him but he also knew they knew nothing and that he wasn't the monster he was painted out to be. He, Peter Cambridge, loved children and would never hurt them.

He was at the checkout with six bottles of the moisturizer when he saw a young mother with her young son, he guessed about two or three. The child was looking tired and was lagging behind his mother. Peter paid for his goods and went out into the car park, popped his bag on the front seat and was just about to get in the car when the child came wandering out of the shopping centre and walked directly towards him. Peter looked around but could not see the mother. There were other men and women in the area all busy with their shopping. Cambridge took a few steps towards the child and with the proficiency of a tiger catching his prey, he had the boy in the car and was driving out of the car park in seconds. His heart was pounding as he pulled into his driveway. The child had said nothing, done nothing, just sat exactly where he had been put. *"It's amazing,"* he thought, *"It's as if he was waiting for me, knowing I would help him."*

"Just wait there now," he said to the little boy and the child looked up at him and smiled.

Once inside Peter went about getting the boy some milk and chocolate biscuits which he ate and drank happily on the floor near the lounge room couch. As Cambridge took the cup from the child he noticed that his pants were wet. "Oh my! Come here little one, you wet your pants. That must be uncomfortable. Let me help." He picked up the boy and took him to the bathroom where he proceeded to draw a bath and undress him. It was during the act of drying the child that the child began to get upset and wanting his mother. "Now, now, don't worry. You've been such a good boy so far," he said in a coddling manner. "Come on. I will take you to mummy very soon."

Peter Cambridge didn't know how things got to the point that they did, he blocked it out but one minute he was loving the child and the child was loving him back and the next minute the child had stopped breathing.

That night he saw on the local news that a two year old child had gone missing and there was a search underway. The news reporter was saying, "This morning around 10.30 young Billy Snowden was shopping with his mother when he went missing. The mother said she had been talking to a friend in the shopping centre and hadn't noticed Billy wander off. She told the reporter she looked everywhere and then the manager of the store rang the police. Anyone seeing young Billy, who was wearing a red cardigan with blue jeans and white sneakers, are to call the Ballarat Police." The news then turned to overseas issues and Cambridge turned the television off.

A week later there was less coverage of the missing Billy Snowdon and gradually it was no longer reported on. The child was never seen again and Peter Cambridge was the only one who knew why. Billy was buried under his house. The death of the child had been an accident and yet he knew he must have been too rough, the child was only two. He had vowed to never touch a child again even though he knew he had a lot to give. He had kept that promise to himself.

Chapter 12

Thomas had seen Cambridge – not that he knew his name – but he knew him the second his eyes spotted him in the crowd. He quickly said his goodbyes to Miles and, crossing the road, began to follow at a distance. His thoughts were rushing and tumbling at such a rate that he didn't know what he was thinking. He was just pursuing, he could not let him out of his sight.

Thomas remembered that the man had taken him to his house and got him a drink of lemonade. Thomas was frightened and sullen and would not speak to him except to say, "Where's William? Where's my mummy?" and the man told him mummy was looking after William because he had hurt himself and that she wanted him to stay with him for a little while. "I don't want to stay. I want my mummy." He had cried and then remembered he wasn't allowed to cry, Mummy would be mad, so he stopped soon after beginning. The man had said, "You will see her soon," and in that, he was correct.

Exactly forty-eight hours after the horrible accident that man had released him onto the road when no one was around and pointed him in the direction of home. In recalling this terrible time he remembered that the man was tall and had a two day growth and smelt of musk and body odour.

Thomas was following in a type of fugue state, it was real yet his emotions were so piqued, so raw and his thoughts so concentrated on what that man had done that he almost missed seeing him turn right at the corner of Regent and Doveton Street. Thomas slowed down; *'Concentrate'* and he shook his head. He watched as the man entered through the garden gate of a weatherboard home. He walked slowly by the house noting the number but kept walking. Thomas's heart was racing; nausea he felt was threatening to overtake him. His legs were slowing and his arms felt like lead at his side. He feared he would stop altogether.

Thomas had no idea how he got home that afternoon but he remembered finding himself on his bed staring at the ceiling. Slowly he looked at his watch and seeing that is was 6.30 pm he got up and went to the kitchen to get a drink. Sharon was peeling potatoes at the sink and looked up, "You look terrible, Thomas, Are you alright?"

He mumbled he was fine, grabbed a glass of water and went back to his room. Thomas knew he could never be settled within himself until he knew who that man was.

After a restless night he rose, showered and dressed. He then rummaged through his wardrobe finding his back pack and went into his father's shed. Once in the shed he selected a number of tools.

Thomas left the house via the side gate, hoping to avoid his parents. This morning he was clear on his direction and what he needed to do. Outside the Regent

Street home he stopped and took in his surroundings. It was a quiet street and there was nobody about. The fence was a high wooden slatted fence with a couple of large gum trees overhanging it. The gate was wrought iron with an intricate pattern on the top one third. It was attached with a chain and hook similar to a farm gate. Slowly but deliberately he unhooked the gate, stepped through and quickly re-hooked it. At the same time he looked furtively about the garden and moved to the closest gum tree and took stock. The house was a weatherboard with a few steps up to a wide verandah and front door with large bay windows either side. It was etched in Thomas's memory although it looked smaller than his four year-old mind remembered.

Swinging the backpack off his back and holding it in his left hand he opened it and withdrew a knife he had secreted away the night before from the kitchen. He re-zipped the backpack and as casually as he could, he walked up to the front door and rang the doorbell.

He quickly glanced at his watch, noting the time as 8.24 am.

After the second ring of the bell the door opened to a man in a dressing gown, rubbing his hair down as if he had just gotten out of bed. Before he had time to speak or react Thomas shoved him in the chest, which sent the man staggering backwards, and at the same time Thomas entered the hallway and slammed the door shut. Peter Cambridge was wailing, "Hey! What the hell's going on?" and Thomas simply showed him the carving knife and screamed at him to shut up if he didn't want to lose his tongue. Cambridge instantly complied. He had been in prison and been bullied and intimidated and he knew the way to survive was to do as you were told until you knew what they wanted.

Thomas glanced about, trying to get his bearings, then said, "Let's go," and indicated the lounge/kitchen area. Cambridge walked in front of Thomas into the lounge and stood by the couch. "Look, if its money you want you have come to the wrong place. I don't have anything valuable. Please." He knew his voice was sounding whiney but he was scared, and his thoughts were racing. *"Was this guy the police? Do they know something?* And then, *"No, he's too young."* All this was rushing through Cambridge's head whilst his attacker was moving his arms about, waving the knife backwards and forwards while staring through him. "What are you saying? I can't understand what you are saying. Please!" But Thomas wasn't listening, he was trying to get control.

Finally Thomas stopped his movements, having gathered some clarity about what he was doing, and where he was. He pointed to the couch and said, "Sit down!" and Cambridge did.

Cambridge tried again, "Please. Just go, I won't tell anyone I promise." And he meant it, the last thing he needed was the police in his home. He then added, "Or at least tell me what you want."

Cambridge stood up then and immediately regretted it. Thomas lunged forward and the knife entered his right bicep, making him scream out and flop back onto the couch. At the same time Thomas landed on his lap, pinning him to the couch and holding the now bloodied knife to Cambridge's throat. Through gritted teeth he said, "Don't move or I will gut you – you bastard."

Chapter 13

It was 4.50 pm and Thomas was back at home, having returned his father's tools to the shed and his mother's knife to the kitchen. He then showered and changed and was wondering where best to discard his clothes from this morning. He was sitting at his desk in his room, unsure how he felt. He recalled the fear in the bastard's eyes as he sat on him with the knife to his throat and then the utter repulsiveness that careened through him at the reality he was touching his monster, his childhood monster. He had sprung up then and dry retched two times and upon seeing the man hadn't moved he pulled up a chair and sat opposite him. "What's your name?"

"I need to get my arm seen to," he cried.

"What's your name?" in a slow steady monotone.

"Oh God, Peter, Peter Cambridge."

"And do you remember me, Peter Cambridge?" and Cambridge shook his head, "No. Should I?"

"Oh yes, I think you should remember thirteen years ago, a bus accident, a little boy, you bringing him here to this." Head twisting right and left as he looked around, "This place?" and he waved his arm with the knife in it around and absurdly he noticed a drop of blood hit the floor and he wondered to himself, *'My blood is in this room, this house, my blood.'* He then looked up and said, "Do you recall that day, Peter?" Thomas was staring with such intensity that Cambridge could not hold eye contact, so he looked away and said in a very quiet voice, "Yes."

"Well, guess what? That was me. Do you know my name?"

"Yes. Yes I do. Thomas Nelson, who went missing after the death of his older brother. Yes. Thomas I know you and I am so sorry but... I sent you home, remember?"

"Shut up!" Thomas screamed. "You fucking creep, you're not sorry. You still enjoy sticking your fingers up little boy's bums? Putting bottles in their bums? Feeling them? Kissing them all over? WELL! ARE YOU?" and he leaned very close and repeated, "Are you, shit head?" Thomas was no longer in control of himself, he was seeing all this from above, like a waking dream, slow motion, he was slowly rotating his head first to the left then the right, he tensed and relaxed the hand that didn't hold the knife. He was seeing Peter cringing away from him now and he realised he was looking about for a way to escape whilst answering his question, "Thomas, no, no, I don't do that, not anymore I realised I was wrong, it was wrong, I AM sorry, I will pay you anything, please don't hurt me."

"A liar as well hey, you told me a minute ago you had nothing valuable. I came here," and he nodded to his backpack, "to teach you a lesson and to do to you what you did to me. Bugger you right up," and he raised his eyebrows and smiled. "But you know what, I have

74

changed my mind. Just being in the same room as you makes me sick in the stomach so, Peter, it's your lucky day."

Thomas saw Cambridge visibly relax, "Oh thank you, can I get my arm seen to now?"

"Sure," said Thomas in a slow elongated manner, "let me help you up," and extended his arm. Cambridge hesitantly extended his good arm, felt Thomas's hand grab his and with a yank he pulled Cambridge half off the couch then released him and at the same time drove the carving knife into his chest. Cambridge had no time to react; he knew there was a carving knife sitting his chest and he was powerless to do a thing. Thomas sat in the chair and watched as the life drained out of Cambridge. He is not sure what he did for the hours after that, could not remember leaving the house or anything although he had the vague idea he stayed in the home a long time.

Five days later there was a news item on TV talking about a church elder of the Anglican Church who had visited a Mr Peter Cambridge only to discover his decomposing body in his lounge room. Police reported that he was a well-known paedophile and had spent time in prison in Victoria and interstate. They had no leads as to the killer or killers and were asking for public assistance. The reporter was saying, "The victim had been interviewed two years earlier about the disappearance of young Billy Snowden but at the time the police didn't have enough evidence to arrest him. There are no clues as to what has transpired in this home."

Three years after Cambridge's murder the skeletal remains of Billy Snowden were to be found under his house after a dog dug up a small forearm in the backyard. The find was reported to police and led police to search the property and recover young Billy's body.

Part 2

Chapter 1

In the year 12 classroom there were eighteen students and their teacher. The room was fairly sparse, with lino on the floor, the typical blackboard at the front of the room and a whiteboard to the right of it. The students were sitting at desks facing the front, most with water bottle opened, along with books and computers. Some students preferred to take notes on their note pads and transpose to the computer at a later date. Any method was fine as long as the work was eventually done. The teacher was just wrapping up the lesson saying, "So, in summary, the point of this lesson was to wrap up the previous two lessons, and try to understand the reason people are so enthralled, still today, with the writings of William Shakespeare, and I would conclude that he provides us with life learnings. We have looked at a number of Shakespeare's novels and found many notable quotes throughout each and every one.

For homework this week I want you to prepare a thousand word essay from the book Hamlet, on the quote: "There is nothing either good or bad, but thinking makes it so." (Act II, Sc. II). I will be particularly keen to see your interpretations of this quote, not in the concept of the play but in its adaptation to life today. As I think Shakespeare wanted us to when reading his works. Think about a situation in your lives, it could be anything. Like..." But the teacher paused and thought and the students sat watching her. With a lift of her eyebrows they knew she'd found an example. These students had been in her English class for two years now and knew many of her movements and idiosyncratic gestures and until the lift of the eyebrows you gave her time to think without interruption, time to collect her thoughts.

So the students had sat quietly and waited for her to collect her thoughts so she could provide them with an example, "The situation could be you are travelling on the bus and realise you have forgotten your wallet. How could Shakespeare's quote above have any relevance to that simple life event?" Sarah Jones sat up and began to speak but she was cut off.

"No Sarah, I want you to consider this towards your own life example and put it to paper for next week when I will be happy to discuss your ideas." Then, looking up at the wall clock, "Goodness the bell will be sounding soon. Let's pack up. Thanks for all your input and as usual if you have any questions between now and then don't hesitate to catch up with me."

Everyone grabbed for their computers, books, papers and bottles and noisily left the room.

Carla Parkinson gathered her folder and headed out the door and down to her office. She had been working as a part-time High School teacher for nearly twenty years and she still loved her work and the students she taught. English was a passion of hers and trying to understand the nuances of language had been a constant throughout her life. She had formed the notion early on in her career that when you understand words within the context of your environment it was a way of survival and she was very focused on trying to teach younger people this; what she referred to as 'the survival tool' to get through life. She firmly believed language and breaking down the meanings of words effectively could save your life.

As she gathered her bag and papers from her desk she was thinking all this and nearly jumped out of her skin when her colleague, Jack Preston, came up behind her and said, "I heard you say you were having tomorrow off, Carla. Are you doing anything special? Need a long weekend?"

"Oh! Jack you frightened the crap out of me. I was deep in thought. No, no nothing, just thought having a Friday off would be good. You?"

"We have a flyball comp in Vic Park on Sunday so I'll be running around there. Anyway got to go. See you Monday."

"Yeah, enjoy the flyball, I might even pop over and take a look."

"Yes, do that," he called as he left the classroom doorway and headed down the corridor.

Carla wasn't 100% sure what flyball was but she knew it had to do with dogs and tennis balls and that Jack loved it.

She walked out into the High School car park, threw her bag on the front seat and eased out of the lot. She intended to head straight home, have a light dinner and get to bed early. She lived alone and was happy, particularly tonight, to have only her own company.

Chapter 2

Carla woke up at 5.36 am and wondered whether she was ever going to stop this asinine and senseless obsession with this date. She doubted it. She had been doing it every year, on this day, May 2nd, for the past twenty-one years. It was inbuilt in her core and to not obey herself on the rituals she made for this day was unthinkable. It would be like a death in the family, a hole so big it was unfillable; so no way was she going to deviate from her task. It was the only time she actually gave in and let herself be vulnerable to her thoughts and feelings. She was well aware it went against everything she knew of language and inner thoughts, her inner dialogue. She knew she could easily avoid this self-pitying day like she did every other day of the year but she wasn't going to. At 47 she was quite successful in her own right but on this day, as she always did; she would wallow and ask unanswerable questions of herself, "What if?" "What would life be like if it hadn't all happened?" "When did it begin?" and "How or why hadn't I done something?" Stupid, stupid, stupid thinking she knew but for her, necessary, a crutch. She needed to feel this emptiness, this void, this vacuum as she had come to think of it; if only once a year and then fill it fast in order to get on with life.

She was very aware it was self-defeating but she didn't care. Today she would indulge in the real person she was underneath – the self-doubting, over analytical, sad, and insecure person who felt there was no real sense of purpose to life. On this one day life just plodded on. The outside world saw the smart, deep thinker with a dry sense of humour and passionate nature for humanity. *"I'll be that tomorrow,"* she said to herself and chuckled.

She got out of bed and showered, leaving the wet towels on the floor, a thing she would never normally do, and wandered into her kitchen-dining room. Carla had lived here with her mother pretty much all her life except when she was married to Roger. That was the time she genuinely was the person she pretended to be today. During that time there was no effort being confident and emotionally attached to life. Five years of bliss back between the ages of 21 and 26 and then, life spiralled into a confusing mess which she had allowed herself to be swept along in. Although, to be honest, she had tried to make sense of it all but in the end she gave up and threw herself into work. At 26 she and her ten month-old son had moved back to live with her mother and she had been in the home ever since. Her mother lived in Ballarat on Prince St and over the years maintaining the house had become a constant burden for Carla, who had no interest at all in painting, decorating and maintaining the outside, or, for that matter the inside of the house, and as such, she spent a small fortune on getting 'handymen' in to do this 'odd job' here or the 'odd job' there. The house was set on a large block that fronted Prince Street but the driveway was entered from the back on Fawler Street. She rarely parked in the back, preferring to park on the street out front. As a young girl she thought the house was a mansion and so did her friends but now it was 'just the house'. She remembers asking her mum one day why she and her dad had bought such a big home when there was only the three of them and her mother had no idea why.

"Ask your father."

And he had said, "Carla, I think having a large house is good for us all to be able to get away from each other from time to time. Don't you?" and as time went on she definitely thanked her father for his forward thinking.

From the front door there was a small entrance way with an old hat rack and on the right was where she had made her office. A very cosy room with white walls and a large window facing the front road, a small two seater couch and her desk tucked in the corner. Carla saw private students in this room every Tuesday to complement her salary from the High School. To the left of the entranceway you entered the lounge and then through to the kitchen-dining room. Because the land was a sloping block the home was a split level with a downstairs section with a spare bedroom and the laundry. Carla only ever used the laundry down there, she never had people over to stay. She had an ensuite off her room which was on the ground level and adjacent to the kitchen. The kitchen was a small but functional room with plenty of cupboards and storage and a large gas stove and oven. She had gotten rid of the dishwasher and the slow combustion stove years ago.

Having fixed herself a cup of coffee and some toast she shuffled into the lounge, put on the TV and table lamp and curled up with her knees to her chin and began to think. In the past, when the 'what if' thinking came about, the day generally seemed to go in the same old fashion. If May 2nd fell on a week day she took the day off. She would arise early and mooch around the house and indulge her thoughts. By mid-afternoon she would be opening a bottle of champagne... Why not? And then over the next few hours drink it and listen to inane pop music and metaphorically 'beat herself up'. She basically never knew what to do with herself on this day, but this day needed to be marked and she marked it her way.

Carla had no idea as she sat on the couch, knees to chin, sipping her morning coffee, that today would bear no resemblance to her usual self-pitying – why me day?

Chapter 3

Carla didn't know how long she had been sitting hunched up on the couch but when her foot started to ache she stood up and kicked her legs about, trying to get the circulation back. She opened the curtains and walked into the kitchen. Even though it was May 2nd she still needed to keep some routines happening. It had been her habit every Friday to spend the morning cooking food which she could freeze and bring out during the week before going to her afternoon school classes. She mainly cooked foods like stews, soups, spaghetti sauces etc. because she knew that if she didn't have a big cook up day each week her diet would be sorely lacking. Cooking for one was impossible.

When her mother was alive they had taken it in turns to cook weekly, which was a good arrangement unless her mother was having one of her 'unstable periods'. During those times, nothing but nothing, got cooked, cleaned or shopped for; in fact daily life and routines were thrown out the window. Carla thought, *"Poor mum, sick most of her life. I suppose she couldn't help who she was,"* then she mused, *"but I wish I hadn't had to live through it all too."* Moving on from those thoughts she said aloud, imagining her mother was there with her, "I think stew is on the menu for this week's culinary delights, mum and perhaps soup too, what do you think?" She collected the onions, garlic, carrots, beef and potatoes onto the bench and went about roughly chopping them all up. Chopping onions was the worst because for Carla, not only did her eyes water and sting excessively, but onions also brought about a sneezing fit and runny nose. Today was no exception and she dropped the knife on the chopping board and turned to avoid sneezing all over the bench before running to the bathroom for a flannel to wash her eyes and a tissue to blow her nose. After the sneezing fit finally passed she dropped the flannel into the sink, the tissues in the loo, washed her face and hands and returned to the kitchen to resume cooking – tiresome but predictable she thought.

She popped the large pan on the gas cooker and sautéed the onions and garlic before braising the beef and adding the beef stock and vegetables. Once it was boiling she reduced the heat and put the lid on. She was just thinking about putting on some music when the doorbell rang.

"Bloody hell!" she said aloud whilst quickly glancing up at the kitchen wall clock. "9.46 am, who could that be?" she asked herself, as well as thinking, *"Good Lord, look at me. I can't see anyone now."* Carla had appraised herself in the mirror when she was washing her eyes from the onions and what she saw was a rather dishevelled woman still in pyjamas, in an old dressing gown which should have been thrown out years ago. In that time in the bathroom she had also noticed the first real signs of wrinkles. Yes, she'd seen the little crow's-feet at the corners of her eyes for a number of years but now they were a little deeper and definitely more noticeable. She had shrugged her shoulders and continued to examine her face. Overall she determined that she was still relatively attractive, her blue eyes, (although right at this moment they were red-rimmed) were still clear and vivid, her hair was straight reddish-brown shoulder length and she had a slightly tilted nose. The only reason she allowed herself to think she was possibly attractive was because she had been told so by friends and colleagues, not because she actually believed it herself. No, to Carla she was 'just Carla'. So when the door bell sounded unexpectedly she added to her commentary, "Shit, shit, shit, shit, shit - not today."

Carla thought hard and fast, it could be one of her students coming by to ask some questions about the current assignment she had set them. It wasn't uncommon but this was a Friday morning and the students should be at school. The doorbell rang again so, with that thought in mind, thinking it was probably a student, she went to the door. She realised she was shaking and knew she had to get a grip. As such she shouted out from behind the door, "Who is it?" At first there was no answer so she called again a little louder. "Who is there? I am not really able to answer the door right now."

A man's voice answered, "Hello. Is that Carla Parkinson?" and Carla answered, "Yes, who wants to know?"

"Ms Parkinson, you may not remember me because we have not seen each other for about twenty years or more but my name is Peter Westmead. My mother was Susan Westmead. I was hoping to talk to you. If it's a bad time I can come back later."

From behind the door Carla froze. The man called Peter then called out, "I am sorry to have disturbed you. I will go."

Carla's mind was racing, "What the fuck!" She felt overwhelmed with memories and feelings. Yes, she had immortalised this day, yes she had indulged herself with self-pity, yes she had questioned repeatedly her actions in the 'things that went wrong' – if that was the right way to express it. But she had never, ever, had anyone speak the name of the Westmead to her in twenty-one years and her shock was palpable.

"Peter! Really Peter! Oh my God. Is this a joke?" With that she grabbed the door handle and swung the door open seeing the back of a tall, slim man with black hair just about to get into his car.

"Wait Peter," she shouted, "I'm sorry, please." As she moved down the garden path she felt like she was in a dream and nothing was real, her feet were moving but she didn't recognize where they were taking her. She fumbled with the gate latch and cursed when it wouldn't open. As she fumbled Peter had come back around his car and stood in front of her. Looking up she said, "I am not ready to see anyone, look at me, but if you would like to come back around 1 pm we could have lunch. I am cooking stew. What do you think?" The words were tumbling from her mouth and she knew this might be a mistake. She didn't know if she could cope with the memories. She actually didn't know this man from a bar of soap, was he who he said he was? And yet, here she was, dressed like – who knows what; asking a stranger to come back and have luncheon with her! Now she knew she was mad. If he was who he said he was then could she bear it? At least when she was thinking on her own she could always put in filters at different points when wallowing in sentimental internal dialogue, it was important to be able to do this – in putting in filters she didn't have to think about things she chose 'not to remember' but this! This would be different, if this really was Peter, if this really was the poor child of Susan Westmead, her dearest and closest friend from childhood, then could she cope with the guilt, the tragedy?

With all this racing through her mind the young man who called himself Peter simply said, "That would be great Ms Parkinson. I will be here at 1 pm. Do you want me to bring anything?"

Chapter 4

Carla shut the door and melted onto the floor. "My God," her heart was pumping so hard she thought she might pass out, "what does this mean? Well," slowly standing up and staring at the closed front door, "well it means I've got three hours to get myself together and then I will know."

In her bedroom she opened the wardrobe and pulled out a cream, long-sleeved shirt, jeans and underwear. Carla, apart from this very day, always ensured she was well dressed and what she would say, "Presentable to the world." As she showered and washed her hair she began to think about Susan Westmead and her son Peter. Part of all her tumultuous life started with them. Well, no, that wasn't true, she berated herself. It started earlier than that.

Susan had been a student with Carla from the third day of high school. She was new to the area and was waiting outside the principal's office when Carla sauntered by with a couple of her high school friends. Carla hadn't paid her any attention until Mrs Coburn popped her head out and called, "Carla Parkinson, could you give me a minute?" Carla was known by the principal because she was a friend of Mrs Coburn's daughter Julie and she had been to the Coburn's home on a number of occasions when they were in primary school together.

"Carla, I'd like to introduce you to Susan Layman, who has just moved here with her parents from Grafton in New South Wales. Susan, this is Carla Parkinson. I have allocated Susan to form 1 E which you are in so I wanted you to take her under your wing, show her about and help her with understanding the school roster etc." It was said in a shrill, yet directive manner and without waiting for an answer she chimed, "Thanks Carla," and disappeared back into her office.

The two girls looked at each other and Carla said, "Come on Susan, or we will be late for Maths. Do you have a locker yet?"

"I have a key but I haven't been shown where it is yet."

"Don't worry I'll show you at morning tea," and with that she grabbed Susan's arm and they took off down the long, now quiet, corridor.

The girls hit it off immediately, being virtually inseparable from that day. Every weekend they would swap whose house they would stay over with. Carla at Susan's Saturday night and the following weekend Susan at Carla's home, although secretly Carla much preferred being around Susan's family because she always harboured a bit of guilt about her own mother. Carla remembered there were times when her Dad had to drive Susan home because her mother was 'having a bad day'. What that meant in Parkinson speak was – her mother was either confining herself to bed and this could last for weeks; or she was so active, talkative, that she was not capable of looking after herself, let alone her husband and daughter or another child visiting. "Well it looks like mum's having one of her 'let's save the world' days," her father would joke, "let's take Susan home before your mother signs her up for the Special Forces to save the white tailed spider," and he would chuckle and Carla would laugh too but they both knew they were in for a rough few weeks.

There were times that her mother was placed in hospital. Carla hated those times more than the times her mother was 'having bad days' at home. Thankfully her father only expected her to visit on the weekends choosing to "Leave the doctors to 'do their thing' and get her back on her feet." On these occasions Susan's mum used to pop in and bring a casserole or some other nice dinner around for her and her Dad. Initially her father was reluctant to accept the help but Susan's mother sent her father around and they sat on the verandah and drank a beer, chatting. Carla didn't know what they spoke about but after that, whenever her mother was hospitalized, the Laymans came over and helped around the home, it seemed that they had come to an understanding and that was great with Carla.

Although her household was chaotic at times there was always a lot of love present but when she was aged nineteen her father died unexpectedly from a heart attack whilst playing golf; he was only 56. It was a terrible time. He had been the family's rock, the mainstay of her existence. Her mother was too inconsistent, too 'flighty' but her father had weathered all the storms sent his way and cared for "my girls" as he would say to her.

Her mother, Margaret, on hearing the news became catatonic and Carla tried to care for her but it was hopeless. Eventually, seven days later, she rang for an ambulance and her mother was admitted, once again, to the acute psychiatric ward but, within a few hours, she was transferred to the general hospital and placed on a drip. A day later she had a nasogastric tube put in place to feed and hydrate her. It was just under six weeks before her mother was discharged from hospital, having missed the funeral and her chance to say goodbye to her loving husband. Carla's memory of the funeral and her mother's absence remained vague. She too was suffering and had no way of knowing what she was supposed to do, or say, or how she was to react. The Laymans were terrific and she supposed that they had taken the reins and organised 'things'.

Upon her mother's release from the general hospital she was transferred back to the psych unit and it was another three weeks and a course of electric shock therapy, otherwise known as ECT, before she was considered well enough to be discharged. During that time Carla visited on weekends and the conversation between her mother and herself was stilted as if they were strangers. Carla recalled feeling guilty whenever she left the hospital and yet could not put a finger on why.

One afternoon it was a sunny day and the nurse had told Carla when she came to the ward that, "Your mum seems a bit more lively this week."

"That's good. Perhaps I could take her for a drive then?"

"Yes. I think that would do her the world of good. Let's wait till after her lunch and her medication and then I think that will be fine. Mind you, only half an hour. She's been so unwell we need to take things slowly." "Sure."

Carla walked her mother to the car park and in the cheeriest voice she could muster, "Look mum, my new car. What do you think? Mr Layman helped me purchase it and it was only $1100. He says it's a real bargain and the repayments are only $11.00 a week. I love it. What should I call her?" Carla knew she was rambling but she actually was genuinely excited about her little white Volkswagon beetle.

She stopped to open the side door and Margaret sat quietly in the front seat. "Where are we going?"

"Don't know. How about a drive around Lake Wendouree and then we can stop in the botanical gardens and have a little walk."

"Sounds lovely, dear."

As they sat on the grass under the huge Monkey tree in the botanical gardens both women were looking at the grass and not talking, each obviously deep in their own thoughts, when her mother quietly said, "I have always felt from the day your father died that I must have imagined him. That he wasn't real. I know that's silly but I only wish I had been well enough to be at the funeral to tell everyone how important, caring and loving a man he was and that I was the luckiest woman in the world to have married him," and she looked up then at her daughter, with tears rolling down her face, and Carla responded, "I know mum. He knew you loved him. It's not been your fault," and they hugged for a long time. No words communicated but their language was poignant.

A week later Carla brought her mother home and life slowly melded into a form of routine and day to day living.

Chapter 5

As they grew into teenagers and went on to university, Carla and Susan continued to share each other's lives, and when Susan met her husband to be, Liam, at age eighteen, Carla met Roger Nelson, but unknown to her then, he would be her husband in the near future too. Like the girls, the men got on well and most weekends they hung out together. Day trips to the Mornington Peninsula, weekends away at folk festivals, catching Saturday night movies. All four were practically inseparable and it was no surprise to anyone when both couples married in the summer of '88. The girls were nineteen and the men both twenty.

Roger and Carla moved to Ballarat North, not far from her mother's home, and Susan and Liam bought a home in Ballarat Central. Susan fell pregnant halfway through her third year of university and as such did not complete her degree in social work but Carla continued to study, completing her teaching degree majoring in English language.

In 1989 Susan had her son and they named him Peter Liam Henry Westmead. Carla was over the moon for the pair and funnily enough it was Roger who started talking about when they would start a family. Carla wasn't keen to start a family until she had gained a few years' experience in the field and, "Really cement my place in teaching, Roger. I think that's important because I want to continue working after children."

"Sure. No hurry," and with his beautiful big brown eyes and cheeky smile he swept her off her feet and said, "Well, we still need to practice for the future," and they laughed as he carried her to the bedroom.

During the first year of Peter's life Carla saw less of Susan, although they regularly spoke on the phone. Roger and Carla babysat on a few occasions just so Liam and Susan could have a break, and Carla was mesmerised at how attentive Roger was to the child. In late '91 Carla was working in her 2nd year of teaching as an HSC English teacher at the local Ballarat High School when she found out she was pregnant. Carla was 25 and although excited about being a mother she was apprehensive too. *"What if the kid's 'not right' like mum?"* and then countering that with, *"Don't be stupid it will be fine."* The school year ended a week after she learnt she was pregnant and she completed the year with great results, with all her 23 students passing their exams. It was an impressive feather in her cap as the principal had remarked at the afternoon tea Christmas break up. "The first person to accomplish 100% success in a class for form 6'ers since Mrs Wells back in 1959. Well done, Carla." She worked up until 6 weeks before the birth and Mr Allen, the principal, wished her well and invited her to apply for any positions in the future should she consider returning to work.

In August '92 her son Samuel was born, although he was never called that, he was Sam to everyone she knew. Roger was over the moon, never had he been so eager to be home early from work. As soon as he arrived home he would rush to Sam and pick him up, even if he was sleeping – which annoyed Carla no end – but the child never seemed to mind, *"So what the heck"* she would say to herself, ignoring her real thoughts which went on the lines of, *"For God's sake I have just spent 3 hours trying to get him down and you come in and wake him up, Oh you are soooo annoying I could throttle you."*

But all in all life couldn't have been fuller, with Carla looking after Sam, the home and her beautiful Roger, the ever considerate and loving husband and provider. They had decided that when Sam was twelve months old Carla would go back to work and Roger would go part-time and care for Sam. Susan had said that she would love to look after Sam the days Roger worked. "Hey Carla, really, I need the money. Liam's still building his business and getting all the plumbing gear is really expensive these days. To be honest I just don't know where the money goes. But the money you give me for Sam will work perfectly in covering those extra pesky bills that pop up out of nowhere. Besides," she said a low but genuine tone, "Peter loves Sam. They play together so well. It will work out fine for everyone. Don't worry."

As it turned out it was only a month later that her principal from Ballarat High rang to say there was an opening for a part-time English teacher starting term 2 next year and would she please consider the appointment. Carla was in two minds. "Look Roger, I know we planned on waiting until at least Sam was twelve months but will the two months earlier make much difference?" She knew she was trying to convince herself more than Roger. "I don't know, Carla. I will have to talk to Thomas about going part time and what that will look like. I have been putting it off 'cos we are so busy and you know Thomas and work!" Yes, she did. Continuing he said, "And what about Susan and Liam, are they ready? Really, I think it would be great but the timing's just not right."

The conversation jostled backwards and forwards for two days after that and each evening, over the dining room table, when Sam was in bed, the wine glasses out, and the TV on in the background. Carla would say, "We need to make a decision, Roger, Mr Allen needs to know tomorrow before advertising. He's keen to get this cemented down and not leave it till the last minute."

Slowly Roger got up from the table, his eyes lowered to his half emptied glass, he reached for the bottle and filled it to the top and lent over and topped Carla's up too. "Well!" She knew she sounded like a whinger, "Look, one way or the other, Roger, we have to make this decision. I've spoken with Susan and she's fine to go, in fact, raring to go." She looked pensively at her husband, who was now pacing the room with concern all over his face.

Quietly he stopped pacing, turned directly to Carla and said, "Congratulations, schoolteacher," with a huge smile across his face and his glass in the air. "Thomas gave me his blessing saying, 'Some things are meant to be, Roger' and I said to him, 'What do you mean?' And he said, 'Well a mate of mine has just come into town and needs a little help so if you want part-time I can give him the other hours.' Can you believe this Carla? Thomas being nice and understanding! Go figure."

Carla was on her feet by the time Roger finished and was hugging him. "This is great. It's amazing how things work out. For everyone. Cheers," and they clinked glasses and gulped down their wine. There were still many questions to be answered. Which days would be best to work to coincide with Susan? How much to pay Susan? How will Sam cope? What's the backup plan if he doesn't settle to being looked after? But for that evening those questions were sidelined as they made their way to the bedroom.

The morning saw them both still very happy. Carla rang Susan straight after breakfast and invited her, Liam and Peter over to dinner that night to discuss details.

Chapter 6

Breaking her from her reverie was the chiming of the doorbell and a quick glance at the clock told her it was 1.05 pm and Peter Westmead was at the door.

She quickly looked at herself in the hallway mirror, wiped off a little tomato paste from her upper lip, flattened her hair and opened the door. Peter stood with what looked like a bottle of bubbly and some flowers, both of which he extended towards her saying, "For you. Thanks for seeing me."

"No please, thanks, come in Peter."

He moved past her and into the hallway and stopped. "You know I vaguely remember coming to your place with mum and dad when I was little."

"Yes, you have a good memory, you would have been only three, but this is my mother's old home, not the house you would have visited." Immediately she felt guilty correcting him, it made no difference which house he remembered but she continued, "I was trying to work it out, it must have been at least twenty-one years since I last saw you," and then as if remembering her manners she said, "oh, how rude, please come into the kitchen and take a seat. Can I get you a drink? Tea, coffee, hot chocolate or something stronger? *"Rambling, stop rambling,"* she berated herself as she walked in front through the lounge to the kitchen.

"Coffee will be fine for now, Ms Parkinson."

"Call me Carla."

Peter sat at the dining room table which shared a spot in the kitchen and she went to work getting the coffee organized.

"So Peter, what brings you to town? *"Lame, Carla, lame."*

"You do, Carla." He stated as a matter of fact, "I need to know what happened to mum and why she died."

And Carla instantly thought. *"Oh my god what can I say. It's my entire fault!"* She remained quiet for some time and he never interrupted the silence and then she said. "It's complicated, Peter, you deserve to know but, firstly, tell me what you have been told." Then holding up her hand added, "But let's eat first. *"Anything to put this off."*

"I'll talk whilst we eat if that's ok. I really don't mean to be a burden. I have vague flashes of memory of mum but it's not much. I was only three but I can still remember her golden hair and whenever I smell roses I think of her too. But what do you think, Carla? Do roses cut it for a mother and a memory?"

Carla had determined not to interrupt him but he really had little to say about his mother. She remembered how Susan's garden was full of the most beautiful roses. Every type of colour you could think of and the deep rich thick smells that wafted around the garden and into the house were just divine. Susan often said her grandmother was the green thumb in the family and, "I guess I got it from her. Mum was never really interested. But gardening makes me feel relaxed and the smell of roses always makes me stop and see things in perspective. You know the other day I was feeling upset about something Liam had said and I sat in the garden for over an hour. I don't know what happened, I kind of blanked out, but when I realised the time I was feeling much better. I realised there was nothing to be upset about after all. That probably sounds crazy to you?" and Carla had thought, *"Yes it did,"* but then a lot of things Susan thought and did seemed a little off tap… but wasn't that part of why she loved her? Susan was always able to see problems from a totally different angle to Carla and, oh how often her wisdom proved right and saved her from making a fool of herself on many occasions. *"The flip side of a problem, the positive versus the negative, always good to have, and Susan always had it,"* she thought.

She gave her head a slight shake and focused on the man sitting before her, who was saying that there were other images but they were fleeting. A black car, Sam – yes he remembered Sam, just – bushes but not roses. That was it. She was definitely feeling she didn't need this. This was not her memory lane and she needed protecting. She did not want this man in her kitchen. *"Filter, filter…"*

Carla had asked then, "How is your father, Peter? How's Liam?"

"He's not well. The booze and smokes are catching up fast. Last time I saw him he wasn't able to walk ten metres without becoming breathless, but he's still smoking and drinking. That was three years ago."

"I lost track of you and Liam after, after…"

"Susan was murdered." Peter completed her sentence.

"Yes. After that. What's your life been like? What do you do with yourself?" Carla knew she was deliberately avoiding the discussion around Susan Westmead, this day, twenty-one years ago.

"Ms Parkinson, Carla," he corrected himself, "I came here to have you talk to me. I need answers. Growing up with Dad was the life from hell and yet I don't know why. The violence when he was drunk, which was most days, the skanky women who haunted the house day and night, getting drunk and high on whatever they could. They'd come up to me and try to be friendly," and at this point he stood and walked to the backdoor and with his back to her he said in a falsetto and exaggerated voice, "Hello, young man. My, aren't you the lovely one."

He turned then and moved back towards the dining room table. "Shall we crack that bubbly? I hate thinking of this stuff. It was a long time ago but you asked." Upon sitting he smiled and said, "Well?"

"Yes. Sure. Good idea." Carla jumped up and grabbed two glasses, apologising for them not being proper champagne flutes. Peter continued.

"You have no idea, and I am not sure I can fully make you understand, they'd breathe their sickly breaths on me and try to cuddle me. It was awful. Then, when I was seven years old, Dad came home with Sally and announced he was getting married. She was hanging onto his arm, swaying about. Her hair was fluffed up, red smears on her face, I'd never seen HER before and to me she looked like a monster."

"Well," screamed Dad, "say something son, give your new mum a kiss."

"I remember I turned and ran out the back door. I was terrified. I didn't really know what it all meant. But," and his voiced dropped so low that Carla strained to hear him, "there was nowhere to hide. He came outside calling me, saying 'come back. If you don't, you'll get a hiding.' I was asking myself why, and I yelled out from behind the tree I was standing behind, Daddy, I don't like the 'monster', I'm scared. My father came down the steps and walked to the tree, grabbed me by the arm, squeezing very hard, whilst dragging me almost off my feet, back into the house. He had his mouth at the side of my head sneering, "You will go in there and you will give your mum a kiss or else – do you understand, Peter?" and yes I understood alright because this wasn't the first time his temper was taken out on me but this time it was different because this time the monster stayed. All the others came and went. But no, Sally was here to stay. I wanted to say I want my real mum, why did she die, why? But I didn't. I had asked those questions before and Dad had just gotten angry and told me 'Life's a bitch, son and there's no point crying over stuff you can't get back. I've learnt that and so will you. Don't ever ask about your mother again, there's nothing I can say. Do you understand?' Peter paused then, took a sip of his champagne and looking at Carla said patiently, "So Carla, I want... no I need to understand why my life turned out the way it did. I am hoping talking to you can help. Honestly I am not here to distress you. I know it seems selfish but I have been thinking about this for a long time. I truly think that if I can understand about mum I might be able to fill a hole that Dad refused to help me with. So please. Can you tell me about mum? About what actually happened?"

"I'll do my best Peter. I can tell you what happened but I honestly cannot tell you why. I need to give you some history and context though." Inwardly Carla felt the bile rising in her gut as she prepared herself to totally relive the past as best as she knew it. Peter Westmead had sat up straight and was looking directly at her. She could see his need, it was palpable in every fibre of his body.

Part 3

Chapter 1

"How do you let him get away with it?" Thomas had asked his father, not for the first time. Oscar and Thomas were in their home office. "I need help. The real estate game is turning to shit and the competitiveness is nothing like we have experienced before. I have Charlie Dawson working nights just to keep up with everything and he's starting to complain and threatening to leave if we don't employ another person."

"Why haven't you then?" was Oscar's refrain and Thomas, who was pacing back and forth, looked at him incredulously and spat out his words, "Because father, Roger is on the books, Roger is receiving a wage and Roger does nothing, bugger all. That's why I haven't employed someone else and you damn well know it. He bludges off your work and mine because you let him. He should be here taking over the rental management which would free up Charlie for sales, which would leave me to do what I do best and that's manage the stocks, bonds and shares. I can't be doing two jobs. He's just lazy, no heart."

"I will speak to him, then."

"When?"

"Tomorrow. He is coming over for morning tea with your mum."

Having the last say Thomas said, "If he thinks he is going to inherit part of the business when he puts nothing in he will have to think again," and with that he stormed out.

When that conversation was taking place Roger had been married to Carla for nine months and he was coming up for his 21st birthday. His mother had called him on the phone and asked him over to discuss plans for his party which he agreed to do the following day.

Roger rocked up to the driveway of his parents' home on his 250 Yamaha motorcycle dressed in his leathers and bike helmet. He had bought the motorbike despite protests from his parents who were fearful he would hurt himself, but even the temptation of a BMW convertible was not enough to sway him from his passion of riding a motorcycle. Roger had been spoilt all his life and he knew it, his brother Thomas knew it and all his friends knew it but his parents saw nothing wrong with this. He had been indulged in every way but after meeting and marrying Carla he was slowly changing and, he felt, in a good way. He noticed that he was less demanding of people's attention and was able to give people his attention without wondering what he could get out of them. He was actually beginning to like himself and enjoy helping others and that, he mused, was all because of Carla. She'd berated him countless times, "People don't owe you anything, that attitude of yours;

'If I want it I should have it" is wrong, Roger." In the intimacy of their bedroom one night Carla had said to him, "Roger, the way you spoke to your mother and father tonight over dinner was appalling."

"What do you mean? They were alright."

"No, Roger they were not, especially Sharon. Didn't you see her flinch when you talked about going on that road trip with your mates on the bikes? She was only expressing her concern for you and trying to understand what it was that you loved about motorcycles and you virtually slapped her with 'You thought having a bike was a good idea too, remember, and now you complain if I choose to ride it!' All I'm saying is, there is a right way and a wrong way, Roger, to speak to people. You were hurtful and you are so busy thinking of yourself that you don't consider other people's feelings. Your mother adores you and you treat her like that." Roger thought Carla's little jibes here and there had been positive on him and it was showing in time with more pleasant and considerate interactions between Roger and his family. Although Thomas was always a different kettle of fish to understand. Roger had been working for his brother and father now since leaving school at eighteen but he hated the real estate game. He had always wanted to be an electrician, and besides, he could never meet Thomas's expectations. He'd said to Carla on many occasions, "Dad's ok, but Thomas! He comes from a different world, I tell ya."

Roger was slowly realizing he was changing because of Carla but also, he thought, he was just maturing. Anyway, it was partly because of that that on the day of having the morning tea with his mother he acquiesced to Thomas. A thing he had diligently and painstaking avoided doing all his life. Roger was nine years younger than Thomas, and he had never formed a close relationship with him. He saw Thomas as nobody really. A person who lived with his parents and ran the business. They shared no brotherly connection at all. Although, and for no reason that Roger could pinpoint, he knew his brother would never let anything happen to him, which was strange because they had never seen eye to eye, yet there was an innate feeling that could not be explained. Puzzling but I suppose that's families for you, he thought.

Roger got off the bike and took off his leathers on the front porch, rang the doorbell, at the same time as turning the door handle and moving into the entranceway calling, "Hi Mum."

"Hello dear. I am in the kitchen."

He planted a big hug and kiss on his mother and walked to the fridge. Sharon was cooking scones and asked him if he wanted tea or coffee. Even though the family had enough money to have a cook Sharon had insisted on doing the cooking herself, she loved it and felt it was the only thing she could really give her boys that money couldn't buy. Not that she had bought much for Thomas. No, he was different to Roger, she mused, far more independent. She did however insist on a cleaner.

Roger said coffee would be fine and they chatted casually about what Carla was up to and how the real estate business was going and general day to day chatting. With the scones out of the oven and the coffee pot brewing Sharon said, "So Roger, two months and you will be twenty-one. What do you want for your birthday and what kind of party do you want?" At that very moment Thomas entered the kitchen and went "Ha, oh yes party boy, what do you want?"

"Now Thomas, don't be like that."

"Like what? When I turned twenty-one you and Dad gave me no choice for a party – remember – part of the business yes but no party! I remember even if you don't. I had already been working the business for three years, getting it back on its feet when Dad had let it slide."

"Oh, Thomas, things were different then, like you said the money was tight and your father and I thought this was the best, AND," she stressed, "I think if you are honest you never would have wanted a party anyway! We would have given you a party if we thought you would have liked it," and she gave him a wry smile.

"Don't stress mum," Roger announced happily as he moved further into the kitchen and began taking a scone and coffee. Roger had been watching the exchange between his mother and brother and he noticed a deep look of contempt on his brother's face towards his mother but as quickly as he saw it, it was gone again and a smile replaced it. "I'll be in the office." Then turning to Roger, "When you two have finished your business will you come and see me? I want to discuss something with you."

Thomas headed down the corridor, popped his head into the lounge where his father sat reading and said, "Don't worry about talking to Roger, I'm on to it, not that it will change anything anyway." Oscar looked up and saw his eldest son and said, "Alright. Thanks, son," and returned to reading. Oscar Nelson was no longer interested in the real estate business, in fact he hadn't been for a long time.

Chapter 2

Sharon and Roger spoke for over an hour and it was decided in the end that he actually only wanted a small gathering of friends and family and that going out for a meal would be best.

"Nothing too lavish, mum. Most of my mates can get out of control with a bit of grog in 'em so this way we can limit their access. Besides, Carla and I have planned to fly to Cairns the next day and our flight leaves at 8.35 am so I will need a clear head."

"I've never been to Cairns. Sounds nice," she had replied idly.

As to what he wanted for his 21st birthday present, that was different. Roger tried to tease out of his mother how much she and his father were prepared to pay but she was vague and non-committal so he said, "OK. What I really want is a leather lounge suite. The one Carla and I have is old, and tatty. One like what you have in the lounge would be great. What do you think?" She looked concerned but laughed it off and said she'd speak to Oscar about it.

With that he jumped up, "I better get going."

"Don't forget to pop in and see Thomas on the way out."

"Oh yeah, thanks. I forgot."

Roger loped down the hallway and up the steps to the second floor. There had originally been three bedrooms up here but a year ago they had renovated the third room for an office. "The office I work in when I'm not at the office," Thomas had said to Oscar.

It was large and bright with two thick leather seats. He had a couple of original paintings on the wall of landscapes by a little-known artist and the desk was huge and made from oak. Along the east side of the room he had a wall full of filing cabinets, with files dating back to 1949 when Oscar first started up the business.

Thomas was standing by the large window which looked out onto the back yard. He was swaying on his heels and from Roger's perspective he looked like the cat who had swallowed the bird.

"Hmm," he thought to himself, *"I wonder what this is all about."*

He gave a tap on the door and entered the office. Thomas immediately turned and smiling said, "You want a drink? I've got whiskey, rum, vodka."

Roger was wary and said, "Are you having one? It's early," and with that he glanced at his watch. He was surprised to see it was fast approaching 12 pm, so added, "Yes, I would love a whiskey and ice."

"Okay. Sit down, Roger, I have wanted to talk to you for a while." He sat and Thomas poured them both a good sized whiskey and handed it him as he sat behind the desk, adjusting a few papers.

"As you know, Dad started the business in '49 and back then it was a very lucrative business given the post-war problems and he's had his ups and downs with the changing tide of the economy over the years. Anyway, I joined the business when I was seventeen and, like I said in the kitchen, I got a buy in when I was twenty-one. I now pretty much run the entire business, as you know."

Roger was wondering where this was going and why the history lesson but said nothing.

Thomas stopped, took a drink and looked at his young brother. He thought to himself, *"Looks like I'm boring him!"* but he quickly suppressed an instant sense of anger. "Anyway," he resumed, "what I wanted to discuss with you was the possibility of you taking on a bit more responsibility." He immediately held his hand up like a shield from any words that might escape from Roger's mouth. "Now, before you react, hear me out. The only reason I am managing to keep the business afloat at present is because I trade in stocks and bonds but I cannot do this efficiently if I am spending all my time running the rental side of the business. Charlie Dawson is great but he is getting fed up. I don't want to hire someone new because that's extra training and extra wages. Roger, you are part of this family and we need you to come on board. I know real estate's not necessarily your thing but family comes first and we are struggling."

Roger was taken aback with this little speech; in all his life he had never heard Thomas speak so passionately and openly to him before. It actually unsettled him a little. *"Geez,"* he thought, *"Perhaps there is trouble for the business down the track."* To his brother he said, swallowing the last of the whiskey, "I don't know. I've got plans and if I am managing the rental side that will take more hours, won't it? I'll need to talk to Carla and, hell Thomas, this has come out of the blue. What does dad say?"

"He was going to talk to you but I decided I would. Look, go home, think about, but Roger, say yes. You're the obvious one. Like I said, we need you." He felt a little bile rise in his throat as he said these last words but he was sick to death of having his younger brother bludge off his hard work.

After Roger left, Thomas thought about all he had done and risked in order to keep the business viable and how, having gotten away with a sloppy scheme in his younger days, he had learnt from his mistakes and gone on to prosper. Thomas allowed himself time to revel in the memory of his early days in the business. A man named Eric worked with his father as a real estate agent when Oscar opened for business back in forty-nine. Eric was only twenty and he was very good at sales. He became more than an employee, he became a close friend of Sharon and Oscar's, and often socialized with them after work. By the age of thirty-five Eric had a wife and three children and life was looking good. Oscar had said that Eric's friendly, laidback nature was an asset to the firm. He had an easy way with people and could defuse a situation very quickly. Like the time a man barged into the office which was established on Sturt Street and demanded to see Thomas. Thomas was only new to the firm and had been learning the trade from Eric and Oscar.

"Where is Thomas Nelson?" the man demanded, and both Oscar and Eric stood up from their desks and went over to him.

"What's the problem?" they both chimed in unison.

"Like you don't know! Where is he? I'll beat the crap out of him, I swear to God I will." Eric took a step back and, putting his hands in the air said, "Sir. He is gone for the day, (hoping to God Thomas didn't walk back through the door right that minute) but I am sure I can assist. Please take a chair and we will talk."

Reluctantly the man sat. He explained that he was a client of Thomas's from the weekend and that he had been shown a home which was perfect for him and his young family. "My wife fell in love with it straight away. A huge backyard, three bedrooms and a rumpus room. Perfect."

Eric sat and nodded and listened and the man continued, "And this cretin tells me," and inflicting a smart arse tone, '*Sir, there is already a bid on the home, you will need to act fast.*'

And I said, "How much have they offered?"

"82,000."

"Okay, I will offer a thousand more."

"I will call the other buyer and let them know their offer has been exceeded."

"I have now been waiting four days. No word from him, no return phone calls, nothing. I demand to know what's going on."

Eric calmly said, "Yes, tell me the address of the home and I'll look it up."

"1800 Lidmore Street."

Eric got up and went to the filing cabinet and pulled the folder, where he instantly saw it was stamped, in big red ink, SOLD. Price negotiated $82.000.00. *"Shit,"* he thought, *"what the fuck has he done?"* but Eric was good with people and he could think fast.

"Mr Langdon, I'm sorry to say that the sale of 1800 Lidmore Street was completed two days ago. Now although I am as livid as you as to how this incident could have occurred; and please be totally assured I will deal with Mr Nelson personally, I think this has happened for a good reason," and here he gave a chuckle, "oh yes, a very good reason. You see it just so happens that there is a home, very similar to the Lidmore Street home, in Plover Street, and I believe you will be very impressed with what I show you."

And that was that, Mr Langdon had his sails taken from under him. He did buy the home in Plover Street and at a much cheaper price. As for Thomas, his father dealt with him that evening.

"What the hell are you doing, Thomas?" Oscar had yelled, the second he came through the front door. Thomas looked at his father very straight-faced, because he knew what he was talking about, and said, "Being enterprising."

"What?" Oscar exclaimed.

"Look, its simple. This guy and his wife loved the house in Lidmore Street. They wanted it bad. I could tell. I can read people. So I spun him a story that I would filter out all other offers over the next week so that he would secure the home for $82.000.00 if he swung me a neat $1,000. He jumped at it. So when that Langdon guy shows up and offers more I simply don't pass it on and then talk to the vendors saying, $82,000.00 is the best offer and if I were you," I stressed, "I'd jump on it for a quick sale and they agreed." He was smiling broadly now, "And I just made myself some nice cash on the side."

Oscar was not smiling, however, he was furious. "That's not ethical, Thomas. We are working on behalf of the vendor and the buyer; you cannot simply siphon off money from people. What happens if that Langdon fellow went to the ombudsman? You are just bloody lucky Eric was there to smooth the way. If it had been left to me I'd have let you hang," and Oscar took a step closer to his son and, staring at him, cheeks flushed and forehead knitted, he said through gritted teeth, "don't ever pull a stunt like that again. I am not going to lose my business over some bullshit act of greed. Do you hear me?" And with a sigh and a drop of his shoulders, went to the lounge and poured himself a large brandy.

Thomas watched him leave the room and he too let out a long breath, but he was ropable, he could not see how his father failed to see the opportunity to make bigger dollars. Yes, he had to admit he had been clumsy, risky even, but he had already learnt from this. He knew he could do better and get more when the next chance availed itself; and it would present itself and he would be there to cash in. There was nothing his father or "Saint Eric" as he came to call him behind his back, could say or do to stop it.

Thomas got up from his desk and went to see his father and told him his request of Roger and Oscar said very little. Oscar thought he knew his young son well and working in the business was not for him but he didn't know what to say, so he simply said "I'll leave it to you boys. You know best."

"Yes," Thomas thought, *"he is tired of the whole thing,"* and with a little charity in mind he thought, "*Well maybe after a lifetime of working, by the time I'm his age, I will be tired of it all too."*

Chapter 3

Roger left his parents' house shaking his head. *"Now, that's weird,"* he was thinking, *"wait till Carla knows."*

He got on his motorbike and merged into the afternoon traffic and headed home. He had the day off today and he planned to spend the rest of it cooking dinner and maybe even a dessert. Like his mother he enjoyed cooking and besides, Carla wouldn't be home till around 4.15 pm because Thursday was her busiest day at school, having a full day of classes.

Once he had taken off the leathers and gotten into his casual clothes he began getting out the ingredients for making a garlic sauce with beef steak and summer salad – even though it wasn't summer. Whilst he trimmed the fat, peeled and crushed the garlic, he went over in his head the conversation he and Thomas had had. Roger thought, *"Hell, taking on a greater role in the business isn't going to be easy with Thomas down my throat. I have managed to avoid him over the years but he'll be on my collar demanding and exacting perfection where there is none to be found. I am not sure at all about this."*

Roger continued chopping and musing about unspoken possible conversations with his brother. *"You need to concentrate, put more effort in, did you ring the customer back? How could you have thought they were going to be good tenants?"* and on and on he imagined his new role to be with Thomas over his shoulder.

"But," he thought hopefully or naively, *"what if he has changed? The very manner in which he spoke to me was a 'change'. I probably don't mind the real estate game as much as I think,"* and then, doubting himself asked, *"what else can I actually do that gives me flexibility? I've got mates doing shit hours, poor pay, and crumby bosses. Least if Thomas gets too much I can go to Dad, it's his business too,"* so his thoughts went around in circles. He imagined telling Carla when she got home, *"Well, what do you think?"* and she'd say something like, "It's up to you. You know I will support whatever you choose."

"Hmm, not helpful," he pondered and when Carla got home he poured them both a glass of red and he related the conversation he had with his brother.

"Well," Carla said, "that is interesting. So what are you going to do?"

"No, Carla, tell me what you think first. What pops into your head?"

"Look, obviously I know the relationship you have with Thomas and it hasn't been great." He just nodded and took a sip of wine. "So you can look at it as a new door opening and a challenge. You are always saying you would probably like the industry if you had more to do. Thomas is offering you a chance to run your own section. You can make it your own with your style and touch. It could be exciting."

Roger looked at his wife and said, "Ok, I'll sleep on it and maybe things will be clearer for me tomorrow." With that he stood up and reached for Carla and they hugged. After a moment he let her go and resumed prepping for dinner.

Roger awoke Friday morning feeling a little fuzzy-headed. He and Carla had polished off two bottles of wine by the time they went to bed the evening before and their conversation had gone backwards and forwards over the pros and cons of Thomas's plea and he was no wiser the next day.

He rang and spoke to his father after breakfast and had little satisfaction there, although he thought he had heard a hint of something in his voice. It was like – he thought it would be great to have Roger around more and see more of him and yet there was a cautionary tone too – but Roger was unable to grasp it.

Finally Roger decided that procrastinating was pointless. *"Why not give it a go. I am young and can always change my mind down the track. Yep. I will go find Thomas."*

Chapter 4

Roger started working the rental portfolio the following week but within a month he was doubting his choice. Thomas was unbearable to work with. He refused to give Roger any autonomy and there were many times when Roger would find him double-checking his work. He would pull a file and ask, "Why do you think these people are suitable for the Alfredton home? It's three men, for god's sake. They'll probably trash the joint," and initially Roger would calmly explain that he had done all the right checks and balances and Thomas would simply make some inane comment on the side and move on. But as his interference continued. The arguments between the brothers got hotter and hotter.

On a Wednesday in late spring Thomas and Roger were in the office in Sturt Street and Thomas had come in waving a paper file around, saying, "This time you have gone too far. What's the meaning of decreasing the rental for the Wendouree Parade home by $10 a week? Who said you could do that?" and Roger had replied that he was the manager of rental properties and he, Thomas, could shove his head up his arse. He had consulted with his father and they agreed there was a genuinely good case for the reduction.

"That's not how you run a business," he said, his eyes mere slits and his tone spiced with venom. Roger threw up his hands, "Why the fuck did you bother to ask me to do this job, Thomas? What is this constant running behind my back? If YOU want to do it so much then have your stupid job back," and he turned to leave the room, then hesitated and turned around slowly and added, "and another thing brother; don't think I don't know about all your dodgy dealings, or the little nest egg you're siphoning off on the side. Does Dad know?" and he stared carefully at Thomas. "Hmm no, I bet he doesn't. That's one thing he wouldn't tolerate, even from you."

Thomas didn't move as Roger turned again and headed out the room, grabbing his motorcycle helmet as he went.

Thomas felt his heart pulsing hard in his chest and his head began to throb. He had had a gut full of his brother and his charity basket cases. How in the hell did he think the business ran? Who does he think he is? Yes his father had been charitable and it had helped the business but that was then and this is now, new times, new decisions! But more strikingly upsetting was his remark about 'the nest egg'. Thomas was indeed putting aside money in a separate account, he had been doing it all his life. He worked hard, harder than anyone and he'd be damned if he was going to share the profits of the business fifty-fifty with Roger when Oscar passed it on. So he had devised a good system for moving money between the various sections of the business, sales, rentals, stocks, bonds and shares to a number of offshore accounts without it ever going through the books, without Oscar knowing. So how did Roger know about this? He went to the bathroom and rummaged in the medicine cabinet and took three Panadol, his head was pounding.

Thomas tried to concentrate on work but found he couldn't so he decided to head home, he was worried and the throbbing in his head was getting worse despite the Panadol. Now, sitting on the back verandah sipping a hot chocolate he was thinking, *"I'll have to talk to Roger and try and see what he knows. He may have just been mouthing off. Wouldn't put it past him. Besides, you have been very careful, very careful indeed. No, there is no way he knows anything."* He began to feel a little better, a little lighter in the head and he had a plan in his mind on how he would approach this problem.

Roger on the other hand had ridden very fast through the streets to put as much distance as he could between him and his brother. He was furious. As he turned into his street he saw Carla pulling into the driveway. She hadn't even gotten out of the car when he was at her door yanking it open and saying something. It was a mumble and jumble of words being spoken into the full faced helmet. "Roger, calm down, what's happened?" she was saying, as she attempted to get out of the car. She couldn't help but smile even though she knew he was upset, and that something bad had happened. He looked so silly, helmet on, arms waving about in the air, muffled incomprehensible words flowing out into the street.

He stopped all of a sudden and looked at her smiling and then she heard him say, "Bloody hell," and then they were both laughing. Roger peeled off his helmet and helped Carla with her books. She said, "No, don't tell me, I can guess, Thomas!"

"I've had it. We need to talk, you have no idea what he was on about today!" and he briefly explained.

"What will you do?" Carla was saying as they entered the hallway, dropping their gear and books on the floor whilst continuing to the kitchen.

"He's always been impossible to work with but he does seem to be getting worse as he gets older, if that's possible! I don't know why I thought he would change, what a laugh." He slumped on the dining room chair. "The trouble is I actually enjoy the job now. I've spoken with Dad but he's no help. I think Thomas has whittled him down over the years. He doesn't know how to approach him and nor do I. He just will not see reason, will not hand over any control. Honestly, Carla, it's an impossible situation. I think for my health's sake I have to quit."

As Carla put the kettle on she said, "Maybe you should have a chat to Charlie and see how he manages Thomas. He's been with the firm a long time. He might have some tips."

"Good idea, hey, beer for me thanks," with a wink. Carla saw her husband physically relax. He never could maintain an angry stance for long and she hoped Charlie could shed some light on how to appease Thomas and keep him at arm's length. With that thought she grabbed his hand and dragged him into the bedroom. "Beer later, Romeo."

After an hour of lovemaking, and showering, Roger was in the bathroom doing his hair when he called out, "Hey Carla. You still there?" and she replied "Yep, just making the bed." "I just remembered, I was so mad with Thomas that I said I knew he was doing dirty dealings

126

and stashing money and that Dad would be very disappointed. I have no idea where that thought came from but it will make him worry because all he ever does is want to impress the old man. What a laugh. Oh and guess what? Remember I told you months ago Thomas wanted me to move to Adelaide to manage rentals over there?" Carla did vaguely remember this. Roger had come home and said that Thomas had been buying investment homes in Adelaide. He had had some inside information that there was going to be an expansion of manufacturing in South Australia and that houses would be a high priority for a growing population. He had purchased three already at a budget price and he wanted more. Carla remembered Roger saying, "Thomas said to me, 'That's where the money is Roger, so pack up within the month and get over there. You and Carla can live in one of the houses and manage the others and keep your ear to the ground for bargains'." Carla called from the bedroom, "Yes I remember, why?"

"He brought it up again. He is not happy that we refused to move and he is getting twitchy, says he needs someone there on the ground. He can't manage it hundreds of kilometres away."

"What did you say?"

I said, "Thomas we don't want to live in Adelaide, all our friends and family are here. And he says – 'Mum and Dad are thinking of moving Roger, the family is leaving, relocating to where the business is best.' Boy, Carla, I can't keep up with him but I will find out from Dad tomorrow. By the way, we still don't want to move do we?"

And Carla replied, "I couldn't leave mum. It would break her heart."

"I know." By this time he had moved into the bedroom and taken her in his arms. He kissed her lightly on the side of the cheek and said, "Dad will put some more perspective to this. I don't want to live in Adelaide either."

Chapter 5

Several months had passed and things around the office had definitely settled. Roger supposed it helped that for four weeks Thomas had been away overseas taking a holiday. Everyone nearly fell off their chairs when he waltzed into the dining room one evening when Roger and Carla were over for dinner and announced, "I've decided to take a break. Get away for a while." There was a collective silence and then Carla spoke up. "Wow, that's great Thomas, where are you thinking of going?"

"I thought I'd go to England and then do Europe. I might even stop somewhere in Asia too. I haven't planned it exactly, I just need to get away." He then looked directly at Roger and said, "Do you think you, Dad and Charlie can handle things?"

"Well sure. No worries, when do you plan to go? For how long?"

"Next week, for about four weeks."

"That's great, Thomas," Sharon had said, "You must send us postcards. Promise."

And that was that. Thomas was gone for the month of November and even upon his return the relative harmony within the office remained.

When Roger had sought assistance from Charlie as to how to manage Thomas he had no advice. In fact he had laughed out loud and clapped Roger on the back and simply said, "Duck and weave my boy, duck and weave."

It was New Year's Eve '91 and Roger and Carla were home having a quiet evening and reflecting on the year that was coming and had gone. Most significant was of course the up and coming birth of their child, due the 8th of August '92, but also the fact that the real estate business was booming and Thomas continued to let him run the rental side of the business with little interference. That was huge. Oscar had also announced over dinner one night that he was going to retire from the business and that he would split it fifty-fifty with his sons, whom he expected to continue running the business.

Carla and Roger couldn't have been happier.

Chapter 6

Carla had risen from the couch and was pacing a little, trying to get her stories, memories and what she had been told by Roger in some semblance of order. "I'm sorry Peter, I have spent a lifetime trying to forget all this. Please be patient."

She then stopped and looked at Peter. "Is this making sense? It sounds strange to my ears."

"A bit. I'm not sure how it all relates to my mother but I suppose we will get there."

Carla looked up at the clock and saw it was coming up to 5 o'clock. "My, look at the time. Peter I am sorry but I am feeling very tired."

"That's OK Carla, as I said I didn't come to upset you. I'll go but can we catch up tomorrow?"

Carla looked at the young man who was only three years older than her son Sam and saw the pain in his eyes. He deserved some explanation even if she didn't understand herself. "Of course. Let's walk and talk tomorrow and then come back for lunch again. Still plenty of stew left over," and they both laughed.

"Thanks Carla, it means a lot to me. I'll get here around 10 am then?"

"It's a date. See you then," and she escorted him to the door and waited until he was out of sight before closing the front door and running to the kitchen to open another bottle of wine.

Ten am on the dot Peter was ringing the doorbell. Carla was ready with backpack and water and they drove to Lake Wendouree, saying little on the way.

As she parked the car near the Ballarat High School rowing club she said, "So Peter, this is where you come in, so I hope what I talked about yesterday begins to make sense. Why I needed to give you some of my history. The long-term relationship with your mother and father, the exceptional person who was Roger but the troubled person who was my husband's brother. The contradictions that these family members exhibited over the years and the influence they bore to some degree on where I ended up, as well as your family."

Peter never replied but shut the car door and they walked down to the path that encircles the lake and began walking. Carla immediately felt better walking than she did yesterday sitting still and reliving hurtful memories.

"So it was Tuesday the 16th of April '93, an ordinary day, with me at home with Sam, who was now eleven months. I'd taken the part-time position and been a month into it. Roger was at work. I was getting ready for High School and packing a bag for Sam. Nappies, bibs, bottled formula milk, a little pot of mashed vegetables for lunch and his favourite toy bear. See your mum looked after him three days a week and we were in this great routine, now that the initial worries on whether Sam was going to settle being looked after by someone else were over. We need not have worried as he never batted an eyelid. He looked forward to staying with you and your mum. I'd drop him off at 10 am and pick him up around 12.30 pm, on Monday; Wednesdays were shorter, only an hour and a half and Thursdays were the long days. I'd pulled up in your mum's driveway and …"

As she talked she began to imagine the entire day as if it was happening.

"Hi Susan," she called from the car and Susan came out with Peter at her side and helped Carla with Sam and his 'stuff'. "I'm running a little late today but will catch up for a cuppa when I get back, OK?"

"Of course," Susan replied, as she took Sam from Carla's arms. Carla rushed back to the car and the three of them stood waving as the car headed out the drive.

Carla was back at the house by one o'clock and the two women quickly fell into stride talking about each other's day and the children and what's for dinner. Had Sam slept? What the boys got up to.

At 2 o'clock Carla and Sam were on the road heading home. Tonight Roger was working late due to a huge increase in rental properties coming onto the books and he found he worked better in the evening when it was quiet. He hated doing it because all he ever wanted was to get home and play with Sam but he thought if he waded through the paperwork tonight he'd be on top of things and he'd give himself some time off later in the week.

Carla had put Sam to bed for the night around 9.15 pm and had just sat down in the lounge and opened her book when there was a knock on the door. She was on her feet in an instant and as she walked up the hallway towards the front door she called out, "Did you forget your key? Hang on," and opened the door. She flinched when she saw, not Roger, whom she was expecting, but a policeman. No, two policemen standing in front of her.

"Yes."

"Mrs Nelson?"

"Yes."

"Can we come in, please?"

She stepped aside and let them enter the hall. Her mind was reeling but she told herself not to jump to the negative. Wait to see what they have to say although she was pretty sure it had something to do with Margaret, her mum; it wasn't the first time the police had come to the house over the years when her mother was unwell. Those times coincided with her having manic episodes and that usually meant she was down the street making a general public nuisance of herself. In the past Carla and her Dad had been embarrassed by her behaviours but over the years they learnt to take it all in their stride.

"Can we go into the lounge?" the officer was saying, "I have some bad news for you."

"*Oh my God,*" she thought. "Is it mum? What's happened?"

"Please sit, Mrs Nelson. What I have to say is very distressing."

"No, I'd prefer to stand." She answered with the authority she did not feel.

"Tonight at 8.37 pm your husband, Roger Nelson, was involved in a fatal motorcycle accident. I am so sorry."

With those words ringing in her ears her legs crumpled beneath her and she landed on the floor. The officers quickly reached for her, brought her to her feet and sat her on the chair.

Through the shock, she heard the officers saying, "Is there someone we can ring, someone who will come over?"

And in a voice that she didn't even recognize as her own she said, "Susan, get Susan," and pointed to the phone on the little table in the hallway saying, "Her number's in the Teledex, get Susan Westmead."

Carla stopped walking and Peter said, "Are you alright? Carla, how awful. Look, if you don't want to talk about it I understand." He didn't know what to do or say and Carla could feel his discomfort.

Saying those words aloud had made Carla shudder. "It's OK. I can't change it and you deserve to have some understanding. You see, Peter, I was in shock and I remember I couldn't do anything. It was strange, I was in some kind of fugue state. The police waited with me until Susan arrived and then they left." Again Carla was in the moment.

The women hugged each other and Susan tried to soothe her with words which she knew were pointless but she didn't know what else to do. Carla was not communicating or doing anything and this frightened

Susan. It was now heading close to midnight and Susan had somehow managed to coax Carla upstairs and into bed. She had refused any medical intervention and Susan was not keen to push the issue.

Once Carla was settled she checked on Sam who was still sleeping soundly. She rang home to Liam to tell him what had been happening and that she was going to stay overnight but would come home early in the morning to get Peter so he could go to work. Liam responded by saying, "No worries, Susie. Give Carla a hug from me. This is so terrible, bloody hell how could this have happened? I love you."

"I love you too," and hung up.

In the coming days Carla had learnt that Roger had left the office around 8.30 pm. There was little traffic on the road. He stopped at the intersection of Sturt and Dawson Streets for a red light and without warning, from behind, a car had come up behind him. The police had estimated it was travelling at least 80kms in a 60km zone, and it didn't stop, it literally ploughed into him and kept going. Roger didn't have any time to react. This information was gathered from the road scene only because there had been no witnesses to the incident. Investigators told Carla he would have died on impact. The only identifying material of the car came from some shattered headlight glass and some paint on the motorcycle, which was white. The police report /conclusion was that Roger Nelson was hit and killed by a car, possibly a 4 WD, travelling at speed at or around 8.37 pm on the 16th of April, 1993. The driver did not stop to render assistance and up until the point of this report no person or persons have been spoken to or seen as people of interest.

The funeral was a small torrid affair lasting forty minutes at the little chapel at the funeral parlour in Doveton Street, North and then a procession just around the corner to the new cemetery. Carla had not been given a say in any of the arrangements. Sharon had phoned her three days after the accident and simply said, "Don't worry about anything, Carla. Thomas is taking care of everything." Then there was silence on the phone and Carla knew she was crying but could not bring herself to comfort her because she herself was too numb, devoid of any ability to assist herself, let alone her mother-in-law.

Carla saw Oscar, Sharon and Thomas Nelson at the funeral but they made no effort to talk to her and, if she were honest, she wanted it that way. As Susan and Liam were also at the funeral Sam was being cared for by her neighbour but Carla was anxious to get back home to be with him.

After Roger was buried and people had begun to drift back to Oscar and Sharon's home for the 'wake' Carla lingered with Susan and Liam, waiting in the background so they could take her home. She could not face the 'wake'. At one point both Liam and Susan grabbed for Carla as she walked towards their car because they thought she was about to faint but she remained upright, tears streaming down her face, mascara running and she turned to them both and said, "How the hell does anyone get through this?"

Chapter 7

Carla struggled in the following weeks to care for Sam. Susan found she was spending more and more time at Carla's home than her own home and although she wanted to do all she could for her friend she was getting tired. "Carla, I know it has only been a few weeks but you need to get some routine into your life. Liam is needing me at home and Peter is out of routine and getting upset. Could your in-laws come over and help you?"

"It's alright, Susan," Carla said, as she sat slumped on the couch in pyjamas and stared out the window. "How can I, Susan? How do I get routine? I can't concentrate, I have no energy, and there is no way I could work. I just don't know what to do or where to start. I know I have to 'get on' but," and she looked up at her lifelong friend, "I'm not sure I can," with a small gulp.

"You need to talk to someone, Carla. A professional. Perhaps you need some medication. I don't know but I do know this cannot go on." There was a long period of silence between the women and then Susan added, "Look, its 5 o'clock. I have to go home. Do you want me to take Sam overnight again? You know he misses you."

Susan was thinking, *"Maybe get her on a guilt trip to help snap her out of it,"* but it didn't work, she said nothing. "Well he can come with me now and you think about what you need to do next, Carla. This cannot go on?"

In a voice very small and quiet Carla said, "Yes Susan, take Sam. Thank you."

By the time Susan had run about getting more clothes and nappies for Sam and gathering Peter up and putting away the play things half an hour had passed. Carla had not moved and as Susan called out "We are going," she noticed that Carla made no attempt to even look at them.

"That's it," she said to herself as she went out the door. *"There better be a plan in place or I am going to ring the in-laws and get them involved. This cannot go on."*

Susan arrived with the children after 12.30 pm the next afternoon, having picked up Peter from pre-kinder group. Upon entering the house she firstly noticed the chill in the air and then the utter silence. "Carla," she called as she put the suitcase with Sam's things down, "Carla!" feeling a little more worried as she walked further in the home. Turning into the lounge she was absolutely shocked and amazed to see that Carla was in the same position, same state as she had been yesterday when she left.

"Carla, for God's sake, it's freezing in here. Have you eaten, slept? Oh my God." Carla did not move, and made no effort to acknowledge she was there. Susan raced to the linen cupboard in the hallway and grabbed a blanket and when she returned to the lounge she saw

Sam had crawled on to his mother's knee and was patting her face, saying, "Daddy, Mummy, Peeper look," and he pointed to Peter who was standing looking a little frightened near the lounge room door. Susan almost wept. Placing the blanket over Carla she moved to the phone and dialled, after two rings the phone was picked up and a woman's voice came over the phone, faint and hesitant.

"Hello."

"Is that Mrs Nelson?"

"Yes."

"Mrs Nelson. This is Susan Westmead. I am the very close friend of Carla, your daughter-in-law, and I am sorry to bother you in your time of grief but Carla is not coping. She has hardly slept, eaten or done anything in the past three weeks. I am very frightened for her mental state. I have been doing as much as I can but I cannot continue to virtually live at her home and I fear her grief is very unhealthy." She was speaking rapidly. She knew she was desperate, had run out of knowing what to do and Susan hated not knowing what to do, how to help, but this was beyond her. There was silence on the other end. "Mrs Nelson," in a slightly raised and panicked voice, "Mrs Nelson, are you there? Have you heard what I said?"

"Yes," came the answer. "I will tell my husband," and with that she hung up.

Susan looked incredulous at the phone. *"The bitch,"* she thought, *"no wonder Carla didn't want them in her life. Hell, what am I going to do?"*

She decided that she would organize some food for them all and try to get Carla to eat and then get her to the shower and if she saw no improvement in an hour she would ring Carla's doctor.

Chapter 8

Back at the Nelson's home Sharon was telling her husband and Thomas about the phone call she had just received. "What do you think we should do?"

Thomas knew what to do immediately. "Well, clearly we need to get Samuel away from her. Her mother's mad and now it seems she is. Look, leave it to me." Both Oscar and Sharon were happy for this precise action and agreed it was best for Thomas to deal with. They were both too tired and knew they couldn't help. Thomas went into the study and closed the door. Walking slowly over to the phone on the desk he picked up the local phone directory and scanned the pages until he found the number for the local psychiatric services and was put through to a nurse.

"Hello, Charlotte Janes, triage. How can I assist you?"

"My name is Thomas Nelson and my sister-in law is behaving very strangely."

"In what way, sir?"

"She is not eating, sleeping or looking after her son. She had a tragedy in her life three weeks ago and she is not coping. I think she is suicidal." Thomas said all this in one breath and without inflection.

"Where is your sister-in-law now, Mr Nelson? What has she said or done to get you to that conclusion?"

"I don't have time standing here and answering stupid questions. I want her seen." Thomas was not one for answering questions at any time but to be thwarted in his ideas by this woman was too much. However he also knew that provoking the woman would be counterproductive so, in as calm a voice as he could muster he continued, "She is at home with a friend who is looking after her but she cannot look after her anymore. I am very worried about her. Her mother has mental problems and I think she needs to be in hospital."

Although this man had not clearly articulated the problem with his sister-in-law Charlotte had elicited an underlying tension, possibly anger in the tone and so in order to ensure she could get a clearer picture of what the situation was she said, "Can you bring her in for an assessment?"

"No!" he shouted and then, checking himself for the second time said more calmly, "I am sorry. I am just sick with worry for her. The truth is she wouldn't come with me." Pause. "No, you need to go there and see her. Her name is Carla Nelson," and he gave her the address. "How long would it take you to get to her?"

Given the small information, but the fact that this Mr Nelson had said the woman was suicidal, Charlotte decided that it would be better try to see her today if possible.

"You said a friend was with her. Can you give me the phone number there so I can speak to her?"

"Yes," and he gave the number adding, "you can ring me on my mobile and let me know the outcome." With that he hung up and returned to the kitchen where Sharon and Oscar looked up at him and said in unison, "What's going to happen now?"

"I have rung psychiatric services and they will assess her and hopefully get her in hospital. If that happens we will need to get the boy and bring him back here. She sounds like she's not capable of looking after him."

Sharon was aghast. "No Thomas, at least not today. The house isn't suitable for Samuel. He's so little. Can't the woman with Carla look after him? We could pay her."

Thomas said he thought that might help for a couple of days until they got organized but only a couple of days. No, Thomas wanted Samuel to live with them and this was a timely opportunity to get what he wanted. Something he wasn't even fully aware of within himself was now being fully realised. He had wanted Roger's boy. He had feared for the child since he was born and the anxiety he felt when he thought about the boy was painful. Now he had the opportunity to look after him and that underlying sense of dread was beginning to dissipate as his thoughts began centering on a life with the child.

Chapter 9

Susan had just settled Carla into bed when the phone rang. She looked at the children, who were playing with Lego on the bedroom floor, and said, "Boys, stay here I will be right back."

"Hello. Carla Nelson's home."

"Hello, my name is William Atkins. I am a nurse with the psychiatric services and we have received a call from a Mr Thomas Nelson through our triage section saying his sister-in-law is unwell and possibly suicidal. I was wanting to gather some more information about what is happening for Mrs Nelson. Firstly, who am I speaking to and what is your relationship to Mrs Nelson?"

"I'm Susan Westmead, Carla's closest friend," and in her mind she was saying, *"Suicidal! Is Carla suicidal?"* then she realised the man was asking her, "Can you tell me how she is presenting to you?"

"Umm, yes, yes of course," and Susan explained that Carla's husband had been killed in a motorcycle accident three weeks ago and that since then she had ceased attending her job at the High School, had eaten very little, hardly slept and today she was too weak to shower herself. "I have had the responsibility of her eleven month-old son, full-time, for the past four days because Carla is unable to care for him at all. Earlier she was managing, albeit a little, but now," and she realised her voice was getting to a whingey pitch. She told the nurse, "Carla looks terrible and sometimes she didn't make sense but now she's hardly speaking at all."

"Is she suicidal, has she tried to harm herself?"

"I don't think so," pondered Susan, "at least she hasn't said so to me. She is just lost," and then she added as an afterthought, "mind you if she doesn't start eating…," and her voice trailed off.

"OK, Mrs Westmead. A colleague and I will come over to assess Mrs Nelson this afternoon around 4.30 pm. I assume you will be there!" and Susan said she would. Susan hung up and went back to the children. She tried telling Carla what was going on but she was unresponsive.

Atkins and his colleague Sarah Ho arrived right on 4.30 pm and Susan let them in and showed them to Carla's room. She picked up Samuel from the bedroom floor and he squealed loudly because he wanted to keep playing but Susan soothed him with little kisses and a promise of ice cream. At hearing the word ice cream Peter immediately jumped up and stood next to his mother. "I want an ice cream too."

"Yes, dear, of course." Then turning to the bed she said, "Carla, this is William Atkins and Sarah Ho, they are nurses from the psychiatric services. Thomas rang them." At the mention of psychiatric services Carla sat up wide-eyed and said, "He what? Why? What's the matter?" She was almost screaming, "I don't need psych services. I just lost my husband, leave me alone. Psych services are for mum. But not me!" and promptly turned her head from them. She felt exhausted with the effort and she began to softly cry.

"Mrs Nelson." It was Sarah who spoke. "We just want to talk to you and see that you are alright. We don't mean to frighten you. Your brother-in-law was concerned after your friend here spoke to your mother-in-law."

Susan felt guilty and said, "I didn't know what else to do, Carla. You haven't eaten properly in three weeks. You are not sleeping and you are growing weak. I thought they would come over and help you. I didn't expect this anymore than you did."

Carla kept her back to them all but said, "It's alright Susan I understand. I'll talk to them."

"Thank you. I'll go and look after the children," happy to have an excuse to get out of the room. To the nurses she said, "If you need me just call," and left the room.

Whilst Carla had been reacting to the nurses and then speaking to Susan William Atkins had been taking in the surroundings. The room was rather chilly and the curtains drawn. Carla looked ragged and her eyes were puffy from crying and lack of sleep. He saw a picture on the dressing table of a very handsome man with brown eyes and a charismatic smile. This he assumed was the husband. Next to that photo he saw a picture of Carla, her husband and a newborn baby. They were looking directly at each other and William could see the love they shared. He thought, "Poor bugger." He moved closer to the bed when Sarah began to address Carla.

"Mrs Nelson."

"Carla."

"Yes, Carla, can you tell me what happened to your husband?"

Carla gulped, she hadn't said the words out loud about the accident and she wasn't sure she could.

A good minute went by and William was about to ask another question when Carla sat up. "He was killed in a motorbike accident three weeks ago and the bastard never stopped, left him in the road crumpled," and then she started rocking back and forth, back and forth and mumbling and crying and then wailing. Both William and Sarah looked at each other and as if they could read each other's minds they said in unison, "We need to speak to Susan," and with that William left Sarah to watch over Carla.

Downstairs Atkins spoke as he entered the lounge area, "Susan, can I have a word? Can you give me a little more detail of what Carla has been like over the past three weeks and how she normally functions?" And Susan sat down and told him about a wonderful, vibrant, intelligent, professional woman who loved her husband and son dearly. A person who is considerate of others' needs sometimes to the point of neglecting her own. She told William about Carla's mother and all her admissions to hospital over the years and how it had been hard for Carla and her father when she was growing up. William Atkins remembered Carla's mother but he said nothing to Susan. When Susan appeared to run out of things to say about Carla, William asked, "So what you have told me suggests this is extremely different from anything Carla has exhibited before. That even the death of her father, with whom she was very close, did not precipitate the extremes we are witnessing today. For him she grieved but in a healthier, functional manner?"

"Yes, that's right."

"OK, thanks Susan, that's been a great help."

William returned to Carla's room and saw Sarah looking quite concerned. "How is she?" and Sarah said, "Not good, she's incoherent and I'm not convinced that she may not be psychotic. I think she needs to be admitted and seen by the psychiatrist. I don't think she's safe to be left here."

"I think you're right, Sarah. Apparently she's lost a lot of weight and is probably dehydrated. Her GP is Dr Sarah Medern at the group practice in Lydiard Street. I'll give her a ring and see if we can't get her into the Base Hospital for a physical work up and then get the psychiatrist to assess her there. It maybe she will be OK with food, fluids and sleep. Let's hope."

William spoke with the GP and an ambulance was called to take Carla to the Base Hospital for admission.

Carla did not resist them when they came. She allowed them to pick her up and place her on the trolley and wheel her into the van. She said nothing that anyone could understand although sometimes she would look up and stare into the air making grimaces and shaking her head.

Susan told the nurses she could look after Sam until Carla was home. "Let her know he will be OK. I will bring her a suitcase of things tomorrow afternoon if she is going to be in hospital more than just one night."

"Thanks Susan, I am sure she will be OK," and the nurses, along with the ambulance, left.

Chapter 10

Thomas took the call at 5.40 pm from William Atkins, a nurse from the psych unit, telling him that at this point in time she was being admitted to the general hospital for a physical work up and the psychiatrist would assess her in the morning. Thomas had thanked him and hung up. He then immediately phoned Alan Turpy. Thomas had dealt with Turpy before and he hated the little man with the squinty dark eyes and pot belly, beer stomach but he was a man Thomas could trust to get a job done with efficiency and diplomacy. He was a venal character but that was exactly what Thomas needed right now. Of course it was imperative that Carla be admitted to hospital before his plan could be acted out. He would have to wait for those nurses… and Thomas was not a patient man. To Turpy he was saying, "OK, it's on. You know what to do?"

Turpy did know what to do. He had been told to wait until Liam Westmead left for work and then he was to go to the door and get in under whatever pretence he could.

It was 7.45 am the following day and Liam had just shut the front door and was getting in the car when he noticed a white delivery van three doors down his street. He noticed it had flowers on the side and thought as he was pulling out of the driveway, "*Well, that's an early delivery, Maggie won't be happy being woken.*" Maggie was a good neighbour and friend and she worked nightshift at McCain's and she was very routine about coming home at 6 am, showering and going straight to bed. He remembered when he was working nightshifts he couldn't go straight to bed. He had to sit up for a few hours, watch TV and unwind with a beer but Maggie, oh no, she was straight to bed, straight to sleep and look out if anyone woke her before 2 pm.

As soon as Liam's car was out of sight Turpy started the van, did a U turn and parked in the Westmead's drive. He jumped out, careful to keep his hat low over his eyes and grabbed a bunch of roses he had purchased the evening before off the front seat and marched purposefully to the door.

When he rang the doorbell he heard a woman inside call out, "OK, what did you forget? Obviously your keys?" and then he heard footsteps coming to the door and the door opened. With a smile as wide as he could muster he said, "Mrs Westmead, I am from the Lily Pod flower and garden store and your husband Liam asked that I deliver these to you."

Susan was amazed, Liam had been a romantic when they first started going out but over the years that had waxed and waned, not that his love for her was less, it was just that things slotted into routine and romance seemed to drop away. "Oh, they are beautiful," and went to take them from his gloved hand, but at the same time he bought his other gloved hand out and in it was a small calibre hand gun. "Don't do anything stupid, Susan, back in the house. Quick!"

Susan backed up and Turpy moved fast to get off the verandah and inside the house, letting the door shut with a bang.

"What do you want? I don't have any money and only cheap jewellery. Please, I have children in the kitchen. Tell me what you want." She was terrified and her eyes never left the gun in this man's hand.

"I want the boy."

Susan looked aghast and stammered, "The boy, what boy, no. You can't hurt them, I won't let you." She was panicked now and saw clearly this man wanted one of the children. Which boy she didn't know but there was no way she was going to let him have either boy. "*Think Susan, think*" she was saying to herself and he was saying, "Look, this can be easy or hard," and with those words she lunged to get the gun but Turpy was too quick and pulled it back. Susan then saw the phone on the wall and grabbed for it and that was when she felt a terrible agonising pain that started in her back and flooded through her chest. She had no time to think, she was dead before she hit the ground.

"You stupid bitch," Turpy said and looked up and saw a child of about four years old staring at him and then he looked to his mother. The child started screaming, "Mummy, Mummy," and Turpy thought, "*Fuck this,*" and ran out of the house, jumped in the van and sped off.

He drove from the house heading north, navigating to the Ballarat – Creswick Road. He knew where he was going, had done this trip a number of times, the Creswick State Forest to a place called Nuggetty Dam. Turpy was thinking ahead, he needed to dump the van and get back to town and ring Nelson. He turned right off the White Swan Road onto a dirt track. The van shuddered as he drove quickly over corrugations and potholes. To the side of this road there were many side tracks, mostly made by dirt bike riders, but Turpy was heading for a spot just beyond the dam itself. He knew this area well because it was a good place to strip cars down that he stole. Usually on those occasions though he had a friend follow him and he'd have a lift out. Today he'd have to walk out. This didn't bother him though, the Federation track back through the bush wouldn't take too long and it would afford him some cover. It was highly unlikely that he would see anyone on the track on a Tuesday morning.

He passed the dam on his right and drove along a narrow off shoot on his left, travelling as deeply as he could into the bush. He killed the engine, checked around in the cabin of the van for anything he may have dropped and then, satisfied he had everything, he got out. Turpy had been careful and had kept his gloves on the entire time so fingerprints were not left.

As he walked along the Federation track he mused over the outcome of his 'assignment'. Yes, he knew Nelson would be pissed that he hadn't grabbed the kid but he wouldn't care too much that he'd killed the woman. That was collateral damage, or was it? He didn't understand Nelson, never had but he had a healthy respect for keeping on his better side. His association with him was limited and he was thinking he would break it after he got his money. There was just something about him that 'wasn't right'. He gave a loud chuckle to himself when he thought *"Ha Ha, like you're intact Alan old matey,"* and then added *"Well, I reckon I are more stable than that guy anyway."*

He came out of the bush at Brown Hill and headed for the milk bar there and bought himself a cold drink, being careful to keep his eyes averted and saying nothing. Outside the shop he got his mobile out and phoned for a taxi and within an hour he was back in his flat having showered and eaten. He had tried Thomas twice since getting home but there was no answer on his direct line at his office. He never communicated with him at home. It was forbidden.

It was nearly 12 midday so he turned on the radio to listen to the news. The ABC reporter came on at 12 o'clock and the major headline was the discovery of a woman at her home, shot dead. The reporter was saying, "This morning at 8.05 am triple zero received a call from a distraught man saying his neighbour had been shot and requesting ambulance and police. Police arrived at the home in central Ballarat at 8.20 am to discover the body of a woman in her mid-twenties dead in the hallway with a single bullet wound to her back. He went on to detail the fact that here had been two children in the home and that it was the screams of the four year old that alerted the neighbour. "At this stage the police are saying little as to why this vicious attack took place."

"Well," Turpy thought, *"now the shit hits the fan."*

Also at that instant his phone rang and the voice on the other end of the phone said, "You fucked up."

"No I didn't. You weren't there, it's worked out for the best, mate. You will definitely get the kid now, no questions asked. The other way you wanted it was flawed. Really, what were you thinking? A kidnapping! How you thought that would work was beyond me. I

want my money and I'm out of here for a month or two."
After a few seconds later the voice said, "OK, usual spot,
11pm tonight," and then the phone went dead.

Alan Turpy was pleased with himself, a quick
$20,000, all in a day's work. He decided that a trip to
Darwin might be in order, especially with winter
approaching. *"Who stays in Ballarat during winter?"* he
thought.

Chapter 11

Peter had seen the man and his mummy and he knew that it was bad. He had screamed and screamed and then run outside, down the drive and into next door's house. His yelling was high-pitched and frantic and Mr Trainor was outside to the boy in seconds. The child couldn't articulate the problem but Mr Trainor knew it must be bad. He had lived in this street for nearly fifty years and he had helped welcome Susan and Liam into the neighbourhood. He liked them a lot, especially as they tended to keep to themselves, but they were always friendly when they bumped into one another.

With Peter's hand in his Mr Trainor had gone next door and saw the front door open. He didn't even get into the hallway before he saw Susan's body. He gasped and ran to her but he knew straight away that she was dead. He reached for the phone and dialled 000 and told them there was a body and he needed an ambulance and the police. After he had completed the phone call he looked around and saw that Peter was gone. He called for him, "Peter, Peter, where are you?" He sensed, more than heard, that he was being watched. He headed towards the lounge room. With heart thumping he stopped motionless as he realised the killer might still be in the house. "*Where is that child,*" he thought. "*We have to get out of here.*" He had many thoughts swamping his mind but he took a deep breath and said to himself, "*At 72 you had a good innings so let's find that boy.*"

He walked purposefully through the doorway and into the lounge where he saw no man with a gun but two little children, Peter and another child, sitting to the right hand side of the doorway watching him. "It's alright little ones. The ambulance is coming and the police," as he put his hand out to the children trying to be reassuring. "How about we go back to my place and Mrs Trainor will make you some scones and drinks? Yes? … you want to do that?" and Peter answered, "Yes, but Sam cannot walk properly yet."

"That's ok, I can carry him," and Mr Trainor picked Sam up and holding him on one hip and Peter's hand in his left, the three of them walked past the body of Susan Westmead and never looked back.

Chapter 12

Carla was admitted to the medical ward where she was sharing a room with elderly ladies. She did not acknowledge anyone. Although her rocking had ceased her mumbling had increased and occasionally the odd word was clear enough to identify but it made no sense. The nurses on the ward, in conjunction with the doctor, set up a saline drip to try and rehydrate her as this was their greatest priority at this point in time. Carla was also given an injection of 2mgs of Haloperidol, a strong anti-psychotic medication the doctor felt would calm the agitation she was clearly experiencing and give her some sleep.

"I think with fluids back up to healthy levels and a good night's sleep we will see a notable difference in her," the doctor had said to the nurse. The Haloperidol certainly did help, within 20 minutes Carla was sound asleep. When she awoke that evening she was disorientated. "Hello, where am I?" she called out and then she heard a quiet but rather raspy voice say, "It's alright, dear, you are in hospital," and she responded with a loud, "Nooooo," and began pulling at the needle in her arm. The night shift nurse ran in, flicking on the lights and quickly surveyed the scene. "Mrs Nelson, please. What do you think you are doing?"

"Getting out, can't stay, get Sam." Carla could hear her words but she couldn't get her words to make sentences. She felt vague, inconsequential, like having no substance. Another nurse came into the ward then and the first nurse said, "Ring Dr King, explain what's happening and get a verbal order for some more Haloperidol. Quick."

Five minutes passed and the nurse, Sister Kennedy, had managed to get Carla to leave the drip in situ and to lay back down on the bed. Carla was mumbling again and she seemed very distracted, often turning her head and then covering her ears. The second nurse came in with a kidney dish and a drawn hypodermic needle. "He's ordered a stat dose of 5 mgs and then 2 mgs PRN orally every 6 hours after that."

"Good," Sister Kennedy said, "she's very upset."

"Mrs Nelson. I am going to give you a needle to help you relax and sleep," and with that she pulled the covers down and gave Carla the injection in the middle right quadrant of her thigh. Carla didn't resist, she was preoccupied with words, words and more words.

The injection took its effect within 20 minutes and again she slept. Carla was still sleeping when the psychiatrist and William Atkins came to see her the next morning. The night shift had left by this time and the day shift nurses spoke to the doctor, giving him a hand over of the patient.

"Alright. So we have a twenty-six year old woman whose husband was killed in a motorcycle accident three weeks ago and she has virtually ceased to function. She appears delusional or at least possibly experiencing some psychotic symptoms. She has been well hydrated overnight but taken no food."

"Yes, that's right doctor," the dayshift nurse said.

"Good, let's go meet her."

Carla was just rousing as the doctor and William Atkins came up to her bedside. She felt very groggy and tried to remember where she was. She thought she recognized the young man but had no idea from where.

"Mrs Nelson, my name is Dr Thallis and you may remember Nurse Atkins who came to your home yesterday." Carla nodded ever so slightly keeping her eyes on the doctor.

"I understand you have had a terrible time in the last three weeks. I am very sorry for your loss. It is an absolutely tragedy and I can only imagine what you are feeling, so please, can you tell me how you are feeling now?"

Carla continued to stare at the doctor. She could see his mouth moving but she wasn't able to fully understand his words. "Sorry, what, what did they give me last night? I can't think."

"Mrs Nelson, let me explain," and, in a slow and softly spoken voice, the psychiatrist explained to Carla where she was, why she was there and that he was there to assess her mental state and determine the next course of action. That being: an admission into the acute ward or some other assistance and support at home. Carla listened and managed to take in the enormity of her situation. She was thinking, albeit very slowly, *No way I am going anywhere near a psych unit. Hell! That's*

Margaret. That's mum, not me!" but to the doctor she coherently gave reassurances that she would eat and look after herself and Sam and, "Oh yes, definitely I will seek professional grief counselling. Thank you doctor, thank you. I just felt so distraught and overwhelmed but… I have had some sleep and feel much better. Thanks, thanks." Looking from the psychiatrist to the nurse and back.

The psychiatrist was happy with his assessment of Carla, labelling it as having an acute reaction to a traumatic and disturbing event that was short in duration and did not require an acute admission to the psych unit. "That's good, Mrs Nelson, you can get ready and leave after morning tea. I will write you up some PRN Haloperidol to use if you are having trouble sleeping." Again Carla thanked the psychiatrist as he and the nurse left the room.

As soon as Carla was dressed she called her mother, who said she'd be there in an hour to take her to Susan's place to pick up Sam. "Oh, Carla I was so worried when I heard you were in hospital," her mother was saying.

"It's OK mum, I am fine now. Just pick me up as soon as you can. Love you." She deliberately made her voice sound more cheery than she felt but she was determined to get as far from hospital as possible.

Carla was waiting outside the hospital in Drummond Street and she could feel a bit of strength returning to her. *"OK, that was not what should happen. Roger would need me to be strong. I can't change what's happened but Sam is the focal point now."* She felt tears rising but held them back. *"I'll be alright."*

Margaret was packed ready to pick Carla up when the police arrived. "Now what?" she thought. Initially they asked if her daughter was with her. They had gone to her house but was told by a neighbour she had been taken to hospital yesterday afternoon. The neighbours had suggested she might be here with her now. "No, I am just about to pick her up. What's the problem?"

"Given our news we would rather break this to her at home but not if she is unwell in hospital."

"Please, I need to pick my daughter up. What's going on?" and they proceeded to tell her about Susan's murder and that Sam was with the Trainors.

Margaret felt like she had been smacked in the face but it wasn't for herself she feared, but for her daughter. *"Oh my goodness, no. She cannot take this. It will kill her."* To the police she said, "What! No! Carla," and in a pleading voice she added, "Sergeant, please let me break the news. Please. She's not that strong." Margaret was scared for her daughter. "I am going to pick up my daughter from hospital now and then we will go to the Trainor's and get Sam."

"Right. We will call ahead and let me Mr Trainor know to expect you. Also we will need to speak to Mrs Nelson. If she could come to the station as soon as possible. It is very important we gather as much information about her friend as possible so we can try and piece together why anyone would want her dead."

Pulling up on Drummond Street Margaret saw Carla leaning against a small brick retaining wall and was surprised at how composed she looked compared to the last time she'd seen her a week ago. Inwardly she wished she was as composed.

Carla jumped in the front seat and gave her mum a kiss. "Let's get Sam, Mum." But Margaret stayed still with the engine off. "What's wrong?"

"Carla, it's Susan," and she told her what the police had said.

Chapter 13

Thomas got to the Black Hill lookout at 10.40 pm and waited for Turpy. Alan was often early to meetings and Thomas didn't like coming in second, it unsettled him, gave him a sense that he was on the back foot and tonight he wanted to be early.

At 10.50pm he saw headlights heading up the hill and then coming towards where he was parked. He recognized Turpy's car, a red Holden something or other. Thomas wasn't into cars. Turpy hadn't even parked before he got out of the car holding the bag with Turpy's pay.

Alan saw Thomas as soon as he came over the rise and lowered his high beam, slowly cruising down to where he saw Thomas getting out of his car with a bag in his hand.

"Good," he thought to himself, *"Get the money and piss off out of this bastard's life."* Turpy had always been wary of Thomas and as he slowed to a stop he felt to his left along the bench seat and was comforted by having his gun, safety off and ready. *"Any smart move by the bastard and he's toast. Makes no difference to me. All I need is the money."*

Alan pulled up about five metres from Thomas and Thomas walked purposely towards him. He rolled the window down as Thomas came to his side and before he had time to say anything Thomas raised a gloved hand and shot Turpy in the side of the face. Alan knew nothing, his body jerked violently sideways across the bench seat and didn't move. Thomas casually put his hand in the window, turned off the engine and lights and quickly returned to his car, saying aloud to himself, "Well, you should be proud of me. That's one way to save $20,000," and he chuckled, let himself get back into the car and backed out of the parking lot just in time, as a group of three cars carrying young men came over the rise but they stopped at the upper car park area. Although he was a little disconcerted at the arrival of the cars he talked slowly to himself, encouraging himself to 'act normal', leave high beam on and get away with the least of attention. Thomas had been up to this lookout many times before and he was reasonably confident at this time of night it usually only attracted the kind of people who didn't want to be recognised. The drug users, drug dealers, lovers who had nowhere else to hang out, and any other deviant you cared to name. Thomas hated them all, 'useless, wasters' to his mind. As he passed the three parked cars the men were all heading for a table lower down on a grassy area below the car park with beers and other drinks in hand talking and calling out loudly to each other. Thomas kept his head down and headed towards home.

Alan Turpy's body was found early the following morning by an elderly couple who had come up to watch the sun rise. Initially they didn't take any notice of the car but as they drove by to leave the woman noticed the window was down and thought that odd.

"The window's down. Not very smart to leave the car open like that," and her husband said, "Let's take a look. Could be another suicide. Last year we had four people kill themselves up here. Don't understand the attraction."

He stopped next to the car and got out. He noticed a man slumped sideways in the driver's seat and called, "Hey, buddy, you OK?" but when he got no answer he moved a little closer and adjusting his glasses he saw what he thought was blood and backed up quickly. "Holy hell," as he rushed back to the car screaming, "Meg. Meg. We got to call the police, I was right, another suicide I'd say."

Police arrived and cordoned off the area. The following day it was reported in the press that a body had been found with a single bullet wound to the head. Police initially thought it was a suicide but analysis showed that it would not have been possible for the man to shoot himself where he was actually shot. Police have concluded that they are looking for a gunman. The man killed was not a local person and police have few leads, but anyone who might have been in the area sometime between 9 pm and 4 am were urged to call police.

Thomas watched the papers with interest and as days passed and reports about Turpy were less frequent he felt comfortable that he would not be connected to the case.

Chapter 14

Carla had jumped out of the car but had collapsed on the pavement when Margaret had told her the news of Susan's murder. She had not moved, simply fallen to the path and lay there. Margaret had tried to get her daughter up but it was no good, she was not strong enough and Carla was a floppy, dead weight. As staff came out having heard her cries for help, someone called the ambulance and she was taken back into the hospital. Margaret explained to the triage nurse what had occurred and she immediately called psych services. Within an hour Carla Parkinson was admitted to the acute psych ward with a tentative diagnosis of crisis reaction with catatonia.

Thomas was informed by Carla's mother that she was being transferred to the psychiatric unit and that she was going to pick up Sam and look after him whilst she was unwell. Even though Margaret had had little to do with the Nelsons she understood their recent loss and wanted to include Thomas and his parents in what was happening to their daughter/sister-in-law and grandson/ nephew. When Margaret mentioned Samuel and that she was going to care for him Thomas said that he thought it would be better if he and his parents cared for the boy because, "There are three of us and we could share the load. Besides Margaret, Carla is going to need you now more than ever and with us caring for Samuel you can give Carla all your attention. Wouldn't you agree?" and he smiled at her and nodded his head.

Initially she replied, "Oh no, Thomas, that is gracious of you and your parents but I should care for Sam." But secretly Margaret was happy for the offer. She loved Sam but she had never been a strong woman and she needed rest throughout the day and having an eleven month-old, 24 hours a day was a big ask.

"I understand Margaret but I insist. We will take," then realising that was not an appropriate term to use he quickly adjusted his words saying, "umm, I mean… will care for Samuel just until Carla is discharged. I will bring him around to see you regularly. I promise." With relief Margaret agreed. Thomas declared he would pick Sam up later in the day from the Trainors and asked that Margaret ring the Trainors to let them know the change of plans. Margaret was instructed to have a bag packed and ready for when he came to her house later that day. Again Margaret allowed herself to be directed by Thomas.

Thomas left the hospital where he had been talking to Margaret and headed straight to find Sharon who was in the kitchen. "Mother, I am picking up Sam this afternoon and I want you to accompany me to pick the child up. It's better you're there with me. Woman to woman."

"Of course. I'll get ready. What's happened Thomas, why the rush?" Thomas told his mother about the shooting of Susan Westmead and Carla's collapse. "Oh, what else, Thomas?" she bemoaned, "what else." But she never offered to see Carla or ask any more questions.

Picking up Samuel from the Trainors went smoothly and Thomas and Sharon had him home with a suitcase of clothes by 6 pm that evening. Oscar was pleased to have his grandson with them and it just so happened over the coming weeks that he tended to do the bulk of the caring. Sharon was aloof and often left Sam on his own in the lounge, in a playpen, which Sam hated. He was pulling himself up now and he would stand holding the bars and cry and call for his mummy and daddy. Sharon hated hearing the child call his father; the reminder of losing Roger was there day in, day out. "This child DOES not replace Roger," she had shouted at Oscar one evening when he remarked she should get closer to him. It made her desperately sad looking at the little boy, but instead of going and comforting the child and seeing this situation as a good thing, it only made her increase the distance between herself and her grandson. Oscar observed there was no bridging the gap for his wife and so made a very conscious effort to try to keep Samuel away from Sharon as much as he could. Thomas was not around during the day but he was very attentive in the evenings and Oscar marvelled at the change in Thomas's demeanour when around the child. Softer, less strident and querulous.

One week after Carla's admission to the psych unit Thomas went to speak with his father. "I've been talking with the doctors at the psych unit and they say she's getting worse not better and they don't expect her to be discharged any day soon. They are both mad, you know that, Dad. I don't believe it is good for Samuel to grow up with them. I have applied for temporary custody." Oscar looked up from his book and went to say something but Thomas warded him off with his hand, "Well, at least until she can prove she is a fit person."

"Really? I suppose that's a good idea, son," and then as an afterthought, "her mother won't have him?"

"No. You know she's been in and out of the nut house and it looks like Carla's of the same genes. Anyway, I have decided that the real estate business is really hotting up in South Australia and I think we should pack up here and go live there. Roger was thinking about it before he died so now he's not around, we should go. What do you think?"

"My God, not this topic again. I don't know what your mother will think. Roger's memories are here, in this home. Look, you have to take things a little slower, Thomas, it's only been just over a month. We need to consider Sharon. I mean, I know we've been tinkering with the idea for a while but this just seems very sudden, I will need longer to consider this." He paused and got up and headed over to the window. "And what about the business here? Our friends? It's a huge ask and your mum and I aren't spring chickens, you know."

"I have actually spoken to mum and she's keen."

With that Oscar swung around facing Thomas. He narrowed his eyes and said in a slow long drawl, "Really?"

"Really. You know how she hates the Ballarat winters and she's of a mind that Adelaide will be a good way of moving on. She's very fragile, Dad. You know, losing two children and she said she hates all the

171

memories here. So again," and he stepped closer to his father and opened his hands in a form of supplication, "What do you think? Charlie can run the business we have here and we will make a killing over there. A new start." Thomas was smiling broadly.

Oscar had never heard such enthusiasm from his Thomas before but he had to ask, "What about Samuel and Carla, Thomas? Where do they fit into this?"

"We take Samuel with us and I'll worry about her when needs be. It will be a good move, Dad. Don't worry. I will organise everything." He turned then and walked out of his father's study saying to himself, *"I'll organise it alright. She will not have her son back, ever."*

Chapter 15

Things moved fast after that. Charlie was told of the plans and after some heated discussions with Thomas, Thomas agreed that he could hire someone to manage the rental side of the business. He then organised a removalist and left Charlie to the task of selling their home for him and his parents. He was keen to get away as soon as possible. But before he left permanently Thomas had one major thing to do and that was to get Carla to sign Samuel over to him. He visited her in hospital and told her they were relocating and that she could join them when she was well but in the interim he needed to have temporary custody of Samuel in case he needed any treatment and to protect his legal rights. Carla had looked at him blankly, her eyes were vacant, her pupils constricted and her movements were very slow and stiff. She was unsure exactly what Thomas was saying but registered somewhere in the background that this was about Sam and she needed to do something. Thomas was looking at her with some sadness which he normally didn't allow himself to register. *"My brother loved this woman and yet neither of them has shown any responsibility for their son. Roger, lazy, allowing his wife to continue working and giving the child over to others to care for! Why. It was always doomed."*

Thomas always knew he was really the only one who was capable of ensuring that his nephew was safe and it worried him that they might have had more children. Then what! No, things had worked out the right way. He thought, *"Best to cut ties completely and she can get on with her life, forget us. Better to get this over and done with, fast."*

"Carla, do you understand? Here is the paper I need you to sign. Will you do it?"

Carla was tired, she just wanted to curl up and sleep and Thomas was stopping her. With great effort she nodded and took the pen. Her hands felt weak and the simple task of holding a pen was almost too much for her. Thomas pointed impatiently at the places he required signatures and she scrawled her name where he said. Immediately Thomas picked up the paperwork, returned it to the A4 envelope, stood up and left without saying another word. For Carla she was thinking, *"Good."*

As Thomas left the single bedroom William Atkins came out of the nurses' station and, spotting him, said, "Hey Mr Nelson, what are you doing down there? This is quiet time, and besides, no visitors in the bedrooms. She is very unwell still and needs rest."

Thomas put his hands up in a show of surrender saying, "Yes, yes I am sorry. I just wanted to see how Carla was and no one was about so I just assumed I could wonder down. I am so sorry if I have upset the routine, nurse, but I didn't talk to her as she was asleep so I just closed the door and was coming back."

"Okay. But please, in future, ensure you announce yourself at the nurses' station."

"Definitely, please let Carla know I popped in and will come back in visiting hours tomorrow." With that he continued walking towards the exit, relieved to know he would never step foot in the place again.

Chapter 16

On the day of Carla's admission she had been medicated with anti-psychotic drugs and over the coming weeks had remained non-communicative, lethargic, and virtually immobile. She managed to shower in the mornings but the nurses had to coax and encourage her to come out of her room. Her medications had been changed and antidepressant medication had been added to the medication regime, leaving her very sedated and her mind very fuzzy. Adding to the staff's concern was her continued refusal to take in adequate fluids and nourishment. The doctors were concerned. "It's been two weeks since admission and I have to say we are not seeing much change in her presentation." Dr Thallis was speaking to the charge nurse of the Unit and Nurse Benson was saying, "I know. Her sleep pattern is erratic, the only food she is eating is what she can pick up in her hand, a slice of ham, a carrot or pea. She refuses to use a knife and fork. The nurses are reporting they cannot assess her thought processes because she only speaks in monosyllables or not at all. The extra introduction of the anti-depressant doesn't seem to have had any effect."

"I think we need to think about electroconvulsive therapy, I am concerned that she cannot continue as she has been. We will reduce the medication and have her booked in for early next week. I am aware that her brother-in-law and parents-in-law are leaving the State soon. I will try to contact them to get permission or otherwise I could speak to her mother, although I am reluctant to put this to Margaret, given her mental state. Anyway leave this to me," and he left to go on his rounds.

Dr Thallis phoned the Nelsons' home and got Oscar. After explaining the situation with Carla, Oscar said he would inform his son who was taking care of Carla's affairs. "He will ring you before the end of the day, Doctor," Oscar reassured him. As soon as Oscar told Thomas, Thomas was on the phone and agreeing to sign the authority to provide six treatments of ECT over a six week period. Dr Thallis explained that it may not require that many sessions but, "It is better to have more approved than less."

Thomas went to the hospital that afternoon and signed the necessary papers and then popped in to see Carla. He was shocked at what he saw. Carla was pale, had lost a lot of weight which she could ill afford and her eyes were like black, sunken, lifeless orbs. He crossed the floor and sat on the bed next to her and put his arm about her. Since taking on Samuel he had changed, he knew it within himself, his thoughts were clearer, more focused on his surroundings, something he had never taken any interest in. He was noting the stark, clinical room in which his sister-in-law was now living. Heavy dark curtains pulled shut, refusing to let in the light. The white painted walls and signs dotted here and there about, 'If you are depressed call this number for help' or 'Talk to someone if you feel down.' 'Push this button for nurse on call.' He felt very uncomfortable in this room. Still holding Carla he said, "Oh you poor thing. It's a tragedy for you I know, Roger, Susan, it's not fair, it doesn't make sense. I miss him dearly even though we didn't see eye to eye." He then turned to face her and holding her face up with his hand gently on her chin he said, "Carla, if I ever find out who the bastard was who hit Roger I will kill him myself," and he gave her a squeeze on the shoulder. Carla looked like she was going to say something but nothing came out. She tried to get her eyes to meet Thomas's but nothing happened. She wanted to tell him, *"Thomas I'm trapped, I need help. And thank you."* But in reality all she could do was snuggle closer into Thomas's arms. It felt good and it was what she wanted. No one had touched her since Roger had died and she felt so alone. She didn't want it to stop. But stop it did, Thomas pulled away and holding her shoulders he said, "I hope you can understand this Carla. You are very unwell and you need to get better and then you can get on with your life. I will look after Samuel, don't worry about that. I will ring from Adelaide and let the doctors know my phone number so you have it when you are well again. Is that okay?"

But she didn't respond, she couldn't respond, it was too much.

Chapter 17

The following week Carla was prepared for her first ECT. She was having bilateral ECT. Dr Thallis had attended a seminar on ECT back in February the same year and he had noted that there was some controversy over the use of Bilateral ECT vs Unilateral ECT but he felt in Carla's case that the double-sided placement of the electrodes would produce a better and swifter outcome. He knew that some patients experience muscle soreness after ECT along with memory loss and confusion and that this is more pronounced with bilateral electrode placement, and that retrograde amnesia was possible, affecting events that occurred in the weeks or months before treatment, but again, he felt the benefits outweighed the risks of a few lost memories. He believed it was a good thing for his patient, given her debilitating grief, and he explained to the nurse who was going to assist with the procedure, "I know some people are against the bilateral use of ECT but I feel it will give her a quicker response and recovery time. I'm hoping in the next weeks and months following ECT we will see a return of any the memory loss and a lift in her mood which will predominantly have her showing more interest in life, better social interaction and," and he stopped and looked around, "and that she will have lost her suicidal drive, _if_ she ever had one." Turning back to the nurse he added, "We get to that point and we can look to discharge. Yes, definitely there is no evidence that ECT causes structural brain damage. So she can only benefit." So with those thoughts in mind he proceeded to the ECT suite with the nurse following behind. The nurse was musing to herself that she wondered who he was trying to convince, her or himself!

Carla did indeed have retrograde amnesia and it took four sessions of ECT before she really appeared to be making headway. The last two sessions Dr Thallis decided to revert to unilateral therapy as a precaution.

Carla's presentation by the fifth session was one with more activity, both physically and mentally. She was conversing with the nurses and fellow patients and it was felt that it was time to sit with her and discuss what had happened and where to go from here. She was still being given medication, although at lower doses, but the nursing staff were vigilant around her because they were well aware, from experience, that when a patient with major depression begins to get more active, there is a chance that they then have the energy to kill themselves where they did not have the energy before. The staff had never established if Carla was suicidal but they were taking no chances. When Dr Thallis had said it was time for a full psychiatric assessment again the staff were relieved as they would then know what they were dealing with. Having had a patient on the ward for seven weeks who had hardly spoken had been challenging.

Chapter 18

"Come in, Carla." She had just entered the interview room on the acute ward and saw Dr Thallis and Nurse Atkins sitting in the room with her file open in front of them.

"Please, take a seat. How are you feeling today?"

"I feel fine, Doctor. The last week or so I feel I can think clearly and my brain doesn't feel like fudge."

"Great to hear. Well, you had five treatments of ECT now and I am thinking we don't need to have the last one. William here has been saying how you have really improved and that you have been conversing with people and even allowed your mother to visit. That is all very encouraging."

Carla looked down at her hands and avoided eye contact. She was feeling really embarrassed if they only knew and she was desperate to be discharged and get home as soon as possible. Carla could hear her father's voice echoing in her mind, *'She's done it again, Carla. That mother of yours, honestly. She knows exactly how to act and behave when she want early discharge. Don't make waves, be compliant, she gets me to come in and say I am ready for her to come home.'* Carla thought,

'Well if that's what it takes, mum. You are my best teacher.'

She looked up and heard Dr Thallis saying, "Do you know where you are, what the date and day is, what year it is?"

"Yes, it's Wednesday, I saw it on the white board outside the nurses' station, yes, Wednesday the 15th of July. 1993?"

"And do you know why you are in hospital?"

"Yes, doctor, I wasn't coping. Roger, my husband, and Susan, my best friend, were both dead within three weeks of each other," and she gasped for a breath and felt a wave of nausea hit her so hard she thought she was going to vomit. As suddenly as the feeling came it subsided.

"Are you alright?" asked Atkins, who had noticed she had gone pale and there was a tremor in her voice and hands.

"Yes. Yes. I just hadn't said it out loud." She determined to herself at that moment that she was never going to say those words out loud again, never if that was how she was going to react and feel.

The doctor was continuing, "Yes, Carla, an absolute tragedy which would test the best of us. Your husband was killed in a motorcycle accident and three weeks later your friend Susan Westmead was slain by an unknown assailant."

This time Carla's body literally jolted off the seat. She found herself standing and then felt, throughout her body, a tingling sensation burning through every inch of her skin. She stared at Dr Thallis whilst at the same time wringing her hands violently up around her chin. "I'm sorry," she stammered, "I know what you say is true now but when *it* happened I couldn't get the reality of it to sit with me. It was like my thoughts were being controlled by someone else. Like I was being told to shut up, don't speak and all will be well. I had no choice but to listen. My own thoughts could not be trusted," and her eyes filled with tears. William handed her the tissue box and she took two, gently blowing her nose. She then sat down and looked up at both men. "Where's Sam? Where's my son?"

It was the first time she had spoken his name, although over the past week she had been thinking of him nonstop. Even when her mother came to visit last week she never made mention of Sam, fearful her mother was going to say something had happened to him. But now, a week later and feeling a little stronger, she wanted to know.

Dr Thallis looked to William who said, "Your son is with your in-laws."

"Oh. Okay. I will call Sharon and have him brought in to visit. I am much stronger now," and she stopped and with a wry smile added, "Anyway I am sure I am close to discharge and that will be the best medicine of all, Dr Thallis, won't it?" and she smiled widely and placed her hands under her thighs to stop them from flitting about. She was now feeling very tired and wanted to leave.

"Carla." It was Dr Thallis and, without acknowledging her previous comment, he asked, "Do you feel your thoughts are controlled now?"

"No," looking up sharply, "not like before. I feel a lot clearer. I know now, what is real."

"Are you having thoughts of harming yourself or wanting to kill yourself or die?"

At that she actually laughed, "No doctor. Never. Why would I want to do that?" and laughed again.

"That's good to hear."

"When can I go home?"

"I'd like you to stay in hospital until Friday and we will reassess you then."

Friday came and Carla was discharged. Margaret met her at the psych unit and drove her to her home. Upon entering the house Carla became distressed and quickly turned to her mother. "Please mum, can I stay with you for a few days, just until I get used to being out of hospital?"

"Of course, darling, of course," and they drove to Margaret's home.

At her mother's home she was pacing and her thoughts were tumbling over themselves. She was fairly confident that she remembered the last two weeks of her stay in hospital but there were definite blanks. After such a long time in hospital she felt disconnected, like she was in a bit of a dream state. She couldn't quite get her mind to make plans. What did she need to do? The energy was draining from her and she decided to lay down and at that point she did make one resolve and that was not to get sick again. She had to keep getting well. *"Yes, when I have done that I will know what to do. I just hope it happens soon.* " She was asleep within a few minutes.

A couple of days later over breakfast Carla could feel within herself that she was stronger and more grounded. It had been the right thing to stay with her mother directly on discharge, rather than to have gone home alone. She put her toast and marmalade down on the plate and to her mother said, "Mum, I am going to ring Sharon today and we can go over and get Sam. I want to go home with him. I feel it's time and I cannot stay here forever. I have to get on and sitting here isn't the answer. *'There I've said it,'* she thought, *'good for me.'* But the look on her mother's face quickly drained her resolve and confidence.

"What is it?"

Handing Carla a second cup of coffee Margaret Parkinson looked at her daughter and said, "Carla, they have moved to Adelaide."

"What do you mean? Mum! What are you trying to tell me?"

"Thomas. The Nelsons, they moved to Adelaide about five weeks ago. You remember Thomas came and visited you. You signed the papers."

Carla had no idea what her mother was talking about and she most certainly did not remember Thomas or papers or anything else. "Where is Sam?" she shouted, jumping up from the table and pacing her mother's small kitchen. She stopped in front of the sink and looked out the kitchen window on to the native garden bed, then, turning like in slow motion said, "What's Thomas's number? I will call him and get Sam back here. Now."

Again Margaret looked at her daughter. "He said he gave you his number when you were in hospital. It must be in your bag."

"Good," and she ran from the kitchen to her room and emptied her suitcase, which she had been living out of, onto the bed but found no phone number, no address, and no trace of Thomas's visit.

Screaming from her room, "Mum. What are we going to do?" and then there was nothing.

Chapter 19

Carla had stopped walking at this point and placed her hand on Peter's arm. "This is where I made the biggest mistake of my life, I think, but I have never really known if it was or whether it was the best decision, Peter," and she looked to the ground. "Peter. I walked away from my son. I did not try to find him. I did nothing. I got well with mum. Sold Roger's and my house. Tried to forget. Worked and this is who I am. My guilt is complete. Or did I do the right thing? Was my son, my Sam, better off with his grandparents and uncle? I told myself yes. Am I a coward? Maybe or was I brave? Oh my God, these are the agonising questions that torment my mind every May 2nd when I give in to looking back. Nothing resolved. No answers. Just a day to remember and try to justify my life."

Peter said nothing.

Carla and Peter completed the six kilometre walk around the lake. "Peter, I am tired and I am sure you have things to do. What about meeting tomorrow at Victoria Park, tomorrow morning? Say 10 o'clock again?"

"Sure, that's fine. Yes, time has gotten away from us. Whereabouts at the park, then? At the public toilet block, the car park and children's playground area. Do you know it?"

"Sure. Sounds perfect." They travelled back to Carla's house in silence, both deep in thought. Carla thought, '*I should ask him what he's thinking but I can't, not yet. I bet I am making this worse!*'

Part 4

Chapter 1

Carla spent a restless night, unable to stop thinking about all she had managed to repress for so many years except for her wallow day, which was now two days ago and was being relived with every minute. She wasn't sure if she could handle any further meetings with this young man who wanted answers which she couldn't give. She felt so completely inadequate when she listened to her own voice trying to make sense of her history. She knew she had done the right thing to move on and not completely crumple under the sadness that life had dealt her, but having Peter around was causing her to self-doubt and feel, if she was honest, sick. Carla resolved to meet with Peter one more time and send him on his way. She would have given him all she could and she needed to care for herself and not allow herself to drift back to those dark days.

She was up early and was at the park earlier than 10 as she was anxious not to be late. Carla saw Peter before he saw her. She was sitting idly rocking back and forth on one of the playground swings and she noticed how he had the look of a person lost and she had an overwhelming feeling of wanting to hold him and tell him it will all be OK. Following that thought she thought of Sam and wondered if what she felt for Peter was really a sense of what she wanted for herself and her son. *"No time for this,"* she thought and jumped off the swing and waved, calling his name. There was a brief pause as they came together and then Peter opened his arms, gave her a hug and a peck on the cheek saying, "It's a beautiful day for, drum roll…another walk," and he smiled a beaming smile whilst grabbing her arm and moving onto the path.

As they walked Carla had said, "So Peter, at this point, I've told you about your mum and the seven weeks after her death.'

"Murder, Carla. She was murdered."

"Yes. It was. I was in hospital and I didn't know anything about what was happening in the world. I was so sick."

"Yes. That was awful for you," and Carla looked across at him when he said this and she thought for a fleeting second, *"Was he being sarcastic?"* but then they were distracted by, "Wow, sounds like a lot of barking going on."

And Carla added, "Look at all the cars, let's go check it out." She needed a distraction. She wasn't sure she could go on like yesterday. It was draining.

"OK," he said obligingly and they turned off the path, heading deeper into the park where the noise of dog barking was happening.

"Looks like some sort of competition, maybe agility." Peter said. "Come on."

He seemed excited now as they walked through the multiple gazebos that were dotted around one side of the oval. There were people walking dogs, people talking dogs, people sitting with dogs in cages. It was a sea of dogs of all shapes and sizes and then they spotted an arena which was made up of orange bunting. There was an open tent on the side of the arena which looked like a place for the officials and then there was, to Carla's eyes, just a general confusion and chaos of dogs and their owners. The noise in the arena from the dogs was great but the handlers in the arena were just as noisy.

"This is funny. I don't think it is agility," Peter said. Scanning the gazebos and the activity in the arena they noticed signs advertising the clubs that were represented and the sport.

"Oh! It's flyball. I have a friend from High School who does this. Talks about it all the time but I have never really known what it was." Now Carla was excited too, as she looked around to see if she could see Jack. Seeing the Ballarat banner she squinted her eyes against the sun and spotted him. "Jack," she called and walked briskly over to him.

He looked surprised. "Carla. Great to see you. So I have finally piqued your interest to come and watch flyball, hey?" and he smiled broadly and in the same movement grabbed her hand and took her across to the ring. Peter followed a good couple of metres behind but when they stopped Carla introduced him. "Jack, this is a friend of mine, Peter Westmead. Peter is visiting for a few days."

"Nice to meet you. Where you from?"

"Originally from here but I've been living in Melbourne for the past four or five years."

"I see," but before Jack could ask more Peter turned and moved closer to the arena to watch the dogs. *'Almost like he wants to be as far from Jack as possible,'* thought Carla but then dismissed the idea as Jack touched her shoulder and said, "If you watch I will take you through it, but in a nutshell the dogs race up over the four jumps, hit a box at the end which releases a tennis ball and the dog must catch the ball and return back over all the jumps with the ball still in its mouth. As that dog is returning the next dog is released to do the same, then the next and finally the last dog; dog four completes the relay. Whilst this is going on the other side is doing the same and the fastest team wins that heat. Easy."

"Wow, Peter and I were watching for a while before we spotted you and you know, it's funny, Jack, some dogs are fast, some slow, some jump high jumps, some low, some have to run twice. It's very confusing," Carla confessed.

"Not really." But Jack didn't have time to tell her all the nuances of the sport. "OK, got to go we are up in two races' time so got to get ready," and he turned quickly and sprinted back to the Ballarat gazebo.

"Peter, Jack's up soon. Let's watch his race and then we can move on."

"Sure Carla. No worries."

Five minutes later Jack and his team were in the arena. Jack had a working dog but it wasn't an obvious

Kelpie or Border Collie as Carla recognized but definitely a working dog.

With barking all around from both teams' dogs, the referee was saying 'watch the lights' and the next thing Jack's dog was off. Carla didn't know where she was supposed to look because the next second it was back but another dog was running up and over the jumps and then it was over. She had no idea who won but it was fun watching.

When Jack had finished he wandered over to her and she was introduced to 'Jack' the Kelpie cross. "Or Koolie," Jack added, "not sure exactly what he is because he is a rescue dog but he's a great boy with a great name," he said, chuckling and scruffing the dog's head.

"Well, did you win?' asked Carla, whilst bending and also giving Jack a head scratch.

"No. But I am happy with Jack. He can be a little devil sometimes in the ring. Gets too excited, so as long as he does clean runs that's good enough. Besides there is always the next race, it's an all-day event you know?"

She didn't know but said, "Well, I am so glad we stumbled across this. Maybe if I get a dog I will try flyball too!" and she backed away waving saying, "See you tomorrow, Jack."

Back on the walking path Peter and Carla fell into a natural, comfortable step with each other. They were both quiet, lost in their own thoughts. Carla was thinking that she may well get a dog and join that flyball game and how it would be nice to have an activity outside of work and the home. Peter, on the other hand, was busy wondering how he could broach the question he had been formulating in his mind since yesterday. They passed a group of cricketers on one of the many ovals in the park and continued in silence for about five more minutes when Peter simply said, without preamble, "Carla, I think we should try and find Sam." *"There it was, out. Let's see what happens now,"* he thought.

Carla heard him loud and clear and she was stunned by the words, the idea, the impossibility of what he had said, she had no words to answer him. She simply stopped dead in her tracks and stared at the back of Peter's head. He hadn't realised she had stopped and had continued to stride forward. He was probably twenty metres in front of her now when he realised, stopped, turned and returned her gaze.

"Did you hear what I said?" although he was 100% sure she had.

And she replied, "Peter. It would be impossible."

"Why, Carla? He's your son. You have been cruelly dealt with. He had no right to keep Sam from you all these years. And," he held his hand up to stop her interjecting, "and, I know what you are going to say. You and your mother signed him over, you made the decision. It wouldn't be fair on Sam to enter his life now! I know all that but Carla," and he took a deep breath, "have you thought it has not been fair on Sam not to have you in his life?"

She stared off into the distance and Peter continued his rehearsed speech. "Carla, think about this. I have grown up feeling incomplete and alone because no one would tell me about my mother. I have felt empty, sad and very angry most of my life. Having sat and walked with you over the past two days and listened to you describe a woman who was bright, funny, smart and loving has filled a gap in me that I never thought could be filled. I feel I have some grounding now, some sense of self and I have you to thank for that. I know me turning up must be hard for you but you have to know you have saved me in a way. So what's to say that Sam won't feel the same? What's to say he isn't out there feeling lost? You said yourself his uncle and grandparents, well especially the mother and uncle, were pretty strange, cold people. Perhaps you owe it to Sam and yourself to try." He wanted to go on but he also wanted her to have time to think. "Come on, let's keep walking. You can tell me to bugger off if you like. I won't be offended." But he knew he would be. Somehow finding Sam had just taken on an even greater urgency in Peter. He felt he was connected to Sam somehow in their shared upbringings, yes, and a connection that had to be put to rights. But he never said this to Carla, who now had a pensive, perplexed look on her face.

They were nearly back to the playground and both had been silent when Carla asked, "Peter. How?"

"How?" he said, crinkling his brow.

"Yes. Peter, talk is easy but the real thing is. How can we find him? I haven't seen him for twenty-two years or so. What if my turning up destroys him, causes problems for him. Destabilizes him?"

"What if it is the making of him?" he retorted.

Carla remained silent again and they continued walking and all of a sudden they realized they had passed the playground and were in earshot of all the barking and yelling of the flyball again. "Oops, gone too far."

That broke Carla's reverie and she turned to Peter and said in a very steady voice, "Can you let me think about this, Peter? Could I ring you, perhaps tomorrow when I have had time to collect my thoughts? I will have you know this idea of yours is not new to me. I've had it many times but I have also buried it many times and I think," and there was a pause, "I think I've buried it for a good reason."

"Of course, of course. You have my number. We will talk soon. Let's turn back to our cars." They turned around and Peter added, "But thanks, Carla."

"For what?"

"For not rejecting the idea outright, thanks for taking the time to think about it. And Carla, I will respect your decision." Peter gave her a quick hug. They got back to their cars and Carla had agreed to call him.

As he sat in his car watching Carla pull out on to Sturt Street he was thinking to himself that, regardless of what Carla decided, he was going to track down Samuel Nelson. He felt it was necessary for his own salvation. But he would prefer Carla to do it with him. He would wait.

Chapter 2

Carla on the other hand was not thinking at all. She felt her mind was blank and there was no way she could form any kind of cohesive, logical train of thought or put a finger on her feelings, *"Numb I suppose,"* she said to herself. She watched Peter get into his car as she pulled out before him. She had planned to do some shopping after her walk but felt too drained, too brain dead, too excited! *"Am I excited? Do I think it is possible? No. Carla, your initial reaction was the right one. It's impossible."*

Carla drove home with the radio on loud so she could concentrate on driving and not thinking. Pulling up in the driveway she looked about her home, garden and sighed, thinking it's so lonely, broken down, and lifeless. Just like its owner. Upon entering the hall area she slipped off her runners and went to the bedroom to get her Ugg boots. There was a slight nip in the air and she decided she'd put the electric heater on in the lounge just to get the chill off the air.

Having done that she noticed it was nearly midday, too early for lunch but not too early for a drink. She went to the fridge, grabbed the bottle of McLaren white wine, opened it and poured herself a generous helping. She then mused, *'Hmm, an Adelaide wine. Is this an omen?'* With glass in hand she went into the lounge and allowed herself to think about Peter's idea.

At first she was ambivalent, often defaulting to her well-practiced thoughts of "Sam is and has been, better off without me in his life," but then she allowed some doubts to creep in. She replayed the things Peter had said in her mind and one really big turning factor was that he had said – 'We should find Sam.' Not I should find Sam. Did that mean Peter would help? She needed to know, she couldn't plan anything if it had to be her, alone. Carla knew she just wouldn't have the strength or drive to seek her son out on her own. She had become an expert in deflecting anything that might arouse the need to act. She drank her wine and back and forth her thoughts went and before she knew it lunch had passed and dinner was closer to the mark. She was feeling hungry and the wine bottle was nearly empty but she had finally come to a decision.

Putting the last of the wine in her glass she headed towards the phone. "Don't hesitate," she told herself and dialled Peter's number. The number rang out and she left a message asking him to call her.

"Damn it," she said, already losing courage and beginning to doubt herself. *"Just my luck he wasn't answering. Maybe it's for the better. Yes I think so."* She remembered she hadn't pulled anything out of the freezer for dinner so decided on fish fingers and fried them along with an egg and then retired to the lounge, putting the TV on with the hope that it would distract her.

When Peter hadn't returned her call by 9 pm she was almost beside herself. She was tired from the last three days and was feeling like an emotional wreck and she realized drinking a bottle of wine on her own had not helped. She decided that she'd go have a bath and then go to bed. She needed work to get things back on track and tomorrow was High School day.

Chapter 3

She set the alarm for 7.30 am with the idea of doing her shopping which she neglected to do yesterday and then prepare some classes before going to the High School in the afternoon but when she awoke she felt flat and deflated and had an anxious, almost nauseating feeling in her stomach. She was thinking it must be the wine she drank but quickly countered that thought with, *"No, it's because Peter never called back. I wonder where he is?"*

She had just finished dressing and was drying her hair when the phone rang. She quickly made her way to it, picked up, "Hello."

"Carla, it's Peter, sorry I didn't get back to you last night. I didn't see the message till after 10 pm and I thought it was too late. What's up?" He sounded breathless to Carla and she said so. "Not really breathless but I am nervous about this call."

"Peter, I have been thinking and thinking and thinking until last night I thought I couldn't think a rational thought again. I wanted to ask you last night. Have you thought about how we can do this? Are you intending to help? Be there with me? Maybe pick up the pieces if it goes wrong? Where would we begin?" She was ranting now, a catharsis of thoughts and questions brimming over, last night it was clear in her head, this morning she wasn't sure.

Peter interrupted, "Absolutely I intend to be with you, all the way. Why don't I come over and I'll tell you what I've been thinking."

"Yes," and she felt her body relax, "that would be good. I have lectures this afternoon but you could come any time after 4.30pm. How's that sound?"

"Great, I'll be there. Thanks, Carla, this is great."

Carla hung up. *"Is this going to be an equally bad idea as the one to give up Sam in the first place?"*

When Carla arrived back from High School Peter was on the doorstep, waiting. With a big grin across his face he stood up, waved and Carla waved back.

"Sorry I'm late," she said, "but I went to the shops after work. I've been pretty disorganised the past few days."

"Do you need a hand?" and moved towards the boot of her car.

"Yes, that would be good."

They loaded the shopping onto the kitchen table and Carla busied herself with putting away and Peter put the kettle on for a cuppa.

"So how was your day?" he asked.

"Not bad. Just a couple of classes today. I enjoy the banter and discussion that kids today bring to the room. Different from when I was at High School. What about you?"

"Oh, a bit of this and that. Just trying to pass the time really."

"You know, I've been talking for the past three days but you haven't told me where you're staying and what you have been doing since leaving your dad's home. Come on, give me the low down." Smiling and pouring the coffee.

"Well, I am not one to talk about myself really. I left home at fifteen and headed to an aunt's in Sydney, on mum's side. One of the few things he told me about."

"I didn't know Susan had a sister, Peter. That's news to me. I never met her all those years we were friends and Susan never mentioned her, I'm sure."

Peter stared hard at Carla and then after a few moments laughed and said, "No. I didn't mean a real biological aunt. No, an old friend of mum's mum who *she* called aunt and Dad just said one day when I was little and he was, as usual, angry with me, "I should send you to your aunt's in Sydney to look after you. Lazy old bitch would probably die before helping out."

"I didn't know I had an aunt, Dad," I said, and he snarled something about, 'Oh yeah. Real loving good for nothing. Didn't even come to your mother's funeral!' I knew not to ask any more questions then. But over time I did get him to tell me she was called Elizabeth Laydonbury, see close to our name, Laydon, and she lived in Bankstown. That was all I needed. I hunted her down via the phone directory and she invited me to visit. I stayed with her until I went to Sydney Uni where I lived on campus, passed my useless Arts degree and then bummed about before coming to see you. The rest is history as they say. Oh! And to answer your other question, I'm bunked down in the joint near the railway station, Reid's. Now that's posh!" looking with eyes wide open and eyebrows knitted. Carla knew the place he meant and saw and heard his satire.

Without drawing breath Peter plunged on. "So, Carla. You ready to find your son?"

With coffee cup half way up to her mouth, "You know what. I am," she said. "I've decided, in for a penny, in for a pound. If we find him and he wants nothing to do with me I haven't lost anything," and clapped her hands together. "But on the other hand if he wants me in his life I have everything to gain." Quickly adding, "But I wouldn't do it unless I had your support, Peter. You have to know that. I am not as strong as people think I might be."

"We'll do it together. Let's crack a bubbly and celebrate our adventure," and he laughed as he moved to the fridge as if he'd lived there for years, and Carla joined in his laughter too.

As the cork popped and the glasses were being filled Carla said, "OK, Mr Detective. Where do we begin?"

"Here," handing over the glass. "First here's to a successful mission. I believe that what you and I have been through we deserve a win."

"Cheers to that," and the glasses clinked together. "Anyway I've given it a lot of thought but I need your knowledge of the family. Thomas, the uncle, do you think he is still in real estate?"

"Well, obviously I don't know but I'd say so. It's where he made all his money on the back of his father's business."

"And can you remember where Thomas said he was going when you signed the papers or where in South Australia he and Roger had discussed moves. I remember you told me there had been discussions of a move before all the tragedies?"

"No, not really," she hesitated, "it was a blur, like I said. Mum was just keeping it together and I was in the psych hospital and Sam needed to be cared for. I was drugged up and having ECT and honestly nothing made sense, Roger, your mum. It was awful."

"No worries," he said. "We will Google search and see what comes up." He went to grab Carla's laptop but then seeing her face said, "Are you OK? You look a little pale."

"No. I just have a feeling, a vague memory or it could be a false memory, of Adelaide being mentioned. Glenelg, Brighton! I don't really know though; it's been a long time."

Peter jumped up with an excited gleam in his eye. "No, that's great, let's start a Google search of all real estate agents in Adelaide and surrounds."

With laptop in hand they moved to the lounge and Carla booted it up, opened Google and typed in Nelson real estate, Adelaide. Instantly a page came up with a Nelson Alexander, Jane Nelson, Karina, Peter, Francis Nelson, Nelson Rd, Nelson the suburb and then together they both pointed on the second page Thomas Nelson and Partners, Real Estate, 135 O'Connell Street, North Adelaide. She felt her heart miss a beat but tried to stay objective whilst asking, "What do you think? You think that's him?"

"Only one way to find out," and handed Carla the phone. "Give it a ring."

"Oh no, this is crunch time," she thought and then heard Peter say, "It's OK, Carla. I am here with you, remember."

"I think it's too late. Look its 5.45 pm, even if it is them the office will be closed."

"Carla, just ring. If no one answers we will ring tomorrow," and placing a hand on her arm he said, "OK."

"But what will I say. We haven't discussed this part yet." She was beginning to panic and felt sick to the stomach and all her doubts were flooding back. *Was this a good idea? It seemed good as a concept but this was real.* And to Peter she said, "I don't know, Peter. I'm worried."

"Shh think, what's the worst he can do? Hang up on you. Well, so be it. Least we have found him and that means we will find Sam. I can't do this for you, Carla."

Peter dialled the number and handed it to her. The phone rang three times and a female voice answered.

"Hello, Nelson and Partners Real Estate. How can I help you?"

Carla did not speak and the woman said, "Hello, Nelson and Partners Real Estate. How can I help you? Are you there?"

Carla took a breath and said, "Hello. My name is Carla Parkinson. I was wanting to speak to Thomas Nelson, please."

"Yes, Ms Parkinson, can you tell me what it's about, I might be able assist with any enquiries you have."

"Ah, no, actually it's a family matter and I need to speak with Thomas personally."

"Well, he is not in the office now but I will take your name and number and leave him a message via his email asking him to call you. Is that alright?"

"Yes. Umm, thanks. Say it's Carla Parkinson, formerly Nelson, and my number is 0079331034."

The receptionist repeated the message and Carla said that it was correct and then hung up.

Slumping back on the couch and looking at Peter she said, "Well, now I suppose we wait," and a very nervous, anxious, twittering chuckle escaped her. What she wanted was a drink. Why she wanted a drink was because she knew she was a coward and a drink would boost resolve. Inside she was shaking.

Chapter 4

Peter left Carla's around 8 o'clock and they had discussed different scenarios of what they would do if this Thomas was the Thomas Nelson her brother-in-law, and where to go from there. One thing they did agree on was that Carla would need to take time off work so they could travel to Adelaide to see Sam. They would take her car as it was a station wagon and could hold their belongings better. Besides, Carla found out Peter's car was a rental. They also Googled different caravan parks looking for onsite cabins with two bedrooms where they could stay overnight en route if needs be. Having done that they estimated how much time and money they would roughly need. "Well, I think we have covered all angles, Carla." Peter had said as he prepared to leave. "Now we just need him to ring."

"He might not, you know."

"I know but like we said if he doesn't we will go to his office and wait till he shows and then he will have to talk to us." With that he grabbed his coat and left.

"Glad you are so confident," she said under her breath as she shut the front door.

Carla had done the dishes and showered and was just settling onto the couch to read because she didn't think she could sleep even if she tried. When the phone rang she jumped, took a quick glance at the clock, 10.05 pm, and picked up on the third ring. "Hello."

"Hello. Carla. It's Thomas. You rang the office today. Why?"

Immediately his brisk voice made her feel angry and so, in a voice she hoped echoed his clipped exchange, she said, "Hello Thomas. How are you too? I rang to say I want to see Sam. It's been twenty-two years, Thomas. I'd love to see you, and Sharon and Oscar too."

"They are dead, Carla. Dad died seven years ago and mum a couple of years later and I haven't seen Sam for over two years."

This made her reel, she hadn't anticipated that. "Where is he? I will go and see him. Just let me know where he is."

Thomas's voiced was raised when he blurted down the phone, "I don't know where he is. He is probably dead from an overdose for all I know. He was a no hoper Carla, he pissed off about two years ago and that's that. So if the purpose of ringing me was to see Sam …you are too late, he's gone. Carla, don't ever ring me again. I don't like history coming to my door."

"But Thomas," she stammered, "I want to come. Perhaps we can meet and you can tell me about Sam, about your life these past twenty-two years."

"No. That is not possible. I don't like memories. I live a quiet life now. Go back to your life," and he hung up.

At Carla's end she was staring at the receiver. At Thomas's end he was staring at the receiver. Neither moved for a long time.

Chapter 5

Thomas had gone as white as a sheet. His mind was racing with thoughts like, *"I knew this day would come, don't panic. You have planned for this, you have protected him all his life, and you can do it again. No bloodshed, no, be smart. Yes I know,"* and with that he picked up the phone again and said, "I want to speak to Geoff," and he heard in the background, "Hey, Geoff, it's for you, some rude prick didn't even ask nicely."

Geoff looked up from the computer he was sitting at, then looked back, typed a couple of more things and hit the save button. He didn't have to ask who it was, he knew if the person was described as a rude prick it could only be Thomas Nelson. Wearily he got to his feet and went over to where the phone was sitting on the end of the bar. "Hello, Thomas," he said in the friendliest voice he could muster, "what's happening, my man?"

"Cut the small talk, are you alone?"

"Yes, pretty much. Mick and Scott have just left the bar and your son Sam is in the cellar stacking wine bottles, the evening's been a quiet one. Why?"

"I want you to listen," and he proceeded to talk to Geoff for the next five minutes. Geoff listened and said, at the end of Thomas's speech, "OK, leave it with me. I'll have to do some wheeling and dealing but it should be fine."

"Good." Thomas then went to his office and made a few banking transactions, poured himself a brandy and drank it whilst staring off into the cloudless night sky. He felt he was able to relax again. He had a plan and it was workable and as such made it so he could breathe. If Thomas wasn't in control, Thomas could not think or function efficiently. Think quick, plan hard, get it done. No turning back. *"Yes, it will be okay, okay."*

Thomas had met Geoff Wright not long after he and the family moved from Ballarat to Adelaide. Geoff had walked into the real estate office and told Thomas, who just happened to be in the office, that he was looking to purchase a business, one in hospitality. He'd been running a pub in a small town near Port Vincent and now he was keen to branch out and relocate to Adelaide as well. He had a couple of sons who were now high school age and it was time they were closer to more educational choices and sports. He'd been looking on the internet for some time now and just hadn't found the right thing.

"Why us, Nelson and Partners? We are new in town?" Thomas was busy and didn't have time for this man. His plan was to set up the office, get the rentals side of the business happening productively because he already had a number of homes and then, and only then, 'as this was the plan' would he look at the bigger picture; and, he reminded himself, looking at the industrial/business side of the real estate industry was the last area to develop, general home real estate would be next; no, this guy needed to leave. Thomas was already pacing.

"Well actually," Geoff was saying, "a bloke by the name of Tim O'Rourke suggested I look you up. Said you've got business nous and know a few tricks of the trade," and extending his hand he said, "Geoff Wright," and Thomas, now looking at the man in front of him, stopped pacing and shook his hand and at the same time ushered him into his office out the back. His office was still incomplete but Thomas had a very nice jarrah desk and two substantial easy chairs erected under a large window looking out into a well-manicured, old English garden with a large oak as a central feature. After inviting Geoff to sit down he said, "Do you want a drink?"

"Well actually, yes I'd love one. I'm parched." Thomas would learn over the years that Geoff Wright had a tendency to say 'Well actually' often and it annoyed him excessively, but that was not the case in this first encounter.

Thomas poured himself and Geoff a generous whiskey on the rocks with a "Dash of water?" and Geoff nodded, with a quick, "Well yes actually. Very nice of you."

Having sat down opposite Geoff he examined him, trying to get a quick but astute first impression before he spoke much more. Geoff was a small rotund man but he looked fit. His eyes were gentle in a sad sort of way. He was dressed in dark slacks and a T shirt that had a logo on it advertising some investment group that Thomas hadn't heard of. Thomas made a mental note to himself to look them up, '*Might be worthwhile, who knows,*' he thought.

"So, Geoff, it was Geoff, wasn't it?"

"Yes, mate."

"You can call me Thomas. So, Tim suggested you talk to me. That's good. I haven't seen him for some time. How is he?"

"Oh! Well actually, you know Tim! Dabbling with a bit of this and a bit of that," and Thomas did know. Thomas knew Tim very well and he didn't like him one bit, but what Thomas did know, is that if Tim O'Rourke sent this man to him he was letting Thomas know that there was money to be made here. Opportunities. A person of possible use. The only thing he didn't know, nor did he trust, was why he, Tim, wasn't taking this advantage himself. Why would he send him to me? Thomas was weary.

Thomas realised he was staring at Geoff and quickly diverted his eyes to his drink and took a sip.

"How about you start at the beginning, Geoff, how do you know Tim and what's your business?"

For the next twenty minutes and another whiskey each, Geoff told Thomas that he was the owner of a little pub near Port Vincent and it was a good business, steady custom but there was no future, no opportunity for expansion. The big outlets like Dan Murphy's were squeezing the little pubs out. People were happy to travel 50 km to stock up rather than use the local 'bottle O'. He'd done well but he felt he needed to expand and the city seemed the right place. He'd met Tim O'Rourke about a week ago. Tim and his wife were on a holiday travelling the coast and staying in B&Bs, getting a feel for what works and what doesn't. He told me one night that his wife wants to run a B&B or something similar so this was a field trip. Thinking, Thomas mused, 'This must be Tim's wife number three or maybe four even! Wow.' He hadn't seen Tim for quite some while and he hoped for it to stay that way.

Geoff continued to say they had decided to stop at small pubs too to get a comparison and his joint was on the course they'd chosen. "Tim and his wife were charming and we all got talking over an afternoon drinks session and that's when I told them of my plans and that I was having trouble finding a suitable place. I told them, 'So far everything I've looked at has been either too run down but in the right place, or too expensive, or it was perfect but the owners didn't want to sell, only lease'."

"Yes, you have to be careful, that's for sure," Tim had said. "That's what we are finding too," and turning to his wife he added, "Aren't we honey?" and he'd squeezed her hand.

"Anyway later that evening Tim had come back downstairs and beckoned me over to the end of the bar. So I say – looking for a nightcap Tim? And reach for a bottle of port, "Port?"

Tim said, "No mate. I've had plenty. No. I just wanted to say that I wish I could help you but with this little road trip and a number of other ventures on the go I don't think I'd be able to really look into things for you just now."

And I says, "Yes, well actually I began looking quite a while ago and I really want to get something soon. It's going to be a new school year in a few months and I was hoping the boys could be settled at the beginning of a new school term if possible so I am getting a little desperate. But you can't rush these things, can you Tim?"

"Look, I know a man, Thomas Nelson. Works real estate, very shrewd, good operator. Here is his number. He hasn't long been here in South but good worker in Vic. Drop in and see him, tell him I sent you. If he can't help you then hold on for another six months and I'll see what I can do." Patting me on the shoulder he added, "I like you, Geoff. I think you're on to something. Timing's just wrong for me."

'Well, thanks Tim. Thanks again.' "So that's it, Mr Nelson, just perchance and here I am. What do you think?"

Thomas looked at his watch and said, "Geoff, it's 3 pm. Obviously I need to have a lot more details, how much can you afford? What's going to happen to the pub near Port Vincent? I will need to see the books."

"Of course. I actually have all that here with me back at the motel."

"OK. Then bring them to me tomorrow at around 11 o'clock and I'll look them over and in the meantime I'll make a few calls. No promises though, OK?"

"No promises. Thanks," and Geoff got up, shook hands and with a, "See you tomorrow," he was gone.

Thomas sat down again, chin on hands and wondered what that was all about.

Geoff had returned the following day with his paperwork and Thomas was not impressed with the manner in which he kept his books. He could also see

215

that Geoff was not a very inspired or creative thinker. In all the time he had owned the pub he had done nothing to attract trade, instead he relied on trade naturally flowing to him. '*The fool,*" he thought.

"Leave this with me and I'll look over it carefully and ring you when I've had time to digest the entire balances and checks."

"Thanks Thomas, I really appreciate this."

As it transpired Thomas bought the pub from Geoff and hired staff to run it but retained Geoff as the manager, overseeing the running from a distance, with the expectation that he would, from time to time, go back and live on site when new initiatives were being tried. He wasn't entirely sure why he was doing this but for some reason he knew it was the right thing to do. If not now, perhaps in the future. Thomas had backed Geoff financially too, with the difference between the pub and the city pub he had hoped to buy. Geoff was now indebted to Thomas and their business venture had proven fruitful.

Chapter 6

Thomas got off the phone to Geoff and started to feel some relief. He knew that Carla wouldn't be put off by his assertions he had no idea of Sam's whereabouts. He felt it in her voice that she would come and see for herself and as such, he had to get Sam out of Adelaide.

Sam got home around 11 pm and Thomas was waiting up. When he came in he called out, "How was your shift, Samuel?" and Sam bounced in and stood by the fire and said, "Well, it was slow tonight but Geoff has asked me to go to some pub near Port Vincent and run it for him for the next two months."

"Really! Why is that?"

"He said the current guy has gotten ill and will be off for at least two months and he needs someone who knows the business and he thought I'd be perfect."

"Hmm, what do you think?"

"Well, the first thing I told him was that you would definitely not be in favour of it. And anyway I'm not that keen. Never been down that way before. But on the other side, Geoff's a good guy and I'd like to help him out. I suggested Davo, you know, my mate from High School, he might be interested 'cos he's been talking about deferring Uni lately, says he's getting itchy feet. But Geoff was pretty insistent that I should be the one. I said I'd discuss it with you anyway. Dad, he wants to know ASAP."

Thomas was measured in his next words. "A nice little holiday by the beach hey! Well, I don't know. When would you leave? Where will you stay?"

"Oh, that's sorted as long as you are okay with me going. I would leave tomorrow and stay on the premises. Geoff had said that he would meet me there to settle me in and introduce me to the staff. He will stay two nights and then would leave the pub in my hands. So what do you think? I don't care either way. I don't want you worrying." Privately Sam was worried. Prior to this, in his twenty-three years, he had never been away longer than a few days when there were school camps or staying overnight with friends. Even on the occasions of the camps his grandfather always accompanied him. He remembered once saying, "Please, Dad, I don't need Grandad around, I will be fine." But his father had said, "Samuel, this has nothing to do with you. Your grandfather loves to help out with the school. You can't begrudge him that!" and so it had always been. Thomas had instilled in Samuel a need to be ever vigilant and wary of people. To be observant and watch for subtle signs such as odd inflections in tone, eyes unable to maintain contact, body stances. It was never a full-on lesson, it was just understood between father and son. Many times Samuel had questioned his father but in the end he had to concur that the world was very unpredictable and being alert wasn't a bad thing. 'You only have to listen to the news and read the papers to know so.'

Whilst he was thinking this he heard Thomas saying, "Well, you know I don't like you going away but if it helps Geoff and you're happy, then alright. Perhaps it will do us both good." Then as an afterthought, "Perhaps I will come down and stay with you for a week. Yes, that would be good, wouldn't it son?"

"OK then," and he went to his room. Sam was thinking, *"That was easy. I expected him to argue. Very odd. Oh well."* But he was nervous at the prospect and sleep was hard to find.

The following morning Sam was packed and heading out the door with a road map in hand, $500 cash from his work and extra money Thomas had given him. He had his box of CDs and an iPod full of music and he had spent most of the morning plotting his course. It was like a huge adventure for him even though the pub was only an hour to an hour and a half away from home. All the same Sam was feeling very tentative and light-headed. Thomas saw him off and said that he'd ring him that night to see how things were going. "Thanks Dad, now are you sure this is what you want? If you are, well, we'll talk soon," and he went to hug his father but stopped abruptly when he saw the look in his father's eyes. *"Is he sad?"* but then turned, waved and jumped off the verandah two steps at a time, threw his suitcase on the backseat of his Holden commodore, which Thomas had bought him for his 18th, and started the car up. It was a good reliable car and he had maintained it well. Waving frantically through the driver's side window he eased out of the drive and was gone from Thomas's sight.

Sam never even turned the music on. His head was filled initially with excitement at this unexpected turn of events that was seeing him, for the first time in his life, going away from his father with distance and time being factors. But he was also worried about this very dramatic change in his lifestyle. He travelled north from Glenelg where he lived out on the Tapleys Hill Road towards Port Adelaide. He turned east along Grand Junction Rd, left onto the Salisbury Highway before turning left again onto the Port Wakefield Road where he began looking for signs to Pine Point, Port Julia or Port Vincent. The trip took him just over two hours and he realised that he had taken nothing in. Absolutely nothing of the landscape, so focused was he on getting to his destination. Sam realised with a slight shock that his forearms were aching from gripping the wheel so tightly and when he tried to remember where he had come from it was a total blank. *'Hell, it's like I warped here! Now that's scary.'*

He had parked the car out the front of an old sandstone building which was two storeys high and had a large thick wooden door with stained glass windows in its panelling. Above the door was a hanging sign *'Just like the olden movies of old England'* he was thinking. The sign read The Rock Hotel. Well, he'd made it. Geoff had told him that he had bought The Rock twenty-five years earlier from an old friend of his father's who was wanting to retire. Apparently it had been in his family since 1836 when it was originally built. Although Geoff had said, "It looked nothing like it does today. Back then apparently it was just one big room. Emanuel Orson, who built the pub originally, hadn't liked the hustle and bustle of Port Vincent and apparently he determined to make his own way by buying land 'up the road' and building half way between Port Vincent and Port Julia. It's called The Rock because Rocks Creek runs alongside the pub. It was the main supply of water for the pub until 1992 when they got mains water. So lots of history. "Sounds good to me Geoff," Sam had chirped. "See you there."

Sam entered through the doorway and was pleasantly surprised to see a long wooden bar that ended just before two large French windows that spilled out into a very green, lush beer garden where in summer tables would be set up for dining. Behind the bar was the usual pub paraphernalia, glasses, spirits on shelves, beer taps advertising the different brands. All things Sam was very familiar with from his job at The Cumberland. His initial feeling was that this was going to be alright and with that he sauntered up to the bar.

Chapter 7

Carla had stood staring at the phone, she was angry, so angry she felt like screaming and hitting something, anything. But she didn't, instead she rang Peter.

"Hi, it's me. The bastard just rang, I can't believe him, he says he hasn't seen Sam for two years, says he's a drug addict, probably in prison. The shit didn't care and when I said I wanted to come over he said it wasn't possible. Who the hell does he think he is? Oh I am so angry, I could..."

But Peter butted in, "Slow down, Carla. I can hear you're upset."

"Yes. I just needed to vent. It was awful. So stiff, so fact is I don't know what to think. If Sam is lost in drugs," and she slunk down on to the phone seat and sighed, "If he is lost to drugs it's my fault. I don't think I can deal with this."

"Carla," in a very calm soft voice, "stop. Think. What if he is just saying that to keep you away? He has never wanted you near Sam and this is probably just another ploy. It sounds ridiculous to me that he wouldn't know where Sam was or at least welcome your input."

"Ha, you don't know Thomas. After hearing his voice I see he hasn't changed. No. You are probably right, he's probably lying but really I have to stop and really consider if this is the right thing, Peter."

"Oh Carla. Look, this doesn't change our plans. Five minutes earlier you knew it was a good idea. Don't let him continue to run your life. Look, we are better off now than five minutes ago. Least we know Thomas is definitely in Adelaide so let's go and see him face to face. Harder to avoid us then. Come on, what do you say?"

She was quiet for a moment and then with a sigh she said, "You're right, Peter. Yes. Tomorrow I will talk to the faculty and get a few weeks' leave and we can head on over to Adelaide in a couple of days." In a quieter and more stable voice she said, "Peter, thank you so much. I actually feel," and there was a pause, "I actually feel alive and, dare I say it, very determined. I don't think I have felt like this for such a long time. A feeling of purpose and it's because of you."

"Carla, it's a two way street. I am beginning to feel less angry and more hopeful. Ring me tomorrow when you know when you can leave and we will plan from there."

It wasn't until Thursday of that week that Carla got to discuss taking time off and she was disappointed when she was told there was no relieving teachers available for five weeks. But they were happy to give her a total of three weeks leave after that. She had explained this to Peter, saying, "Well, we can leave Friday 13th June at the earliest. Least that will give me time to get the car serviced." Carla was thinking, *A lot has happened since May 2nd and by June who knows what*

223

I'll be thinking. Funny Peter didn't seem to flinch when I told him about the delay. He'd said, 'No worries. As long as you and I can still find Sam that's all that matters after all this time.' Yes, you never do know what is around the corner.' And she smiled to herself.

June 13th came in no time and Carla had tossed back and forth her decision. *"I think it would have been far better to just have gone when I first said yes. The waiting has been hard,"* she thought. She also felt like the wallowing day had extended to weeks instead on one day a year and that was exhausting her and yet countering that was the overwhelming sense that even though she'd done nothing yet, somehow she had achieved a lot, a personal lot, a growth and a more positive outlook and it made her feel good inside. Carla had packed the car on Thursday evening with tent, sleeping bags, pillows and all the camping gear she could fit into the station wagon. She and Peter hadn't discussed accommodation apart from looking at cabins but she wanted to be prepared to camp as well. She was never one to waste money on expensive accommodation when camping was an option.

She had picked Peter up outside the Burrumbeet Caravan Park just before the entrance to the Western Highway at 8.30 am Friday morning. As he got in she said, "You never did tell me when you moved out here. Mind you, I was a little worried when you said you were staying at Reid's."

"It was alright there really, but one of the occupants had mentioned there was an onsite van going here and I thought it would be nicer for privacy."

"And has it been?"

"What?"

"Been nicer, and private."

"Yes, it's been useful to reflect and consider where I am now compared to before this all came about," and with that he smiled and in a very enthusiastic voice said, "Great. Let's get going."

She eased out onto the road again and looking across to Peter with concern in her voice said, "You look tired."

"Oh, it's a long story but needless to say I bumped into an old mate from school, we had a long night catching up. Few drinks. You know how it is? In fact I might sleep for a little while. Wake me when you need a rest." With that he tilted his head to the left and closed his eyes.

Whilst Peter slept Carla had been enjoying the names she saw on the signposts and was wondering what had inspired people to give them the names they did. Dadswells Bridge, Horsham, Dimboola, Lillimur, Nhill. But when she saw the signs to Rainbow and Jeparit, she realised she had travelled this road before. She recalled Jeparit as being a pretty old town and its claim to fame was a famous prime minister, Sir Robert Menzies, who had been born there. However what she most remembered was going to Jeparit one summer with Susan, Liam, Roger and some of her uni friends. It was stinking hot and they camped at the Jeparit caravan park which backed on to the Wimmera river. They stayed five days and all they did was have fun, drink too much, go for walks along the river watching the waterbirds, swim and make love. She remembered they had travelled in Roger's old Holden and he'd just gotten past Great Western when it had a flat tyre. It took him and Liam over an hour to fix it. She and Susan had sat under a small tree and waited as the trucks sped by and the boys struggled. Finally they got it done but Liam had worried all the way that they hadn't done the wheel nuts up tight enough and twice they had to stop to check. Carla was smiling to herself as she remembered Roger and his loving nature. It was hard to believe that Susan and Roger were both dead and poor Liam had lost his way through booze.

She was beginning to feel very sad with the memories and so she determinedly decided to focus on her life and where she was headed now. She remembered being relieved she could drive 110 km. *"Ridiculous being only able to do 100km on a highway in Victoria,"* she'd thought. After about another 45 minutes she was definitely starting to feel fatigued. A few minutes later she was coming into the township of Keith.

At Keith she stopped and woke Peter, who had slept soundly. "Time to get lunch, stretch, toilet and look about," she chimed. It was a chilly day but the sun was shining.

Peter stretched and rubbed his eyes. His face was crinkled with sleep lines from squashing his face into his left cheek. "Where are we? Hey, looks like a good bakery there. I'm starving."

"I packed us a lunch. Sandwiches, fruit," Carla said.

"Hmm, thanks but I really want a pie and chips."

Secretly Carla did as well but ignored her want and opened the picnic basket and began to set it out on the picnic bench whilst Peter was in the shop. The big trucks rolled on by along the highway or stopped for food and a rest themselves and there was a general hustle and bustle happening in the small township.

They had both finished eating. "Well, I'm feeling very refreshed for food and a sleep. How about you?" Peter was saying.

"I'm a bit tired. I haven't done any long distance driving for a while. And," she turned to Peter, "you were out of it, weren't you? Did you know I stopped at Bordertown and at the fruit and vege pit stop?"

"Nope. Out like a light I guess. What were you doing at Bordertown?"

"Oh. Just needed to stretch my legs and fill up with petrol. The little rivulet they have in the park just as you come off the highway looked too inviting to ignore. Actually I thought you would have woken. Amazing."

After throwing the rubbish in the bin Peter said, "I'm going to walk up the road there," pointing along the road, "to the IGA and get some ice and some beer. Want anything yourself?"

"Yes. Thanks. But I'll come with you." As they walked Carla looked down the road as they crossed to the supermarket and noticed a large pub and a sign to a caravan park. "This looks nice, doesn't it? Perhaps we could stop for the night, have a counter meal and do the rest of the trip tomorrow. What do you think? Beer, wine and rest!"

"You think? Maybe we should just get this last leg over and done with and start fresh in Adelaide tomorrow. It's still early."

"Yes, you're right. I think I am just stalling," and she gave a big wide smile and walked into the shop.

Peter drove the next leg. They had just gotten to the other side of Keith when to their left was a sign to Mount Monster. "What a name, hey. I wonder why someone would call a mountain that!"

"Who knows? Funny though. Maybe there are monsters there or something spooky like that story about Hanging Rock in the Macedon ranges, Woodend."

Peter looked across to her and said, "Hanging Rock, never heard of it," and Carla proceeded to tell him the 1900 story of Miranda and how she and her school friends go for a picnic at the rock with their teacher but Miranda disappears and the teacher is obsessed with finding her. Peter was unimpressed with the story but it passed the time.

Before they knew it they arrived on the outskirts of the Adelaide Hills around 5 pm as night was setting in.

Peter said, "OK, let's get a motel tonight and plan what we need to do over a nice relaxing dinner and then we go back to the motel for the drinks we bought in Keith." Holding up his hand he said, "I know you like camping and not wasting money but my treat. Just tonight! Besides, it's dark," and he quickly put his hands back on the steering wheel.

The first Best Western they came across they booked in. Carla felt quite conspicuous arriving at a hotel with a very young, attractive man. "I feel like everyone is watching us," she whispered to him and he just smiled tapping her lightly on the shoulder. "Come on, who cares. We have better things to worry about."

The next day they got up and having Google maps open they made their way to 135 O'Connell Street, North Adelaide. Peter parked and they put money in the meter. "Are you sure you don't want me to come in with you?" he was saying, as she adjusted her coat and hat. The weather was damp and chilly and Carla was feeling cold inside.

"I think it's better if I see him first. Get a sense of how things will be. But thanks." Touching his arm, "It's been a long time but as I said last night, Thomas was always very particular and suspicious of people he didn't know and I think if I turn up with you he will possibly refused to help at all. I know," seeing his expression change, "I could be totally wrong but you have gotten me this far. Let me do this on my own."

He nodded and returned to the car to wait.

Entering the real estate office Carla was greeted by a young lady with dyed brunette hair tied in a bun on the top of her head and thick make-up. "How can I help you?" she chimed with exaggerated happiness at seeing a customer.

"Hi. My name is Carla Parkinson and I would like to speak with Mr Nelson, please. Thomas Nelson." Adding quickly, "It's personal and very important."

"I'm sorry, but Mr Nelson never sees anyone without an appointment but more importantly than that," she said, her eyes large as emus and a hand flick of invisible hair. "He's not in and probably won't be until later today."

"Oh. I see. Can I leave a message? Or better still can I have his phone number, please?'

"Absolutely not. But I will send him an email and he can contact you. Now, your number?" Carla left her number and leaving the building she stressed to the receptionist, Sue, according to her name tag, that it was extremely important and to please make sure that the message was conveyed to Thomas as soon as possible.

"I'll try. Bye."

Back in the car Carla told Peter what had transpired, "So I guess we wait, then," she ended.

"It's only 9.30 am, let's go for coffee and have a wonder along the Torrens to pass time. Your favourite thing Carla, walk and talk," and he smiled his typical cheeky, charming smile.

"He's getting to know me well," she thought. "Yes, good thinking," she said to him.

With coffees in hand, coats done up high against the wind and chill, sun in their eyes they walked along the well-manicured track of the Torrens River but spoke little.

Then her mobile rang. "Shit. Fingers crossed." She looked at the phone, noted the time as 10.06 am and answered. "Hello, Carla speaking."

"Hello Carla," and she grasped Peter's arm and mouthed, 'It's him,' and pointed to the phone at the same time.

"Thomas. Thanks for ringing back so quickly."

"Carla, what do you want? I told you over the phone I don't know where Samuel is. Haven't known for two years. What do you want from me?"

"Thomas, I'd love to see you. Catch up. Talk about Sam and where you think I might start looking for him. Please, Thomas." She knew she was sounding like a child wanting a lolly but couldn't help herself.

"Not possible. Lct the water continue to flow under the bridge, Carla. It was over a long time ago. No good can come of trying to find needles and answers in haystacks," and once again he hung up and once again both were left looking idly at their respective phones.

"OK. Plan B, Ms Carla Parkinson," and he turned and began walking back in the direction of the car.

"Plan B!" she called as she hurried to catch him up.

Chapter 8

Peter was driving as they followed Thomas at a safe distance to what they hoped was going to be his home. They were laughing now saying, "Look at us like characters from some cheap police show following the suspect."

"Yeah," said Peter, "but little do these two dumb cops know that the suspect is heading anywhere but where they want him to be going! They end up back in Ballarat," and they laughed again, both knowing they were covering with banal humour for the stress and concern they were both feeling.

They watched as Thomas pulled into his driveway in Glenelg. Peter had pulled over and Carla said she wanted to wait for fifteen minutes before going in. "Give him time to settle before we see him. Peter, I know I've said this before but Thomas will not welcome us. And he has a very bad temper. And he will not appreciate what we are doing. I have been told, and 'should' obey. That was a Roger saying. He'd say, Carla, my brother has spoken and I MUST obey or else it's trouble. And then he'd laugh so loud and then deliberately do the opposite…, if it suited him of course. They definitely battered heads those two," and the thought of Roger made her sad but also very determined. To herself she said, *"I am going to find our son, Roger, I will."*

Jolted back from her thoughts Peter was saying "It's OK, we aren't here to see him for a social visit, we just want some answers about Sam. Carla, just stick to our guns. Honestly, it wouldn't surprise me if Sam opened the door."

As they waited Carla took in the home. The street was decorated with Jacaranda trees and elms along both sides. Thomas's home had an ornamental wrought iron gate that was operated by some sort of electronic device but it appeared it was not operative at present, as the gates were open when he arrived and remained open. The grounds were immaculately tended with beautiful flower beds either side of the paved circular driveway that wound to the large double panelled, wooded entry doors. Beyond the flower beds were crisp manicured grassed areas. To the right of the driveway and further to the back of the home Carla saw a gazebo and large exotic trees that she could not recognise but knew them to be old. "Beautiful home," she murmured to no one in particular. And Peter did not answer or acknowledge her. He was surveying the grounds and home with an entirely different view. That of escape. *"If this guy is as bad as Carla portrays then we better have a plan to get out of there in a hurry,"* were his only thoughts at this point in time. He also reminded himself to make sure the keys to the car were handy at all times and the car remained unlocked. He worried that another car could park in front of them and make getting out slower but there was nothing he could do about that.

Fifteen minutes later they were on the verandah ringing the doorbell. Carla and Peter both stepped well back from the door.

After a second attempt Thomas opened the door and inanely Carla chirped, "Thomas, how are you? This is Peter Westmead. You remember Susan, my best friend, the one who, well, this is her son," and then she stopped. And then she waited. Breath held, eyes fixed on Thomas's face, hands clenched. She thought, as she saw the cold and controlled countenance of Thomas, that she might wet herself and berated herself for not going to the toilet earlier. She noted in this minuscule timeframe that Thomas's face had not aged all that much from when she last recalled seeing him, some twenty-two years ago.

She felt a pressure on her left upper arm pushing her to the side and Peter stepped forward, hand extended saying, "Hello, Mr Nelson," but Thomas did not acknowledge him. He remained fixated on Carla's face and said though gritted teeth, "I told you not to come. You are not welcome. Get off my property!" at the same time as turning and closing the door. Carla, in the meantime, was wondering how it was possible to go from being totally confident, having rehearsed conversations in her mind, over and over again, to instantly being unconfident, unsure of her entire being. In her mind she saw herself talking to the last year 12 class she took only – what was it? Eight weeks ago! – when she asked the students to consider Shakespeare's quote from Hamlet "There is nothing either good or bad, but thinking makes it so." (Act II, Sc. II), my God, I am doing that, and with that thought and resolve she said, "NO! Thomas. I will not go, I can't go, don't you understand? I can't go until you tell me where my son is."

Thomas stopped and turned back to Carla. "Your son, YOUR son, don't be so dammed stupid. You gave up your son at eleven months old, remember!" he shouted. "You've never wanted anything to do with him all these years. Why now?" he blurted. "Why now? Answer me that!"

"Thomas," Carla said, trying to keep her voice calm, "Thomas, perhaps we could come inside and discuss this?"

"You will not step foot in the house. You abandoned your son so you need to take responsibility for that."

"But Thomas, it's been so long. I want to tell you how I have wanted to see Sam with all my heart but with me being so sick after the death of Roger and Susan and..." but Thomas wouldn't let her finish.

"I don't care one iota about you. You are dead to me. Your son is dead to me. You have wasted your time. I told you on the phone he is a no hoper, drug addict and for all I know he's dead or in prison. Go back to Victoria and leave me alone. You came far too late. Too late. Do you hear? GO."

"Not until you tell me what happened, why he took to drugs, where did you last see him. Did you get the police to find him?"

"Get off my property, Carla, or I will call the police to have you removed. Take your new toy boy and stay out of my life."

Carla was about to arc up when Peter grasped her firmly on the elbow and said, "Come on, Carla. We won't get anywhere here," and he turned her around. Even though she didn't want to go she knew she had to and allowed herself to be steered back down the driveway to the car.

Once at the car she seemed to curl into herself. She was deflated and angry and guilty and very, very nauseated. "I feel sick," and with that she vomited, emptying all her lunch on the verge and over her shoes. Peter didn't go to her but waited till she had finished and handed her some wipes. "Come on, let's go book into that caravan park we saw backing the river and then we will work out Plan C," and he smiled that lovely smile that Carla was beginning to love seeing. He was still talking. "We knew it wasn't going to be easy. Look, he didn't do anything that we didn't expect. Did he?" and Carla knew he was right. What had she been thinking? Thomas helping her! Ha! No chance. Yes. Peter was right.

"Well OK. We are here now let's look to Plan C, whatever that is!" and for the first time when thinking of Thomas and her past she laughed, feeling perhaps things will be OK.

Having gotten an onsite two bedroom cabin they were now sitting on the small verandah drinking wine and thinking about their next move. "I feel so bad, Peter. You have no idea. It seems finding him won't be easy."

"Don't give up yet. Assuming Sam's still in Adelaide I suggest we take some time and check out the night life district. You know, the Kings Cross of Sydney or the St Kilda of Melbourne. It's a very long shot but it is a start. That, of course, is if Thomas is telling the truth. The other point of call could be prison, but let's look there as the last resort."

"Hmm but we don't even have a photo of him and there's no way Thomas would give us one. I think it's hopeless."

"Oh ye of little faith. Come on, let's start tonight and see what turns up."

They cooked a small meal on the scant kitchen appliances within the cabin and stopped next door and socialized with some of the local residents. At 10 pm they decided to head out.

It was a quiet night and windless but kind of warm compared to a Ballarat winter's night. "Not bad tonight is it? How do you want to do this?" Peter asked.

"Well, all we can do is ask people if they know a person called Sam and I'll describe... hey... that's it!" and she started scratching about in her red carry all bag.

"What are you doing?" Peter asked as he watched tissues, make-up, pens, address book, and other paraphernalia get dumped unceremoniously onto the front seat of the car. They were in the central CBD in Elizabeth Street.

"I have a picture of Roger in my bag. I've carried it around forever. Sam looked like Roger as a baby so let's assume he grew up to look like him too." She was smiling broadly, "I know the picture is older than Sam would be today but it might help."

"Good thinking." He responded with high laugh and then said, "This lot will probably be suspicious of people asking about one of their own, what do you plan to say?"

"I'll tell them the truth. I am looking for my lost son."

"Okay then, let's see how we go."

Locking the car very carefully and making sure there were no valuables in sight they moved off into the night.

Chapter 9

"Shut your fucking MOUTH! You stupid devil," he yelled and followed it with a punch to the face, hitting the girl squarely in the side of the head and sending her reeling across the dirty trash-ridden floor to land heavily on her side under a crate that had been used as a table. She lay there unmoving, but he was at her side and still yelling. "It is all your own fault, mole." Kick, "You think you can make a phone call and I wouldn't know. I KNOW. I can read your stupid brain." Whack on the back. She was in a foetal position now, hands covering head. "Get up, you shit. NOW! Before I get really angry."

She felt him move away from her and knew she needed to do as he said. She was tired, hurt all over but acutely aware of her surroundings. This was nothing new to her. At nineteen she had put up with this practically all her life. Father, mother, siblings, boyfriends, all the same. But she had learnt to survive in this world through drugs and sex. Both worked hand in hand because without it she'd never be alive now. She knew she'd have to kill this bastard. It was her or him. His rages were getting worse. At first when she'd met him six months ago he was funny, euphoric on occasions and he made her laugh. Using together was fun but experience already told her it wouldn't last. She'd been using meth for eighteen months now and it was the same thing. The newbies would enjoy the hit, feel great, and be really dare-devilish. The danger she loved. But give them a couple of months, some even less, and 'the party' was over. The shit set in, and 'bang', sleeping with a fucking monster. They all varied but the outcomes were the same. She or they would have to go or they'd kill each other. This bastard, he was a great supplier but he was mad. She had no idea if he was mad before the Ice or because of it but she didn't care either. She was in survival mode now and needed to think.

Elly had a backup plan always and that was her older sister Jenny, who lived in the CBD of Adelaide and had helped her out on a number of occasions since she had moved to Adelaide herself; but the last time she saw Jenny she was a mess and told her, "Elly, just piss off. You came here, I didn't ask you to. I can't do this! I am sick for Christ's sake, look at me!" and her hands had drifted from the top of her head towards her feet to amplify her condition. Elly had looked then. Her sister, eight years her senior, was skin and bone, teeth rotting, hair lank, clothes in rags. Her squat was shared with numerous homeless people who came and went and Jenny had said she had given up. Crying, she implored her sister, "Elly, go back to Melbourne. Go see Aunt Mary in Bayswater. She will help. I know she will. Don't go near Mum, though. Just don't. Look, Mary said to me years ago that she would help me and I told her to get fucked. Elly," through the sobs she implored her sister, "Go see her. It's too late for me," and then wiping the tears and snot on her bare arm she screamed, "GO. Now. I cannot help you," and crumpled to the floor.

That was only two months ago and Elly's predicament was the same as it had been when she had run to her sister. Drugs, violence, madness, hunger, desperation. She was stirred from her thoughts with him yelling, "Hey, Ell babe. Come on here, look what I've got for us." Wary but also knowing she had to go, she walked gingerly to where he was sitting on a dirty mattress with a syringe ready for taking. "Babe. I'm so sorry. It's crazy here. I just thought you were calling the cops. I can't get my mind straight sometimes. Here, have this," and he handed it to her. Without hesitation she injected herself and passed the needle back to him. He smiled, "Beautiful."

Later that night, Elly never had a clue what time it was, she unfolded herself from his arms and dressed. Unlike her sister she was still reasonably healthy and her clothes were quite new. *'Thanks to Target,'* she thought. In an oversized jumper and jeans she slipped out of the room and went to the bathroom down the hall. There was no electricity or running water but someone, she had no idea who, always had water next to the toilet. She went and flushed the paper and urine down with the water and moved out into the night. Elly's head was not clear and she was feeling extremely anxious about something. She couldn't put her finger on it. She hadn't eaten all day but had no appetite. She was cold and tired and aimless. Sitting in a doorway in the alley from which she had emerged she put her head in her hands and tried to think what to do.

Carla and Peter had been moving along the street and Carla had approached many single people and small groups of people asking the same question and showing

Roger's photo with the same response, "No never seen him," or absolutely nothing, or on one occasions she was told to, "Piss off." By midnight they decided to call it quits.

"I'm buggered. Let's call it a night," Carla said, catching Peter on the arm to stop him moving forward.

"Yeah. OK. Do you want to stop for a drink? Rethink our plan?"

"Yes. Why not. What about here?"

They were standing outside a dark shop front called Devlo's Nightcap so they entered and sat at a table in the shop front window and ordered vodka for Carla and a beer for Peter. They both sat silently reflecting on the evening and recognising it was a fruitless effort. However both were also determined that they had the time, "So why not continue at least for a few nights longer?"

"No harm done. If we get nothing, well we will pressure old Thomas again."

"Peter is always so upbeat, positive," she thought.

Their night-time routine continued for another five nights of street scouring. If nothing else both of them agreed that it was fun talking to random people. Some were either really interesting and in for a chat, or others wouldn't give them the time of day and expressed their desire to be left alone in the most colourful and imaginative ways. Mostly though, people tried to assist.

She'd gotten used to the distinctive smell of the night crowds. The musty, old, almost rotting atmosphere that screamed with smoke, both tobacco and cannabis, alcohol and decay. Some people they had approached seemed so sick, weary and old that Carla wanted to help with money or take them somewhere for shelter but Peter was very clear about "No strays, Carla. It's too dangerous. Be sensible. You know it!" and she did, but it didn't help her in not feeling she needed to do something. She wondered if this life went on in Ballarat and if it did she was going to see if there was anything she could do when she got back home to help. Every street and park and mall seemed to ooze with an underlying grating, desperate human need. Or was she projecting her own needs? She wondered. She wasn't sure how to describe her nightly forays into the seamier side of Adelaide life and she actually deliberately stopped herself from thinking too hard, because when she did that she was overwhelmed with sadness and guilt that she had abandoned her son to this life. Carla had fought hard to fill the vacuum she had experienced from the loss of Roger, Susan and Sam by avoiding thought and avoiding any emotional ties to anyone. Blotting out painful thoughts and memories and building up a convincing story that she had done all the right things had worked well. Don't be around the Nelson family because that would upset them because you are a reminder that they had lost a son and brother. Don't be around your son because he is better off not growing up in a home with a mentally ill grandmother and a weak mother. Yes, these plans and tactics had worked well and fortified her ability to cope with her losses and it meant she had lived. Running around now, looking for her son, who probably wanted nothing to do with her, was causing doubts and bringing back old hurts. *"Protect yourself, stupid."*

Peter was talking to her. "Carla, let's go to Devlo's early tonight." They had been frequenting the café each night before retiring. "Oh, why?"

"We need to decide where to go from here."

"Yes. I was thinking that myself."

Ten minutes later they were seated in the café with a number of patrons coming in and out. It was much busier at this earlier hour. Cappuccino in hand, Peter said, "I want to go and see Thomas again. He has to give us more."

"He could have been telling the truth, Peter. But we should talk to him, I agree, even if it's just for me to say goodbye and totally close this little chapter we have opened." She sighed. "I don't regret any of this you know. I think you are wonderful, truly," and she smiled and tapped his hand lightly.

"Don't give up yet."

They stood and paid for the drinks at the counter and entered busy Hindley Street. The people traffic they were used to, the night creepers, night owls, all manner of night folk, were not out and about yet. They walked towards their car which was parked further away this night than usual due to some night roadworks and the earlier hour in which they had come. Once they were on North Terrace they travelled north and were just passing the Holy Trinity Church when they both heard what sounded like a cat mewling.

"Keep walking," Peter said, placing his hand firmly on her arm, leading her on.

They had now passed the church, and had turned left up the narrow roadway where they had parked, when the noise they had heard seconds earlier became more distinctive. "That's not a cat," Carla said, in a frightened but whispered voice. She was staring into the shadows of the church grounds, where an alcove of the building was jutting out from the side. "It sounds like it's coming from over there," and she moved, without hesitation, to slide between the church's ornate iron fencing on her left and some green corrugated iron fencing that had been put there from the building site next door, to her right.

Shaking his head in frustration Peter followed. He didn't call out or speak because he was concentrating on taking in their surroundings and where the best escape routes were. *"Again,"* he thought. *"Clearly,"* he was saying to himself, *"squeezing between this iron fence and temporary corrugated fence is not the best way to flee if this turns out to be trouble... and this will be trouble."*

Carla was walking tentatively too. She was also aware that what she was doing was dangerous but she had felt so helpless these past five nights that something in her just wanted to help someone, somewhere!

Underfoot was bitumen, clearly she was walking on the area where the churchgoers would park. There were no cars about and, as she left the safety of the light in the narrow roadway and got closer to the church itself, the area became darker and less distinctive. The noise that had attracted her though was getting closer and she now clearly understood it to be sobbing, sniffing. She could also hear talking but she was pretty sure it was only one person's voice.

Then she saw a person huddled against the church wall, it was sideways to her and hardly moving.

Carla stopped and Peter came up to her. Before she could say anything Peter had moved forward and she heard him say, "Hello. Are you alright? Can we help?"

The noise stopped and they were able to see it was a young girl. She looked wet and Carla thought she was naked.

Chapter 9

Getting up from the footpath Elly decided she would try and find her friend Jo who she knew would be either in the Adults Only men's club or on the job, either way she just had to hang about the club till she saw her. On this night she had waited for a few hours and then been moved on by the bouncers who didn't appreciate hangers on. "Jo's not coming back tonight so just move on, Elly." They knew her well enough but there were rules and she moved on without argument. Finally as daylight started to wend its way through the night sky and dull shadows were being cast off the buildings she decided she had little choice but to return to the squat.

Even though she had only been in Adelaide for eight months she knew the streets well and avoided certain areas which were notorious for gang related 'stuff'. "You get caught up down there and there's no telling how you'll come out," Jenny had told her in the early days, and she had taken the advice to heart, even though no one else had warned her. In thinking of Jenny she thought she'd try and see her tonight, especially as Jenny had looked gross the last time she'd seen her and she worried about her sister. With that in mind she entered the derelict building which she called home and went to her room, hoping the hell that Baz her 'boyfriend' would be there. Moving towards the broken window that gave her a view of the building next door she rattled about under it pulling up a few loose floor boards to find her blanket, clothes, toothbrush and toiletries. Placing her hand purse, which held some make-up and some loose change, in the hole, she covered the boards over again. Elly then grabbed the blanket and wrapped it around her and lay on the dirt-sodden mattress and thought, *"I feel like shit. Where's Baz? Bastard better not be long."* She was withdrawing, she knew the feeling too well and the only way to get through was to get more. She hoped Baz would be out scoring and be back soon. If not, she'd have to get it herself and there was danger in that, greater danger for her than Baz or any of the other creeps she'd been with. Too much giving to bastards who only cared for one thing and that was themselves, their survival. But Elly was a survivor too. She spotted people's uses and she knew what she wanted, that being drugs and that was what men did best for her.

Elly thought that she had slept a bit but, upon awaking, she was very uncomfortable and very much in need of a hit. She sat up and looked around. *"Where is the bastard?"* as she shed the blanket and grabbed her brush that was caked in her hair. "Fuck the drugs," she said out loud as she combed her hair and tried to get her thoughts straight as to what she needed to do. *"Get some Ice and then figure out the rest, you stupid bitch."* Then, just as she made her way to the door to leave, Baz came in.

"Elly, Ell, come on." She was wary now. She could tell he was off his face and something had excited him. She noticed blood on his shirt and knuckles. *"This is bad, stay calm."* She went to him, big smile across her face. "What you got for me?" instantly touching his crutch, "let's get on."

"Hmm. Yes. Feel this. You need this? I need this," and he began undressing and pulling her down with him. The sex hurt and he stank of blood, and rotting and sex and she was totally absorbed in nothing else but getting this over and done with and then getting drugs. When she knew it was over she leapt up and grabbed his clothes, throwing them down upon him. "Come on. I need some now, you filthy bastard. I don't give a shit what you've done, just get me some stuff. Look," and then quieting her tone, "look, hit now and then this is all yours," and she bared her arse to him. Baz leered and slapped her in the middle of her back, sending her sprawling on the ground. He seemed to have the energy of ten men and within seconds he had her on the mattress again, raping her.

She had, in the past, been okay with this but she had usually been off her face too, and everything and anything was good, Godly, loving, mind-fusing but she was not in that state now. Hell, no. She was scared, had no energy and ached, her senses were focused on escape and the need for relief. Relief from life, the pain, the memories of a father clawing her body, licking her little face, talking, talking, talking, shit knows what, hurting, hurting, why? Why? "Honey," she whispered, "honey, hit first, please, you know it will be better." Slap, across the face, "SHUT up HONEY!" She fought but he was strong so she steeled herself, saying, *"Let it ride, go with it, it will finish."* She was not sure at what point she stopped hearing his laughter or feeling his fists but it did end. Elly got up. She ached everywhere but still her need for drugs was great. She began to cry whilst picking up her clothes and then a greater feeling overtook her, she realised, "I need my sister."

Elly walked to her sister's squat, having left Baz naked on the mattress. She was dressing as she entered the street. At Jenny's she stood outside the door. "Hey Jenny, let me in, please, come on, please." Banging the door she found it opened easily and as such stepped in. She hadn't gotten a metre into the room when Jenny came rushing towards her. Jenny was flying, slapping her arms wildly, there was a man with a knife, running at Jenny. Elly saw blood on her sister's hands, on her sister's chest and at the same time she was catching her, catching Jenny as she stumbled back with the unexpected impact of her sister's body ploughing into her. She managed to see the bottom half of a man as he ran past them both. She and Jenny were now on the ground, Jenny on top of her. Wriggling quickly from beneath her sister she looked upon a face that was alien to her. Elly knew it was her sister but she also knew Jenny was gone. There was blood everywhere, on her, on Jenny, "OH NO!" stab wounds, blood everywhere, looking around, in the room, more blood, Jenny gone. Elly stood and continued to look down and around, frozen to the spot, all empty, vacant, no thoughts, no words, no language, all gone. She had no idea how long she stood there with her sister's body at her feet but then her eyes landed on the drugs on the floor near a mattress. Elly took a step over her sister's tiny body and reached for the drugs and the needle.

Chapter 10

All Elly was aware of was two voices. "Are you alright?" "Yes, can we help?"

"Who the fuck. Stay calm. Don't move. Open your eyes, careful, dark, blood, naked," was all she was thinking.

"My God, she's covered in blood, Peter. We better call an ambulance."

The word ambulance kicked her into motion, "No. I'm ok please, don't call anyone, I am ok. Please." Elly heard herself speaking whilst uncurling and getting to her knees.

Carla and Peter looked at each other and it was Peter who said, "Come on then, she doesn't need help."

"Good thinking. Bugger off you bloody arseholes!" Elly said to herself.

"Don't be stupid Peter, we can't leave her here, like this! For goodness sake we have to do something."

"Stupid cow, just piss off and leave me alone," Elly's next thought.

Carla was at ground level now with Elly and she told Peter to go to the car and get her jacket out of the boot. He turned and had left reluctantly, "Only because the car's not far, Carla." He reminded her, "This is bullshit, you know that!" But then he was gone.

"This IS bullshit. Peter's right. What am I doing?" But she remained down on the ground with Elly. She wasn't sure what to say or do so waited quietly until Peter returned with the jacket.

"Here, put this on." But the girl was hesitating, "Please. We want to help."

Elly had begun to see some use in these two. *"Well I suppose I need help. Okay, let her give it. Can't stay like this, can I, got to move, do something?"*

So Elly took the proffered jacket and stood, putting it on. Carla was also on her feet again saying, "Is there somewhere we can take you? Hospital, family, friends, please, what can we do? You can come back with us tonight, get cleaned up and we can take it from there if you prefer."

At hearing this last statement of help Peter said in a tense but quietly restrained voice, "You have to be joking. Carla! No way. Think, will you!"

But Carla was on a one-way mission, even though logically she knew it was stupid and that there was probably nothing good to come of any of this, but she was prepared to ignore common sense. *"Why?"* she asked herself, *"What's this girl to me?"* but there was something else happening within her body, her core which ached and longed to be appeased. Carla didn't have words for this just an inner knowing. So aloud she said, "I think it will be alright, Peter. I don't know why but I think it will." Her internal dialogue was working overtime, *"I suppose if I wish enough for something it could come true. I wish to help this girl, I wish to help my son, I wish to help Peter and shit yeah, I want, and need, to help myself. It can happen."* She reflected on how, in such a short time, she was already changing, but she was scared, terrified if she allowed herself to be honest. Twenty-two years of protection from any emotional involvement to this! An avalanche of humans needing help, Peter, Sam, this girl. Carla was not sure of anything right at that point in time. She was blacking out within her own thoughts, a numbness was beginning to settle in, *"Oh! No. I cannot get sick."* It was just at that point that Peter's voice broke through.

"So you want to help someone you don't know." He was incredulous and his face spoke a thousand words. 'You want to take," and he pointed and sneered at the same time, "this to the caravan park? With us! What if she kills us in our sleep?"

Hearing this something inside kicked in, it was her more professional persona, her other self. She answered whilst putting her arm through the girl's arm, "Oh don't be so dramatic. Until we know what's happened here there is no evidence to support your conjecture that this girl is going to harm anyone. I think we can help here Peter, that's all," and that stated she immediately had all the usual Carla self-doubting thoughts. *"You are probably the single most stupid person I know, Carla Parkinson,"* and with that she ushered Peter aside and walked herself and the girl through the gap in the fences and up the street to the station wagon. "What's your name?" as they got in the car.

"Elly," she replied in a tired and timid voice. *"Yes Peter boy. Don't be so silly. Madame two shoes is helping little 'ol me. You arsehole. Now this could be fun!"*

In the car Elly had managed to repeat her desire to have nothing to do with the ambulance or police when Carla had asked again. "No, please. If I can just get cleaned up I will be out of your hair. I promise."

Back at their cabin Elly showered whilst Peter sulked in his room. He had told her outright. "This is your mess. Don't include me. I thought you had more sense. What about Sam, Carla?" and she had replied that nothing had changed with the plans that they had made that evening, before finding Elly.

"We will pack up and see Thomas on our way out. I need to see him one more time."

Emerging from the bathroom Elly saw the little two seater couch made up with a sleeping bag and pillow and made her way over to it. "Thank you. Can I just lay down? I'm really tired."

"Yes of course. You don't want anything to eat or drink?'

"No. Just rest."

"Okay, let's talk in the morning," and Carla watched as Elly got into the sleeping bag and curled up on the couch looking very squashed, but there was nothing she could do about that, and when she saw her close her eyes she picked up her hand bag, phone and iPod and took them into her room and turned off the lights. *"Just in case Peter's right,"* she thought.

Carla hardly slept that night, worrying about Elly and running scenarios through her head about what she had to say to Thomas. Try as she might to shut her brain off she could not and the more she stewed on decisions made tonight the more her scenarios of conversations got wilder and more fanciful. At one point she smiled at herself, *"Always the heroine in these conversations with myself. Yep. The intriguing things I say, the wisdom I purport, the admiration I engender. If only."* Carla was well aware that what she thought she would say or do in any given scenario was never anything like what she did in the real situation, so she added to herself, *"Shut up, Carla. Go to sleep!"* But sleep was not for her, not tonight.

In the other bedroom Peter was also not sleeping. He felt nauseated and cold. The person in the next room was not part of his plans. He was not happy to have an uncalculated risk. Not now, not when they were close to maybe finding Sam or at least possibly getting a bit more closure from Thomas. Peter was convinced that quiet persuasion and a dogged approach to any problem was the way to go. It had worked with Carla. She didn't want to consider the trip over here at first but he had been patient, pointed out positives and dispelled worries with solutions and reality and she came around. But now she was wrecking it. Why? That was the question rolling about in his head. What was this about? For the first time he was unsure how to approach this new dilemma. He glanced at the bedside clock and saw it was 4.42 am. *"Hell,"* however he must have gotten to sleep soon after that because the next thing he heard was people moving about in the other room.

Carla had gotten up around 6.30 am, no longer able to lie in bed. The morning was very cold so she had quietly put the heater on and then the kettle. In the quiet of the cabin the kettle sounded like a steam train and she quickly turned it off and put a pan of water on the stove to boil instead. Elly was curled up in the same position as when Carla last saw her and she appeared to be asleep. Upon looking at her face she could see a number of bruises to her right eye and Carla thought her nose might be broken. If not broken then very swollen and bruised too. Not for the first time she thought, *"What's happened to this girl?"*

Even the opening of the fridge and the clinking of the cups from the cupboard sounded amplified ten-fold and obviously it was loud, because soon after Elly began to rouse. She opened her eyes and took in a coffee table, clean! A warm blanket, clean! TV on the wall. Smell of coffee! She needed the toilet but was scared to move. *"Think,"* she thought. Then images returned to her and she remembered Jenny and she sat up like a bullet, clasping her head in both hands and moaning, "Oh no, no, Jenny. Please no," and repeated this over and over whilst rocking back and forth.

Carla had put down the coffee cup and was at her side. She did nothing, but sat on the couch and held the girl. Peter could hear this exchange from his room and wanted nothing to do with it but he too needed the bathroom and he knew he couldn't simply wish this all away. He had to be part of it or he'd have no control and that wasn't an option.

He got up, wrapped a towel about himself, gathered his clothes for the day and opened his bedroom door. He noted the girl in the sleeping bag rocking back and forth and Carla with her arm about her, gave a quick nod of recognition to Carla and went straight to the bathroom. A minute later Carla heard the toilet flush and the shower going. She was keen for a shower herself.

When Peter emerged from the shower he glanced at himself in the mirror, something he avoided normally but it was too late. And there he noted the welts and scars his torso carried from beatings and lashings he had experienced from childhood. A childhood he had spent most of his teenage and adult life trying to disconnect from. Its evil had penetrated his heart and he hated it when he was reminded of it. He thought ironically that he had behaved similarly to Carla. She had avoided her past in order to move on and *"so am I."* He knew avoidance worked mostly, thank goodness, but there always seemed to be the need to tweak it, to fill an unforeseen gap that liked to raise its head and try to take you back, back down memory lane, back to hell. Why this happened he didn't know, but he was a fighter from his past, as Carla was in her way, and he would continue to get through it. *"Scars and all,"* he thought, as he quickly covered his body up. Back in his room he packed his bag and determined to join the women with a fresh approach.

Both Carla and Elly at this stage had moved to the kitchen table and were both drinking coffee. Carla had given Elly a set of her clothes including bra and underwear and although Elly was slightly smaller in frame the clothes looked quite good on her. "Sorry. My feet are too big so I can't help with shoes," and Elly had simply smiled at her.

"Good morning, ladies," Peter announced. "Now I'm clean and slept I feel much better. How are you both?" and he headed for the kettle and put it on.

He looked at Carla from behind Elly with a look and shrug of the shoulders that asked, "Well, what's the story?" and Carla shrugged back with an, "I don't know" look.

Peter pulled up a seat and, looking straight at Carla, said, "I'm packed, we need to be out of here by 10 am. Elly, where do you need dropping off?"

Elly looked up, the first time she had actually looked at either Carla or Peter properly, and said, "I don't know? I have to get away, my sister, she's all I have here and," with a slight gulp, said matter of factly, "she was killed last night. It was her blood on me. They will kill me too if they find me. Please, I don't know what to do."

The questions were running through both Peter and Carla's brains but it was Carla who spoke. "Oh my God, we need to go to the police, Elly. Your sister, oh no!"

But Elly was on her feet in a flash. "Don't you get it? It's drugs, it's sex, it's life, it's survival, it's death, oh God, Jenny told me not to come here. I have to get away. The police can't help. They will get me just like Jenny. In the end. Please can I go with you? You said you were packed," and she looked at Peter. Her eyes were brimming with tears and she looked terrified.

Peter very calmly asked her to sit down and talk quietly. "Look, we don't need the world to know. Do you have other family here to help you?"

"No, I'm from Victoria. I've only been here eight months," and now she began to cry. Elly was crying for herself, for her sister, for ice, heroin, ecstasy, cannabis, any bloody thing, she felt shit, and she didn't have to explain herself to these morons. "Please just help. You have to trust me when I say I am now in trouble, in danger!"

Carla was worried for Elly and Peter was worried for himself, for Carla and for finding Sam but he could read people well. Well… he liked to think he could, and he could see that Carla was not going to leave this girl, she would not abandon her. So, despite his reservations he announced, "Well, it's settled then. Elly will have to come with us. We will give her a lift to Ballarat, where she can catch a train to Melbourne or where ever she came from and get herself safe," and he smiled at them both. "Yep, one hitch hiker for the trip isn't such a bad thing, is it?" He felt he could cope knowing they'd still be roughly sticking to plan and be rid of her within a day or two.

Both women said in unison, "Really?'

Chapter 11

Against Carla's better judgment and Peter's protestations Elly had insisted on going back to her squat and getting her meagre belongings. She had assured them she would be okay and would meet them after they had finished speaking to whoever they had to see that morning.

It was agreed they would meet up at Delvo's, no specific time but somewhere between two or three pm would be good. Carla did not know if they would be delayed in seeing Thomas so thought it better to have a later time to meet.

They had packed the car and, having finalised their bill, left to see Thomas. Elly wanted to walk back to her squat but Carla was having none of it. "No, don't be silly, we can drive you." But Peter had taken her aside and said, "It's a good idea if she walks, Carla, please think about what we are getting into because if she was telling the truth then we shouldn't be seen with her. We don't need to attract attention. Especially the attention she's talking about. This is already a harebrained idea!"

"You are right, Peter. I will start thinking more level-headedly," and as an afterthought she gave Peter a hug and said, "Thank you Peter. Thanks for helping. I know you are not happy about this but I can't leave her."

"I know, come on let's get this show on the road."

Elly walked off in the direction of the CBD and as they drove towards Glenelg Peter commented, "Do you know what you want to say?"

"Not really, I just want to tell him we have tried to find Sam but no one knows anything and," she stopped and thought, "and would he please let us come in and at least tell me about my son? Yep, I think that's all I want. Then I will never bother him again."

"Okay then. Let's see how it goes," Peter chimed, hoping his uplifted mood would strengthen her resolve. "If nothing else Carla, you at least know you've tried."

As they turned into Thomas's road and were looking for a place to park they noticed the car in front of them pull into the driveway.

"Okay, well I presume he's home then. We'd better hold back, Peter. I don't want a scene in front of anyone." Then, as an afterthought, because she could feel herself becoming anxious at the thought of talking with Thomas again, she added, "How about, if we wait say, fifteen minutes for this person to leave and if they haven't gone by then we will bugger off, do a little shopping for the trip home, pick up Elly and be gone. You OK with that?" and without waiting for a response added, "like you said, we have tried and it will be a pity but really it was always going to end this way, wasn't it?"

"Hm, maybe, maybe not but… sure, we can always try again in a few months' time," and he smiled when he saw her face looking like someone had just been zapped with an electrical current. "Just kidding. Just kidding." He laughed.

Peter had seen a parking spot just across the road from Thomas's driveway so he did a U-turn, parked and cut the engine. The car had pulled up at the front and Peter could see the person in the car fiddling about, "Looks like he's getting stuff off the back seat," as he observed the person pulling a bag over to the front. The next moment the car door was kicked open and a young man emerged. Both Peter and Carla strained to look at him but his back was to them. Then he turned, arms clasping an overnight case, and moved to the boot of the car. At that point his face was clear and Carla gave a short gasp and grabbed Peter on the arm, "It's Roger! Well, his face, Peter. Don't you see? It's him. It's Sam. How the hell can that be?" but she knew. "Thomas… the bastard WAS lying!'

Peter was sitting staring blankly and didn't answer.

As Sam struggled with his overnight bag and then the suitcase from the boot, Carla said, "Come on. Let's go." But Peter said, placing a restraining hand on her arm, "Perhaps I should approach him first, test the water. We hadn't thought about this happening."

Carla was jumping about in her seat, "Yes, no, maybe, what about together, I don't know, oh, if you think that's best."

Peter did. He alighted from the car and walked confidently up the driveway, directing himself straight at

Sam. Sam caught movement at the corner of his eye, stopped struggling and turned to face the stranger.

"Hey," in a bright, cheery voice. "Looks like you need a hand."

"Yeah! It's stuck on the boot hinge. I was in a bit of a hurry this morning and just threw stuff in."

"Let's see if I can help." Both men then bent to the task and released the suitcase with a force that sent them both tottering backwards. "Whoa," Sam exclaimed, "thanks, mate. You here to see my father?"

"Ah, no actually I'm here to see you, Sam."

"Do we know each other?" and thought, *"I hate it when people remember me but I don't recall them, it's embarrassing. I definitely don't remember the face."* To Peter he added, "I don't actually recall you."

"No you wouldn't, but you and I have history. We knew each other when you were a baby and I was three years old. Sam," he continued, "I'm here with your mother," and he pointed to the car.

Upon seeing Peter point towards her Carla got out of the car and slowly crossed the road, walking hesitantly up the driveway towards them. Her heart was pounding and she felt light-headed. She was so unprepared for this that she thought she might faint. *"Keep going, hang in there, he's your son."*

At the same time the curtain in the front room of the house opened slightly and Carla saw Thomas looking out. *"Oh shit,"* she thought. *"Oh. Well, what will be, will be."*

As Carla got closer she heard Sam saying, "What the fuck are you on about? What do you mean, my mother? My mother's dead, you moron."

"No. I'm not Sam. He's telling the truth." Carla was surprised at her very steady voice because she felt nothing but unbalanced within herself.

Sam stared at her and took a large step backwards as if she'd struck him, and in a way she had. He would never be able to articulate it but he knew it was true. But how? He was in shock and unable to speak. Carla moved a little closer and again he stepped back. "I don't understand what's going on," as his head swung from Carla to Peter and backwards towards where he knew his father was.

Almost on cue Thomas emerged from the house and his face was contorted and strained with visible anger. He was yelling and waving his arms. "Get off my property. I have told you to go. Leave my son and me alone. I will call the police and have you physically removed. Go."

Carla looked at Thomas and the feeling of insecurity and imbalance was replaced with extreme agitation and anger. "Your son, Thomas? Don't you mean nephew?"

"No. I bloody well do NOT. He is my son. I raised him. You didn't want him. I have the papers, Carla. Remember that."

And Sam interjected, "What are you saying, Dad? What is she saying? Please...," looking around frantically, "please someone explain what the fuck is going on. I feel sick," and it was true. Sam had been feeling sick all the way home from Port Vincent to the point that he had pulled over once and vomited on the side of the road. He knew his father would be unhappy with him returning without his say-so but he had to get away from that place. He had to get home. Sam also knew that in the end his father would forgive him and understand. But this! He felt like he'd walked into some time warp or was in a dream. This wasn't his world. Again he looked from Carla to Peter then to his father, waiting... expectant. *"Dad will fix this,"* he thought.

"Don't give them the time of day, Samuel. Please go inside. I will deal with this," Thomas said, reaching for Sam with the intention of getting him to head indoors. But Sam flinched his arm away, "I'm not going anywhere until I understand what's happening here," and he crossed his arms tightly about his chest with a very stubborn look on his face and an expression that said, *"And you can't make me."* Inside he was trembling and bile had risen to his mouth, he gulped for air trying to hold it down.

Carla went to speak but Peter quickly jumped in, spraying his words, with arms gesturing up and down and around.

"Okay. She's your mother. He's your uncle. Your father died in a motorcycle accident. She got sick, he took you and she's here to find you." Relieved it was out there he instantly regretted it as he watched Sam's face.

Sam gaped at him and said in a low and slow voice, "And who are you? My brother?"

"No. No mate. Don't worry about me yet. You have enough to take in. So, for now though my name is Peter, Peter Westmead.' And he extended his hand but Sam simply stared at it.

"Whoa. Okay, stop," and turning to his father he said, "Dad, explain. None of this makes sense."

Thomas was glaring at Carla but he responded to Sam by saying, "Can you go inside and after these people go I will explain it all."

"No, Dad," he screamed. "No. Explain it now! I feel sick to the point of spewing all morning and now this," and he pointed squarely at Carla.

Thomas began to shake his head and looked as though he was asking himself questions, troubled by inner thoughts, pacing. All of a sudden he gave a bit of a jolt and said, "Yes. Alright, what he said," nodding towards Peter, "it's true. But, I believe I am your father in all manners. She," pointing to Carla, "abandoned you. I'm the one who raised you. It's been twenty-two years, Samuel. Where has she been? Answer that, Carla. Why now, Carla?" and he spat her name like it was poison in his mouth. Carla was feeling diminished and speechless and was spared by Sam who was saying,

"Why did you tell me both my parents were dead? Why not the truth, why not let me know?"

"I was protecting you. You didn't need to know about your biological mother. Can't you see she didn't want you?" This got Carla's attention and she butted in.

"Sam, that is simply not true. Perhaps we could head into town, get a coffee and talk. I can explain most things, not all, but I can't do it here in the driveway. You said you feel sick; do you need to freshen up? Please, we need to talk away from here. I haven't come to cause trouble. Honestly, Thomas. Honestly, Sam." All were silent and she added, "You look like your dad, you know."

Peter excused himself and went back to the car, where he phoned Elly and explained they may be late, "Perhaps closer to three than two," and apologised. "I'll ring when we are half an hour away." She was fine with that.

Walking back from the car he thought he saw some sort of metal jutting out from Thomas's coat pocket. He couldn't be sure but he thought it could have been a gun and he hurried up to Carla and leaning in to her said very quietly, "I think he has a gun. Let's get out of here. Now!" but she didn't seem to hear him. She was staring at her son, at his confused and distressed expression and she was thinking, "*I've only caused damage. Sharon was right, all those years ago when I tried to make contact. She told me Thomas and Sam had bonded and that coming between them would be a cruel thing after two years. Sharon's words and her own weakness was some of the reason she never pursued her son. Now, here I am hurting him and destroying the life he has known. She hated herself for it and hated the fact that she had let Peter Westmead cloud her judgement of all these years. Yes, they had to go before more damage was done.*"

Still arguing with herself she was countering her doubts with her maternal instincts that told her to stay and explain. However, Carla was an expert in walking away, it was her default to 'unpleasantness', her barrier. So she turned to Sam and Thomas and said, "I'm sorry to have upset you, Sam. That was not my intention. I can see that my coming was a mistake," and turning to Thomas she said, "Please tell him the entire truth, Thomas, and tell him about his father, your brother, my husband and how we loved him dearly. Will you at least do that?"

Thomas didn't move, he was thinking, *"Good, I can fix this with Sam. My god, why did he come home anyway. He has caused this mess. I had it covered. It shouldn't have come to this."* He was angry. "Don't tell me what to do, Carla. Sam," he yelled. "Get in the house. NOW. I will explain later."

Sam turned and looked at his father and he could tell instantly that his father was building up to an explosion of words which usually came when he felt he was being thwarted or someone had done the wrong thing by him and Sam was always fearful when Thomas got like that.

"Bye Sam; but if you want to talk here's my phone number," and she handed him her High School business card which also had her hand-written mobile number on it. Sam took it without speaking and Carla and Peter headed off down the drive.

Sam was torn but knew he had to make some decision and make it quickly. He turned to Thomas and said, "I'll be back in a minute."

"Don't go, Samuel. Stay with me, you're better off without this." But he was talking to Sam's back. Sam was already halfway down the driveway calling out, "Hang on. Where do you two think you are actually going? You can't just drop some shit about you being my mother and then leave. Shit man, what do you think I can do? Just forget this little scene."

Carla and Peter had stopped by the car and were looking back up the driveway as they waited for Sam to catch up. He stopped and shrugged, "Well?"

"I don't know, Sam. I don't know what we were thinking, we thought we'd covered all the scenarios of catching up with you but we should have known it was wrong. I was selfish," and she began to cry but kept her eyes on Sam.

Peter butted in, "Look, I'm sorry too, Sam, but we need to get out of here. I am not comfortable knowing your uncle has a gun on him. I don't know him but I don't trust anyone who carries a gun. Come on, Carla," and he jumped in the car. Carla stood facing her son. Her emotions were racing and she recognized within herself it was love for a stranger and yet, somehow she knew him, every part of him. "It's weird, isn't it?"

Sam said "Yes, if that's what this is, then weird will do. I need to know more, damn it. I have to understand. Look, where are you staying? I'll drop by once I sort stuff out with Dad, uh," and he let that thought trail off.

Peter wound down the window. He was clearly agitated. "Come on," in a very loud voice, "let's get some distance happening, he's coming down the driveway," he was shouting now. Sam looked back and saw Thomas had the look that even he, Sam, had learnt to avoid over his lifetime. When Thomas was looking as he was there was only trouble brewing and Sam knew he had to move fast. He glanced again at his father, noted his father with his hand on his left hand pocket. *"Shit,"* he thought. "You go, I'll be okay. I'll ring you when I can. GO!"

She jumped in the car and Peter took off. In the rear vision mirror he saw Thomas and Sam standing in the middle of the road staring at the back of the station wagon.

Sam faced Thomas. "Have you got a gun there?"

Ignoring the question Thomas said, "Why did you come back, now, of all times? Why are you here, Samuel? I sent you away, you weren't meant to be here," and then he realised what he had said.

"What do you mean you sent me away? Why? Because of them? Because what they said was true? Why wouldn't you want me to know the truth, for fuck's sake?"

"Don't speak to me like that. I forbid it. Yes, yes I know. Just wait, I can't think. It's being done. I will."

It was definitely time for Sam to quieten down. He knew his father's moods and strange antics and his current state only spelt trouble if not handled well. He remember a few years back confronting his father when they had argued over whether he should be attending college and 'doing something with his life' and Sam had said that he didn't feel he had a life and that he had wanted to know more about his mother. Thomas, as he had always done, at the mention of Sam's mother said matter of factly, "She is dead to us, Samuel. Don't ask again." It was his stock standard answer. But when Sam dared to press the point he became enraged, yelling loudly, pacing, rubbing his head but none of it was directed at Sam but totally at himself, as if trying to straighten out his thoughts. Sam, angry himself had shouted at his father. "What are you on about? I have no idea what you are saying. You always go off like this, talking crap, when you're angry. Well, it's stupid. Stupid, you hear! We should be able to talk like adults; this jabbering you do doesn't help anything. Nothing ever gets resolved with you unless everyone does what you want. You're mad," and he began to leave the room, shaking his head. Thomas said his name, the words had jolted him and Sam thought he would see his father making a concerted, and deliberate effort, to stop pacing and quieten his mumblings, he repeated his son's name and added, "Get out of my sight. Quick, hurry, pleeeease," and Sam had run. He never knew what Thomas might do when he was in these 'moods' and he never wanted to know. It was innate in him. An instinctual knowledge to never push past a point and Sam certainly wasn't about to change that now.

"Stay calm and talk quietly." Looking at his father he said, "Dad. You must know I need to understand. I need to know. This might be what I have been missing. It will not change anything between us. Dad, please."

"No, son. I won't, I can't let you leave. I'm scared for you. I can't protect you if you go. Samuel, you are in danger. I know it. Please son, I've looked after you all this time. Trust me now."

"No Dad, you have always said that and I've believed you but I don't think this is danger, this is important. I think this woman coming here has put you 'in danger'. Of what I don't know." But Sam's words were lost on Thomas and Thomas's words were lost on Sam.

They had both walked back towards the house whilst this interaction was taking place. Sam saw his overnight case and suitcase still on the ground next to the car and decided. He was no longer thinking, he simply turned to his car, grabbed the suitcase and overnight bag, flung them back into the boot, slammed it shut, jumped in the driver's side and sped around the circular driveway. Thomas hadn't moved, he was rigid, feet riveted to the ground, but his arms were moving. Sam looked in the rear view mirror as he stopped to check for traffic and

271

saw his father remove the gun from his pocket and look at it and then look at the car. "Holy hell," Sam said aloud, "Holy bloody hell." He kept driving.

Chapter 12

Peter and Carla were heading back into the CBD and Delvo's café. Both were distressed and unsure what to do. "Look, let's pull over and think. I feel like shit and I need to be standing and moving," she said, turning to Peter who was holding the steering wheel so tight his knuckles were white.

"Good idea. I feel sick too, in fact I need a drink." He pulled into the Safeway car park. They both got out and started pacing about, not talking but lost in their own thoughts. Peter was conflicted about the very violence that Thomas had exuded. Peter knew violence, had grown up with it and had learnt well how to detect it early and avoid it. He knew one thing; he did not ever want to encounter Thomas Nelson again. *"He's sick, that one,"* he thought. He felt sorry for Sam. He had looked so confused, so lost. He couldn't blame him.

Carla, on the other hand, had only thoughts of regret and repulsion for herself and the wrong she had done. She was busy self-berating, running over old self-deprecating thoughts. She was beginning to feel a dark cloud coming across her. Unbidden she called out, "No, please, no. I can't do this. I can't." She was working herself up into a state. Peter was broken from his reverie when she had called out and was running towards her. As he got closer he could hear her phone ringing and reached through the window of the car. "Do you want to take it?" Absentmindedly she took the phone. "Hello."

"Hello. It's Sam," said the voice and she responded, "I'm so sorry, Sam."

"Don't worry. I don't have time. Where are you? We need to talk." He was almost hysterical. "Quick." Carla beckoned with her hand for Peter to come to her, "Wait, Peter, here," shoving the phone towards him, "you talk to Sam."

Peter listened to Sam's urgent request to know where they were and Carla heard him saying they were in the Safeway car park. Still in Glenelg. Not far from his house. And then "Do you know it?"

"Yes. Stay there." Both men hung up at the same time.

Sam pulled up three cars away from them and came over.

Everyone began speaking but it was Peter who seemed to be more in touch with what was happening. "Mate, get your breath, breathe." Sam was pointing in the direction he had come from, his home. "Yes Sam, I know. He has a gun. Why the hell do you think we left?"

"For Christ's sake," and he ran his hands through his hair, "I've seen him mad but just now. I'm not sure I know him." He bent forward then, placing his head down, hands on knees.

Peter said, "Look, I think we need to have more distance from your Dad right now. Don't you?"

"Uncle. Remember the little bomb you two just let off up there. UNCLE," he yelled.

"OK, uncle. Look Sam, just calm down mate. We are not the bad guys here! I'm no expert but I don't think he's 'quite right'. I've lived with violence but that was something different. I just feel we have to get going."

"Yes, you're right," Sam was thinking, *"Something's tipped him over the edge this time. He is always a bit tense but this is different."*

"Sam." It was Carla and she had moved up next to him. "Sam. Do you want to come with us? We can't stay any longer in Adelaide. We have plans and we will need to stick to them." Carla agreed with Peter, they needed distance. "We're travelling back to Ballarat today. We'd understand if you don't want to go away. Obviously I don't know anything about your life or what you do but we'd love to have you come with us."

"Great idea, Carla. Definitely, please Sam. We have been looking for you for the past five days and it would be great to clear all this confusion up, mate."

"Let me think." And all three went quiet. Just then it started to rain and although not heavily it was enough, with the wind that was accompanying it, to make Carla hug herself and suggest they at least get in the car whilst they decided what to do. "Besides Thomas may be trying to find you, Sam," and to herself she added, *"or me!"*

All three were in the station wagon now and Sam began, "What about my car? I don't think I should go back home just yet." Sam was acutely aware that Thomas was wanting to know about why he was back but with him in the mood he was, he was scared.

"Does Thomas have a spare key?" it was Carla who spoke, and Sam nodded. "Then leave it here. Text him where it is and that you'll be in contact soon and chuck your bag in our car. Look, no pressure. Your choice."

Sam was so conflicted, *"I don't know these people, but I want to know their story, or is it my story? Dad will be even more upset if I just go. Hell, it was amazing he let me go to Port Vincent. No, there's some truth here I need to know and if these people aren't staying then I have to go. Stuff Dad, no, that's not fair. Oh my head."* His thoughts were racing but the one thing he did know as sure as anything was – he was scared. Scared like he had never been before in his life. Earlier this morning he was a bit worried about how he was going to make his father understand why he had left the pub in the lurch – now though, there was that problem to conquer and an even greater one – the possibility he was going to travel to Ballarat with a person who claimed to be his mother, his dead mother! And some bloke, hell, who knows where he fits in. But Dad knew her, admitted as much so he had to know. "What a bloody mess."

"Sam, Carla." It was Peter again, "We need to decide and decide quickly. I don't feel good being here."

"You're right, Peter," and turning to Sam she said, "Well Sam?"

"Okay. I'll get my bag and lock the car. I'll text him on the way."

"Let's go," said Peter with an overt sigh of relief.

Peter threw his mobile phone to Carla as they pulled out of the car park and said, "Give Elly a call, will you. I said we'd call half an hour out and she said she'd be at the pickup point. We are much earlier than we said so I hope she can be there." Sam was curious as to who they were picking up but he was too tired and distracted to bother asking.

The three of them travelled in silence until Peter pulled over outside Delvo's and Elly jumped in with a small backpack.

Elly was looking cleanly dressed. Hair tied back and lots of make-up. She seemed very happy with herself and was talking ten to the dozen upon getting into the car. "Hi. What's happening? Who are you?" staring at Sam.

"Elly. This is Sam and he will be travelling with us back to Ballarat. Sam, Elly."

"Hi," they said in unison.

Carla turned fully to the back of the car as Peter pulled out from the curb and joined the afternoon traffic. She stared at Elly, saying, "Have you taken something? This trip was contingent on you stopping the drugs, Elly."

"I did. My dealer came by just as I was getting my stuff and invited me over for some food and offered 'one more for the road,' I couldn't pass that by, could I?" staring defiantly at Carla.

"Don't mess this up, Elly. You told me about an aunt and I suspect your aunt doesn't want drugs in her home. If that's where you are heading."

"Yeah, yeah, I will go there first. Check it out. Jenny said she might help. Lives in Croydon or Ringwood or Bayswater. Can't remember. It will come to me. Okay, I

277

haven't got any more. Let me enjoy this last hit," and she closed her eyes and began jiggling in the seat and waving her hands in the air and singing.

Sam slowly slid closer to his door, thinking, *"This is great, a junkie as well as two strangers. I must be mad."*

Peter turned the radio up to block out Elly's singing and Carla turned back to the front. All of them revelled in their own preoccupations.

Every now and again Elly would sit up, move forward leaning over the front seat and say something that no one understood. Carla was thinking, *"Like a word, salad, yep, off her tree, jabbering away,"* and as quickly as she would sit forward she'd flop back and mumble away to herself again.

They had been travelling about two hours when Elly's behaviour became very erratic. Her gesturing was getting more pronounced and she started yelling, "I need a pee, I need to get out, I can't stay in this bloody car." At one point she grabbed Peter by the shoulder and made him swerve. "For fuck's sake, you stupid little bitch, we almost had a head on." Carla had grabbed the dashboard and was flung right and left in her seat. "Shit, lucky the seatbelt held," she screamed glaring at Elly.

"Settle down," Sam yelled, trying to get her to sit back in her seat but she would not be appeased.

"Peter, you better pull over at the next safe spot. She's probably starting to come down and being cooped up isn't going to help. Besides you need a break too."

"Okay," and Sam piped up, "Yes, I need to get away from her and stretch."

Elly didn't react, she was beginning to undo her jeans.

"Peter, hurry mate or she'll piss in the car."

As luck would happen he noticed a truck parking place on their right and he slowed quickly and drove into the area, stopping the car about 300 metres from the main road. Elly bounced out and without even stopping to look for privacy dropped her pants and urinated at the side of the car.

"Bloody hell? Skanky cow!" Sam murmured as he diverted his eyes and got out of the car himself.

"Sorry Sam. I'll explain everything," said Carla. She thought, *"this poor boy, what must he be thinking."*

Once out of the car Peter was saying, "Now what? I think this is going to be bad." He was struggling to contain his anger. His legs felt like jelly after nearly hitting that car back on the road and he worried that the people in that car may have called 000 and reported a car driving erratically. The police were the last thing they needed.

"I'm so sorry. I seem to keep making mistake after mistake." Carla sat on a log and stared in the direction of Elly who was now simply pacing up and down around a large, half-dying gum tree that looked like it would drop nearly all its limbs given a strong wind. "Poor thing. It's so dry these days. It takes a toll on the trees." Carla knew she was distracted and had no rational thoughts for what she needed to do. The situation was impossible and it was, again, her fault.

"Well people. Now what? Ideas, clues," and Peter told them of his concerns about the police.

But before anyone could answer Carla jumped up and called, "Elly where are you going?"

"Get stuffed, you stupid cow. I need to score and unless that dumb arse," pointing widely between Sam and Peter, "is driving me back I'm out of here."

"Elly, you can't walk back to Adelaide. Come back here."

But Elly kept walking.

"Shit, just what we need; a withdrawing junkie out here in the middle of nowhere. Whose great idea was this?" Sam demanded of Carla and Peter

"It was mine and I'm sorry I didn't think it through. I just thought I could help. Dumb, dumb, dumb."

'Yeah," interrupted Sam and with an exaggerated sarcastic tone said, "You just thought, hey, since I want to 'help' I will collect a few no hopers along the way. Better the odds. Might 'help' one of them if I can't help them all! Oh Jesus, this sucks."

"No, Sam." She was serious and very determined to have him understand. "I had given up hope of finding you and I suppose, for some reason or other, I thought, I haven't bothered to help anyone in the past and this girl needed help. Look, Peter and I had discussed it. We were prepared to travel with you if you were withdrawing and had wanted to come with us."

Sam gaped wide eyed, shook his head like he was trying to move a blockage, "You what, what are you talking about? Me withdrawing, from what? Why the hell would you say that?" and he took a large step close to her, anger clearly on his face.

"Sam," yelled Peter, "step back from her. Calm down. Listen, we have looked for you over the past week because Thomas told us he hadn't seen you for two years and that you were probably a drug addict and in prison. As we looked we came across Elly and Carla thought she could help her and Elly wanted help. Or at least said she did. That's why we decided it was time to leave, finding you was impossible. We turned up at your place this morning to have one more shot at Thomas. At least see if he would tell her," and he pointed to Carla, "something she could go on with, to narrow the search to find you! And if he wouldn't, well at least she'd have known she tried." He ran his hands through his hair. "Mate, she has been very angry at Thomas because she believed he had abandoned you two years ago. That he hadn't tried to help you and your drug problem. She felt it was her fault. But then, you pulled up. She"... now pointing at Elly, who had stopped pacing and was sitting quietly under the tree again and not looking at all as if she was heading back to the road. "She IS a big mistake but we need to think of where to go from here? I know you don't know us but we don't know you. Look you might go into withdrawal for all we know too. None of us know what to expect but we are here in the middle of nowhere," and he stopped abruptly. Sam was laughing, laughing loud and Elly had looked up and she was laughing too and Carla could feel a hysterical laugh burbling up from her also.

Still laughing Sam said, "That's precious. Do I look like a drug addict?"

"Well," twisting his lip in a slight sneer, "no, but that's what we were told."

Carla piped up then, "Look guys, there is so much we need to talk about and yes I was probably stupid but we still need to figure out what we do now. Should we try to get her back?"

Both men said together, "No idea."

"Okay," looking at her watch, "it's just after three, why don't we get back in the car and drive on? See how things pan out. Elly looks a bit calmer now."

Elly had stood up and was walking over to them. "Sorry everyone, went a bit crazy. More panic about not having anything than withdrawal. No panic now. Back to normal," and she smiled at them all.

"Okay, let's get going. Carla, you drive."

Chapter 13

They hadn't gotten too far down the road when Elly's behaviour became erratic again. Her mood seemed to be swinging from passive to irritable in short periods of time with the slightest thing setting her off. The song of Melissa Etheridge set her off in screaming out, 'Does he love you like I do do do, stimulate you, oh yeah!' and being very suggestive to Peter who was in the back seat with her. "Back off, Elly." Then minutes later she would be tearful and then the Green day song sparked her up with her calling out, "The best days of my life. The best days of my life," before bursting into tears again.

"I can't take this, Carla," Peter called from the back. "Turn the bloody radio off. Look, I think we need to get off the road and camp the night. Let this cow settle. Or let me out and I'll hitch a ride with normal people."

Carla had seen the sign to Keith as the next town and was thinking it might to OK to go to the caravan park that they had spotted on the way to Adelaide but Peter said he thought that was a bad idea because of Elly's unpredictable behaviour. Just then Carla spotted the sign to Mount Monster on the right and indicated right without asking what anyone thought and, strangely enough, no one questioned her. Fifteen minutes down the road she turned right onto a corrugated dirt road and then left at the sign indicating the conservation park. The little road was flanked by spindly bushes both sides and then it opened out to the Mount Monster car park. Carla slowed down but didn't feel this was the best place. "Not sure we should camp here. Obviously it is where people camp but I'd rather have a more secluded place. If you all know what I mean." No one spoke.

She continued on the one-way track and just as she was beginning to think they may well have to go back to the car park camping area Peter called, "You found the perfect place," and Sam and Carla looked where he was pointing and there was a beautiful body of water set into a hill cutting. There was sparse vegetation surrounding the water which helped with them deciding on the best place to pitch the tents. As an aside comment Sam noted, "Doesn't matter where you go there is always graffiti, hey," and they turned seeing spray painting on the rocks identifying who had been there. "I've seen more than that,' it was Elly. She had gotten out of the car and was heading down to the water. Peter shook his head at her in bewilderment but said nothing. Carla said, "I have no idea what that means."

Peter added, "Alright. Let's set up here. It's perfect, No one around and we can get just try to chill. We have all had one hell of a day and I am tired out." Looking about they spotted a flattish piece of land to their right which was protected from the wind.

"This is great, Peter. OK, Sam. Would you like to drive back to Keith and get some supplies?"

"Sure. Or do you want me to help here?" secretly hoping they said no because apart from one school camp he had never been camping or put up tents.

"No. Peter and I can do this. I'll make a list for you though. What do we want for dinner?"

"Anything is fine with me, probably just a barbie and drinks, I sure need one."

With the list made Sam set off. Elly had wandered back to the car and grabbed her bag. She then mumbled something that Carla missed before taking off on foot in the direction of the bush on the other side of the old granite quarry. Carla was about to call her back but Peter put a hand on her arm and said, "Let her go. She won't go far, I'm sure and beside she can't get into any trouble out here. Come on, let's set up camp before it gets dark."

Carla and Peter worked in virtual silence and Carla felt the calmest she had for some time. She gave the smaller tent to Peter to put up for him and Sam whilst she had the bigger tent for herself and Elly. "I think whist she is still unpredictable I would prefer to have the bigger tent," and Peter had agreed.

Carla's tent was a sturdy, one central post tent and only needed sixteen pegs and it was up in no time. Peter's tent was a double room dome tent and she ended up having to help him with threading of the poles and getting the fly on properly. Using up energy was therapeutic for them both. The camp was looking good now and they started to collect some firewood and organise a place to prepare food.

Sam was back within the hour, armed with beer, champagne, red wine, 2 bags of ice, sausages, potatoes, silver foil and nibblies. "A smorgasbord," he said and smiled. Carla noted how like Roger he was at that very moment and it took her breath away.

"Fantastic, I'm starved," she said.

Knowing that Elly couldn't go too far no-one bothered to look for her but as the sun fell completely away they were getting a little worried and doubted their decision to leave her alone for as long as they had. Just as Carla got up and was saying, "I'll grab the torch and go and see if I can find her," she came into the camp area. She looked terrible and Carla rushed to her. "Elly, you had us worried. Come over here to the fire, we are about to cook, so good timing." She took Elly's hand to direct her to the fireside. "You feel cold. I'll get you a coat."

Elly allowed herself to be led to the fire and put on the proffered coat. Her makeup was running and she had obvious scratches up her legs and arms and a small gash under her right eye.

Peter went to say something but Carla nodded her head, indicating she wanted her to be left alone.

Sam said, "I'll put the billy on, coffee or tea?"

"I might have a beer, actually," said Peter and went to the Esky.

"Yeah, I'll join you."

Carla said, "Me too," and to Elly, "What would you like to drink? Wine or beer? I think it might help knock the edge off whatever you are going through."

"No. I want to sleep."

"Alright, Elly dear," Carla crooned, "I've made your bed in the tent with me. Go lay down. It's a good idea. Do you want to eat first?" and Elly nodded her head, got up and went to the tent. Fully clothed except for the removal of her boots she got into the sleeping bag and was not seen again until the next morning.

"Phew," said Carla, "that's a relief. I was getting very anxious there for a while."

"She'll be okay and she will probably sleep all tonight and tomorrow if we are lucky. She's been doing this shit for a while." It was Sam who had spoken.

"We can't know that, Sam, but I suspect you are right."

"I've seen and heard about this stuff, having worked in pubs for years and I've had mates who use too. Speed, or actually ice mostly these days. It's becoming a real problem and the violence associated with it is awful." He looked at them both then and added, "Yes, observed it but never, ever taken it. In fact, I don't smoke cigarettes and my only indulgence is alcohol. I'm a bit of a fitness nut if you really want to know." Peter was watching the snags fry and had placed the potatoes in earlier. "So what can we expect then, Sam?"

"Well, it varies of course from person to person but what I've seen and heard is they use for a few days nonstop and then crash, and there's all these changes in them. Unpredictable, violent, some even go completely mad, hallucinations, hearin' voices, suicidal. You can't tell really. I'm guessing with her, seeing her this afternoon whatever she had this arvo topped her up and now she's in comedown mode. The withdrawal phase can be the ugliest, so let's hope I am right when I say she'll sleep all night and with luck all day tomorrow."

"Well, she slept okay last night. We had her at our cabin and I didn't hear boo from her."

"Well, let's just see," and Sam took a plate of snags and a silver wrapped potato from Peter. "Smells good."

Carla was piling a couple of snags on her plate and getting some bread and without looking at Sam said, "I wonder why Thomas said that about you then. You know, that you were a drug addict and in prison?"

"I've been thinking about that and it's odd. Did he know you were coming?" Looking straight at Carla

"Well, no. But I did ring him and ask about you and basically that's when he told me not to come. Maybe he knew I would regardless."

"When was that?"

"Oh, four to five weeks ago, I think," looking at Peter, who nodded yes.

"Well, that's when I got asked to manage The Rock. I was to stay there for a couple of months but I couldn't cope and came back early. It's starting to make sense."

"Glad it is for you, mate," Peter said. "It's a bloody mystery to me."

Chapter 14

No one had said anything and yet each of them knew they were putting off the inevitable, the time they would have to talk… really talk to each other. They finished eating and sat comfortably enjoying their drinks and the sunset, which was deep red in colour and truly special. Carla called out when she saw the first star in the sky saying, "Star light, star bright, first star I see tonight, wish I may, wish I might, have this wish I wish tonight," and Peter said, "And what would that be?" and she shrugged and said, "You know," with a glint in her eye, "I cannot say or it won't come true," and they all gave a small chuckle.

"Okay then," Peter exclaimed, "time to break the ice."

And Sam quickly said, "Hey, mate. If you've got Ice, I'm not a fan, AND," in an exaggerated tone, "don't let little Miss E," pointing to the tent where Elly slept, "know about it!"

"Ha! Ha! A comedian in our midst. Did you think your son would turn out to be a comedian?"

"Sadly, I didn't know how he would turn out," and she turned and looked at Sam, the ice was broken.

"Okay, let's," a pause, "talk."

Sam went to the Esky and grabbed three stubbies and handed one to Carla and Peter. They opened them simultaneously and Sam chimed, "Well, here's to getting to know you both," and they clinked stubbies with a, "Cheers to that."

After several deep swallows Peter said, "So, who first?"

"I suppose I need to start." It was Carla.

Taking a big sigh, and with a shiver as the night air cooled her skin, she said, "I have gone over this in my mind once a year with regular monotony and then I have pushed it back to the recesses of my mind for another year. I am not proud of decisions I made and I will try not to make excuses. You must also understand there are parts that I simply don't have answers to – things just happened," and she fiddled with her stubby and then took another swallow.

Both Peter and Sam were looking at her and saying nothing.

"Sam, I met your father when I was nineteen. I was best friends with Susan Westmead, Peter's mother. We had been friends since school. That's the connection to Peter. Anyway. Susan married Liam Westmead and not long after I married your dad, Roger, Roger Nelson. Susan got pregnant with Peter and three years later I had you. It was the happiest time of our lives and we all socialized and helped each other out all the time. When you were ten months old your dad was killed in a hit run accident. They never found the person who did it. It was awful, he was a beautiful man and he loved you dearly." She stopped talking for a while and then continued, "I fell to pieces." Looking up at Sam she wanted him to understand the depth of her loss, his loss. "Sam, you can't imagine, one minute you are saying, 'Bye, I love you', as your husband, your best friend, your confidante, as he leaves for work. I'm standing there with you, our gorgeous boy, on my hip, waving. I'm not saying to myself, 'Great knowing you'. No, I am thinking, 'what's for dinner'? And 'Oh great, our favourite show's on tonight. I'll get Sam down after dinner and we can curl up on the couch together. They are the thoughts flooding through your head when someone leaves for work, Sam," and again the pleading in her voice. "Sam, you never consider that that is the last time you will see that person." Another gulp of beer, "My mother, your grandmother, she's dead now, but she was not a well woman and was not able to help me and look after you. Susan came every day and took you to her house, cared for you and brought you home in the evening and I did my best to get through the nights. The next day she was on the doorstep again gathering your bag for the day and taking you off. I was supposed to get better, move on, but I couldn't or I wouldn't. I don't know." With imploring eyes she looked to Peter, "Your mum was such a good person," and she dropped her head, placed her stubby down and reached to the fire with both hands, rubbing them together. She was beginning to feel really cold now.

Settling back again she calmly stated, "Three weeks later Susan was murdered."

"What the fuck… no way, why… how? Shit mate," Sam's words stumbled out and then he shut up. He didn't know what to say or where to look. He felt very uncomfortable.

"It's OK, Sam." To Carla he said, "Go on."

"She had done her best and in the end I was taken to hospital. Susan still looked after you. I think she was getting a little annoyed as I was seemingly getting worse not better and I had been stubborn and was refusing help. I was told of the murder the day I was being discharged, I was placed in the psych unit after that and was there for seven weeks. I distinctly remember feeling like I was being enveloped in a black cloud and it was suffocating."

"So who killed his mum? Susan. Why?" Sam was leaning in towards Carla now. He stood quickly and said, "Hold that thought, I need another drink. Anyone else?" Carla looked at her beer and declined, thinking, "*I will once I get through this though.*"

Sam returned to the fire and, handing Peter another beer, sat.

Carla said, "Sam, believe me. We don't know who or why Susan was killed. I believe the case is still open but there have never been any leads. Not one. She had no enemies. Nothing."

"This is unbelievable."

Peter spoke then. "I remember a bit of that morning. I remember a man, flowers, mum shouting, a loud bang, mum lying down and blood. Even at my age I knew what blood was. Then someone from next door came and took you and me to their house." Peter was staring into the fire as he brought the memories of his last look of his mother to the surface.

The three of them sat quietly. Sam wanted to speak but could feel it wasn't the right time to ask questions and he got up and added wood to the fire, sending sparks into the air. "The police said that it was clear from the little evidence they did have, and from what the neighbours heard from their living room, that Susan was protecting you both. She apparently shouted you will never touch these children and then there was a loud bang. Unfortunately the neighbour was elderly and by the time he got outside he only saw the back of what he thought was a flower delivery van. No number plates, no ID of the driver. It was useless. He then rushed to the house and saw Susan in the hallway injured or dead, he didn't know. But he was in a dilemma, go back to his house to ring the police or get you both away. He chose to get you both out of the house so by the time the police were alerted the trail was cold. I ask myself why? Susan was a beautiful, loving, caring family woman who would never hurt a hair on anyone's head. It was so wrong." She thought of the Forrest Gump movie just then and pondered, "*If life is described as a box of chocolates then why had someone as wonderful as Susan had a bad batch?*" Then, shaking her head realised that Sam was speaking.

"What did the police say then?" Sam was getting a little angry and Carla could hear it in his voice.

"The police surmised it was a bungled robbery attempt."

Peter said, "It's strange, though. Why did mum say you won't get these children? I've been thinking about this, Carla, since you told me this last month. It seems to me that we had something to do with this."

"You two! How, what, why?" Her voice stuccoed when she spoke those questions because she had mused on that question in the past. '*Why had the*

gunman wanted the children? What was he thinking?
And she had gone around and around in circles in her
mind until she couldn't think at all. To Peter and Sam
she said, "I suppose we will never understand what
transpired that morning." She heard within herself a
voice that was resigned to the unknown, and a mind that
did not want to dwell on a question that no one could
ever answer. Knowing why it happened would still not
satisfy her, still not make a semblance of sense.

Sam stood again, it was totally dark now except for
the area around the camp fire. "I have to have a pee,"
and he wondered off to the other side of the station
wagon where there were a few spindly gums.

Peter said he was up for another drink and Carla
decided it called for something stronger. She was
drained and exhausted. She got up and pulled out, "A
nightcap? Irish whiskey, anyone?"

"Whoa, hell yeah. You kept that hidden," laughed
Peter. "I could have done with that as a warmer upper
after all our failed attempts traipsing the streets of
Adelaide, Carla," and although she couldn't see his face
very well she felt his warm smile.

"Hmm, yes. I thought if we found Sam it would be
the time. And look," raising the bottle in the air and
pointing in the direction of where Sam had gone, "we
did it. I don't know how to thank you, Peter."

They didn't see Sam until he was well within the fire
light. "Getting quite cold and dark about." He
commented, "Did I hear Irish whiskey? Now you're
talking." So three Irish whiskeys were poured. "This
smoke is bad," Carla commented, waving her hands
frantically about, "I will stink of smoke."

"Point your little finger at the smoke like this," and Sam pointed his right hand little finger to the fire and waited. "See, it's not coming over here. Magic. An old granddad trick."

Carla laughed and gave it a try. "Look, it's working," and Sam laughed and then turned to Peter.

"Geez Peter. How did your family cope?"

"It was tough. Dad took it hard and it's not been easy. But let's not talk about me now, there's plenty of me time over the next day or so. To be honest it's been a hell of a day, so I might finish this," raising his glass, "And hit the fart sack. Leave you two to chat."

Carla and Sam looked at each other and both agreed that they were tired too and it was best to call it a night. "There is so much water under the bridge we can never cover it all in an evening anyway," Sam said.

Chapter 15

Thomas was left standing in the driveway looking at the gun in his hand and staring at the back of Sam's car. If any of the neighbours had been watching they would have seen Thomas slowly put the gun back into his jacket pocket and turn, face livid red, and march stiffly to his front door which was swinging open in the slight breeze. They would have known to keep well away. They would have sensed deep anguish and distress and understood that nothing good was going to follow.

Thomas was beside himself with worry. *"Sam, how can you ever understand what you are doing? What we have done to look after you?"* His head was pounding and his thoughts were loose and he was struggling to grasp a single thought and process it. From the moment Sam was born Thomas had been consumed with a deep and penetrating need to protect him. He understood that his brother William was there and guiding him and that between the two of them they had failed to protect themselves from the bus and the 'man' but they would never fail to protect their nephew. That was never an option. Thomas remembered the first time he had gone to the hospital, three days after Samuel was born, only to see his younger brother gurgling over the child, swinging him in his arms, making silly noises and placing the child in the little hospital cot and then turning his attention to Carla. Neither of them were looking at the child, anyone could have taken it. He, Thomas, considered it. William considered it. But just as he moved inside the doorway of the ward Roger saw him. "Thomas, come in and meet Samuel William Nelson, or Sam to us all," his voice was so bright and the pride was undeniable. He grabbed Thomas's hand and dragged him towards the cot but Thomas hadn't been able to help himself. "You should be more careful leaving Samuel unattended, Roger, and you, Carla. You must know from the news that 'things' happen to children."

"Oh! Thomas. Don't be so dramatic. Sam's here in the room. Nothing can harm him," and she had grabbed Roger's hand and again their focus was away from the baby.

"Just trust me. Both of you. You must be careful." He remembered going over to the cot and picking Samuel up and holding him very close. Upon touch he was gripped by a strong tightening of the chest and what he described to himself as an electric zap, that although it only lasted a few seconds, coursed through his body like a jolt of lightning and the bond was sealed. The two of them were more than life, more than, uncle, more than any words could ever describe. Thomas remembered trying to articulate what had just occurred but he could not. Had they seen it? Did they already know? He had waited, there in the hospital room with Carla in the bed, Roger at her side and he with the child in his arms but they said nothing. They had not understood and that was a problem. A big problem.

This is where Thomas's thoughts were as he tried to settle his breathing and think. He had helped them protect their child, a child they never appreciated with their lackadaisical manner. They were too focused on themselves. He supposed it was a sign of the times but he would be vigilant and be ready to act if there was any hint that the child was in danger. It was his duty. Hadn't he done what he and William needed and wanted? Hadn't they saved Samuel from the harms of the world? And now! What? *"I need to control myself"* but he was struggling. He was beside himself, feeling almost paralysed. Then he had a flashback to the day he saw William hit by the bus, the man, the pain that happens when you aren't looked after. How adults let you down. He, Thomas, had not cared for Samuel all these years to sit back and let him be drawn to danger now. Aloud he said, as he walked to his kitchen, "No Carla, you are not fit. You know that," and as an aside he mumbled, "Who was that man with her?"

At the kitchen sink he ran the cold water tap and splashed water all over his head and neck. He was talking more rapidly now but his sense of paralysis was lifting. *"I understand,"* and *"Yes I will think of a plan."* "Don't be stupid," he shouted, "I have looked after him all this time and I will again. Yes, William, I know he doesn't realise the danger. I can fix it," and on and on his one sided conversation went until he left the kitchen saying, "If you would just shut up I could think." Silence ensued as he made his way upstairs to his bedroom and changed his wet clothes. "Thank you."

William's voice had lived with him forever and Thomas had learnt it was louder and stronger whenever he, Thomas, felt weak or troubled and William always helped, put him on the right path. He loved his brother dearly and he knew he would help now but as Thomas had gotten older he had become more and more exhausted with the chatter, the mutterings and directives. There had been times in his life when he was unable to go against William's wishes even though he thought them radical and unnecessary and yet, he mused, in the end things worked out for the best.

Thomas now lay prone on his bed and thought what he could do and William was there, adding his ideas. Thomas hadn't realised but he had in fact fallen asleep and it was now 3.30 pm. He wondered why no one from the office had called him and asked if he was alright and when he rang in his receptionist said, "Yes, Mr Nelson, yes, you told us you would be out of the office all day today. No, there are no messages for you. Will you be in tomorrow?" and Thomas had replied in a bewildered and distracted way, "Yes, Mary, yes, usual time." After hanging up the phone he noted to himself that he had in fact, over the past fortnight, lost chunks of time. He certainly had no recollection of phoning work.

Thomas made himself a toasted sandwich having eaten nothing since six am this morning and he began to feel better, less light-headed, clearer in thought. His problem was simply, Sam must come home, Sam cannot survive on his own and Sam cannot stay with those people. He refused to recognize Carla as a relative or mother. He rationalized that she had signed him over and the deal sealed, the cooling off period over. Thomas allowed himself a smile at that reference to the real estate business. "Ha," he said aloud.

He went to the hallway and picked up the phone. Geoff answered after three rings, "Cumberland. Geoff speaking."

"Hello Geoff, I was wondering if Scott was there."

"Yes, in the bar getting ready for the afterhours drinkers. Why?" he added suspiciously.

"No reason. When does he knock off?"

"Not till 11pm on a Tuesday."

"Any chance of getting in a casual to fill his shift tonight? I need to talk to him as soon as possible."

"Do I have a choice, Thomas?"

"No." Then as an afterthought he added, "Geoff, it's very important."

"Yeah, well everything is important to you, Thomas, at this rate I'll have no employees if you keep asking for them. First Sam, and now Scott. Will he be gone for long?"

"Not sure. Hope not. Just ask him to come to my house now and I'll talk to him and let you know. Okay?"

Then Geoff quickly added, "Hey, what's up with Sam, anyway? Just up and left the Rock. Is he back home, does he want Scott's shift?"

Geoff heard 'no' and then a buzz of the phone. Cut off.

With a sigh of resignation he hung up and went to the bar to speak with Scott.

Scott Asher was thirty-two and Geoff's younger sister's son. Scott had been a troubled boy from primary school age and adulthood hadn't done anything to quash his impulsive nature. He was one of those people who acted before they thought and it had gotten him into trouble all his life. He had been expelled from school at the age of fifteen for repeatedly flaunting the rules and when he arrived at school one afternoon intoxicated that was the last straw. "Mrs Asher, we've done all we can but we can no longer tolerate Scott's overt disobedience of the school rules and it is not fair on the other students." June Asher had pleaded with them to give her son another go but they refused.

"I'm sorry, we've done all we can. We suggest you see a child and adolescent counsellor or a youth drug and alcohol counsellor, Mrs Asher." The principal knew however that any form of help would probably never happen given the poverty of the family.

Scott then spent time roaming the streets by day and getting into trouble by night, His mother had no control and it was a mystery to Geoff how it was that she had raised four other sons basically on her own who had grown to be decent chaps, yet Scott was so different. He had tried to help, be a father figure for Scott, but just when he would think he had achieved a breakthrough with the lad he would somehow sabotage his own efforts and trouble would be back at his door. "It just doesn't make sense to me." He had told his sister the last time Scott went to prison, "Why does he bring this on himself? When you actually sit down and talk to him he's not a bad guy. Seems he just can't keep out of trouble."

"I know, Geoff. I just despair. And I give up. This time he's gone too far. Broke into Al's house and stole all his coin collections and all the garden equipment. His own brother, Geoff. How could he? Bloody drugs, it's the ice these days," and she had cried.

"You did all you could, sis," and he hugged her.

Scott had served a few months in youth detention and two adult imprisonments, all for drug-related crimes such as possession and cultivation of cannabis, receiving stolen goods, multiple traffic offences and exceeding the prescribed concentration of alcohol. His latest sentence was two years with a fourteen month minimum, the longest yet, and the judge had told him if he didn't stop behaving like this the next sentence could see him in for five years. Scott had finally been given a scare. He had said to June in a phone conversation from prison, "This is hell, mum, that's it, I am not going back to this shit hole again. It's got to stop," and June Asher had smiled and thought, "Yes, at last perhaps he can settle."

Scott had been thirty then and upon his release he came to live with Geoff in Adelaide, where he was guaranteed a job and a chance to get his life on track.

To all intents and purposes he had done that over the past eight months. He was complying with his parole order, he worked his shifts, paid his bills and apart from coming to work a couple of times stoned he was going well. He hadn't made many friends and Geoff thought that was probably a blessing in disguise. "Fewer people to influence him," he told his sister, and she'd agreed.

Now Geoff was worried. He was pretty sure this had something to do with the fact that Sam had left The Rock and was home or at least on his way home. Geoff had been informed about three hours earlier by Eva, the waitress at the pub. She'd rung and simply stated Sam had left and wasn't coming back and what did he want to do? He had told her not to worry and it was only a temporary position and did she know someone who might be able to step in at short notice? And she had said she did. "Good, go ahead and get them on board. We will worry about anything else later," and hung up. Staring at the receiver he was thinking, *"I'd like to wring Sam and Thomas's necks. What a carry on. They need to leave me out of their crap."* Geoff went out to the bar and Scott was standing staring at the wine glasses. "Hey there, Geoff. What's happening?" and without waiting for a reply added, "Just can't decide if the larger glasses should go from right to left or vice versa! What do you reckon?"

"Hmm, what about the larger glasses on both ends and meeting in the middle with the smallest; that way you don't have to walk as far."

"Not bad thinking, Unc," and he slapped him on his back exposing his well-tattooed forearm. "So what's on your mind?"

"Scott, let's have a drink and sit down."

"Okay, this seems serious. What have I done? Or not done?"

"No. NO, it's nothing like that, we just need to talk."

Scott shrugged and poured himself a beer and Geoff a bourbon and coke. Carrying them over to the table he placed the drink in front of Geoff and said, "Just the way you like it, sir," and grinned from ear to ear. Geoff looked at his handsome, boyish face and thought, "What a shame he has had so much trouble. He really is a nice bloke."

Both took a gulp of their respective drinks and Geoff took a big breath in and said, "You know Thomas Nelson?"

"Yeah he kind of owns the pub with you. Yeah. I met him when I got out. You told me he likes to meet the people who are going to be working at the bar and around his son."

"Yes, that's him. Well he has asked to speak with you. I don't know what it is about but I think it could have something to do with Sam," and he proceeded to tell Scott briefly about why Sam had really been sent to The Rock pub. "I could be wrong but anything to do with Sam evokes a strong reaction from Thomas. Always has."

"No worries, I'll see what he wants."

"Scott. I want you to listen to me. If you don't like what he is saying tell him no. You are doing really well this time around and me, and your mum, are really proud of you. I don't want Thomas to bugger this up for you."

"Don't worry. I'll hear what he has to say. Can't be that bad? Right! Anyway I don't want you to get into any shit."

"Scott," Geoff almost shouted his name. "That is my point. It is not about me. I can handle Thomas. He's pulled in all his tickets on me long ago. I stay on here 'cos I've got nowhere else and Thomas and I have an unspoken understanding. We go way back. But having said that, he is an odd one, Scott, and I don't want you messed up in anything dicky. You hear? Listen to him and if you're not sure say you'll think about it and come back here and we will decide if it is in *your* interest and not just Thomas's. Say you'll do that, Scott. For your mum's sake, mate." Geoff was more worried as he sensed that Scott did not understand his cautionary warnings.

Scott downed his beer and said, "I hear Geoff, will do. When does he want to see me?"

"Now." In a soft defeatist tone, "You know the address?"

"Yep. Can't forget that fancy house."

Scott gathered his smokes, helmet and keys and headed for the back entrance where he had parked his scooter. He had bought it not long after getting out. It was cheap to buy and run and he liked pottering about on it on his days off. He had a smoke before donning the helmet and heading to Thomas's home.

Chapter 16

Scott pulled up at Thomas's half an hour later. He removed the helmet and left it on the bike, running up the steps two at a time, hitting the doorbell without breaking stride.

Thomas opened the door almost immediately and exclaimed, "Scott. Thank you for coming so quickly. Please come in." Thomas had put the phone down from talking to Geoff earlier and decided he needed to freshen up. He had showered again and put on a suit and so when he answered the door Scott's first impression was, *"Hell, he's going out to a ball. Do normal people sit at home dressed like that?"* He didn't have time to think further on it because Thomas was saying, "Please come in, can I get you a drink, tea, coffee, something stronger?"

Scott said, "Oh, yeah, wouldn't say no to a whiskey, thanks." He thought asking for whiskey would show he was a bit more refined than just a beer drinker, which of course, was what he really was.

"Whiskey it is," chimed Thomas. "Let's go into the study," and he turned and walked into the study on the right with Scott walking behind.

Thomas poured them both a whiskey on the rocks and told Scott where to sit. They sat opposite each other. Scott was feeling nervous now and Geoff's words were ringing in his ears. *"Hear what he wants to say and then tell him you will think about it."* He stared at his glass and then piped up, "Well, nice place," hoping to break the ice.

"Oh thanks, yes," Thomas said absently and then added, "Now Scott I've asked you here to put a business proposal to you. You know my son, Sam," and Scott nodded. Thomas continued, "He has been coerced into leaving Adelaide with a man and a woman." Scott looked up at Thomas,

"No kidding."

"Yes. And I want him to come back. The woman is filling his head with nonsense about being his mother and he is believing it, even though it is absurd."

"Wow. That's weird. Sam seemed too earthy. Rational."

"Yes, I thought so too but I haven't been able to talk to him and so he is being fed lies. Scott, I want you to persuade him to come back."

Scott jumped up. "Me. Why me? Why don't you?"

Thomas felt a strong pang of anger at Scott's jumping up and questioning him. He took a breath and said very measuredly, "Because he will not listen to me just now. He will listen to a work mate, a colleague. I am sure when you tell him I am happy to have mediation with these people he will come home."

"Medi what? Look, I'm not that good with big words, Mr Nelson. So you think Sam will listen to me. I think you're crazy."

Thomas was beginning to feel this was wrong but it was too late now, he had played his hand. Scott saw he was strained and seemed to be distracted and he said, "Look what if?" and then he seemed to rethink what he was going to say and said instead, "Can I have a beer?"

Thomas looked at Scott and stood, going over to the mini bar and getting out a Crown Lager. Handing it to him he said, "I am very serious, Scott, and I think you can help me. I will pay you well to find Sam and bring him home."

At the words pay well Scott lost all defensive thoughts and was now listening, and Thomas had noticed the shift immediately. *"Ha,"* he said to himself, *"Money opens the way."*

"Sit down Scott, and let me tell you my plan and if you don't like it, fine. Okay?"

"Okay." He was all ears now and the distrust and awkwardness he felt only a few minutes ago had dissipated.

"I will pay you $10,000 now and $10,000 when Sam is home."

Scott's mind was reeling. *"Shit, $20,000, that's amazing. No way I can say no to this. But play it cool Scott."*

"Well, that sounds fair to me Thomas, um sorry, Mr Nelson." He had blurted this out before he could temper his words or listen to his own counsel. It was out his mouth in a second and it was a done deal.

"Thank you, Scott. Now what type of car do you have?"

"I don't have a car. I have a scooter, it can take a pillion though." He was aware he was talking quickly. He wanted this job now.

Thomas held up his hand. "Don't worry, I will give you a car. In fact, if you bring Sam back within the week, you can have the car too. How's that sound, Scott?" Thomas was smiling inside for the first time since Carla had phoned four, or was it five, weeks ago. He had lost track. He knew Scott was hooked and he'd do anything for him now.

"Scott, I don't want Sam hurt but I am going to give you a gun to take just in case you need to scare off the woman and man he is travelling with. Do you know how to use a gun, Scott?"

"Yes Mr Nelson. No worries." Scott was not a violent man but he had, on occasions, toted a gun for protection and had injured a man in self-defence when he was twenty-five. He was never charged with the crime. It had sickened him but it was over drugs and he knew it was either shoot the bastard or be shot himself.

"Alright then, it's set," Thomas said. "I want you on the road now."

"What time did they leave?"

"Around midday some time," and looking at his watch he said, "They are at least six hours ahead of you which means if they are travelling straight through to Ballarat they would already be close. I am hoping they will do an overnight stay which will give you time to catch up to them. I think it will be easier to get to Sam on the road than once they are at their house. But either way you need to get going," and to add to the urgency he raised his voice claiming, "Now," and he handed Scott a piece of paper with Carla's home address.

"OK. I'll just stop and get some clothes and supplies."

"No." Thomas butted in. "I have packed you a bag with everything you'll need. You are close to Sam's size so I think you'll be okay. There's food in an Esky and here," he reached into his coat pocket and produced a set of keys, "the keys to the car," and tossed them in the air for Scott to catch.

"Well, I better ring Geoff."

"No, I will let Geoff know what's happening. Please let's move."

"Okay."

Out on the drive Thomas pointed to a 2010 Ford Ute. "It's full of petrol. Clothes and food in the back. Here," and he handed Scott a mobile, "ring me when you find them and then keep me up to date. My number's set in there." Lastly he handed him his gun and a box with ammunition. "I am relying on you, Scott."

"You have thought of everything," as he jumped in the car. He was just pulling away when he stamped on the brakes, wound down the window and said, "Hey, what car are they driving?"

"Oh yes, a cream 1999 station wagon, a Mitsubishi I think."

Scott put his thumb up and drove out of the drive.

Part 5

Chapter 1

Scott was in a world of, *"You have got to be kidding me, this is such easy money, must have done something right."* "Well," he said aloud, "Now I just need to catch up to Sambo and bring the bugger home to daddy."

Scott had been travelling about two hours and it was getting close to eight o'clock. He'd been up early that morning and was beginning to feel tired. He decided to pull into Coonalpyn, a little township on the highway, and fill up with petrol, even though he hadn't even used a quarter of a tank yet, and get a pie, maybe some beer and some more smokes. He was also keen to by papers for a joint.

Having filled up, and complete with his supplies, he pulled back out on the highway and travelled roughly another hour listening to the pop music station but he was getting overwhelmed with sleep again.

He thought, *"No need to bust my arse. Like Nelson said, they are probably in Ballarat now, nice and cosy indoors and here I am buggered and needing a rest. He wants Sam back in a week so a week it is."* With that thought he determined to find a nice byway and settle in for the night.

Another twenty minutes and he came across a siding with public toilets and a picnic table. He parked the car and went to the back of the Ute to see what Thomas had packed. He was impressed, there was a swag and an Esky with ice and food and stuff to heat up beans and water.

Scott got busy setting up his camp via his headlights and soon had a fire made. He wasn't all that hungry, having eaten earlier, but he opened a pack of nuts that was in his pack. Cracking a beer and smoking a joint he felt very pleased with himself. By around ten pm he was bored with his own company and the rattle of traffic streaming by so he decided to get some sleep and get an early start.

Next morning he was up at dawn and wishing he had a shower to jump under. Instead he had to make the best of splashing his face with water. He couldn't be bothered relighting the fire and decided to grab breakfast along the way. Within fifteen minutes he was in the car and heading in Melbourne's direction.

At a town called Keith he stopped for breakfast, pulling in at the BP service station which advertised bacon and egg rolls and a coffee twenty-four hours a day. He parked and was just getting out when he noticed a cream 1999 Mitsubishi station wagon pull up and Sam and another bloke get out of the car. *"Shit, you're kidding me. What are the chances?"* He ducked back into the car for fear they would see him and waited.

After ten minutes Sam and Peter emerged from the service station with an armload of goods which Scott decided was their breakfast, along with four coffees. *"Hmm. Why four coffees?"* he thought. *"I was told there were three of them. Better be careful."*

He waited a full minute and then followed at a respectable distance. They turned west back up the highway but then under a kilometre turned left at another servo. The road was fairly straight with farm paddocks either side. Scott noticed a small but distinct hill in the foreground, orange-looking from the distance, and he mused that it was funny for a small hill in all this flat land. He then noticed the station wagon indicating right. He slowed, watched them till they were no longer in sight and then turned right himself on to a dirt road with corrugations. He imagined the dust would be huge if it were in summer but being winter and with overnight dew the road was fairly dust-free. Again he noted the indicator, this time left, and it disappeared from sight. Scott turned left and saw he was entering a conservation park. The track in was narrow and trees were either side. Scott was beginning to feel quite excited at the prospect of catching up even though he had no idea what he was going to say to Sam when he did eventually show his hand. After a short time he saw through the trees, as he drove slowly along, that the car ahead had stopped so he quickly pulled over, cutting the engine.

He got out of the car, careful not to slam the door, then turned back to the car and threw his mobile phone on the front dash. He didn't want it to ring whilst he was watching them. He noticed a number of rough tracks, all leading to where the car Sam had been driving was, and thought this must be a pretty frequented local spot. He was also thinking to himself that he was hungry, and wanted a coffee. He hadn't gone 200 metres when he saw the car and a couple of tents and decided to sit quietly and see if he could determine what they were doing.

Sam and Peter had pulled in and had taken the breakfast to the make-shift table. Carla was up, putting empty beer bottles into a bag and gathering other rubbish. "Hey, how'd you go?" she called, when she saw them.

"Good, is Elly up yet?"

"She's just gone to the loo and will be with us shortly."

"How is she this morning?" Sam asked.

"Still very temperamental and jittery."

Peter piped in, "I was right when I said to you, 'Don't get involved Carla it could be trouble' and she's trouble."

She heard the accusation in his tone and said, "I know Peter, but I just had to do something to help. She seemed so fragile and vulnerable."

And Peter thought, "*We've all been there.*"

Carla continued, "I think I was lucky to get a few hours' sleep. Can't wait for a coffee, guys."

When Carla had entered the tent Elly had woken and was totally disorientated. She was thrashing in her sleeping bag and screaming out. Carla tried to pacify her and tell her she was alright but she had lashed out, hitting her fully on the side of the head, making Carla fall into the tent wall and cry out herself.

Sam was then at the tent pulling the zipper up and trying to see what was happening but as soon as he pulled the flap back and went to step in saying, "What's happening?" Elly bolted out, pushing him to one side opposite Carla, who was still reeling from her head slapping. Peter was quick to react, grabbing Elly as she launched herself at him with eyes bulging as if being pursued by demons. He managed to grab her, somehow locking her arms in so she could no longer hit out, although he copped a couple of good kicks to the shins for his effort.

"Hold her," Sam called and Elly screamed "Help, leave me alone, please, don't," and other such demands. She was clearly distressed and tormented. "I think I frightened her." It was Carla and she was in front of Peter now. "She is really on the edge."

"God knows what these drugs do to people. She's still clearly withdrawing or whatever it is 'they' do."

"What are we going to do?" Peter said through gritted teeth, whilst he battled to contain the struggling Elly.

"Elly, it's Carla," then really quietly, "Elly, you are alright. No one is going to hurt you. Peter has hold of you and is looking after you." Then confirming, "Do you understand?" She waited and asked again, "Elly, do you understand?" and Peter felt, and Carla saw, her appear to get some recognition of who was there. Carla remained talking to her in a calm voice and finally she responded.

"I'm sorry," in a quiet, shaky voice. "Carla, Peter, I am okay, you can let me go," and slowly Peter relaxed his grip on her. He was thankful because he didn't think he could have held her much longer anyway.

Elly then slid to the ground, rocking backwards and forwards, sobbing and banging her arms to and fro across her body.

"Sam, get the fire going, it shouldn't take much, I can see some embers, and get the billy on."

"I'm sorry. I was so scared I didn't know where I was. I feel bad."

"It's okay. Don't worry. Are you okay to get off the ground and come to the fire? We don't want you to hurt yourself." Elly nodded weakly and Peter took her by the arm and helped her up. Once on her feet she ran into Carla's arms. "I'm cold."

"Here," and Peter handed her his jacket. All four of them had sat up then and although there was little conversation all were on edge, worrying if they could trust Elly not to 'flip out' again. Carla estimated it was about four o'clock before they had all settled back to sleep.

Chapter 2

Scott could just hear the conversation. He was wondering what would be the best way to approach this. At first he thought, wait till Sam is on his own and then just nab him but Sam was strong and he'd probably alert the others. So then he wondered if he could simply ring Sam on the mobile and explain the situation. He could say, 'Listen mate, come back with me and let your old man give me my money and the car and then I'm out of your hair and you can do as you please.' *"Yes"*, he thought, *"Sam would be reasonable to that idea."*

He went back to his Ute to get the phone but as soon as he had it in his hand he saw there was no reception. "Damn it," he exclaimed under his breath.

"Okay, next plan," and he smiled to himself. Scott was feeling like a real live private investigator and he was enjoying himself. The trouble was he didn't have a plan one, let alone a plan two or three for that matter. He jumped in his car and rolled a joint and sat and thought.

Elly had come back to camp and was looking worse than the night before, if that was possible, her hair was dishevelled, she was dirty from head to toe, what make-up was left was smeared on her face. She seemed shaky on her legs and she was sweating profusely.

"Are you hungry?" Sam asked, "Got an egg and bacon roll for you and a real coffee," and he stood up to let her sit by the fire that they had rekindled.

"Um, thanks. I feel like shit and my stomach aches." She took the proffered food and took a small bite but found it very hard to swallow. Elly looked around. "You've got to take me back. I can't handle this. I need to score, I'm not ready to go to my aunt's. It's too soon." Her voice was beginning to rise and they all could see they were going to be in for a long day.

Carla said, "Elly, you are through the worst of it. I promise. We can't take you back, it's not safe for Sam and there's no life for you back there."

"Shut up, you stupid bitch. You and all your 'let me help,' well guess what? You don't help," and she threw her food down on the ground and stormed off to the tent.

There was silence for a minute and then Sam said, "Anyone with any bright ideas?"

Peter said, "I could take her back and drop her somewhere and get back here say by the end of the day. That would work out well. You guys get 'quality time' and we get rid of her," with a nod back towards the tent.

But Carla said, "No Peter, that's not going to happen."

He turned on her, hands imploring and voice raised, slight anger to his tone. "Why is this so important to you? She's not family."

"No. She's not but she's young and needs our help. I can't turn my back on her."

Both men looked at each other as if having some silent knowledge that only they knew.

"Fine, play it your way. I'm going for a walk," and Peter left, heading back along the road deeper into the conservation park.

Scott watched Peter coming towards him. *"Shit, shit, shit,"* there was nothing he could do but sit there and hope this guy wasn't the nosey type and would keep to the road and not venture over to where he and the car were. As luck had it Peter had his head to the ground and was walking with purposeful stride. *"Looks pissed off,"* thought Scott. "Well, a little trouble in camp, hey. Now I know what I can do."

Chapter 3

Peter was fuming. He could not, for the life of himself, understand Carla's infatuation with this girl who had ruined everything. "*She doesn't even know her. Why bring this trouble on? This can only end badly.*" He walked along the winding road lost in thought until he came to the car park at the base of Mount Monster. He looked about and noticed the sign pointing out the 'nature track' and decided that he would follow it. He was already finding the exercise was helping to clear his thoughts. He started up the gently sloping hillside, noticing lots of dry tree branches all over the ground from what were, he supposed, gums and wattles. After no more than a few minutes he came to a post which held pamphlets. He reached into the box and pulled out a white brochure with the heading, 'The Gwen Ellis walking track – Mt Monster'. He decided he may as well go on the walk for want of anything better to do. The walk wound its way around the base and middle of Mt Monster. He learnt from the brochure that there were golden wattles, sticky wattles, echidnas, broom bush, which he especially had noticed on the road coming in, and other species of flora. The Crooks family were pioneers in the area and the trail was dedicated to Malcolm Crooks' daughter, Gwen Ellis, but the best part of the walk was the mount itself. It was a beautiful granite rock, so serene and majestic, and at the top he had a glorious view in all directions of the farm lands below. He heard and just quickly caught sight of a mob of 'roos which bounded off upon his approach. Peter was smiling now and feeling much better than he had earlier. The walk had afforded him time to put things into perspective and he felt rejuvenated. He hadn't realised how long he had been on top of the mountain until his left leg began tingling and when he stood it was pins and needles all over. He stretched high and long and then took another look about. *"Thanks, Mt Monster,"* he thought as he began to descend. *"Amazing what you find is in the middle of nowhere."*

Peter returned to the camp at around 12.40 pm and saw Carla and Sam talking near the camp fire. Elly was not in sight. "Hey, guys."

"Peter. Where did you get to? We were a bit worried."

"Just walking. Mt Monster's great, not very big but plenty of mystique and just what I needed to calm down. What have you two been doing?"

Carla and Sam had decided that they probably needed to stay another night just to keep Elly focused and help her see that she was doing the right thing and they told Peter this.

He didn't say anything just busied himself with the kettle and began building the fire up.

Elly appeared out of the tent and went straight to the pool of water. She threw a towel on the ground and stripped down to her bra and pants. She didn't care that they were in watching in the distance, as far as she was concerned they could all get stuffed. But then she thought how nice they had been to her, *"strange really"*. Elly walked to the water's edge but the second her feet hit the water she sunk down mid-way to her shins in black, slimy, sludge. "Oh shit," she yelled and Carla, Sam and Peter all looked more intensely. Elly had by that time managed to get herself back on the edge but she was stinking now.

"Hey, Elly," Sam yelled, "love the way you wash!" and she could hear them all laughing.

"Yeah, very funny Sam!" she retorted loudly and again heard peals of laughter. She smiled then and thought, *"Well, looks like I have to swim."* She looked around and noticed to her left a rocky outcrop entering the water and bypassing the ground. Scrambling over the rocks she could see the clear water and slowly immersed herself. It was cold but she felt invigorated and renewed. As she floated about she thought she would be OK now. That perhaps Carla was right and this bad feeling could pass and she, Elly, could restart her life. She thought of Jenny and that brought her up short. She swam back to the rocks, where she sat in water to her waist and scrubbed her legs, hair, arms and then scrambled back over the rocks to her towel.

She dried off and put on clean clothes and returned to the campsite looking and feeling far more settled. *"Good,"* thought Carla. "Come over Elly, and join us."

"Okay, I need grab my brush." Then with brush in hand she sat next to Carla who was stoking the fire. "We are just deciding who would do the drive into Keith and Sam says he will go."

"I'll go with you, Sam."

"No Elly, that's not a good idea. But I tell you what. What do you want me to get you? Anything, just ask." He put his hand up straight away and with a smile added, "No drugs, though."

"Very funny. Okay, I would love some smokes, deodorant, tampons and jelly babies."

Sam looked a little uneasy but said, "Yep, no worries. What brand do you smoke?"

"Anything or a pouch of tobacco is fine."

"Carla, Peter, what do you need?"

A few hours later, list in hand to cover them for another night in the bush, he jumped in the car and headed back into Keith again.

Chapter 4

Scott looked up when he heard the car engine, *"Okay. Shit, what to do."* He decided he would follow the car because at some point he had to move and this seemed like the best time given that that guy had walked past him once already. He may not be so lucky the next time. He started the engine, did a U-turn and travelled back along the road hoping no one would be coming in the other direction, it was a one way track after all, but he didn't want to risk passing the campsite, not yet. As he got close to the T intersection of the road leading into the park he saw Sam in the station wagon drive past. "*He was on his own. Great, what luck? In fact everything is working out brilliantly,*" thought Scott, as he found himself following the station wagon once again.

Sam drove to the IGA in town and with list in hand proceeded to wander up the aisles checking things off. He felt very embarrassed and slightly unsure of how to proceed when he got to Elly's list but he managed. He was looking in the meat department when he felt a tap on his shoulder. Jumping and turning at the same time he couldn't believe his eyes when he saw Scott.

"What the fuck," he exclaimed and then covered his mouth remembering where he was. "Scott. What the hell are you doing here?"

Scott gave Sam a hug and at the same time was saying, "I'm on my way to Melbourne. Got the shits with the Cumberland, you know, I was never there forever, man. Then when you pulled the pin I thought, hey, if he can, I can. But I am shit at organising and it's taken me this long to get my act together and move."

Sam by this stage had stopped his gaping and in a quiet voice said, "Mate, disorganised for you means a few too many joints," and he laughed heartily.

"Yeah, you're right there but hey, what are you doing here? Where are you staying, Sam?"

"We are staying out at Mount Monster, camping another night. What about you, where you staying?"

"Nowhere at this point in time. I don't think I could drive another minute."

"There's the caravan park just down the road there."

"Naw, it would be nice to have some company. Why don't you come with me? We can hang out at the pub for dinner."

"Sorry Scott. Sounds good but I have to get back, they are waiting on me."

"Oh! Who are they?" and Scott did his best sad face impression.

Sam picked up a few chops and snags and started moving towards the register when he remembered Carla's last minute grocery item. "Sam, Sam," she had yelled as he was pulling out, "Fish fingers. Get fish fingers, they are great on the barbie."

"Really? Sounds gross to me."

"Argh, believe me, you will want them all the time once you try them… oh but they can't be cooked in the sausage fat. Now that would be gross." Sam had laughed and said, "No worries, Carla." So remembering that now he ran back to the freezer section and grabbed a pack of twelve fish fingers. *"So, a quirky side to my mother,"* and he smiled. He was brought back to the now with Scott saying, "Maybe I could come with you. We can catch up. Meet your friends. What do you think? Would they mind?" Sam wasn't sure but he didn't want to disappoint Scott. He and Scott had gotten on well over the last eight months that Scott had been at the Cumberland so one night with a friend was OK with him. "Sure. No probs. Grab yourself what you need and follow me." He was hoping he was making the right decision but it was too late now.

Sam drove into camp with Scott close behind. He stopped nearer the pool of water and Scott pulled in alongside. Getting out he waved up to Peter and Carla who were now standing side by side looking and wondering who this other person was. Sam went over to Scott and beckoned him to follow him up to where Carla and Peter were. Scott was tentative and looked about, trying to size up the situation. *"Seems okay. No problems. Just got to get Sam on board,"* he thought, as he quickened his step and joined Sam.

Peter had been watching the men closely and now turned to Carla and in a low voice said, "How bloody unbelievable. Is this more trouble, Carla?"

She nodded. She was not a suspicious person but she was worried and looked around to see if Elly was anywhere in sight.

"Carla, Peter, this is Scott. Scott works with me at the Cumberland," he paused and then with a smile said, "Well, he did until a couple of days ago apparently and now he's off to Melbourne."

"Hi," Scott said, and extended his hand to Peter and smiled at Carla. "Truly amazing to have met Sam at the local supermarket."

"Hey, better get the goodies," and Sam jogged back to the car. "Hold up. I'll help and get my stuff too." Scott didn't want to be left with Carla and Peter on his own.

Elly meanwhile had heard the new voice and came out of the tent to see what was going on.

"Fuck, now what?' she exclaimed and Carla quickly went over to her. "All's good. We have a visitor. A friend of Sam's. His name is Scott."

Elly looked away, dove her hand into her pocket, grabbed her cigarettes and lit up. She had been fighting strange and sometimes wonderful, sometimes frightening, thoughts since leaving Adelaide and although she thought they were easing she couldn't help but think *"New blood."*

Elly had spent a lot of time in the tent but she hadn't been sleeping all that time. She was wondering what it was like to kill someone, anyone, and she had decided that it would be awesome. Then she had decided it would be wrong, or right, or simple. She was so scattered in her thoughts and she had fought against them and they had been abating. Right now though, seeing Scott, the thoughts came back stronger and with conviction. Carla was talking to her but she hadn't heard a word, boy she was sick of this bitch. "Look leave me alone will ya," and she marched down to where Scott and Sam were getting their groceries and supplies. "Hi, there," she chimed to Scott and he responded in kind.

"Elly, this is Scott, Scott Elly," and then with a chuckle, "So while you're here, Elly, you can carry this up to the camp," and threw the bag with the meat at her, which she promptly missed and it broke on the ground. "Shit."

"No probs, the meat's sealed. All good. Besides a little gravel never hurt anyone!"

She bent and picked it up and the three of them walked up the slight incline to the camp and once again the fire was being restored.

Carla said as they approached, "Let's all have a drink and get to know each other," looking directly at Scott.

"Sure." They fumbled about the camp getting seats, drinks and some nibblies.

With the fire built up and dinner decided all five sat drinking beer and talking about general bits and pieces skirting around the big question, the elephant in the room, the imposer, the question Peter wanted answered. "So Scott, why are you going to Melbourne? Why now?"

"No real reason, time for a change. My uncle's great but I get restless feet. Old Sammy here took off to Port

Vincent so I thought it was time I made a move," and he smiled broadly. "What about you lot? What's the go here?" Sam, Peter and Carla all looked at each other wondering who was going to say anything when Elly piped up.

"Carla here is trying to save me from the drug world." Curling her lip up and nodding her head in Carla's direction and then turning back to Scott. "But I've changed my mind, but they won't take me back. I'm stuck out here in this shit hole instead."

"Hey, that's enough and unfair," Peter exclaimed.

"Oh fuck off, you loser," and she took off towards the Esky, grabbed another beer, stamped back to the fire place, grabbed her smokes and headed to the pool. The other four were silent watching her as she walked to the water's edge and sat on the rocks staring at the water.

"This is too much." Peter was red faced and pacing.

Carla was saying, "It's the drugs, it takes time, we have to expect this."

"Well YOU might but I don't. Look we came to find Sam, now we have two hangers-on." He was yelling now, "This is fucked," and he took off towards the road, walking from camp.

"Hmm," mumbled Sam, "this is going well."

Scott looked at Carla and Sam and said, "Look guys, okay she's withdrawing, is she? What from?"

"Not a hundred percent sure mate, but I reckon ice."

"Okay, that explains it. How many days?"

"Only two that we know, almost three." Carla was sitting quietly trying to think how all this went wrong. In her mind she was saying that it seemed like a good idea at the time and then she laughed out loud.

Both Scott and Sam looked across to her, "What's funny?"

"What's funny, what's funny is how I stuff things up. What the hell was I thinking? Peter was right. It was you I wanted to find not some stray waif. I think I will have to take her back to Adelaide tomorrow. I've stuffed this all up. We have had no time to ourselves. My God, I'm selfish."

Sam came over to her. "Let's see what happens when Pete and Elly have calmed down."

Scott then spoke again, "Listen guys, I think I can help to reduce the tension." They both turned to him. "I've got a little weed, perhaps that will just knock the edge off. I've seen it help with other guys." Seeing the look on Carla's face he quickly added, "It's no big deal."

Sam was quick to say, "Good idea, mate. Yes, the lesser of two evils."

"I don't know," said Carla but she wasn't convinced and she could see the merit in it.

"Okay, I'll go talk to her," and Scott put his beer down and headed to his car, picked up his little stash and went down to Elly.

Scott rolled a joint and Elly was, as he had predicted, a little calmer. So too, was Sam, who had decided that a joint wouldn't hurt either. He'd never been much of a smoker but things were weird at the moment and a bit of 'comic relief' seemed like a good idea. Peter had returned within fifteen minutes of leaving and Carla filled him in. He made no comment but replenished his drink and began putting the meat on. Carla seeing this began cutting up some bread and salad, and warmed up a separate pan for her fish fingers. Things seemed to relax a bit. When Sam had said, "Okay, I'm off to join them," Carla looked a little worried but Peter said quietly, "Don't worry, I'm watching them."

The evening was going fine with Carla providing the food and Peter helping clear up whilst Elly, Scott and Sam sat huddled laughing and smoking. To some extent Carla was happy that Elly had stopped her violent outbursts but she was a little concerned about Sam who was looking worse and worse as the evening continued. "Sam, are you alright?"

And Sam had replied, "Yes," and then immediately jumped up, staggered into the bush and could be heard vomiting. This caused Elly and Scott to laugh heartily telling Carla to, "Relax, he'll be okay, just not used to it." Peter on the other hand was furious but said nothing.

Sam finished being sick and went off to the tent. He wasn't sure where his head was but the alcohol and the joint hadn't done him any favours. Peter left soon after Sam crashed but he'd decided to sleep in the back of the car, the idea of Sam getting up in the night and being sick again was too much for him. Scott, Elly and Carla watched them go their separate ways and then Carla excused herself soon after although she was a bit concerned leaving the two of them up together. *"Mind your own business. They are adults after all,"* she berated herself.

Chapter 5

Scott was the first up and he waited till Sam came out of the tent. Once Sam had been for a slash Scott nabbed him and said, "Sam, mate. We need to talk."

"Sure, but I feel shit."

"Listen, let's walk."

"No, I need caffeine before do anything,"

"Okay, lets drive to the servo and get everyone a drink and then we can talk too."

"Great plan. OK."

Sam saw Carla's tent moving and wandered over and yelled, "Yeah ladies, Scott and I are off to get coffees and brekky, be back soon," and Carla mumbled, "Sounds good."

"Get me some more smokes." It was Elly

As they drove back into town, Sam said, "So Scott, you've quit the Cumberland, hey! Not exciting enough for you in Adelaide?"

Scott looked over to him and said, "Yeah, something like that." They sat silently for a few minutes more whilst an old Bob Dylan song hummed on in the background and then, whilst looking straight ahead, Scott said, "Actually, I'm taking you back to your Dad."

"What? What the fuck are you talking about?" Sam screamed, turning violently towards Scott.

"Hey, watch the road, steady," Scott yelled as Sam swerved on to the wrong side of the road. He corrected the car and slowed a little. "I've got to take you back, Sam. He's paying me, $20,000. He wants you back. Is worried for you. Look," holding his hand up and cutting off Sam, "look, I've thought about it. I drop you off, get paid and you can do whatever you want. Hey, I could even wait for you and drive you back. What do you think?"

In very slow and deliberate words Sam said, "Scott, I am stopping this car now and getting out. I don't need this shit. I am not going back to Dad, and by the way he is not my father. He's been a lie all my life." He paused then and let out a deep sigh. His head was aching and his stomach was feeling very queasy. "Scott. I'm not going back yet, maybe later but not right now and you cannot make me. Carla is my mother, whom I've never known and I intend to learn who I am. I have never felt right, something always felt like it was missing. I always had this empty longing but never known what it was. I think it is this and I am not going with you. Sorry."

They had entered the township and the servo was up ahead.

"Okay, let's get food and coffee and think about this."

"Okay," said Sam, but added, "there is nothing to discuss, Scott."

They ordered breakfast and a coffee and were sitting at a small wooden table and Scott made one more plea for Sam to "be a mate, just pacify him for a few minutes, once I have the money you are still free to leave."

"Am I Scott? You can guarantee that, can you?" and Scott looked up from his eggs and bacon and saw something in Sam's eyes and posture that told him his plan may not be that simple.

Sam said, "Look Scott, let me explain something about my life, something I never thought about until Carla and Peter turned up. All my life my father, now known as uncle, has kept me under wraps. I have been a prisoner without knowing it. My school days were completed under the watchful eyes of my grandparents. I wasn't allowed to walk home with friends, ever!" he emphasised, "I used to say 'Why," and the answer was always the same, 'You can't trust people.' Then they'd tell me some horror story of children being molested and kidnapped and, you know Scott, after a while you begin to believe it. You begin to look for the bad, before the good in people. One of the reasons I left Port Vincent was not because it was dull but because I was scared, I was away from home and surrounded by the unknown. I couldn't handle it and that's my legacy, Scott, my legacy from Thomas and my grandparents and why? I need to know who I am, why all this has happened to me. As I said I have always felt an emptiness inside and I need to understand more, not be dragged back. He will imprison me, Scott. I won't get away. He has done it before."

"Wow, that's tough." Scott wasn't sure where to look or what exactly to say to all this but added, "At least you had people that cared for you as you grew up," suddenly looking melancholy. "Anyway, what do you mean, he's done it before?"

Sam got up and stretched and said, "Let's walk. I feel better when I'm moving."

They paid for breakfast telling the lady behind the counter they'd be back for takeaways soon.

Outside it was just beginning to get light. Sam hadn't realised they were up so early and thought, *"No wonder I feel sick."* The two men walked side by side and Sam started. "When I was thirteen I had a friend called Greg Houser. Greg was eleven months older than me and he liked to tease me that he was so much worldlier. Anyway, I liked him a lot because he was funny and he never seemed worried or scared and I felt safe around him. Greg's parents owned the local fish and chip store and he was always saying, "Come home with me, after school, my dad makes the best fish and chips" but Dad wouldn't hear of it. "But why? It's only for half an hour and I'd come straight home. Please Dad, please." Sam could hear, and see, himself standing in front of Thomas at the kitchen table after dinner, feeling timid, worried, scared but really wanting to go to Greg's.

"Let the boy go, Thomas, my granddad said, but my grandmother and father overruled him and that was that." He stopped and looked at Scott. "You have to understand, Scott, I never asked for much." Scott didn't reply but Sam knew he was listening. "Hey, look up there," and he pointed. "A pole with a jeep on it. Why on earth would you put a Land Rover on a pole?"

"Beats me." Scott shrugged and then, noticing a little building to his left and said, "Hey, there's a kind of demonstration house too, period like." He turned from the Land Rover on the pole and peered into the little model building protected by security mesh to see an olden day kitchen on one side and a bedroom on the other side. "Nice. Better than my prison cell," and he laughed.

"Yeah, looks good doesn't it?" Then looking to his right he exclaimed, "Oh! Look, gold, Scottie." Sam was staring at a little rain water tank, and realised he was parched, "All that bloody alcohol and smoke," and he reached for a tin cup that was attached to the tank and drank greedily. Scott followed suit.

They decided to turn around and return to the servo and order breakfast for the others.

"Anyway as I was saying; I was furious, it was so unfair and I screamed at Thomas and Sharon and Thomas went into one of his 'moods' pacing, rubbing his head and ears, mumbling and Sharon flew into a rage yelling, "Look what you've done now!" It was chaos and I took off. It was about six pm and it was getting dark. I bolted out the door with Oscar calling for me to come back. I ran down the driveway towards the iron gates but stopped. I didn't go any further. I wasn't brave enough so I sat at the gate and cried my eyes out. Anyway, the next day I was escorted to school but I had determined to go with Greg to his parents' shop that afternoon despite them all. Greg was waiting for me outside the school entrance and waved and I said goodbye to Sharon and ran towards him. As I neared he said, "Hi, well can you come over?" "Yes, no problem" "Great. You'll love my mum and dad." School finished at 3.30 pm and instead of going through the front gates where Sharon would be waiting we went out the back gates and through the local park. I was feeling scared, excited, brave, weak, it was amazing. Greg must have noticed because he asked, "Hey, you okay? You seem jumpy. Are you sure it's okay to come home?" "Yep say I." We got to the shop and went in. Greg's dad was behind the counter. Greg had told me that he starts preparing the shop to open at 3.30 pm when school gets out 'cos that when kids come in and they are really hungry. Mr Houser straight away said, 'Hello there, Sam. Come for the best fish and chips in town have you?" Greg's father was named Petro but everyone called him Pete, he was a large man with thick black hair and a large moustache which covered his entire top lip. He had a big stomach that seemed to move when he spoke. I giggled when I saw that but answered "Yes sir." He said "Good then go out back and get a drink and I'll call you when they are ready". Greg and I moved into the house part of the shop and it was amazing. The furniture was old and musty with a funny oily smell. It was nothing like my house. I had only ever been in people's houses that were new, expensive, you know, what you'd call clinical. Anyway this was homely and messy and I remember thinking, I could live here. It feels right. Greg's mum was in the kitchen. "Mum, this is Sam and he's come for Dad's famous fish & chips." "Ah Sam," she exclaimed, "come in, sit down, do you want a drink? Biscuit? I've just made some". I had looked at Greg and he nodded and I said, "Yes please," and they were delicious." Sam stopped walking. "Scott, I was totally spellbound by this entire outing. I completely forgot about my fears, home, Dad, Sharon, Oscar. I had never known this feeling, a sense of, I don't know, it's hard to explain, anyway, the feeling. It took over." They started walking again and were soon back at the servo. They entered and ordered takeaway egg and bacon rolls, cigarettes for Elly, five coffees and a two litre bottle of

Coke and then stepped outside to wait whilst Scott had another cigarette.

"I must be boring you but you need to understand why I can't come back. Not just yet."

"No, no, go on," and blew out a large cloud of smoke.

"Well, we'd been in the kitchen about twenty minutes and Pete came in with the fish & chips wrapped in white butchers' paper and handed a package to me and Greg. I looked at it and was very unsure and Greg laughed, "Here look," and he ripped open the top of the paper, threw his hand in and came out with a very hot chip. It was funny he started juggling the chip from one hand to another dancing about going "Ouch, hot, hot" and we all laughed. I felt like someone else that day. Then I opened mine and Greg's dad goes "see no dishes either." This food was the best food I had ever tasted. We were still sitting about the table, Greg, me and his mum, talking about school and stuff when there was a commotion in the shop. Greg's mum got up and said, "I'll go see what that's about. You boys stay here." I was instantly scared. I knew it would be my Dad and this was going to be trouble. I quickly got up and followed Greg's mum. "Hey, where are you going Sam?" Greg called after me and I told him the truth and I hurried away; "Sorry, Greg, I lied. I didn't get my Dad's permission to come. I think that's him out there. I have to go." I burst through the shop door and Mr and Mrs Houser were standing together behind the counter saying nothing. Thomas was pacing about ranting and cursing at them and then he saw me. "Get over here, now Samuel!" and I quickly went through the little counter door. He came over to me and grabbed me by the arm and pulled me off my feet flinging me across the shop towards the front door. I heard Pete yelling, "Hey, be gentle with the boy, he's done no harm." But Thomas didn't look back and I was literally thrown in the car. The journey home was terrible with the incomprehensible muttering of my Dad. When we got out of the car Sharon then grabbed me and that was that. "You are a wilful, nasty boy. Look what you've done to your father, look how upset he is. Why did you do this? Anything could have happened to you," and then she wrinkled her nose and said to me, "You smell, get inside and get those clothes off and wash yourself. We will talk about this later." And I ran. Anything to get away from them."

Sam stopped talking and dwelt on the memory as Scott stood looking out to the freeway where the huge trucks were rumbling past with regular monotony. "Bit of an overreaction, then?"

"You could say that," and Sam smiled, "Anyway, suffice to say I never went to Greg's place again and was told never to associate with Greg, which was pretty hard when we went to the same school. About four weeks later Greg was no longer coming to school and the fish & chip shop was put up for sale. I don't know what Thomas did but I knew, even at thirteen, that he was behind it and I hated him for it. So you see I have been," and he rubbed his hand across his forehead, "if not a prisoner, I have been an emotional captive all my life. Scott, I am not even prepared to think what he might do if I return this time. I have texted him since I left trying to make him see it will be alright and I will be home when I learn more but he hasn't replied."

Scott said, "Yes, well I must say he was a bit intense the day he asked me to get you. To be honest it was be a bit unsettling."

"See, he's just a little crazy when it comes to me. That's the bloody trouble with my family, they don't talk." He paused then and said, "I really don't know anything about any of them," and he placed his hand on Scott's shoulder. "Don't make this hard Scott, just keep going. Please, mate."

Scott thought about that and in the end he said, in an enthusiastic, upbeat voice, "Brekky should be ready, let's get it and head back to camp. They'll be wondering where we are," and he slapped Sam on the back.

Back at camp Elly was up but still quite uncooperative with Carla and Carla was getting very frustrated with her negativity and resistance. "Honestly Elly. I haven't kidnapped you, you know. You're the one who said you wanted to come along and start afresh before you got too entrenched in the lifestyle of drugs and prostitution."

"Bullshit. I think they are your words, Carla. Yes I agreed to come along but I'm not sure now. I think it's too hard. I am so confused. Look, I know deep down you are a good person trying to help but I have to know if it's your help I want. I am sorry for being difficult it's just that…," and she looked down, "it's just that it's complicated. My life, Jenny, drugs, they help me escape, not think so much. You know, Carla," and again she looked down, "I just don't think this is the right time. I was making decisions because I was scared. You and Pete were there. I get it but not now, please."

"Oh Elly, I hear what you're saying but why not give it a go and see how you cope once you're back with family. If it doesn't work you can always return, at least knowing you gave it a shot. You have actually come a long way these past two days. Really, you have. Think about it. What do you say?"

That conversation was about an hour ago and they hadn't spoken since. Peter had kept his distance.

Elly was walking around and had wandered up the dirt road about two times looking for Scott and Sam. "Where are they? I need a smoke, for fucks' sake," she said accusingly to Carla.

"I don't know but I sure could do with a coffee right now."

Just then they heard the car and both looked relieved.

Scott and Sam got out of the car carrying the food and coffee. "Hey," with a beaming smile, "how are things?"

Carla answered, "Fine now you're here," and Elly quickly piped up, "About time, I'm starved. Did you get some smokes?"

"Oh sorry," looking at Carla. "We got talking and hadn't realised the time," Sam said, ignoring Elly

The girls got stuck into their eggs and Scott stood, saying, "I'm thinking of heading off guys, got to keep moving, so nice knowing you all."

Sam mouthed a silent 'thank-you mate' to Scott.

"Wait." It was Elly. "Where are you going?"

"To Melbourne, check it out, look up a couple of guys I know. Chill."

"Can I come with you?"

"No Elly," Carla piped up in alarm, "what about seeing your aunt, remember what we were talking about this morning. You know, at least giving it a go!"

"Will you shut up? I'm done with you, Carla and 'giving it a go.' I want out of here. Scott, can I? Can I travel with you?"

Scott looked around and shrugged, "Sure, get your stuff. I want to hit the road sooner than later." Elly turned and ran to the tent.

Whilst Elly was packing Peter came over to Scott and said, "Listen mate, do you think I could travel with you two as well?"

Both Carla and Sam looked at him but said nothing.

He continued, "It's just that I think it would be good for Carla and Sam to have some privacy and what better way than in the car!"

Scott thought about that and considered what Sam had told him this morning and said, "You're right. Yep, get packed. This is going to be cosy," and winked at Sam.

Peter went over to Sam and Carla, "You guys okay packing up camp?"

"Sure," said Carla and gave him a hug which Peter returned and with a big smile he said to her quietly, "Don't worry, I'll pop into your place in a few days and see how you are getting on." He gave Sam a slap on the back, grabbed his stuff from the back of the car and was waiting with Scott by the time Elly emerged.

Within ten minutes the camp was cleared of the Ute, Elly, Peter and Scott. Sam and Carla both looked at each other and Sam said, "Well, it's just you and me now. Let's pack up and get on the road too."

They worked quietly, pulling down the tents, tidying up any rubbish into bags to dispose of at home and generally ensuring the site was the same as when they came there two days ago.

With the car packed they jumped in and Carla noted, "We've done well, they are only a couple of hours ahead of us. Might even overtake them if they stop somewhere."

"I think Scott's keen to get some distance between him and Adelaide."

"Really, why's that?"

"Let's get going and I'll explain along the way."

Chapter 6

Sam filled Carla in on what Scott was really there for and she was shocked. "Thomas really is possessive of you, isn't he?"

"Yeah, I know. I feel sorry for him really. I have always known he loved me in his own way but it's been smothering and now, knowing what I know, I don't know how I feel."

"That's understandable." Then with a shake of the head, "I still can't believe he'd offer $20,000 and a car to get you back! Amazing."

"Well, thankfully Scott saw sense and didn't push it. Besides he still got $10,000 and a car, so not bad work, although I hope he lays low for a while. I don't know what Thomas will do but I'm pretty sure he won't call the cops. He'd have a hard time explaining himself."

"Well, that's Scott's problem not yours Sam. Scott made his own decisions. Least he's seen sense and didn't try anything silly to get you back. I actually like him."

"Yeah, he's a good bloke finally heading in the right direction in life. Had it hard along the way."

They had been travelling for around an hour and a half when Sam said, "Hey look, a hitch-hiker. Don't see many of them these days. What do you reckon? Pick him up?"

"Sure, we have room."

Sam slowed the car and then shook his head, "Carla, its Peter, look!"

"My God, you're right, what's going on?"

They pulled up just in front of him and Sam and Carla both jumped out of the car. "Peter, what the hell's happened? Where's Scott and Elly?"

Casually Peter said, "Hi guys, I thought you'd be along soon. Get in the car, I want to put some distance between us and this place." Once in the car he said, "Shit, what a carry on. Come on."

Carla said she'd take over the driving and Sam jumped in the passenger seat. Turning to Peter he said, "Well, what's the story?"

"Well, first, have you got some water? I've been waiting for a while?" Sam threw him a bottle and he took a long drink. "We were travelling along alright, Elly in the middle and me at the window but she was getting really pesky and nagging Scott for a smoke. "Come on, Scott, give me your stuff and I'll roll us a joint," that kind of thing and when he wouldn't give it to her she started making suggestions." Raising his eyebrows and shaking his head he continued, "I was feeling really uncomfortable but thought I could cope, it wasn't that far to travel but when she became openly vulgar talking about sex and what she'd do, well I cracked it I'm afraid. I shouted, "Stop being filthy, Elly,

346

shut the fuck up and leave Scott to drive in peace." Scott hadn't been saying much at all at this point in time but then he said, "Hey Peter, leave little Elly alone, man, if she is keen to give us a little pleasure why not," and turning to Elly he said, "Hey little princess, I've got some really good stuff you might like in the back. What do you think?" I couldn't believe my ears. I shouted at both them, "That's it, let me out. NOW." I knew you guys would be along soon enough so I wasn't worried, I just had to get away from them. So he pulls over and I get out and here I am!"

"Oh, that's so sad. She said she wasn't ready to change."

"Well, I would have done the same Peter, if that was me," Sam said, supporting Peter, and turning to Carla added, "We can't make people change or help them if they don't want it. Her choice, the options were there."

"I know but she's so young. I hope she lets her aunt know that she's probably not coming, if she told her at all," and then looking at Peter in the rear view mirror she said, "Least you're okay, Peter."

And smiling at them both he said, "Yes, I'm good now. What a nightmare."

They made it back to Ballarat well before dark and over the following four days Sam and Carla began to get know each other. Carla had been musing about just how different the three of them were and yet, how they were entwined. *"Peter was amazing,"* she thought, *"To have lived with poor Liam and his violence, drunkenness and whoring and yet turned out to be this thoughtful and insightful young man."* Carla had been surprised to learn how much Liam had changed since Susan's murder. Oh yes, he was a lad who liked a drink but he was loyal to Susan and a great friend to Roger and her. She wondered if things would have been different if she had been well enough after the tragedy to help him. If they could have supported each other. *"Well too late to ponder that now. Too much time has passed."* And Sam, her boy, growing up always believing his mother was dead and that Thomas was his father. What had Sam said the other night? That he loved his father, Thomas, but it was never right, he had had a nagging sense of loss and a sense of living someone else's life. *"How profound,"* she thought. And me, well I can see myself now for being pathetic, truly pathetic, to hide in a veil of black, and provide myself with an excuse never to get emotionally hurt again. Yep, bury myself in work, justify the giving up on my son with words, me, the English teacher, the words master, the word convincer, the word cajoler. And who have I kidded all my life with words, thoughts and justification? *"I've kidded myself."* Again for the one hundredth time since Peter Westmead landed on her doorstep she berated herself for what could have been. *"If only I had fought."* Another sigh. *"Too late, Carla. Too late. Time to concentrate on the here and now, where to with these two lads, where to with me?"* Yes, Carla saw her future as finally having a direction and one that could have options, different from the routines she had cemented for herself.

It was Saturday morning and their fifth day home. Carla and Sam were sitting at the dining table drinking their coffees when the doorbell rang. "Right on time," and Sam got up and let Peter in.

"Coffee, Peter?" Carla called from the dining room.

"Yes, please. I actually slept in so I haven't had one yet."

"No worries," Carla said, "Pot's hot, help yourself."

"Oh, I brought the papers too."

"Great." Sam and Carla said in unison, "I bags the sport section."

"I bags the crossword."

"Fine. Looks like the news for me, again," said Peter. "Very predictable, you two!" and smiled.

Peter made himself a coffee, and sat at the table with Sam to his right and Carla to his left. "So, looks like you two have now gotten to a point of playing happy homes?"

Both Carla and Sam looked up. "What's that?" Sam asked. And Peter said, waving his arm across the table at them both, "This, you two, sitting happy at the table, playing house. Is this how it's going to be?"

"Not sure what you're saying, Peter?"

"Oh no, you wouldn't." Both Sam and Carla were confused and Carla in particular was not liking his tone.

"We have no idea what you are on about, but you better spit out what's on your mind, mate."

"Well, what's on my mind is," and he looked from right to left, "is, that it is time for you two to have a reality check. Yep, that's what's on my mind. Sam. Carla."

"Peter, please. We don't know what you are talking about," and added "You're scaring me a little," and she got up from the table but kept a close eye on him. She noticed he was wearing a large jacket which she hadn't noticed when he first came in, as she was too interested in the paper. His hair was a little dishevelled, which was unusual for him, and looking a bit more closely he looked like he hadn't slept for a couple of nights. Moving towards him she put out her hand and was about to place it on his shoulder and in the same motion started to say, "Peter, are you alright, you look..." when Peter looked up at her and pulled his body sharply way from the proffered hand and said, "I'd sit if I were you, Carla," in such a way that she had no doubt he meant it. She sat and he put his hand into the inside of his jacket and placed a gun to the table.

Sam jumped up and back and his chair fell crashing to the ground. "For fucks' sake." Looking about wildly, "What the fuck is going on? GET that thing out of here," he yelled, "GO ON – PISS off. What the hell's gotten into you?" He had gathered his balance and Carla had instinctively backed away from Peter and was at Sam's side.

In what she hoped was a calm voice she said, "Put that away before someone gets hurt, Peter, and please leave. We don't know what this is about but I will not have this in my home. Please leave or I will call the police." Her heart was thumping in her chest and she knew her voice sounded tiny and that she was obviously not in control. She lifted her arm and wiped sweat from her forehead.

Peter had not moved but was watching the two of them. In a slow and deliberate, controlled voice he said,

"Hurt Carla? Before someone gets hurt. Is that what you just said to me? It's too late for that, don't you think?"

"This is nuts. I'm calling the police," and Sam went to leave the room but had only taken two steps when Peter spoke again.

"You had better turn right around and sit down, Sam. I don't want to hurt you," *"Yet"* he thought, pointing the gun at Sam's back. Sam turned around slowly, saw the gun aimed at him and quickly went to the table and sat. Peter pointed to Carla to do the same. They looked at each other and they both recognized fear and confusion on their faces.

"Smart boy. Smart girl. Now that's better," and he smiled a perfect smile at them both.

"Alright Peter, you have our attention; please, tell us what you want." She was determined to try and not let him know she was shitting herself. Then a crazy thought popped onto her head. *"I feel like I'm in a movie, ha, this isn't real"* and then, *"Shut up idiot, it's happening."*

Peter said nothing for a good minute and they sat still and waited.

"So, now you are listening I want to tell you a story. Remember I've been listening to your stories, so now it's time for mine," his eyes darting between the two of them. Then raising his voice he said, "Ready?" They said nothing. "WELL," he yelled, and then in a quieter voice said, "I asked a question, people. Are you ready for a story?"

"Yes. Ready."

"Good. Okay, let's start with you Carla, this goes," and he stopped mid-sentence as there was a knock on the

351

door. They all looked from one to the other and although Peter looked worried and his grip on the gun had gotten tighter, he shrugged his shoulders and said with a smile, "Hmm, looks like we have company. Sam, up," pointing the gun dismissively at him. "Let's go see who's here." Looking at Carla he said, "Don't try to play the hero, Carla," and then laughed, "Ha, you, hero, very unlikely, Carla. You only think of yourself. Don't you? But in case you do think to do something... remember Sam here will get hurt. Understand?"

'Yes," her eyes were downcast, she did not want to look at him.

Chapter 7

When Peter had been knocking on Carla's door he had been unaware that he was being watched. Thomas had been on the other side of the road in his car for the past two hours. He had been wrestling with himself as to when he would go in. He knew his son, Carla and the Westmead boy had been together often over the past four or five days and he wanted to time his arrival without the Westmead boy being there. *"Damn, too late."* There he was, at the door. *"Pretty heavy coat,"* he thought ridiculously, *"Not even that cold for a winter's day."* Thomas didn't know what to do now. It had been at least a further fifteen minutes since the Westmead boy had entered. As he stared at the front door he spoke, "No. I know, William, I won't leave it any longer." He cocked his head to the side, listened and said, "Okay." He opened the door and got out of the car, walked purposely to the front door and knocked. He had knocked twice and was about to knock a third time when he noticed the doorbell and reached to ring it. Just as he did the door opened and Sam and the Westmead boy were standing in the doorway.

"Dad." Sam moved forward, reflexively wanting to grab his father and hold him close, but the muzzle of

Peter's gun bought him to a quick stop and he added, "What are you doing here?"

"I want you to come home, son." A simple statement. A simple plea. For a split second he thought, *"No, not your son,"* and then countered that with *"Yes, he is my son."*

Sam looked squarely at his father, noticing for the first time that he had aged and he looked very dark under the eyes, and again he was taken with an impulse to hold his father and protect him. Instead, in as strong a voice as he could muster, he said, "You better leave, Thomas. This is not a good time. I don't want you here." But Peter piped up and said, "Hey, that's not very friendly, Sam, Daddy here has travelled a long way," and looking at Thomas added, "Haven't you, Mr Nelson?" and beckoning with his free hand, "Come in, come in."

Thomas pressed his way between the door and Sam and then walked purposely into the hall, waiting to be directed into a room. "Straight ahead, Mr Nelson," Peter chimed, "straight ahead."

Carla jumped up from where she had been told to stay. "Thomas. Is this your idea?" she spat accusingly. But one look at him made her think it was not. He looked so haggard, crumpled, lost, he looked like he had a fever, beads of sweat were forming on his forehead.

"Are you alright?" she asked, tentatively.

"Course he is. Aren't you, Thomas?" Peter said snidely. "Get Thomas a drink, Carla."

"Yes, of course. Thomas, what can I get you?" But Thomas just stared at her and mumbled something which she couldn't grasp.

354

"Not really. Just wait. Give me time. Soon. Yes, I will." Thomas knew he was being incomprehensible and he was fighting within himself to get control. He needed to talk to Sam. He needed Sam to come home. He couldn't cope with him away. He had suffered, worrying about him and the dangers he might have been facing. He stood in the middle of the room as the three of them stared and finally he managed to say in a firm and clear voice, "We'd like a strong coffee, please Carla," and wiped his hands through his hair.

Peter in the meantime had released Sam and had moved back to his chair which was positioned nearest the kitchen door. "Good, now sit down, Thomas. You are just in time for our party," and Thomas sat, thankful for the offer.

Carla reboiled the kettle and busied herself with clean cups and taking orders. Sam wanted water, Peter wanted nothing, she got Coke, Thomas his coffee. Peter had taken off the jacket and was saying; "Now where was I... yes, Thomas, good timing I was about to tell Sam and Carla a story." He looked at Carla and said, "Hurry up, Carla," in a slow drawl, "we are waiting."

She placed the drinks on the table and quickly sat, Peter continued.

"Carla, do you think it was coincidence that I turned up on your doorstep the day of my mother's murder?"

She looked directly at him. "I didn't think anything. I was shocked. I was surprised," and after a small pause added, "I suppose I never gave it a thought. Why?"

"Well, it wasn't a coincidence. I have planned this for a long time. I've told you about my childhood and the women in it. I've told you about my father and the abuse I suffered at his alcoholic hands but I hadn't told you everything. I haven't told you the violence was horrific, depraved. Beatings no child deserved, Carla. Not one. And after a really good flogging I was locked up in the bedroom cupboard and left, sometimes for an entire day. Do you know what that felt like? It was terrifying. I was in pain, I was cold, hungry and in the dark. And worst of all I had no real idea what I had done wrong. I would come out of that cupboard declaring I would never do it again. But I did not know what IT was so I could avoid it in the future. I'd say to myself, 'Okay, it must have been that TV show. I won't watch that again, or I didn't eat enough food, or I ate too much, I smiled too much, cried, I DID NOT KNOW. Always on edge. Don't relax, Peter, look out, oh no he's smiling, there's trouble. Never an end to it, Carla. I'd sit and cry for my mum, but she never came, she wasn't around. No, some bastard had murdered her. And I would call out, 'Please daddy please, let me out. I will be good.' But you know, Carla," Peter was looking directly at her now and she noticed he had snot running out onto his upper lip, "Do you know what? The beatings and the confinement, all I really understood was that Dad hated me." He paused and openly waved the gun about. "Liking the story so far?" and he sat back in the chair realising he had been leaning over the table towards her. He wiped his nose on his sleeve and continued, "I made up stories in my head about how my mum would come back, she wasn't dead, she'd save me and she'd kill my dad." He stopped, looked about … "Oh, you looked shocked, all of you do, well, maybe not you, Thomo," and laughed. Carla and Sam looked at Thomas then and he looked as if he hadn't heard a word. Eyes down, hands wringing, coffee still untouched, head shaking and breathing laboured. "You OK, Dad?" and Sam touched his father.

"Shut up, Sam." It was Peter. "This is my story, remember. You listen. Thomas, if you don't shut up I will shut you up. You hear." Sam looked scared and squeezed tighter on Thomas's arm. A gentle – please Dad, stop – type of squeeze. With that Thomas seemed to physically relax. He slowly placed a hand onto Sam's and sat quietly but did not speak. "Good. Now, oh yes, I was telling you, I hoped mum would come back and kill Liam. Well, she didn't. You know, Carla," he pointed to her, "I think mum would have killed him given what you have told me of her. I think there is no way she'd have let me suffer." He seemed to have an involuntary tic of the head and added, "Anyway, I managed to fulfil that bargain with myself when I was just eighteen."

Sam looked at Peter, "You killed your dad?!"

"Yes, of course, he was a miserable fucker and I helped him find peace like all good sons. He had stopped beating me when I had hit my teen years, but he had devised another, worse punishment for me." He laughed out loud and Thomas jumped. "Wouldn't think it was possible, would you? But yes. When he was drunk and not with some slut he'd get all teary and bemoan the loss of 'my Susan'. He'd say she was the greatest thing I had and then she was gone, oh why? Why? And he'd try to hug me and the stink of his breath made me sick. I'd run into my room but he'd sit outside with drinks and smokes and…," and again he stopped and looked at them. "I was trapped again. Bigger room but trapped.

You have no idea how many times I had to open my door and step over him as he snored and pissed himself. I hated him and what he was. Trapped, trapped." He seemed to have drifted into a memory and Sam and Carla gave each other an acknowledging look that screamed, 'We are in big shit' but both of them knew they had no idea what to do. So they sat, and waited. And Carla added, having remembered something he had told her on their journey, "But Peter, you told us you left home at fifteen and went to an aunt's home in Sydney."

That broke him from his inertia. "Ha, Carla, Carla, you are so gullible, so ready to believe the best in people, believe in their potential, but what about ours?" Pointing the gun at Sam, "Hmmm… No. Everything is a lie except this. My story," and again the gun was swinging about from one to the other. "The fact that I came and what is happening now. This is the truth. Do you get it! This is not a lie, NOT like you, Carla," he snarled. Then he gave what Carla thought was a knowing smile. *"But knowing what?"* she thought.

Sam was looking at Peter and decided to speak. "Peter, why didn't you get help? Tell someone? Why stick around? You said you were a teenager."

Peter turned and yelled at him, "Shut up, little boy who got the world. Shut up. Whinger who has been so sad because 'something did not feel right.' Just shut up. This is my story, Sambo. Shut the fuck up." Looking at Carla he said, "Get me a beer. It's early but I'm thirsty." Carla got up immediately and asked if Sam or Thomas wanted one but both said no.

Beer handed over in stubby holder and after a long swig he continued, "One night a friend of his called from the pub and said, "Peter can you pick your father up.

358

He's pretty wasted?" So I picked him up from a pub, it wasn't the first time, mind you. Anyway, he was drifting in and out of consciousness. I drove out to a place I know in the State forest and bye, bye daddy. No one would ever find him. I never reported him missing and the funny thing is no one came looking or asking. That's how relevant my dad was. Funny hey, those old mine shafts. I bet there are plenty of bodies in them."

Everyone was quite except Thomas who, although still resting his hand on Sam's, was back to constantly mumbling and fidgeting in the chair.

"Anyway," Peter continued. "This is the real point, the real clincher about how we all come to be here now. You've been waiting for this, haven't you both?" Sam and Carla said nothing, both were frightened and their thoughts were racing but to no definitive point or action. Neither of them had experience of aggression or abject hate. This was so alien to them that they were paralysed. "Now I am taking you back to when Dad was alive and I was a kid... One day I'm locked in the bedroom cupboard in Dad's room which was not normal. Normally it was in my cupboard where there was a cupboard inside the wardrobe. Anyway, details, details, I digress. This particular day Dad was drunk and had dragged me into his room and was giving me what for when the phone rang. Opening his wardrobe he threw me in and added he'd be back. I heard the key twist and the phone ringing, and then his voice. It was just another happy day in the lives of the Westmeads. After a little while I could actually see a bit due to a little light coming under the door from the window. In my cupboard it was black but I had made it comfortable enough making sure I didn't fill it with too much junk. So, I'm in Dad's cupboard and I am very, very sore and uncomfortable so I started to shuffle shoes, clothes and boxes about trying to get a space to curl up in. I was about twelve years old, I think. Anyway," another pause for a drink, "I grabbed a box and put it to the side of the wardrobe and noticed another box, smaller and quite squashed where the other box had been on top of it. I reached for it and popped it on my knee. At first I thought it was empty. I pulled out some jewellery, a couple of hankies, some make-up, and thought it must belong to one of the 'women' dad had brought home. I was about to fling it as far from me as possible, which," and he smiled broadly to them all, "wasn't far. Remember folks, I'm in the cupboard... Oh come on! That's a joke, people. Lighten up." Another broad smile, another drink. "So I picked the box off my knee and was about to toss it when I saw a book on the very bottom. I picked it up and do you know what it said?" looking around at their faces. "No. Not going to guess. Come on guys guess... Thomas you guess," and Thomas looked up, his eyes were so bloodshot and wary that Carla doubted he had clear sight, but he managed to say, "I killed your mum?"

"No, it didn't say that you idiot." But he looked at Thomas and said, "What did you mean by that?"

But Thomas was crooning now and talking directly to someone. "I know, it's too late, I will, William, please don't worry."

Dismissing Thomas, Peter turned to Sam and Carla, "He's seriously fucked, Sam. Daddy's mad." Neither responded. "Okay, I will tell you. It said, 'The diary of Susan Westmead – Do not read'. I was only twelve but I was overwhelmed, I grabbed that book but couldn't make out the words in the small amount of light and my reading wasn't the best then so I hid it on me until I could find a proper place to read it. It was an amazing feeling but terrifying too because I knew my father would not want me to read it. I wasn't allowed to talk about her let alone read her diary. Dad let me out two hours later." Peter stopped for effect and waited for some comments, throwing his left palm hands up. "Well? Drum roll, what do you think so far? Good story or what?"

"Peter," it was Carla, "Peter the story is terrible. Did the diary help you?" and he mimicked her in a whiny voice.

"Peter that is terrible, did the diary help you? Well Carla, yes. It did. It helped a lot. It helped me to get to where I am today if you want to know."

"Peter, I need to go to the toilet," and Sam stood.

"So do I," and Carla stood.

"Both of you sit down. You will go when I say so."

There was a tense moment then when Peter marched behind them all around the table and seemed to be sizing them all up. "I've had a chance to get to know you all. Well, maybe not you so much," hitting Thomas on the head lightly with his gun. "You're a strange one from all accounts, hey Sam. You know I feel sorry for you, Thomas. You took the kid in, raised him as your own, and got no thanks for it. Bloody ingrate, I'd say," Staring straight at Sam. "Did he beat you? Have you kiss drunk women, deprive you of food, clothes? That's right, just look blank at me, but I know the answer. NO, he did not. Oh, poor little Sam, he didn't have the cuddles of a mummy but he had everything else and a nice grandfather. Mate," Peter was now yelling, "you had nothing to complain about. Nothing."

In a quiet voice Sam said, "I see what you mean Peter. I'm sorry. Sorry for everything." There was a silence and then Sam spoke again, "But I do need the toilet. Urgently."

Peter looked about and after a pause, "Everyone empty your pockets. NOW," and they did, even Thomas. There was a motley collection of dirty tissues from Carla, a wallet and keys from Thomas and the same from Sam. "Is that it? Where are your phones?" Carla pointed to the lounge room and said, "In my bag," and Sam indicated the kitchen bench which Peter saw. Thomas said nothing and Peter had him stand and frisked him. Laughing he said, "I feel like a cop on telly."

"Okay, one at a time, I'll be standing in the doorway here. Any smart moves and I think Thomas will be the first to go," and then eying Thomas quizzically said, "Still not sure what the whacko meant about my mum." A big shrug and in addition, "Naw, just whacked, I'd say."

Sam left and returned two minutes later. Carla left and returned in similar time. Thomas didn't move. "So, everyone comfortable now?" and then as an afterthought, "Let's move to the lounge actually, get the fire going." He herded them into the lounge and the heater was fired up. It was clear to Carla that Peter was enjoying this, toying with them, but she was still totally at a loss as to what this all meant. Five minutes had passed from the kitchen to the lounge and everyone was seated on the three seater couch with Peter, his back to the heater, addressing them like he was in school.

"Where was I? Yes that's right. I'm out of the wardrobe and have the book with me. I politely thank my dad for letting me out and he orders me to my room. I'm happy about that. Other times he had let me out he's made me apologise to whoever was there or do chores or cook something, so being sent straight to my room without food was fine by me. In the bedroom I firstly sought out a very safe place to hide the book. I don't want Dad to find it – ever – I decide under the mattress. The old 'hide the book under the mattress trick.' He laughed, "A bit of Maxwell Smart in us all," and he shook his head when he looked up at the three of them. "You guys are too serious." There was a short silence and he began, "So, under the mattress I put it and wait. I know that he will be back and want something and I was right. I had just secured the book when Dad came to the door, opened it and said, "I'm going out. Don't answer the door, I'll be back soon."

"It was a relief, it meant he was off to the pub and I would have the house to myself until he came back which was always late... yes dad, see ya," I say.

"I waited half an hour even though I knew he wouldn't be back for ages. Whilst I waited I went to the kitchen and made a sandwich with vegemite and went back to my room. I eventually got the book out and began to read. It was hard at first getting used to mum's writing but she wrote in the diary every day! I knew there must be more books because this one was dated 1993 but she had mentioned things like *'Liam and I went to the Bayside restaurant for lunch and it was as good as last year. I had the same salmon and salad and Liam had a steak. I looked up last year's entry and amazing I had ordered the same. This salmon is the best in the world! And it was this year too. I am very lucky.'* And things like that. She was happy. All I had was this one half year of my mum but it was special. I pretty well know it off by heart. Read it so often. There is one entry though that is the clincher, the words that show the betrayal, the broken promise, the contempt for me and my mum and, if I am fair," raising his eyebrows and looking directly at Carla, "and my dad. Do you remember, Carla? It was all written in my mum's diary. Everything."

Carla was looking at Peter and said, "I remember your mum kept a diary and yes, she wrote in it every day. She was a stickler for it even if nothing happened. She said she never wanted anyone to read them, it was just her way of clearing her head from the day's business."

"Well, old man will you shut up." This was directed at Thomas, who was visibly getting more and more fractious.

"Dad, take it easy. Carla, do you have anything Dad could take? Something to calm him a little. I don't know what's wrong. I've seen him bad but not like this." He look at Thomas and then to Carla. "Shit, this is my fault, I should never have left him. I'm sorry."

"I'm sorry daddyo. Why don't you stop the whinging for once in your life?"

Carla spoke then, "Can I go to the bathroom? I have some Valium left over from mum. They are probably out of date but might still work!"

"Go, quickly, I am even getting sick of my own voice. Hurry, we don't have all day!" Peter was now pacing and waving the gun about and Sam was getting very nervous indeed but he was more concerned with Thomas.

Carla jumped up and literally ran to the bathroom. Sam could hear bottles clinking together and something clearly fall to the ground. There was then a bang as the cupboard door shut and Carla's footsteps could be heard returning to the lounge. With hand outstretched to Sam, "Here, there's two there."

"Thanks," turning to Thomas he said, "Here. Take these Dad, it will help." To his surprise Thomas didn't hesitate, swallowing the two with ease. He turned to Sam and thanked him and sat back in the couch with his eyes closed.

"Good. Some peace. Okay, its good you remember she wrote a diary, so you know what I say next will be the truth. Yes?"

Carla nodded but did not look at him. She had seated herself on the floor with her back on the couch to give Sam and Thomas more room. Also she was feeling like she was losing a part of herself. There were sparkling lights flickering in the periphery of her eyes and she wanted to concentrate on what Peter was saying but at the same time was terrified she was going to blank out. Whilst in the bathroom she had resisted taking her migraine medication but did take two Panadol instead. The migraine medication usually made her sleepy and she didn't need that. Not now, not with this 'situation.' She was beginning to think about 'this situation' but was brought up quickly with a kick to her heel. She let out a scream and bent her legs up instinctively. Peter was crouched next to her, having warned Sam to stay still with a finger slice action across his neck, and said, "Concentrate, Carla" in a very steady voice. "This is your story now. It's where you come in." She sat up straight, kept her knees up to her chin and gave him full eye contact. "Go on then."

Chapter 8

Peter went on to explain that he had been in his room, he was sitting in the doorway so he would hear when his father was coming in. He got to an entry dated March 21st 1993. He told them he had memorised the entry word for word.

"So here it is, Carla. Do you remember where you were that day?"

"No."

"You and mum were having lunch together at the Lakeview hotel. Remember now?"

"Peter, we lunched there often. It was our spot, especially when we had a tough week and wanted to wind down, debrief, and say what was on our minds. We were close and discussed everything and the Lakeside was 'our place'. I might not remember that specific day but I know it makes sense she would have written about it." She paused and looked over her shoulder at Sam and Thomas and then back to Peter and added, "Peter, what is this all about, please? Enough is enough, if you want to frighten us you have. Please leave us. We've done nothing to you but befriend you. We..." but she didn't get any further.

Peter pounced. He was at her side in a split second, the gun to her temple, and through gritted teeth he said, "You insightless, stupid cow. You have not only hurt me, you have destroyed everything. I think you don't even know it, do you?"

Sam was on his feet now but he was incapable of speech because Peter had moved quickly to him the minute he moved and had hit him so hard in the face that Sam thought his jaw had been broken. Thomas grabbed his son and made him sit. He seemed calm and coherent and he glared but said nothing to Peter. Instead he spoke quietly to Sam, "Stay still, son. Are you alright?" Sam nodded and held his face. He felt like crying but fought within himself to not let Peter see any more of his fear than he had to. Sam had felt fear all his life but it was nebulous, not real, and unsubstantial fear, it never had anybody. He was understanding now that this was what real fear was. He was in danger, the danger Thomas had protected him from, told him of. It was all true. His father had whispered to stay still and calm, "I will protect you." Sam knew he would and he did as his father said.

Peter had turned back to Carla. His face was red with rage and it was obvious to her he was on the verge of getting very violent if she didn't shut up. She was confused and baffled but the swiftness of his movements towards Sam convinced her that there was more trouble to come if she didn't listen. She had lost all sense of time.

Peter straightened up and positioned himself back at the heater. "I have all day if you want it that way, although it hadn't been my plan. ... Yes I have planned this, people," and with a nod of the head and curl of his lip he said, "Although I hadn't banked on the old man there. Now, no more interruptions. The diary entry 20th March 1993 Mum writes: *L and I have been away for a week and I have been looking forward to catching up with C and R. I phoned C the minute we got home and said I'd book the Lakeview for lunch the following day. C was happy.* She went on to talk about their holiday up in Beechworth but I won't bore you with that. March 21st 1993 Mum writes: *C and I were lucky today and got a window seat looking across the road to the lake. I never tire of watching the swans with their babies and the people feeding the ducks. I told C about the holiday and she told me about Roger wanting to take her on a trip to Fiji but C isn't that keen. She also told me Thomas wanted them to move to Adelaide but C isn't having any of that. I said why not go to Fiji? And she said she's scared to fly and said she might fall out of the sky and I told C that if something ever happened to her I would help R and S 100%. C told me ditto, if anything happened to me I can count on her helping L and P 100%. C even said 'like they are her own family'. That makes me feel good. C is the best ever friend.* Do you remember that conversation C? Do you remember saying you would help 100% with Liam and I if anything happened to mum? Well? Answer!"

Carla had paled, she now had a sense of what this was about and she felt sick, she did remember and they actually said it often after that and she had meant it. Hadn't she!

Peter waited and when she didn't speak he said with a wave high in the air, "Well, silence tells it all doesn't it, Sam? A big fat NOTHING is what Dad and I got from the best ever friend." He knelt beside her again and with the gun close to her ear he said, "Cat got your tongue, C?"

"No. I do remember and I meant it but I got sick, Peter. I explained that to you. Roger was dead, Susan was dead, I ended up in hospital. I was no good to anyone. Let alone you and your Dad."

"THAT'S NO EXCUSE best ever. You promised, you had an obligation. You told me yourself how mum helped you when Roger died, day in, day out, looking after Sam, trying to look after you. She kept her promise AND she also taught me my life's lesson."

He was toying with her, with them, and they were all numbed. They were not used to anything like this. Was she meant to ask, what life lesson? Or would that trigger more violence. She didn't know and in her mind she was running a dead end commentary until she heard Thomas say, "What was the lesson?"

"Oh, old man thanks for asking. The lesson of survival… kill or be killed. I remember the day she was shot and she was a tiger protecting her cubs and she was going to kill that bastard but he had a gun. Oops, like mine," and he stopped to admire the gun in his hand. "What chance did she have? None is the answer, you morons, my mum had no chance. I've thought about it and it was obvious to me she was showing me the way and I have lived it and perfected it and it works. Kill first, ask questions later." Peter was literally beaming now as he spoke but Carla was not following any of it. Thomas however, said, "So you have killed not only your father but others too?"

"Yes. Little things at first. No torture, not like the torture I suffered, quick, clean. I didn't like it but I am

370

my mother's son." He put his hand to his chin, stroking it with his index finger in an exaggerated, musing way and said to no one in particular, "I wonder how it would have been if C had kept her word! If C hadn't been so pathetic, so devoid of any ability to protect anyone or anything, how it all might have been. I suppose it was my mother's only fault that she didn't see the fault line that runs through you." Then, looking at her, "Why is that, C? What was it about my dad and me that you hated? No, not just Dad and me, what is it about your son, too," pointing to Sam, "that made you want to abandon him? Were we so bad? We were children for God's sake! My Dad, was he so bad? Tell me, I need to understand how a simple promise made and broken has gotten to this." He laughed then turned violently towards her and yelled. "I AM WAITING. THIS IS NOT A JOKE. Carla. I need to know."

She knew she needed to speak but at the same time knew she had no answers and nothing she could say could help this situation. "Peter, I cannot account for how I reacted to the traumas I suffered. It's not an excuse; it just is. Your mum and I never expected to have to really act on that pledge. We were young, healthy, had two beautiful children, husbands, it was grand. It was just things people say."

"No Carla. Don't try and cop out. This was a promise between friends. Life-long and you know Mum kept hers." He was snarling now.

"I loved your mum and would never want to hurt her, you or your Dad. I couldn't help it." She was thinking on her feet now, even though she was still on the floor. "Peter, people suffer trauma and when that happens there is what I describe as a vacuum, a void, a vacancy, call it what you will, and as humans, we have an innate sense that this must be filled; that we could not function in a vacuum. An empty hole in the middle," and she touched her stomach absentmindedly. "It is centred in the middle and then travels throughout the body. I could feel it as a physical entity, and I needed to fill it as soon as possible. Some people believe this is anxiety but I was never convinced and believe it is deeper and more intricately personal, linked to the actual trauma. And compounding the vacuum's size are factors such as when the trauma was experienced, who was there at the time? How old the person was? How the person perceived the event and what they were thinking at the time and the strength of the individual's inner nature as to how they fill it, to survive. You say Susan had the kill instinct but we don't know that, she was definitely a protector. Could she have killed? I don't know?" She looked at Peter now and he looked like he was about to say something but she quickly pressed on. "So what I believe is that people display incredible ways in which they fill the vacuum. It is so complex that understanding it even to a small degree is hard. Peter, ask yourself, why does one person get depressed or have avoidance issues – like me, or become schizophrenic or suicidal, homicidal, or develop personality disorders with varying characteristics? What is driving the behaviour? How does the behaviour assist them? I believe it is to fill a void with whatever a person has at hand, at the time. I became catatonic, I could not function with the loss of Roger and then your mum and over the years I have come to the conclusion that that was the only way I could have survived. To close down. I also have the genetic vulnerability from my mum's side. And," looking at her son, "The decisions I made about Sam were so he could survive. I didn't know I was perpetuating trauma. I thought Sam was better off with Thomas." Her voice drifted off, "I am so sorry."

Clapping sounds, first quiet and then getting louder, and Peter clapping his left hand across the back of his right hand which still held the gun. He threw back his head and gave a loud snort, "Hell, nice speech. Been practicing that?" But without waiting for an answer, as it was a rhetorical question, he continued, "I guess you have, but what a crock of shit. The fact is you need to die. You are poison, you lose your husband and every other person who comes in contact with you from then on gets shit for life." Cocking his head to the side and licking his lips he added, "Here's the list, Carla. It's got nothing to do with empty bellies and stuffed vacuum cleaners, it got to do with total selfishness, you are upset 'cos Rogers gone, you leave Sam to mum's care, mum gets killed by some bloke. 'Who is that bloke? Why?' We never know, random." He paused for effect, "Very strange but you, instead of helping anyone, no, you then totally abandon the world for a little 'me time'. Sam is sent away, Liam is forgotten, I am forgotten." Peter is now pacing and waving the gun erratically, and with raised voice, "The bloody promise is forsaken Carla! Nice legacy," and he pointed the gun directly to her chest. She flinched, waiting for the inevitable but strangely she felt calm. Strangely she could see some sense in his words. But what of Sam if she is dead? With that thought she went to move but found her legs and entire body anchored to the floor. Immovable, happening again. Not even any voice. Becalmed, stalled, off into a safe place.

Peter was slowly pulling the trigger but stopped because Thomas had raised himself slowly off the couch and was saying, "Please, put the gun down, son, you have it wrong. There is so much you don't understand. Please listen to me."

Peter pointed the gun to the floor and said, "Go on. This better be good."

"Carla." She dipped her head to indicate she had heard him and then very slowly, not taking her eyes off Peter, she put her hands behind her and onto the edge of the couch and slowly heaved herself up to a sitting position to be next to Sam. He touched her arm gently. A reassurance.

Chapter 9

"I don't hear voices. I hear William, my brother. He has been with me all my life, always looking after me, protecting me. Not like mother or father, oh no. They let that bastard Cambridge get me, they didn't care. But William and I got him. He got what he deserved."

Peter said with obvious control, "What the fuck are you talking about. Sit down, you pathetic fool." But Thomas kept talking.

"William has always been talking, sometimes he is whispering and I have to strain to hear him but other times, like now, he is very clear and precise. William was the one that saved Sam. We have protected him all his life. He never got hurt, harmed or abandoned and that was because William didn't want anything to happen to him. That's why Roger died."

Carla gasped, she found her voice, "What do you mean, Thomas? What are you saying?"

He turned to her, "I asked him the night he died. I said, Roger you need to give me Sam. I can protect him, you are not serious enough for this. You don't understand the dangers. I will care for him with mum's help." He stopped and, thinking back all those years ago, the scene was very clear. He looked at me and laughed and said, "Thomas, I always thought you were mad but this just confirms it. Do you honestly think Carla or I would simply hand you Sam. You're a joke and so is this bloody job. I quit, if only to get as far from you as possible. He never wanted to understand, to know us. William told me that."

"Thomas, what did you do?" Carla was shaking now.

"I did nothing. Fate got him. Fate dictated that he should die. An opening to save Sam, save the child. A child is more important that an irresponsible adult, Carla. William and I saw this as an omen and we planned."

"Oh my God, no! Thomas. You killed Roger, your brother? No!"

"I did NOT kill my brother. We would never do that but I cannot say I was too upset because Roger was careless and he died being careless with that motorbike of his."

Carla had a sickening feeling in the pit of her stomach. She wasn't sure anymore what the truth was and then she made a momentous leap. Slowly and deliberately she said, "Thomas, did you have anything to do with Susan's murder?"

Thomas slumped back on the couch, making Sam and Carla scrunch up. "Yes," and hung his head in his hands.

It was Peter who was now screaming and he lunged forward and dragged Thomas to his feet and flung him to the opposite side of the room. With teeth clenched he said, "Tell me what happened before I shoot the shit out of you."

Thomas has fallen heavily on his right side and was very breathless. Through deep rasps he said, "I will," deep intake, "just give me a moment… to catch… my breath."

Sam went to stand but the look on Peter's face stopped him and he sat back. Carla was not thinking, just staring at Thomas as he was readjusting his position on the floor and was now sitting with his back on the wall.

"Well!" Sam could see Peter was on the brink. His entire persona was stiff and there was a flush of red in his face underlying a simmering volcano ready to crack at any moment. They were all in danger and all helpless.

"Roger's accident, fatal death, fate's hand." Whack, no one saw it coming, Peter was one minute standing in front of Thomas, the next moment he had slapped Thomas with his gun hand so hard that Thomas had fallen back on his right side, blood pouring from a gaping gap on the left cheek and nose.

"Leave him alone." Sam was at his father's side in a flash. "Dad, you okay? Hell," and he was fiddling in his pockets looking for a hanky. Finding nothing he ran over to the kitchen and grabbed the tissue box.

Peter had stepped aside and said nothing. It was like looking at someone else doing the slapping and nothing to do with him. The movies.

Sam had stemmed the flow of blood and Thomas was asking him to leave him, he was alright. "Let me finish," looking at Peter.

"You wanted him to tell the story. Bloody well let him." Sam had never felt so angry, never really witnessed violence, only heard about it, seen it in the news, TV and the occasional time at school but whenever there were any fights he ran in the opposite direction. Thomas had trained him well. He had been strict, odd at times but 'well that was dad.'

Thomas was looking at Carla now. "When Roger wouldn't listen to us we weren't sure what to do but believe me we never intended death. But when he died and you were not functioning, your mother was no help and Sam was given to Susan Westmead, we decided to talk to her." Peter had moved cautiously to the kitchen, grabbed a chair and was now sitting near Thomas but positioned to have Sam and Carla in clear sight. They had returned to the couch.

Susan had been looking after Sam full time for a couple of days and she was happy when I called and said I wanted to come over. "I'm so glad you have taken the time, Thomas. I am so worried about Carla, she's getting worse, not better."

"We were in the small rumpus area, you and Sam were playing with some toys and looked very happy. I remember thinking this is a nice, safe, good place. Your mum asked me if I wanted some tea or coffee but I declined. I said to her, Susan I will take Sam now. I believe he should be with family. I know you will agree."

"I see your point, Thomas, but I can't make that decision. Carla has asked me to care for Sam and we made a promise to each other." Thomas looked to Peter, "She said, we have a pact, if someone in one of our families needs help we will look out for them. You will understand I can't go against that." Now everyone was looking at Carla.

She shouted, "You can all get stuffed I was sick. Roger was dead, I wasn't coping. I wasn't in control." Then she clamped her mouth with her hand, shook her head and mumbled, "I'm sorry."

"There were lots of mistakes, Carla. We have thought on this. But there has been good too." They all saw Peter flinch at this remark and waited but nothing happened and he remained silent.

"Susan said that if Carla agreed then that's fine. I couldn't wait and to be honest I didn't trust you, Carla. Your genetic pool is flawed, mum mad, you mad, not safe, child, not safe. We had to act and William knew what to do. Get the boy."

"Peter, I'm thirsty, can I get water?"

"You go, Sam, but don't try anything funny."

Sam got up and they could hear the cupboards opening and shutting and then the tap running. Sam came back with two glasses and handed one to Thomas and one to Carla. He looked at Peter and he nodded his head. Sam returned to the kitchen, repeated the sequence, returning with water for Peter and himself.

"I hired a man I had used in the past, to kidnap Sam. He bungled it. Your mother attacked and he shot her. Of that I am very sorry. Peter, I killed him for it."

This time it was Sam who gasped but he said nothing.

"I then had more sway to persuade Carla to hand over Sam to me."

"How was a kidnapping going to help? How, why, shit I don't get it, what were you thinking?" Sam and

Peter were both on their feet but it was Sam who had spoken.

"I don't know. William couldn't explain it when I asked. We were thinking fast, the window of opportunity was on us. Sam, you needed protecting, I protected. That has been my real job."

"You idiot. You didn't protect. You had my mother murdered and my life was stuffed because of it. You didn't protect ME. No one protected ME." And two tears dropped from Peter's eyes. "Well, an eye for an eye."

Without warning Peter turned the gun on Sam, "Sorry buddy." The gun fired but in the split second of the gun being turned to Sam, Peter saying the words, the gun going off, Thomas had risen from the floor and flung himself in front of Sam, collecting the bullet on the upper right side of his back.

Chapter 10

Carla's friend Jack from flyball and High School had been thinking about Carla for a few days, wondering when she'd be back from her leave. He had tried to ring her about a week ago but the phone had gone straight to voice mail and he wasn't sure if he should leave a message or not. There had been an opening at the High School for an English/History teacher full-time and he wanted to let her know, in case she was keen to apply. He remembered her mentioning that there were times when she thought full-time would be good. Yesterday he had finally gotten hold of her and she'd been quite excited and invited him over for lunch to, "Catch up on all the goss." He was pleased and said he'd be there around 1.00 ish.

As Jack was raising his hand to ring the doorbell he heard shouts and then a bang which made him jump back from the door. He stared at the front door for a few seconds and then decided, *"That was a gun, get the police,"* and he turned from the door, leaped off the verandah and ran, digging into his coat pocket and grabbing his phone at the same time. When he thought he was at a safe distance from the house he stopped and hit 000.

"Police, fire, ambulance."

"Police."

Thomas convulsed and slammed onto Sam's lap, one knee landed on Carla, one on the floor. Sam gently grabbed his father in two arms and, trying not to cause him pain, rolled him gently onto the floor, all the time crooning Dad, Dad. Carla was on her feet and screaming but the punch from Peter's left fist sent her careening to the floor where she lay dazed and in pain. Peter was saying, "You bastard. Get away from him, Sam, that bullet was for you. You need to die. Imagine these two then, left without their golden boy," and he was raising the gun one more time.

Peter was crying now. "I told you, Carla, but you don't get it do you? You don't see the misery you have caused. We all have to die. You want to die."

He heard the sirens then and stopped. It was the only chance she thought she had. Carla Parkinson stood up quickly and although she felt weak and faint she screamed and screamed, "RUN, RUN SAM, RUN." Peter turned to her and shot in her direction and she dropped. Sam had made it to the front door and the bullet clipped the doorframe and wood splintered but he grabbed the handle and was out the door. The police were entering the driveway and Sam headed straight towards them. Peter stood on the verandah and fired another shot, again missing Sam. The next shot Sam heard was from the left and behind him. Even in this panicked state he thought, *"Strange, from the left and behind, two bangs."*

At the police car an officer had beckoned him to get down and get behind the door which he did. He looked back to the house to see Peter Westmead's prone body.

There was pandemonium, sirens, the ambulance arriving, Sam was dazed but fine. He did not want to enter that house.

Slowly Carla Parkinson and Thomas Nelson were placed on gurneys and taken to the St John's Hospital. Thomas was in a critical condition and stayed in intensive care for ten days. Carla was luckier, the bullet had lodged in her hip bone and miraculously missed all vital structures. "You'll possibly be left with a permanent limp, Ms Parkinson," her surgeon had said.

When Thomas had recovered he was interviewed by police and told them what he had told everyone that day at the house. For the first time ever Thomas Nelson did not have William Nelson talking to him. He missed his brother. He did not understand why William had left him. His soul mate, confidante and adviser… simply gone. Thomas was bereft. He heard the police saying he was being charged for the 'cold case' murders of Turpy and Cambridge, that the court-appointed psychiatrist and an independent psychiatrist would interview him and determine his capacity to stand trial. Thomas never stood trial, he was transported from hospital via ambulance to the Thomas Embling forensic psychiatric hospital and four days later he was found dead, having taken his life swallowing chemicals from the kitchenette in the general community room. He had nothing to fill, his loss of Sam and William left him devoid of all feeling.

Peter Westmead was written up in the papers as a mentally-disturbed young man who had sought revenge for the death of his mother twenty-two years ago. He had killed two innocent people, Scott Asher and Elly Simpson, in his determined obsession in getting back at Carla Parkinson, who was shot by Westmead. He also shot and nearly killed Thomas Nelson, former resident of Ballarat. Peter Westmead died from a single bullet wound to the right temple, inflicted from his own gun. He also sustained a bullet wound to the abdominal region from police fire.

If Peter had had the time he would have told Sam and Carla all about Elly and Scott. He would have told them that what he said about Elly getting very amorous and suggestive was true but he had gone along with it. It was he who said to Scott that he thought that if Elly needed some loving they shouldn't deny her and Scott had reluctantly agreed. Scott wanted to get as far from Adelaide as possible and stopping for 'side of the road sex' was not in his plans. Scott had pulled over and Peter had urged him to find a secluded spot up a very bushy dirt track. Elly had jumped out of the car and Scott went to his pack to roll a joint. Peter had quietly, unbeknownst to Scott, spotted the gun earlier and it was now that he secured it from the glove box. Joint smoked and suggestions from Elly to 'do it' in the car. Peter had agreed happily, told them both to jump in. Then leaning through the passenger door window he produced the gun and shot Scott first and then Elly. As he turned to go to the highway to wait for Sam and Carla he laughed and said aloud, "Well, that's how to cure a drug problem!"

Carla was released from hospital after four days and Sam was helping her with home-based physio as well as helping her get back and forth for check-ups with the hospital. Jack had been coming over every couple of days and it seemed to Carla that there was something happening here. Memories of a closeness, something she had pushed away all these years, and she wondered if it was because she felt more whole, complete. Her son was home with her. They didn't know in what direction their lives were going to go but for now they had agreed to take it slowly.

Sam was in a quandary, he had been left a lot of money, the business, the home at Glenelg, everything from Thomas. Geoff had been over to see him and he had said that he would help him however he could and Sam was grateful for that. But Sam had a nagging feeling, or was it a voice, or something not quite right, an inward sense of anxiety. He had been thinking of late, *'Peter had made some sense.'* Yes, he could see how Carla had made a huge mistake, done the wrong thing by Peter and his family and as such… she had done the wrong thing by him. He couldn't blame Thomas, his Dad, he had tried to protect him and he had seen, *'Yes, Dad had seen the truth of the situation,'* she was trouble and he saved him from a possibly worse fate the day he took him away. Sam would ponder this a lot over the coming months. What should he do? How to fill the vacuum he felt now that his father was not there?

THE END